MARC WEITZ

He Who Fights with Monsters

First edition

ISBN: 978-1-7341006-0-0

This book was professionally typeset on Reedsy.
Find out more at reedsy.com

"He who fights with monsters should look to it that he himself does not become a monster . . . when you gaze long enough into the abyss, the abyss also gazes into you."

Friedrich Nietzsche

I

A Love Story

1

The Caribbean Sea

The twin diesel engines hummed, vibrated throughout the ship. The bow sliced through the sea smooth as black slate, radiating symmetric ripples into an expanding triangle from the stern. It was the moment when the dark, silent night gave way to the first faint glow of dawn.

I sat in my cabin in an armchair, wearing a suit, dress shoes, and no tie, a book closed on my lap. I ran my fingers along the binding and felt the grooves of the pages shut tightly together. I wanted to read but instead found solitude peering out the window, contemplating what we had just gotten away with.

A knock on the door startled me from my thoughts.

"Come in."

The door cracked open. A soldier not more than twenty-five years old looked in. "They're coming after us."

I sighed. "How did they find us?"

"The president had a tracking device on him. We missed it when we searched him."

"Damn." I looked intently out the porthole but couldn't see anything in the darkness. "How are they coming? How many?"

"It's two Zodiacs. Ten men each. Our drone has them on video. They'll reach us in ten minutes."

"I'll be right up," I said.

"James says for you to wait here."

I put the book down on the end table, stood up, and walked toward the armoire, where there sat a silver metal case. I took a key out of my pocket, placed it in the lock, turned it till the buckle clicked open.

The soldier hovered uncertainly in the doorway.

I opened the case, finding a carefully placed and well-maintained Remington 700 long-action rifle. I removed it, grabbed some bullets, and loaded it.

"Sir, James says that you're safer here in your cabin," said the soldier.

He watched me push passed him, rifle in hand, and into the hallway of the rundown former luxury cabin cruiser. The frayed green carpet offset the brown hardwood paneling on the walls. I passed empty cabins until I reached the stairwell. A brass sign with a lightbulb glowing inside through the cutout, stenciled lettering read "Sundeck" and showed an arrow pointing up the stairs.

A flight up and I found myself on deck, where the scurrying of our mercenaries contrasted the glasslike Caribbean Sea. A tall soldier stood stoically in the commotion, ordering the men into place. They took cover behind the walls at the stern of the ship. Each man with an assault rifle strategically positioned, looking over the wake into the gradually brightening dawn.

I approached the commander. "It's the Venezuelan Presidential Guard who's found us, I imagine."

James turned to me. "I gave orders for you to wait below deck."

"How long before they reach us?" I replied.

"They're eight minutes out."

"Where do you need me to be?" I asked.

"In your cabin."

"I'm the only one with a long-range rifle. All of the other men are using standard Kalashnikovs. It would seem that I could be of use. I'm also the head of this organization."

"But I run the military operations. Period," said James.

4

"Where do you want me?" I repeated.

"I don't have time for this. Go take a position at the corner and stay behind cover. If shit gets intense, go to safety."

"Fair enough." I moved to the where James had pointed. It was at the stern on the port side. My spot was protected behind the metal wall of the ship. I leaned against the railing and braced my rifle so it was stable.

Men coordinated our defense, shouting orders in English, Spanish, and French.

James put his hand on my shoulder. "Watch the horizon. As soon as you get a shot, take it. If they get aboard, go back to your cabin, shut the door, and wait with your pistol."

"Got it."

"Good." James ran off, shouting over his shoulder, "Aim for the skipper!"

Everyone had his position and orders. The three decks of the stern were dotted with men draped over their rifles scanning the horizon. The scurrying settled into tense silence. The engines groaned. The waves lapped at the side. A white, rippling wake swished off from the stern of the ship. Someone coughed. The light of dawn intensified gradually over the placid Caribbean Sea, revealing the hills of a few tropical islands that stood like dark lumps on the edge of the sea. Just two or three light whiffs of cloud hung in the sky, one side lit by the approaching dawn, the other dark and foreboding.

I peered through the scope of my rifle. My eye strained at the horizon, looking for the first signs of the approaching Zodiacs. I felt my heart beating heavily in my chest. I closed my eyes, took a deep breath, exhaled slowly, reopened my eyes, and returned my focus to the horizon. I concentrated on a spot off in the distance, resting my gaze there for a few seconds to let my iris adjust to the darkness. The line between sea and sky was indiscernible. I saw nothing. I turned my focus to another spot. My eye settled in. I struggled to see any movement in this blankness.

"Do you see anything?" someone asked.

"Not yet," I said.

I moved my scope farther to the right. Waited. Settled in. Darkness, gray, black, blue, mixed into a dim blur. Then, a splash of white. Then nothing.

Then another splash of white. Then another.

"I see them!" I shouted, breaking the silence. "Eleven o'clock!"

I heard the men shifting their positions.

"What do you see?" James replied in a hushed tone from somewhere.

I stared more intensely through my scope. "One boat," I said. "It's too far for a shot."

"I see a second," said another voice from elsewhere on the ship. "Three o'clock."

"Fire when in range," said James.

The Zodiac appeared more clearly through my scope. I remained focused as it sped closer, now able to distinguish the individual men on board. I fixed the crosshairs on the skipper at the controls. He was just entering range. The Zodiac bounced very little on the smooth predawn sea. I held my fire, needing him to be closer.

"Stay cool," said James calmly, anticipating what I was thinking.

I took another deep breath and concentrated on the man at the controls. The strike force wore black from their boots to their balaclavas. The skipper moved up and down, in and out of the crosshairs of my scope. There was no sure shot. I just had to do my best. I spread my feet and planted them firmly on the deck. The rifle was flush against my shoulder, my hand holding it firmly under the barrel, leaning it solidly on the railing. The rifle was a part of me, part of the ship, connected to the skipper by an invisible line. We were all linked. I squeezed the trigger. The rifle recoiled. The bullet left the chamber, sure of its destination. Across the sea it traveled its course, finding the Zodiac's skipper and striking him down. The boat swerved out of control to the right and came to an abrupt stop.

"Woohoo!" came the cheers from our men.

"Now the other," someone shouted.

I took my eye away from the scope and spotted the other boat. The sky was brighter now, and the other boat was much closer. I turned toward it and aimed my rifle in its direction. I looked through the scope. I could easily see the skipper.

"Hurry up," said another voice. "We're almost in range of their guns."

6

At first, I didn't understand because if we were in range of their guns, they would be in range of our guns. But then I realized that there was a heavy machine gun mounted on the front of their Zodiac.

"Don't rush him," I heard James say.

I tried placing my feet solidly, but unlike before, it just wasn't comfortable. My rifle wasn't settling in.

"The first boat recovered with a new driver," one of our soldiers shouted.

I put the second skipper in my crosshairs. I took a breath, exhaled, and squeezed the trigger. The shot went off, but this time disappeared harmlessly into the sea, as I knew it would.

"Shit," I said just as the heavy machine gun on the second Zodiac opened fire, peppering our ship with unrelenting firepower. We could do nothing but take cover behind the metal walls, metal walls that proved too thin to protect us from the heavy rounds. I flattened myself against the deck as bullets clanked through the metal around me and whizzed over my head.

The barrage lasted almost a minute until, ominously, the heavy gun stopped firing. I heard the motor of the Zodiac reach the ship. The Venezuelan Presidential Guard shouted to each other in Spanish. We were being boarded. Our men opened fire. Commencing a close-range firefight. It was loud.

"Joe, go back to your cabin," I heard James shout from somewhere.

Being in the corner, I was a bit away from the action toward the middle of the stern. I scrambled to my feet and saw many of our men down. The Venezuelan Presidential Guard stormed over the ship's walls, and the other Zodiac that I had briefly slowed now joined the action with a second wave of men.

"Fall back to secondary positions," yelled James. He must've planned for this, knowing we were outmanned and outgunned. My head spun in confusion. There was little I could do to help, given my long-range rifle. I was not a solider. I had never been a soldier. I was an internet billionaire in his mid-forties who had a hobby shooting long-range rifles. But I also ran a nonprofit organization that assassinated corrupt world leaders. In this case, we had kidnapped the Venezuelan president and his entire criminal cabinet to bring them to justice in The Hague. And now his elite Presidential Guard was coming to rescue him. We either fought them off or we died.

Hunched over, I ran inside the ship, almost missing the door to the stairwell. I grabbed the door jam and pulled myself through and down the stairs to the interior of the faded elegance of the hallway. Muffled sounds of gunshots and shouts penetrated the hall. I reached my cabin and pulled open the unlocked door, entered, and shut it behind me, turning the lock on the knob, pushing the bolt shut, and fastening the latch. I stepped back and stared at the triple-locked but fragile wooden door. I dropped my rifle and held my hands out in front of me. They were shaking.

I heard one of our men shout, "Guys, I'm trapped on the starboard side, need backup—" and then his voice was gone. The voices of the Venezuelan guard grew stronger. We were losing the firefight. I had to help somehow. I ran over to the bed and ruffled through my bag, pulling out my pistol. I verified that it was fully loaded, cocked it, and took a deep breath. "I can do this," I said to myself. I unfastened all three locks on the door and yanked it open. I stuck my head out. The hall was clear.

I jogged to the stairwell and down two more decks into the hull of the ship, where the walls were now metal and covered with chipped and stained gray paint. Halfway down the hall, I reached a door, turned the handle, and pushed it open.

President Juarez sat alone in the room, handcuffed to a metal chair fixed to the floor and wearing a black suit, a white shirt, and a red tie.

He looked up at me with a smile. "You have about two minutes left."

I said nothing.

"You look nervous," he added.

"I'm fine," I said nervously.

"Give up now, and I'll let you continue to live. We could even do business together."

"Doing business nor continuing to live holds no interest to me."

The sounds of boots and men yelling echoed off the metal walls in the hallway outside.

"¡Estoy aquí!" yelled the president. Then turning to me, he said, "Last chance."

The door was kicked open with a bang. Three of the Presidential Guard entered, dressed from head to toe in military gear, rifles, and boots.

I pushed the barrel of my pistol against President Juarez's temple. "Don't move or I'll shoot," I said to the soldiers.

"Drop it," one of the Presidential Guards said.

"These men are crack shots," said the president. "You've got no chance."

They were sizing me up for the shot. The president was right. I had no plan and no chance to get out of this.

"You're going to die," the president said.

"I don't care. I'll take your corrupt ass with me." I felt my finger squeezing the trigger, when three shots rang out in succession. The three Presidential Guards dropped dead, revealing James and two of our men standing behind them.

"Fuck!" I shouted in relief.

"We're clear," said James calmly.

"What happened? We were losing," I said.

"We took care of it," said James. "But this is all that's left of us on board." James motioned to the two men behind him.

I swallowed hard.

"We got more of our men waiting for us at the airport in Bonaire."

I turned to President Juarez. "Looks like you're going to trial after all."

2

Utah State Prison: Two Years Later

T he gray, snowy streets blended seamlessly into the darkening skies and the clouds hanging ominously over the Utah State Prison. Dampness infiltrated everything, making it impossible to imagine being warm and dry ever again.

At a large encampment by the road, thousands and thousands of people had set up tents, of all colors and quality. Throngs of people bundled into down puffies gathered around campfires, holding up signs, playing music, or shouting over barriers at the multitude of police who were doing their best to maintain order. Police cars were parked everywhere with their lights flashing. Barricades were set up in such a way as to give the protesters their space but keep the road clear. The police were uneasy. A few military vehicles with soldiers stood back in reserve. Media vans with their aerials raised to the sky were parked everywhere: local news, national news, foreign news, reporting live, CNN, BBC, Al Jazeera, Fox News.

Away from the crowd and inside the quiet of the prison, a guard put his thumb on a scanner to the right of the door while another put his thumb on a scanner to the left of the door. The light turned green, and the metal door slid open to reveal a second door with a sign that read "Death Row."

Chris Billingsley followed the guards inside. He was in his early thirties, Caucasian, short brown hair, glasses, tweed jacket, skinny jeans, and carried a satchel with a laptop. Each guard punched in a code that unlocked the door.

Death Row was a hallway with six gray metal cell doors, three on the right, three on the left, staggered so the prisoners couldn't communicate. There was a slot for food and a small window.

Two more guards patrolled the hall, walking like caged lions in a circle, spit shields in front of their faces. They wore uniforms different from the guards who managed the general population: black with a white shoulder patch saying, "Execution Squad" and a representation of a noose beneath the lettering. As Chris and his escort, a guard named Holsbrooke, entered, the first death row guard broke from his patrol and acknowledged them by nodding. He led them to one of the cell doors. The guard rapped on it. "Prisoner two-four-two-eight-three-oh. You have a visitor. Put your hands through the slot."

"Don't ya think this is a little silly?" came a voice from inside.

"It's procedure, Joe."

"Of course it is. All right, I'm ready. Slide it open."

The guard slid the slot open. Two white, middle-aged, hairy hands emerged from the slot. The guard locked a pair of handcuffs on the wrists. "Okay," said the guard. Joe pulled his hands back in. The guard shouted "Opening!" and unlocked the cell door, sliding it open to reveal the owner of the hands: a man standing in the middle of the cell with a commanding presence and a big smile on his face. He had scruffy brown hair, was clean shaven, and wore orange prison garb.

"Hi, Chris," said Joe. "Welcome to my home...for now. I'd offer you some coffee, but my espresso machine is in the shop. But my last meal is coming in an hour or so. You're welcome to have some."

"I'm trying to cut down on my caffeine," said Chris, unclear how to respond and instead examining the cold, concrete cell. The walls of the ten-foot-by-ten-foot cell had a two-toned paint scheme with a light grayish-green color on the bottom half, sharply delineated from a dark grayish-green for the upper half. There was a metal bed hanging by a chain from the wall, allowing it to be raised when not in use. In the back was a stainless-steel toilet fixed to the back wall with a sink next to it. In the far corner sat a small desk with paper and a pen, a modest chair pushed underneath. There was a roll of toilet paper, a toothbrush, toothpaste, and soap. "You don't have any personal items, photos?" asked Chris.

"They won't let me. I'm dangerous, you know," said Joe. "Did you have any trouble getting through security?"

"Only with the massive demonstrations outside."

"I heard," Joe said.

"You've got a huge following. Demands for your pardon are coming from all over the world."

Joe shrugged. "Shall we get started with the interview?"

"Ah, yes," said Chris. "We don't have much time."

"We got plenty of time. I get shot at dawn."

Chris winced. "May I use your desk?"

"Of course," said Joe. "Sit there. I'll sit on my bed."

The guard had watched the initial exchange. "If you need anything, Mr. Billingsley, we'll be right outside the door. But you'll be fine with Joe." He slid the door shut, leaving Chris and Joe alone in the cell.

"That's the only friendly guard I've met so far," said Chris.

"They're not bad guys," said Joe. "They just deal with a lot of bad elements."

Chris pulled out the chair, set the laptop on the desk, and switched it on. He opened a new document and typed, "Interview with Joe Levy, Condemned Prisoner on His Final Night." He turned the chair perpendicular to the desk to face Joe. "Before we start, I was wondering if I can ask you a few things about why you chose me."

Joe laughed. "You mean because every news agency in the world wants to interview me?"

Chris nodded.

"You were a good college football writer."

"College football? You want me because I used to write about college football?"

"Yep."

"Not my time spent covering wars, human rights violations, and criminal regimes?"

"That also influenced my decision."

A small laugh escaped from Chris. "You have a sense of humor for someone on the eve of his execution."

"Meh, what are you gonna do? Life is full of darkness, death, and plenty of major and minor bad things. It's always been my philosophy to oppose misfortune with humor. It's my way of giving death the middle finger."

"Are you worried people won't take you seriously?"

"Not at this point. I'm on death row."

"I see what you mean," said Chris.

"Did you ever watch *M*A*S*H*?" asked Joe.

"When I was a kid," said Chris.

"I grew up on it. The main character, the surgeon Hawkeye Pierce, remember? All he did was make jokes, all the time. Some of the doctors considered it silly and unprofessional to be making jokes while operating on young men torn to bits in the Korean War. Yet it became apparent throughout the show that Hawkeye Pierce was the most professional, the most skilled, the hardest working, and the person who cared the most. It was probably because he cared so much that he needed to make jokes to shield himself from the awfulness around him. Perhaps he wouldn't have been able to handle the stress of his job otherwise. Humor is common amongst doctors."

"But what does college football have to do with this?"

"Football is an analogy for life."

"I don't see the connection. You're a billionaire who started an international aid organization with the stated mission of helping people by assassinating corrupt world leaders."

"You're a good writer. Too many modern sports writers cover college football with no imagination, dryly recounting the events of a game, like minutes of a meeting. You write like one of those old-time sportswriters, using analogies, nicknames, allusions, colorful imagery. I see the games in my head, the grit, the struggle, the crush of the pads, the cunning strategies, the bonehead mistakes, the coaches taking advantage of weakness or playing to their teams' strengths."

"I'd like to think I've accomplished much more since then."

Joe's expression turned serious. "Your work uncovering corruption in governments impressed me. And your narrative writing ability comes through in those more-serious pieces. I chose you because you will tell my story in a style that people will read and enjoy. You see through bullshit. You wrote about first-world corporations that support third-world governments under the guise of democracy; politicians catering to their own corrupt interests at the expense of their people. You tackle corruption with facts and have shown a willingness to push back against those in power. And you're young, early thirties, right?"

"Thirty-two."

"You're still hungry. My story could make your career. You'll push it. If Barbara Walters came in here, it would just be another big interview for her. Then she'd move on with her life. For you, it's a big deal. I need you to see through the bullshit that has been my life. I mean, what I was trying to accomplish with my life, taking down criminal regimes that steal from their own people. So, there you are. Have I answered your question?"

"I believe so. That said, my anti-'bullshit' cuts both ways. I'm going to ask you honest questions and press any issue that needs pressing. What I write may not be what you want."

"I wouldn't expect anything less. Shall we get started? My last meal comes in an hour. A two-star Michelin-rated chef was flown in to prepare it."

"Really?"

"Nah, not really."

Chris turned back to his computer and asked, "Do you have regrets about what you did?"

"Nope. What I did was right."

"Do you think you're wrongly accused?"

"No, I'm rightly accused."

"Why did you do it?" asked Chris.

"Do what?"

"The killings."

"Aren't these the type of questions you'd usually ask at the end of an interview?"

"It sets the scene. Why did you do it?" Chris repeated.

Joe's expression turned serious. He sighed and gazed around the room, the humor suddenly removed from his face. "For Liz," he said.

"Your wife?"

"Yes, Liz was an idealist. She wanted to save the world. I wanted whatever Liz wanted."

"Let's hear your story from the beginning," said Chris. "Where were you born?"

3

The Royal Road to Romance

I was born Joseph Levy in Denver, Colorado, in the mid-seventies. I was the only child of two middle-class parents. My dad got fired from job after job, not because he was incompetent—far from it. He was brilliant but fiercely independent. He didn't like being told what to do. He couldn't sit through bullshit meetings. He'd take off whenever there was nothing happening. Most bosses don't like that. He eventually became a computer salesman in the 1970s. This was back when computers took up a whole room, had 8k of memory, and cost $10,000, which was a lot of money back then.

Sales suited my father because none of his bosses cared what he did so long as he was selling, and he was their top salesman. His technique involved taking long naps during the day, disappearing in the afternoon to play tennis, and rarely coming into the office. But he returned phone calls and was available to his customers. He made his clients look good, which made them look good to their bosses. My dad didn't have much energy for corporate bullshit. The company threw award dinners for their best salesman. My dad would win and then drop the trophy in the trash on his way out the door.

My father lived below his means, bought used cars, and lived in a modest home. He saved his money and invested in income property: apartment buildings. This was in the late seventies, before the middle class figured out investing. He retired in his early forties.

My mom was an intellectual. I'm not sure the workplace suited her either. She could write well, spoke a few languages, and had a penchant for the arts. She worked as a journalist for a bit, but she was too creative for the corporate world, and I'm not sure they ever knew what to do with her or she with them. For a while, this creativity found an outflow in painting, writing, and a spell as a professional interior designer with her own practice, but her frustration with the business aspects and dealing with snooty clients quickly killed the pleasure of the creativity. Ultimately, she spent her time raising me and satisfied her artistic side by becoming a patron of the arts, rather than an originator.

I never fit in growing up, starting with my clothes. I dressed like my dad, polo shirts and chinos. Surf clothes were popular, colorful t-shirts and shorts. It was useless arguing with the other kids that Denver was nowhere near surfable waves. After I pled with my parents to buy me "cool" clothes, they bought me one t-shirt and one pair of shorts. I found acceptance on the day I wore my Maui and Sons t-shirt and shorts, but after that one outfit was exhausted, it was back to the world of the uncool. When the weather turned into snowy winters, the kids switched to trendy skiwear, which was more appropriate for Denver but still not my style as I didn't like skiing either. I hated that clothes were so important to social standing.

Coloradans were very outdoorsy, with some of the best skiing and hiking in the world. My parents viewed outdoor activities as a waste of money: all that expensive ski equipment, lift tickets, and gas up to the mountain resorts. As such, most of my childhood was spent indoors watching TV. I watched every episode of *Three's Company* five times. When Nick at Nite came into existence, focusing on the golden age of television, I immersed myself fully in the past: *Donna Reed*, *Car 54, Where Are You?*, *Mister Ed*, and *F Troop*, among others. I could speak fluently about these TV programs with older baby boomers, those who had actually grown up when these shows first aired. When they asked me how I knew these shows, I answered ironically, "I grew up with them."

I did not know it at the time, but I craved more substance. In those early days of basic cable, it was tough to find quality TV. Then I discovered *Night*

Flight, a show on the USA Network that ran all night on weekends. It was a variety show with everything from music videos from around the world to movie shorts, documentaries, and independent films. It was through this that my eyes opened to the world. I learned about "Free Nelson Mandela" by the Specials and watched Jim Jarmusch films like *Stranger Than Paradise*. I would come to school Mondays anxious to discuss these films, but it was just met with derision. "How was *Stranger Than Paradise*?" they asked me for weeks afterward. (It is important to note that I received vindication years later, when one of my classmates attended NYU film school and admitted that his professor showed this film as an example of good filmmaking.)

All this left me despondent, bored, and unmotivated in school. I graduated with lousy grades but was still admitted to the University of Colorado, Boulder because of a clerical error in the admissions office.

All first-year students are required to live in the dorms, even those raised locally. My mom suggested that I live in the music dorm, which made no sense because I didn't play any instruments. But she figured that I might meet others with common interests because I liked music, something she apparently found unusual. At first, I did not fit in there either. My childhood had been rather sheltered, and I did not know what to do with all this freedom. I spent much of my time in the TV room at the dorm, wishing I had my own TV so I would not have to watch everyone else's programs.

The University of Colorado was much larger than my high school, and soon I met other weirdos, people who dragged me out to see what was happening in town at night. I had never gone out at night before. It seemed daring. In the early nineties, Denver was still a cow town on the edge of the Rocky Mountains. Things closed early. Even the 7-Eleven closed. The only professional sports teams were basketball, the Denver Nuggets, and football, the Broncos. The poor Broncos. They lost four Super Bowls. John Elway was the town hero.

But Denver actually had a burgeoning beat scene, written about by Jack Kerouac in *On the Road*. There were two bohemian coffee shops in Denver: Muddy's and Paris on the Platte. Muddy's sat in a rundown firetrap built from brick and wood, located in the notorious Five Points neighborhood.

It had bookcases full of books on warped and crooked wooden shelves that would give you splinters. The seedy tables, chairs, and couches were built solid, like furniture used to be, worn from years of use, filthy and cozy at the same time. Actors put on plays, and there were open mics for poets and musicians. Muddy's opened in the evening and refused to close till almost dawn, serving java, espresso, and tea to those needing an all-night place of ideas and thought, away from the cowboy and sports bars of Denver. To me, Muddy's was the real world. Being there in the middle of the night felt like I was part of some intellectual movement I only knew from films. I was comfortable being an intellectual poser, for I knew nothing at the time and had read very little. But being in that environment spurred my curiosity to search for a larger world.

College opened my mind. Here were other people who liked old music and movies. Kids who had interesting suggestions on books to read, movies to see, and things to explore, things that gave me ideas. All those years watching TV were not wasted. I began to compare the fictional world of TV to the real one. Soon, I wanted more reality. I expanded beyond Muddy's, looking for real life. One of my neighbors had an ancient jeep, lifted with huge tires. We drove into the nearby mountains searching out old gold-mining towns, discovering secluded lakes, hippy colonies, sleepy mountain coffee shops, dilapidated mines. Every sign-less dirt road was an invitation. Without someone telling me what to do or when to go to bed I felt overwhelmed.

Drinking and partying were important activities to most students at CU. On any given night, a house party could be found in the student neighborhood called the Hill. You simply walked in uninvited, even if you didn't know anyone, contributed five dollars to the keg, grabbed a plastic cup, usually from Liquor Mart with an alcohol molecule drawn on the side, took a draft of beer, and sat down on an old couch. Most of the time, I did not even know whose house it was. I found this cool at first but soon got bored because I did not know how to talk to girls. Most of the time they grew tired of me giving them looks without actually making a move. Sometimes one would talk to me after a few drinks, but I was not on the same page as the normal girls.

I didn't get normal girls, and they didn't get me either. Our conversations soon petered out with us staring awkwardly at one another. I then found myself going through the homeowner's CD collection to see if they had anything interesting.

Until college, I never knew that learning could be so engaging. Most teachers from high school gave only rote, half-assed lessons with little enthusiasm. They watched the clock as much as the students. It wasn't unusual for the teachers to have a television rolled in so we could watch educational programming, or not. Educational programming somehow included the Anita Hill hearings and a miniseries about George Washington starring Barry Bostwick. This was the American public-school system. Only now do I realize the disservice done to me.

College was different academically. I majored in computer sciences, because I always had a knack for computers. It was cool but not something I wanted to dedicate my life to. I had little idea what I wanted to do with my life. Then I took a class on the foundations of government. The course started with the creation of democracy in ancient Greece and carried forward into modern times, passing through the Middle Ages, the Renaissance, and Communism along the way. The professor, Mr. Collins, was brilliant, an underwater archaeologist who spent his summers diving the submerged ruins of ancient Greece. More than his brilliance, I was captivated by his enthusiasm and storytelling. Calling his lectures entertaining would be doing them a disservice, because it would take away from their academic credibility. They were enthralling. There was a better way than what I knew in high school. Here was a professor who put effort into his courses, enjoyed his work, and enjoyed inspiring students.

I took more classes from Professor Collins, signing up for his graduate-level Modern Government course. In the first class, he warned everyone that this was a serious class requiring a lot of work and advised dropping out now if we wanted something easier. I'd heard professors say this before and figured it was bullshit. It was not. By the second class, half the kids were gone, which surprised me that so few people wanted such a challenge. I did not mind the work because I liked Professor Collins and the subject matter. It was a lot of work. In addition to the course reading and writing assignments, he required that we subscribe to the *Economist* and *Foreign Affairs* magazine. Neither publication was cheap. Certain articles were assigned. It took me a while to adjust to the dense, informative, and objective writing, nothing like the lightweight journalism put out by *TIME* or *Newsweek*. (Recall too that this was the 1990s, when *TIME* and *Newsweek* were still making something of an effort.) However, my perseverance with both the *Economist* and *Foreign Affairs* paid off. The articles were fascinating and covered a much wider array of issues in the world than most of the popular publications.

Professor Collins course required so much work that I actually left a football game at halftime. I could not concentrate on the game anyway, as the homework problems stimulated me to such an extent that I was thinking of my responses between downs. My eyes were opening, and after all, this was ideally what college was for. I added international relations to my computer sciences major.

I had never traveled internationally or even outside the state of Colorado. Despite now focusing my studies on international relations, the idea of travel had not so much as occurred to me. Then one day I was perusing the stacks of the campus library, something I now loved to do. I would press my fingers against the bindings of the ancient books, feeling the old covers, imagining and desiring the knowledge inside, smelling the well-worn pages, fearful of my own passion to read everything. I came across the nonfiction travel section. There were many old travelogues there. Books about Marco Polo, by Evelyn Waugh, by Mark Twain. I knew those names. But I was all at once struck by the title of an old, tattered book sitting amongst the travelogues, looking lonely and worn. The title was *The Royal Road to Romance*, by Richard Halliburton. My first thought was, *What is a romance novel doing in the travel section?* Why was it so thick? Why was it so worn? I picked it up. There was a checkout card in the pocket of the inside cover. The book was written in 1925 and had last been checked out on the 21st of March 1935. It had been sitting untouched on this shelf for nearly sixty years. I imagined all the generations of students who must have passed through this library. Kids in the 1950s listening to "Johnny B. Goode," listening to the Beatles in the 1960s, the Bee

Gees in the 1970s, and Duran Duran in the 1980s. I imagined their clothes, their dress and attitudes. All that time this book just sat there. I flipped to a page and read:

Youth—nothing else worth having in the world...and I had youth, the transitory, the fugitive, now, completely and abundantly. Yet what was I going to do with it? Certainly not squander its gold on the commonplace quest for riches and respectability, and then secretly lament the price that had to be paid for these futile ideals. Let those who wish have their respectability—I wanted freedom, freedom to indulge in whatever caprice struck my fancy, freedom to search in the farthermost corners of the earth for the beautiful, the joyous and the romantic.

When Richard Halliburton wrote this book, he was twenty-one and about to graduate from Princeton. He wanted to see the world. I was just his age. My naïve college mind only understood the word *romance* to mean love. Maybe I could be forgiven because in the popular culture every TV show, song, and movie concerned itself with romance as love. He meant *romance* in a way that was new to me, an idealized view of the world. In this case, that was his passion and magic from experiencing everything out there. Seeing the Taj Mahal, Paris, Africa. These too make your heart skip, differently from seeing a girl, but still romance.

I was hooked from the first page. I read about how he told his parents that he was going off to be a vagabond around the world after graduation instead of getting a proper job. He packs up the little stuff he needs, hitchhikes from Tennessee to New Orleans, and talks his way onto a ship bound for Europe, working as a deckhand. Without realizing it, I had slouched down to the floor, leaning against the antiquated book stacks, reading undisturbed in this forgotten section of the library for hours, till I was roused by the public announcement that the library would soon close. It was almost midnight.

Richard Halliburton had written five books in all. Six, if you include his *Book of Marvels*, a compilation condensed for kids. There were fewer tourists back then, and his experiences were real and mostly unplanned. He traveled to rarely visited countries and found himself invited to dinner by the American ambassador. Sometimes he hired a local guide and wandered off into the jungle for weeks. He visited the pyramids, sitting on top for hours just contemplating their immensity. He tried to run the original route of the Marathon in Greece but found himself not quite in good enough shape for it. He swam the Panama Canal, even paying his fare to go through the locks, a fare based on tonnage that came out to thirty-six cents. His best story was in the book *The Flying Carpet*, in which he hired a pilot and a biplane to fly around the world in 1930. One night in the Sahara he landed next to a fuel dump and camped beneath the stars, listening to records on a wind-up Victrola, miles away from civilization. From that day forward, I read his books in a constant flow, sleeping little at night and reading in the back of my less-interesting classes.

I was graduating in a few months, and I had not known what I wanted to do, until it became obvious: I would vagabond around the world like Richard Halliburton. Prior to his travels, he had not been anywhere either.

One spring afternoon, I emerged from reading one of his books. I had that engaged but worn feeling one gets after hours rapt in a book. I called my dad to tell him I was going to be a vagabond.

"What about getting a job?" said my dad when I told him my plan.

"You never liked working, Dad."

"I had to pay my dues, and working taught me a few things that brought me to where I am now."

"You think I should languish in a miserable job till I figure things out?"

"Find something you like to do," he said.

My mom picked up the extension. "I worry about you traveling. You've never been anywhere. At least sign up for a program first. Maybe study abroad or even take a tour." I considered my mom's answer a positive, as she was not entirely opposed to the idea.

"Your mom is right," said my father.

Richard Halliburton had no international travel experience when he vagabonded around the world. However, the world was a different place in 1922. Everything was safer back then. World War One, or the Great War as they called it then, not exactly knowing that the sequel would soon be coming, had finished a short three and a half years earlier. While crime and violence against tourists were almost nonexistent back then, lack of communication and primitive infrastructure were the challenges of the time. But Richard Halliburton survived just fine, traveling until age thirty-nine, when he was drowned in a typhoon attempting to sail a Chinese junk from Hong Kong to San Francisco for the World's Fair. I would not be sailing any Chinese junks. I simply wanted to hitch a ride on a ship and then vagabond around the world, meeting people, working when necessary. I had to figure out a way to make that happen.

4

A Successful Losing Record

During my final year, I joined an intramural ice hockey team—this was an informal league, just for groups of friends to play for fun. They made me team captain and center, which said a lot about the skill of our team, since I was a lousy hockey player. No one cared. I named our team Disease Control, and I was the center for Disease Control, and yes, I know that it is really the *Centers* for Disease Control. One guy on the team, Dustin, couldn't play at all, but it was fun watching him try. One time, he called a timeout because he couldn't corral the puck. This was not in the rules as far as I know, but for some reason, the opposing team went along with it.

After the games, the team went to a sports bar on the Hill that had afternoon specials on pitchers of beer. The place was wide open with bench seating at communal tables and televisions hanging from every wall showing the NCAA tournament. After the hockey game, the beer always tasted better, and the buzz felt so much sweeter.

There was also James on the team. I had met James in Professor Collins's course my sophomore year. We discovered that we both liked hockey and became fast friends. We decided to form an intramural team later with Dustin, who was also in the class. A few other random guys were added to the team by the league. Dustin was tall and thin with tangled blond hair, like a surfer. He was one of the most laidback guys I knew.

James was a contrast in personalities. He was an art major with an amazing ability for drawing, but he came from a military family and eventually wanted to join the army. He was tall, broad-shouldered, strongly built, and looked like a soldier. He had good genes, bright and athletic. Despite his lack of hockey skills, he kept in shape by running and playing pick-up basketball. On first impression, he looked like the type of guy you did not want to mess with, but once you got to know him, he was a big teddy bear. Charismatic and gregarious, girls liked him. Qualities that I lacked. Things came easily to him. I could imagine him going places. I knew he wanted to be in the Special Forces. I had no doubt he would achieve that.

"Congratulations on a zero-win season," said James as we raised our glasses of Fat Tire beer, a popular local beer that had not yet gone fully commercial.

"At least we made the playoffs," said Dustin.

"What kind of horrible league sends a winless team to the playoffs?" I asked.

"It's not much different from what the NHL and NBA do now. I mean, more than half the teams make the playoffs now, some with losing records. What's the point of the regular season anymore?" asked Dustin.

"The regular season was supposed to determine the best team. But they don't care anymore about who's the best. It's just about generating money from the playoffs."

"Playoffs test a team's mettle," said James. "The best teams need to step up when it counts."

"Teams and sports are streaky. Often a bad team has a good run against a good team on a bad streak. Then the whole season is wasted."

"Hey guys," said Dustin. "What if Disease Control wins the next four games in the playoffs? We'll be champions with a four and ten record."

"My point exactly!" I said.

"The English Premier League works that way," said James.

"What way?" I asked.

"The team with the best record is the champion, period."

"Baseball used to do that," I said. "Until 1969, there were no playoffs.

The first-place team in the National League played the first-place team in the American League. They played 154 or 162 games back then. After 162 games, there was no argument who was the best."

"Maybe you're right," said James. "They would only have a playoff in the event of a tie for first place, which made it so exciting. Like the famous game between the Dodgers and the Giants in 1951, when Bobby Thomson hit his 'shot heard around the world' off Ralph Branca? The fact that we're talking about that forty years later, an event which happened before we were born, and can name the players involved, tells you how exciting it used to be."

"Playoffs have diluted the thrill of sports," I said. "We get short-term excitement but miss the ultimate fun and significance. The gravity of the competition is lessened."

"And now we have more rounds of playoffs in baseball," James said. "It gets ridiculous. You're right that the heroics are less memorable."

"And interleague play is coming too," I added.

I took a sip of my beer, and feeling slightly buzzed, I blurted out, "I'm thinking about vagabonding around the world after college."

James turned from the TV to face me. "Vagabonding? What does that mean? Like a bum?"

"I mean, you know those books I've been reading by that guy Richard Halliburton? Well, he just bummed around the world for a year after college, hitched rides, worked odd jobs, et cetera."

"Go for it," said Dustin.

"Most Europeans and Australians do it right after school. It's like a birthright. It's not a big deal," said James.

"And Israelis too, after their mandatory military service," added Dustin.

"But I've never traveled anywhere," I said.

"Oh," said Dustin. "Maybe not go Full Monty, then. Start slow. Take a tour or do a program."

"I hate tours and group activities, and I feel like I need to do this on my own."

"You'll get eaten alive," said James. "The Aussies and Europeans go in groups of friends, I think. There are, like, backpacker trails and hostels. I don't think anyone is doing what you're considering."

"I'm not sure if that's true," I said.

"My friend's cousin," said Dustin, drinking his beer, "was in Berlin, and he met a girl who he thought was cool. She asked him if he wanted to smoke some pot, and he's like 'yeah,' so he goes with her to this party, and they have coke, but then the party gets raided, and he's thrown in jail by the cops. Meanwhile, his wallet has disappeared with like $1500 in cash. He was told by the police that this is a common scam. He lost all his travel funds and had to come home."

"This was a guy you knew?" I asked.

"No, just what I heard," said Dustin.

"You really shouldn't go off on your own at first," added James. I had a sense that James was trying to be polite and did not want to say outright that he did not think I was up for traveling on my own, but without being a hater or straight-out discouraging me.

"But I don't want to take a tour. I don't think that's any fun at all."

James took a sip of beer. "Why not do what I'm doing?"

"What's that?"

"I'm going on that archaeological dig with Professor Collins this summer in Israel before I start Officer Candidate School. It's not a tour. It's an academic project. It's probably too late to apply. But ask him. He likes you."

"I heard the professor talking about it, and I remember people applying months ago. He only takes a few select people. Besides, it's not traveling on my own."

"Baby steps, Joe. Baby steps," said Dustin, watching the television.

I began to wonder if anyone had any fun traveling or if it was just a series of unfortunate events. Others told me equally dire travel stories. "Did they have any fun?" I would ask half-sarcastically. At which point their tone would change. "Oh yes! Except for that part." I didn't get it. Were people just trying to add drama to their travelers' tales, or was there really a problem here? I had been telling people my idea for the last few weeks as if I were definitely doing it, but really, I was surveying their opinions, gauging their reactions, trying to decide if I was bold enough to go off on my own like

Richard Halliburton.

5

Forestry Industry Magazine

I went back to my dumpy college apartment. Even for a college student, it was pretty dumpy. It was in an old two-story motel converted into an apartment building. It really did look like something out of a David Lynch movie. All the apartments were studios, because again, they were formerly motel rooms, with brown linoleum floors and kitchenettes that could be hidden behind wooden doors that never slid properly in their tracks. The place smelled like old carpet and disinfectant. I left Coke cans strewn about the floor, adding to the motif. I used to love Coke. I, being a completist, also had an apartment with a cockroach problem. There was an MTV show at the time called *Joe's Apartment* about exactly this, a guy living in an apartment filled with cockroaches. Needless to say, the place did little for my love life. No interesting girls lived in my building, and any girls who visited did so once and never returned. Even my mom only visited me one time.

The place's great advantage was its location just across the street from the football stadium. I could roll out of bed on Saturday mornings and practically be at the game. Campus was a block away. If the traffic lights were in my favor, I could cycle from class to my apartment building in twenty-six seconds. It was also downhill.

It was April, just a month away from graduation, and I still had no idea what I was going to do, get a job or vagabond travel. I was now scared of chickening out of the vagabond idea. *Chicken out* was totally the right term because it was something I wanted so badly but was too scared to do. In retrospect, now after years of travel, I realize just how chicken shit I was, and everyone else too who warned me against the idea. I would have gone and had a great time. It turns out that other travelers, particularly white Americans, love to tell horror stories to scare each other and make their travels sound more daring than they really were. That's a big reason why most independent travelers you meet are not from America. Americans are rather found traveling in tours with detailed itineraries.

My mom pressed me to look for jobs, and so I did. I worked hard one week, sending out seventy resumes to companies in Denver, Los Angeles, and New York. I only received one response—a research company in New York called me for a phone interview. And I never heard from them again. No one wanted to hire me. It was an achievement getting seventy people to agree not to hire me, as it's hard to get seventy people agree on anything?

The job search was getting desperate when my mom set me up on an interview by way of a favor she pulled through an acquaintance in one of the many women's groups she belonged to. It was a shipping company that handled logistics for the logging and transportation of wood from the forests to the mills and then to the markets. They had an opening for a college grad to work in their main office in Denver. My mom said it might lead to "opportunities," without specifying what that meant, and at worst would be a "good experience" as my first job out of school.

An interview was arranged, and one day in April I put on my ill-fitting suit that all parents got their kids in the event they needed to look professional. I took the bus into downtown Denver, to an office building just off Sixth Street. It was a modern building with a security guard in the lobby. I searched the directory for the location of my interview and took the elevator to the thirtieth level. The company's office occupied the entire floor. It was crisp, clean, and modern with elegant carpets, plants in pots for decoration, tasteful abstract art on the wall, and a few glass-walled conference rooms with stunning views of the city. The place smelled like new furniture and burnt coffee.

The University of Colorado forced me and all graduating seniors to take a career advisement course that advised us on how to conduct ourselves in job interviews. Per their instructions, I showed up early with five copies of my resume, printed on good-quality bond paper and neatly kept in my faux-leather document holder that I had picked up from Staples for $7.

The receptionist was just a couple years older than me and pretty. "Can I help you?"

"I'm Joe Levy. I'm here for an interview with Robert Chittenden."

"I'll let him know you're here. Have a seat."

I sat down in the reception area and decided that it was proper to page through the magazines on the table. I soon found myself reclining with *Forestry Industry Magazine* and crossing my legs comfortably. The magazine was full of beautiful pictures of the forests that this company was cutting down and turning into wood products.

"Joe?" came a businesslike voice. I looked up. It was Mr. Chittenden, a tall man in his mid-forties wearing a shirt and tie, but no jacket.

"Good morning," I said, shaking his hand. He had a firm handshake, like you were supposed to have.

"Come with me," he said. We walked beyond reception and down a hall. On the right were offices facing out with views of the city of Denver. On the inside was cubicle after cubicle. I looked in on the cubicle workers as we passed. Some were on their phones, some on their computers; all had tidbits of their personal lives posted on the walls: pictures of family, friends, cats, exotic locales where they probably wished to travel, and sometimes a *Dilbert* or *Far Side* cartoon.

Mr. Chittenden's office was in the corner. It was large and looked out to the west and south, toward the mountains.

"Beautiful view," I said.

"Thank you. Sit down," he said, gesturing toward a chair.

I sat and took out a copy of my resume printed on bond paper from my faux-leather case and offered it to him.

"I already got one," he said. He put on a pair of wire-rimmed reading glasses and stared down at his copy of my resume on his desk. After ten seconds he looked up. "My wife is on the Denver Art Museum council with your mom, I hear."

"She's involved in quite a few things."

He returned to silently scanning my CV. I could only imagine what he was thinking, reading the bullshit that college grads are told to put on their resumes. Things like: two years working at a discount store in high school, International Relations Council in college, "showed strong leadership skills in group projects," "volunteered in a cultural exchange program." God bless Mr. Chittenden for reading my resume with a sense of importance. "I see you like history and government. You've taken a lot of classes."

"It's fascinating to me to see how it influences our lives today," I began. "So many of our institutions come from centuries of—"

"Where do you see yourself in five years?" asked Mr. Chittenden.

"In five years?" I hadn't thought about it. I didn't think anyone would actually ask this cliché question. Mr. Chittenden watched me thinking and knew I had not considered it. *Stupid college kid,* he must have thought, *no direction.* "Running my own business?" I offered. This was a revelation to me, as I had never known this was something I wanted.

"I see. Are you not interested in a future with Denver Logging Logistics?"

"I am," I said, trying to recover. "My mom said that there are opportunities within DLL for entrepreneurs. People who come up with better and smarter ways of doing things and avoid the stagnation that can afflict established businesses." *Nice recovery, Joe,* I thought. Looking back at this exchange years later, I realize how ridiculous it is to ask a college grad who is interviewing for an entry-level job where he sees himself in five years. I mean, good if he or she has a plan, but come on, no one knows how the career of a twenty-two-year-old will turn out. A first job is only for the experience. The idea that any twenty-two-year-old, or me in this case, would be expected to work for DLL for the next five or fifty years was silly.

"That is true, Joe," responded Mr. Chittenden. "I come up with new ideas all the time."

Phew!

"How are you with computers?"

"I'm a double major in computer sciences."

"Oh, right," said Mr. Chittenden.

"But like most people my age, I can pretty much figure out any program put in front of me."

He looked over my resume a little bit more out of politeness. "Did your mom tell you about the job?"

"A little. Something about exploring new routes of transportation."

"Sort of. You'll be assisting the guy who is doing that. Basically, we have a new software system to track our shipping routes. We need someone to go through the old paper system and put the data into the computers."

"Data entry?"

Mr. Chittenden hummed. "Maybe. I guess it's that. There will be other opportunities in the future, but that's where we are now." Mr. Chittenden looked at his watch. "I have a meeting at two. Let me give you a brief tour on the way out."

He led me back to the hallway, where I was shown the break room and a coffee machine that had been left on too long and turned out to be the source of the burnt coffee smell, and more of the cubicles. I was introduced to Jan, an overweight middle-aged woman for whom I might be working. She was very polite and was, Mr. Chittenden told me, "a very nice lady that DLL couldn't do without." She smiled.

After the interview, he shook my hand firmly again and then distributed me into the elevator area with a pat on the back. I reached the pavement in front of the building. I stopped, looked up at the sky, soaked in the sun, and breathed in the crisp air of a spring afternoon in Denver. I ripped at the knot of my tie and went to catch the bus.

6

Drunk Dialing

"They really liked you!" my mom told me later. "Cheryl says her husband is going to offer you the job. I'm really proud of you."

I sent Mr. Chittenden a handwritten thank-you note, as was expected of me. And a few days later, he called to offer me the job. I accepted and said thank you.

The next day, in a late-April snowstorm, I trudged across campus to my economics class, lost in thought, my Walkman in my pocket, the earphone wires threaded through my winter coat and out my collar and tucked into my knit cap. The B-52's *Cosmic Thing* album played for me alone, drowning out the world around me and providing a soundtrack to the falling snow. Maybe my subconscious chose that album for a reason that morning. *Cosmic Thing* was a classic album, the band's best in my mind, and I had listened to it a million times, so it should not have been a surprise when the song "Roam" came on. I woke to my surroundings with an awful feeling in the pit of my stomach. I remembered that paragraph from *The Royal Road to Romance.* "I wanted freedom, freedom to indulge in whatever caprice struck my fancy, freedom to search in the farthermost corners of the earth for the beautiful, the joyous and the romantic." I stopped in my tracks and looked around the white campus. CU had a beautiful campus, and when it snowed, the familiar landscape was transformed into something totally different. To my right was the bridge where a small scene from *The Glenn Miller Story* was filmed. Glenn Miller graduated from CU. In life he quit a good gig with Ben Pollack's orchestra to go off and do his own thing, to create his own sound, to follow his dream.

I turned around, away from economics class, and found myself walking back across campus toward the History Department. It was in one of the older buildings on campus. I climbed the steps to the second floor, finding the office marked as Professor Collins's. The door was open.

I found the door ajar and knocked. "Professor?"

"Hi, Joe." He knew me, but I had never really interacted with him much beyond our classes.

"I know it's not office hours, but do you have a sec?" I asked.

"Come in. What's going on?"

I sat down without being asked. "Your program this summer... You're taking a few students to Israel. I was wondering if it would be possible to get in on it?" I said, leaving the question hanging in the air.

Professor Collins paused, his face grim. He leaned back in his chair and then his face brightened. "Maybe, actually. We took applications and did interviews six months ago, but something has come up. Someone in the group is having a little trouble, uh, fitting in, let's say. He isn't getting along too well with the others, to put it politely. I'm not sure I like him myself." He smiled. "As a professor, I probably shouldn't say that."

"I don't want to take anyone's spot," I lied. I knew who the person was. He was a douchebag, typical cocky-ass frat boy. There was usually one in every class. He was that guy who always had to offer his opinion, right or wrong, to show how smart he was but which had the opposite effect. Sometimes, when a student asked a question, this guy would answer instead of the professor. Professor Collins would then politely correct the response. He was the type who would stand up during the applause for an on-campus production of a Greek tragedy and shout "bravo!" I saw him once at a party feeding drinks to a freshman girl who appeared ambivalent about his attention. James had told me that he was not looking forward to spending the summer with this guy.

"What's going on with you?" asked the professor. "Why didn't you come to me earlier, when everyone else was applying?"

I told Professor Collins the story, about Richard Halliburton, about my chickening out, about DLL, about my taking baby steps toward what I really wanted.

After hearing me out patiently, he leaned back in his chair and silently drummed his fingers on the desk. "I wouldn't do this for everyone. But you've taken five of my courses. You're a good student and clearly interested in history. Plus, you're more pleasant to have around than the other guy. If you're absolutely sure, I can make this happen."

"I'm sure. Absolutely sure," I said.

"Keep this under your hat till it's official. I have to handle this delicately."

A few days later, I was in Professor Collins's class. The douchebag guy was sitting in the back, his feet up on the chair in front of him, his hat on backward, his arms folded, and staring straight down at his desk unhappily. He said nothing during class. I took this as a good sign and felt an evil pleasure in his misery.

Class finished, the students packed up their notebooks and books.

"Joe, would you mind staying a moment?" Professor Collins said.

"Sure," I said as normally as possible, my heart in my throat.

When everyone and the douchebag had cleared the classroom, he said, "You're in."

"I'm in?"

"You're in."

"YES!"

"You have to get moving quickly. We leave in three weeks. You've missed most of the group meetings, but I know you can make it up. Get together with James, and he'll help you too. We meet tomorrow night at eight. You need to be there."

"Most definitely. I'll be there."

"It's too late to get you a student visa, but you can just enter as a tourist. The length of that visa should be enough time for the summer. Are you a licensed scuba diver?"

"Uh, no."

"Get scuba certified, and quickly. Call the Boulder Dive Center. They'll get you through a beginner and advanced course." He wrote down the number.

"Thank you," I said.

"Get going," he said, smiling.

But I wasn't excited. I left class with another awful feeling in my stomach. *Freedom, horrible freedom.* What had I done?

I couldn't concentrate that afternoon, so I decided to go for a jog, which I rarely did. I was in terrible shape. I put on some running shoes and ran for ten minutes up Boulder Creek and then back. I felt a little better.

I called James. "I'm in."

"I heard," he said. "Congratulations! It's so much better that you're going to be on the trip than that other guy. Dude! We're going to have such a blast!"

"Are you sure this is a good idea? I mean, maybe I should take that job."

"Are you crazy? You're going to spend the summer in Israel looking at archaeological treasures. We'll be like Indiana Jones."

"But my mom lined up this job for me with DLL. She pulled a favor. It's a good company."

"I'm not going to tell Professor Collins you're even thinking about this. You're being a wuss. Come, let's go get a drink."

"No, I can't. I need to work on a paper."

"When's it due?"

"Umm...in a couple weeks."

"Oh god, you're turning things in early again, aren't you? You're probably almost done with it, right?"

"I just need to proofread it one more time," I said. "I want to turn it in tomorrow. Turning things in early helped me turn my grades around."

"Fuck that. Come out with me now. You'll turn it in thirteen days early instead of fourteen. Meet me at the Sink in thirty minutes."

The Sink epitomized college bars. It was located just off campus in on the Hill. I only appreciate now just how loaded with college atmosphere this place was. The Sink itself was on the triangular corner of the street leading to the main part of the Hill. It had opened in 1923. It was grimy, as all proper college bars should be, filled with wooden tables with names etched in by years of student drinkers, graffiti scribbled all over the walls per tradition, and the scent of stale beer. State law forbade entrance until age twenty-one, meaning it was all upperclassmen. Freshmen and sophomores were relegated to house parties. Entry to the Sink was a rite of passage.

I walked across campus, passed the theatre where the marquee advertised Matthew Sweet. It was a weeknight, and there were only a few students in the bar. REM played over the speakers loud enough to enjoy but not enough to drown out the important intellectual conversations that all college students have. I arrived before James and sat at the bar. The bartender, a girl about my age, asked me what I wanted. I ordered two Fat Tires.

"You knew," he said as he sat down next to me, taking up his Fat Tire.

"It's the best beer," I said. "I hope they never go mass market and ruin their image."

"Okay, dude," said James, jumping right into my issue. "What's bothering you?"

"I just want to be sure I am doing the right thing. I mean, aren't I here in college to get a job and pursue a career?"

"Yeah! A career you want. Traveling will help you find it. That DLL job sounds miserable. Do you want to be that middle-aged middle manager, in the middle class, living his middling lifestyle?"

"Well, I—"

"You know you don't. You've gone from wanting to vagabond around the world for two years by yourself to taking a boring job instead of spending the summer in Israel. Come on, dude. You're just scared."

"But maybe this would open up the future for me. I could take this job, get some experience, move up, work for a few years, save some money, and then travel. It would be the right thing to do."

"Listen to yourself. Would Richard Halliburton take that job?"

"You've never read his books."

"But I have heard enough of him from you. You're chickening out again. This is normal. Listen to your inner self, not society's idea of the 'right thing.'"

"You're right. I just need this little push."

James had emptied his glass already. "Finish your beer. I got the second round." He signaled the bartender girl. "Two more Fat Tires and two shots of Jäger."

"Oh, god. I don't want this to be one of those nights. You know I'm not a big drinker."

"Beer with me," James said. The beers arrived, along with the shots.

"I'm not good with shots," I said.

"You just need practice," said James. James saw the hesitant look on my face. "Here's how you do it," he said. "Pick up the shot."

"Now?"

"Come on, dude. You're being really wimpy tonight."

"Okay," I said, picking up the shot.

"Hold it between your fingers. Let out a breath like a sigh, throw the shot down your throat in one motion, without tasting it. Don't sip it; it's not wine. Then immediately take a swig of beer to chase away the bitterness. Got it?"

"Got it."

"Go!"

James exhaled between pursed lips and threw back the shot, then grabbed the beer and took a big gulp.

I followed, drinking the shot instead of shooting it, the horrible flavor making me to shudder. I slammed down the shot glass triumphantly and downed nearly my entire Fat Tire, trying to rid myself of the bitterness.

"That wasn't so bad," said James.

"Yeah, exhilarating!"

"Oh my god," said James, looking across the bar. "I know one of those two girls from calculus math mods. I always see her in the tests." Math mods were a series of independent study classes. Instead of a traditional math class, you bought a textbook, checked out instructional videos, and then took the exams in your own time. You simply had to finish by the end of the semester. Everyone waited until the last minute, of course, but I took mine early.

I turned around. There were two cute girls. "Oh yeah," I said. "I've seen her too, the blonde, right? Smoking hot. She's always got her head down studying, not paying attention to anyone or anything around her. That is so cool. But I don't know the brunette."

"Hey!" said James to the girl. "Are you in math mods?"

The blonde looked at James. "Oh, yeah, hi."

"Are you nearly finished with them?" James asked her.

"I've been done for a while," she said. "You?"

"Soon. This is Joe," he said, introducing me.

"Hi," I said. "And this is James."

"I'm Jen, and this is Elena."

Jen had sandy blonde hair, wore a t-shirt and jeans, a fleece vest, canvas pants, and Birkenstocks. Very Boulder.

"Nice to meet you," said Elena. She had shoulder-length brown hair, glasses, olive skin, and also wore jeans with a t-shirt.

"You have an accent?" I asked stupidly.

"I'm Israeli," she said, "from Haifa."

"We're going to Israel this summer," said James.

"Maybe," I interjected. "I have a job lined up."

"He's going," said James.

"Okay?" said Elena in a very American way. "Where are you going?" she asked directly to me.

"The program is run by a history professor and archaeologist here. Do you know Professor Collins?"

"No," she said.

I told her about the program, that we'd be visiting Israel and diving the ruins at Caesarea.

James read the vibe between Elena and me and played the wingman by talking to Jen. Elena was here for her last year in school. She was an artist who had learned to ski on trips to Europe when she was a kid, so she wanted to study in Boulder. She was sweet and seemed interested in what I had to say in a way that I felt from few girls. She was clearly bright and spoke Hebrew, English, and Italian. She had traveled a lot and spoke of London,

Paris, and Italy as though they were regular destinations.

James ordered more drinks for all of us. James was a drinker, and like most people who liked to drink, he was pushing everyone else to have more. After the girls had a couple drinks, plus another Jäger shot, Elena said, "Jen and I have to go. I have to get up early tomorrow, but it was nice talking with you."

I didn't want her to go. "Hey, when do you head back to Israel?"

"I'll be there all summer," she said. "If you're there, we can meet up."

"Okay, can I have your number or email?" I asked, surprised at my confidence.

"Sure!" she said, getting a pen and paper out of her knit purse.

She handed me the piece of paper. "It was nice meeting you! Call me," she said. We hugged goodbye, and the girls left.

"Dude," said James. "She was so into you."

"Maybe," I said.

"She's Israeli," said James teasingly.

"She'll be there this summer too."

"Imagine that," said James, stroking his chin and grinning.

"My mom and DLL will be so disappointed," I said.

"Oh, god, please. What about Professor Collins? He made space for you. Your mom will eventually understand, and DLL couldn't care less."

"But I told DLL I'd take the job. They're counting on me."

James laughed. "They're a giant logging company, cutting down forests. Somehow, they'll manage without you and the vast skills that you bring to them, 'adding value' as an entry-level college grad."

"You're right," I said, lifting my beer glass. "Oh, it's empty."

"Have another," said James. He ordered two more.

"I think I've had too many," I said.

"Sounds like fate to me," he continued. "She's from Israel. How random is that?"

"A pretty girl is not a good reason to go to Israel. A pretty girl is not a good reason to do anything."

"That's not true," said James. "Pretty women have changed my life for the better!"

"Oh, come on. You were so hung up on that Emily girl last year. You were a complete mess, and she just toyed with you."

"That is not entirely true," said James pridefully. "But that's not what I am talking about. Remember when I went on Semester at Sea a couple years ago?"

"Yeah?"

"Think about it. It was a study abroad program where I sailed around the world with 350 other twenty-one-year-old students for 100 days, visiting ten countries. It was amazing!"

"I remember. I was completely jealous."

"Do you know why I went?"

"A girl? You never told me that. Which one?"

"I never told you about her because it was nothing, but she had a huge impact on me. Two years ago, I had a crush on this blonde girl who was in a few of my classes. She was tall, athletic, tan. But she always ignored me. One day I ran into her at Costco. I got up the guts to talk to her, and she was actually nice to me. I couldn't believe it. I thought it might go somewhere, so I asked her out. And she turned me down flat, saying, 'I'm not dating anyone right now because I'm going away on Semester at Sea.' 'What's that?' I asked her. That's how I first heard of it, and that's why I applied, all because of a pretty girl."

"But she just gave you a good idea."

"I got another story. Do you know how I got into drawing?"

"Another girl?"

"Yeah! I was ten years old. I had a crush on Becky. All first crushes are on girls named Becky. She was always drawing in class, and I found out she was in this after-school art program. I begged my parents to get me into the class. My parents were just happy that I wanted a hobby beyond playing Atari."

"A girl got you into drawing? Drawing is a huge passion for you."

"I took the class for a girl and then fell totally in love with art instead of the girl. Nothing happened with Becky but look where I ended up. I am at

CU on a partial art scholarship." James took a sip of beer. "Chase that girl Elena to Israel. Chasing her is the right thing to do and in line with your interests."

"You're right! I'm going to do it, and it's not just the beer talking. Fuck DLL. Fuck the cubicle. I'm going to Israel, and then I'm going to vagabond around the world."

"All right, dude! Give me five." James put his hand up. I gave him five. "Yeah!" I yelled. Everyone in the bar looked at us.

"Now, let's go quit your job," said James.

"Uh, what? *Now?*"

"Yes, now. You won't do it in the morning."

"But"—I looked at my watch—"it's 10 p.m."

"So?"

I took another gulp of beer. "All right, let's do this."

James lived near the Hill. We just walked a few blocks to his place. His roommate, Sara, sat on the couch, wearing a t-shirt and shorts, legs tucked under her, watching the *Real World*.

"Sara, could you mute the TV?" asked James. "Joe needs to quit his job."

"What?" said Sara. "You guys are torched."

"It has to be done now," I said.

"I'm staying out of this," said Sara, switching off the TV and getting up from the couch to head to her room.

"Do you have the number?" asked James.

"Umm, I think so," I said, fishing through my shoulder bag. "It's in my black book. But wait, no one will be at the office. It's ten o'clock at night," I said, slightly slurring my words.

"Oh," said James disappointedly.

"Wait!" I said. "I have Mr. Chittenden's home number. My mom gave it to me."

Sara poked her head out of her room, overhearing the conversation. "You guys aren't serious?"

James's face lit up. "Do it."

I boldly dialed the number. A little girl answered on the second ring.

"Hello?"

"Hi, is Mr. Chittenden around?"

"Sure, hold on," said the little girl. I heard her put the phone down. "Daaaaaaaad," she screamed. "Phooooone."

There was a short pause. Sara walked from the door jam and stood behind Joe. "This I gotta hear."

Mr. Chittenden picked up the extension. "Hello?"

"Hi, it's Joe Levy."

"Okay," he said, pausing. "You're calling me at home. Is this important?"

"Sorry to bother you, sir. I just wanted to inform you that I cannot accept the job with DLL. But thank you for your time and everything."

There was a short silence. "I'm not sure why this couldn't wait, but thank you for letting me know. All the best. Good night."

"Good night," I said.

The line clicked off.

"What happened?" asked James.

"It's done."

"How'd he react?"

"He didn't care," I said.

"Of course not," said James. "Did you expect him to say, 'No, DLL can't do without you. You were our future. Whatever someone else is offering you, we'll double it'?"

"You're evil," said Sara. "You had him do this completely loaded."

"Shut up," said James.

"You shut up," she said, hitting James on the shoulder.

"He did it of his own free will," said James, grabbing Sara playfully. They began poking at each other.

"Guys, stop," I said. "I have one more call to make."

"No way!" said James. "Oh my god, this is awesome!"

"What, who's he calling now?" asked Sara.

"You'll see," said James.

I dialed the familiar number. "Hello?" came the voice from the other end of the line.

"Hi, Ma," I said.

"Hi," she said. "Hold on. Let me get your dad."

I heard my dad pick up. "Hi, Joe. What's going on?"

"I have some news to tell you, and I didn't want it to wait till morning."

"Is it bad?" asked my mom.

"Depends on your point of view, but I don't think so."

"Do you have a cold?" asked my mom.

"No."

"You sound sick."

"I'm not," I said, hoping my mom would not catch on to my buzz.

"What's the news?" my dad asked.

"I'm not taking the job with DLL. I've decided that I don't want to work in the corporate world. At least not now. I have an opportunity to go to Israel with one of my professors this summer to work on an archaeological project, and then I think I'll travel for a bit."

"Have you thought about how this will impact your future? Your career?" my dad asked.

"I have. But I don't want to be tied down to a desk at this age. I'll have plenty of opportunities going forward."

"That DLL job is a good one. It'll be a good start for you."

"Look, Dad," I said, "all you wanted your whole life was to be independent. When you tried to go the corporate route, it didn't work out for you. I know you've never been out of the country, but traveling is something I want...need to do."

My mom chimed in. "You were all set with the job at DLL. Why not just do it for a year and see how you feel?"

"It's too late," I said.

"What do you mean?" asked my mom.

"I quit."

"When?" my mom asked.

"Just now."

"Just now? At 10:30 at night?"

"I guess so. I called Mr. Chittenden at home and told him."

There was a pause, and then my mom broke the silence. "I guess it's done, then."

7

The Real World

I woke the next morning on James's couch, where Sara had been sitting the night before. The TV was left on and still showing the *Real World*. An MTV logo in the corner indicated that it was a *Real World* marathon. My mouth felt like cotton, and my head was pounding. We'd had a lot more drinks after my phone calls. "Oh my god! The phone calls." The reality of what had happened the night before hit me. "Shit, shit, shit. What'd I do?" It was 9 a.m. on Wednesday. I would call Mr. Chittenden at the office and apologize. He'd totally understand. I went to pick up the phone, but then stopped. *I'm being impulsive, just wait a bit.* I drank some water and used the bathroom. The doors to both Sara's room and James's room were closed. I could feel the anxiety running down my arms.

I put on my shoes and walked out into a beautiful morning in Boulder. The sun was shining, and it was a crisp 55 degrees. My anxiety faded during the walk home. There would be no DLL. The buyer's remorse was gone. I was going to Israel.

That morning I called the dive shop in Boulder. There was a beginner's course offered that weekend and advanced the following. I signed up for both. The next few weeks were busy, occupied with finishing classes, graduating, and getting ready for my trip. I had already applied for and received my first passport earlier in the spring in anticipation of my now-postponed vagabonding trip. I had optimistically applied for the passport with extra pages. I thumbed through the empty pages, filled with potential.

Scuba diving was easy for me. I passed the classes with little problem. It was another skill that would open more opportunities. I attended my first orientation meeting for the trip. There were six of us. James was there. Professor Collins told us what equipment to buy and everything we might need. James was an amazing friend. He took me to REI and imparted all his travel experience to me. He showed me what backpack to get (small and reasonable, fifty liters), what kind of clothes to bring (quick drying and cool), stuff that travelers needed but I did not yet know existed, like one of those shammy-type towels. "According to *The Hitchhiker's Guide to the Galaxy* the towel is the single most useful item in the universe," James told me.

My parents were supportive when I talked to them the next day. I'm guessing that they had discussed it and decided that going to Israel with friends and a professor was a much better idea for a twenty-two-year-old than sitting in a cubicle in Denver. They helped me with buying the equipment along with some spending money—not a lot, but enough for me to eat and drink a little beer.

Graduation came. The speaker, whose name I can't remember, was a local entrepreneur. But his speech was memorable. "In wanting to be successful in life, you've already made your first mistake: going to college. It didn't help Bill Gates, Steve Jobs, Richard Branson, or Larry Ellison."

I called Elena for a date, but she needed to leave the country early, a family thing back in Israel. She told me to email her when I arrived.

Everything came about quickly. Soon I was packing up my dumpy apartment. The furniture belonged to the apartment. All I owned were clothes, my computer, some cookware, and a lot of CDs. Those would remain in boxes at my parents' house. I said goodbye to the cockroaches and closed the door forever to the University of Colorado.

On June first, my folks dropped me off at Denver International Airport. I was on my way.

8

Israel

The plane touched down at Ben Gurion Airport. It had been a long couple flights with a connection in New York City. The five others in Professor Collins's group slept en route, but I was too excited. I watched the in-flight movie, browsed the in-flight magazine, paged through the *SkyMall*, and read as much as I could of the Lonely Planet. I pulled my carry-on from the overhead bin. Despite James's help, I had entirely too much stuff. As soon as we walked off the plane onto the jetway, I felt the Mediterranean heat. This was my first time through passport control, and I wasn't nervous so much as curious. That said, when the officer asked me my country of residence, I said "Boulder County." He still let me in.

Professor Collins was already in Caesarea. The six students in our group were to stay the night in Jerusalem and take a bus up the next day. We changed dollars into Israeli shekels. One of the girls in our group, Holly, arranged a minivan taxi to take us to the hotel. As we drove into town, I saw the Dome of the Rock, the Western Wall, and so many things that I had only seen on TV. The light of dusk was settling in, just perfect for photographers.

"This is incredible," I said to James. "It's like the set of a movie, but it's actually real. There are signs in foreign languages. People look so different."

"Dude, you sound like a total newbie. Keep it to yourself."

We were put up in a comfortable but dated hotel near the Old City. There was a slow, tiny elevator that took us to our floor. James and I were sharing a room, which had two twin beds, a bathroom, and a shower. It was clean but had an old hotel smell that reminded me of my apartment in Boulder. The view looked down a narrow, winding street. A vendor across the way sold souvenirs, Orange Fanta, and an array of Cadbury chocolate. It was here that I discovered Top Deck, a bar with milk chocolate on the bottom and white chocolate on top.

"I'm going to go wander around," I said. "You wanna come with?"

"Nah," said James, "I'm not feeling well, and I need some sleep. You go."

"Come on, dude. This ain't like you to want to sleep. It's my first night in a foreign city."

"I know, but I still have that cold from last week. I feel disgusting. You go, man."

I hesitated.

"What's up?" asked James.

"I kind of just need an introduction. You know, new city and all."

James rolled his eyes. "Look, Joe. Go walk around. Nothing is going to happen. There's almost no crime in this city. There are soldiers everywhere. Your odds of being bothered by terrorists are very low. Just get a map and go."

I got a map from reception and spread it out on one of the tables in the lobby. The Old City was just next to the hotel. I put the map in my pocket and decided to wander around. I took a left from the lobby and walked up the cobblestone path to the Old City. It had just turned dark, but the winding passageways were brightly lit by incandescent bulbs strung above. Many tourists wandered about. The shops were just rented spaces in ancient buildings. Throughout were food stands illuminated by single lightbulbs, one with a hunk of meat on a vertical skewer. It smelled really good.

"How much for that?" I asked the man in the stall. He held up some fingers. I gave the man some shekels, and he sliced off a few strips of meat and put them in a pita along with some vegetables and covered it with a white sauce. My god was it good, salty, flavorful, the yogurt sauce a little tangy. I walked up a few more doors to a sign saying "falafel." I'd heard of that. I paid some more shekels and received falafel in a pita, also with yogurt sauce. Falafel is crispy fried balls of mashed chickpeas with spices.

I ignored my map and continued walking. I reached an area that said it was one of the Stations of the Cross. These were the places, actual places, where the real Jesus stopped on his last day, marching to his execution. A video game arcade was oddly placed next to one of the stations. This must've been where Jesus stopped to play Pac-Man.

The narrow alleyway opened unexpectedly into a large space that became the Wailing or Western Wall. Bright floodlights shone off the wall in brilliant contrast to the night sky. In front was the square, busy and animated with life. Some were tourists taking pictures, and others were Jews in prayer. There were separate men's and women's areas. I witnessed people writing wishes onto notes, stuffing them into cracks in the wall, and hoping god would make them come true. I approached one of the vendors selling pens and paper. I wrote my wish and placed it in a crack. I ran my hand down the ancient stones, feeling the millennia of history that had passed through here, the stone polished smooth from the touches of the people who had come before me. In America, our history only went back a few hundred years. The idea of thousands of years was unfathomable.

From the square, I continued through the tiny alleyways, peeking in the shops, and sometimes just sitting and observing. I looked at my watch and was surprised to find that it was well past 2 a.m. It had been thirty-six hours since I last slept. I was overstimulated and had no desire to sleep. The streets were empty of sightseers, but the nightlife had taken over. A few bars were open and raging. I entered the Arizona Bar in the Muslim Quarter. Inside they were playing eighties music, and a large number of backpackers from all over the world were drinking beer and talking. They were mostly from Western Europe, Australia, and New Zealand. I sat at the bar and ordered a cheap beer.

A moment later, I was chatting with a couple Aussie girls. They were on their gap year and simply traveling the world, staying in hostels, and working small jobs whenever they needed funds. They were attractive and had no trouble finding work as bartenders, paid under the table because they were not permitted to work. Business owners took advantage of their illegal work status. Getting paid involved arguing with their misogynistic bosses, who often just gave them half, knowing they had no recourse. One owner threw their pay at them, yelling at them as though he had been the one who was wronged.

A couple English guys who knew the girls joined us. Soon, a large crowd of us were chatting, drinking, and solving all the world's problems. We discussed Israel's place in the world and then the Sykes−Picot Agreement, an arrangement between the British and French to split up the Ottoman Empire's portion of the Middle East after World War One.

I was surprised at how knowledgeable everyone was. I had heard that the education system was better in Europe and Australia, coupled with a more-informed worldview. But I also realized later that independent travel attracts people who are generally more intelligent, educated, curious, ambitious, and, quite frankly, interesting. As much as I loved Boulder, randomly finding seven other people who could have an intelligent conversation about World War One half-inebriated in a bar at three in the morning would never happen.

I struck up a conversation with Barbara, a sun-bleached Aussie girl who had been traveling the world for the last five years and would soon be going back to Melbourne to start her PhD. She had a million stories, good and bad. And though I never saw her again, I bring her up because she said something I would never forget. When I asked why she had decided to travel, she said, "Pink Floyd."

"Pink Floyd?" I asked.

"Do you know the song 'Comfortably Numb'?"

"I do, a little," I said. I had actually seen parts of *The Wall* on *Night Flight*.

"I never want to become Comfortably Numb. Whatever I do in life, whatever decisions I make, I don't want to be in a situation where I am unhappy and become Comfortably Numb to it. Now, I always ask myself that question. Have I become Comfortably Numb?"

And from that night on, "Comfortably Numb" became the theme song for all my travels and my life.

* * *

Dawn broke through the windows of the Arizona Bar. It suddenly occurred to me that I had to be up and ready by 7 a.m. I had to go. I said goodbye to everyone without exchanging emails and went outside. Shopkeepers were opening. Food places were already open, serving breakfast, tea, and coffee.

Rather than find my way back on foot, I hailed a taxi drifting by.

"Old City Hotel," I said.

The man behind the wheel nodded and began driving. I leaned back, starting to feel really sleepy. The dawn sun shone off the golden dome of the mosque at Temple Mount. My eyelids were getting heavy, and I was so busy luxuriating in the joy of being free, travel, and having met such great people that I didn't notice at first that we were driving out of the Old City.

"Sir," I said, "Old City Hotel?"

"Yes," he said.

"Do you speak English?"

"A little."

"Where are we going?"

"Old City Hotel."

"Are you sure?"

"Yes, yes."

We were still driving away from the Old City. I looked back, knowing the hotel was somewhere in the other direction.

"You're going the wrong way," I said. "It's that way."

"No, this way," he said, getting irritated.

Earlier in the year, when I was still considering my big vagabond trip, many of the horror stories I had heard were of people getting ripped off by taxi drivers. "They're the worst," I was told. One person told me that they walked or took public transportation whenever they could to avoid taxi drivers. Or maybe I was being kidnapped.

"It's that way." I pointed. "Turn around."

"It's this way," argued the driver.

"Goddamn it, that way," I shouted.

This began a heated argument, with him turning around and yelling at me in Arabic instead of focusing on the road. I yelled back till I just said, "Let me out."

I tried the door. It was locked.

"Wait, wait," the driver said as we turned a corner, and he stopped.

"Old City Hotel," he said. I looked up and saw we were indeed in front of the Old City Hotel, but it was not the one I was staying at. This one was in the newer part of the city, taller and a little dirtier.

I wondered if I had made a mistake or if there were possibly two. Didn't they have copyright laws in Israel to prevent there being two Old City Hotels? Maybe it was a chain.

"Wrong hotel," I said.

"No, Old City Hotel. You said Old City Hotel."

"Forget it," I said and got out, the door now unlocked with the car stopped.

"You pay,"

"No," I said. "This is the wrong place."

"Old City Hotel," he said, pointing to the sign.

This went back and forth until the receptionist came out and asked what was going on.

"This is the wrong Old City Hotel," I said. "I'm at the one actually near the Old City, but he won't listen to me."

"This happens a lot," she said and explained to the taxi driver in Arabic what had happened. She was so nice that I held back from asking about the stupidity of there being a second Old City Hotel in the new city.

He threw up his hands in frustration and gestured for me to get back in the taxi, which I did. We followed the directions given by the receptionist until we found the correct Old City Hotel. He told the price, the equivalent of $20. It was way too much, I knew, but I was exhausted and paid it, feeling ashamed for not arguing harder. I walked upstairs to my room to find James sitting on the bed, ready to go. "Where the fuck you been?"

"I was out."

"It's time to go, dude. I was just about to raise alarms and tell everyone that you were gone. For now, I just told them you were slow getting ready."

"It's fine, dude. I'm here." I looked at my watch. It was 7:30. "Oh shit," I said. "I am really late. No worries, though, I haven't even unpacked." I just grabbed my backpack. "Let's go."

Everyone was downstairs, waiting. "There you are," said Holly, the de facto student leader of the group and the one making all the arrangements. The bus to Caesarea was idling. I boarded it, and as we drove away from the hotel, I was starting to fall asleep when I snapped awake. "Oh shit," I said to no one in particular. "I left my credit card at the Arizona Bar."

"Oh, no," said James.

"We got to go get it," I said.

I leaned over to Holly. "Hey, Holly."

"What?" she said, already annoyed at me for holding everyone up.

"I left my credit card at a bar. We need to go back and get it."

"Oh god," she said, rolling her eyes. "Where?"

I told her where to go. The whole bus waited for me while I walked into the Arizona Bar and bugged the woman cleaning up to give me my credit card. As I got back on the bus, James said, "You fucked up your first night out in a foreign country, but at least you went and did it."

9

To Megalomaniacs!

I crashed, sleeping the entire two-hour ride from Jerusalem to Caesarea, after not sleeping for almost two full days. James shook me awake when we arrived. I didn't know where I was at first. I was trembling and feeling feverish. It was nearly 100 degrees out and getting warmer. The heat, the sleepless night, and the aftereffects of the alcohol made everything worse.

Caesarea sat on the coast of Israel. Our home for the next three months was a couple of large tents near the archaeological site. The girls had one tent, and the guys the other. Professor Collins greeted us as we got off the bus and showed us where to go. I carried my backpack in and found the cot that was to be my bunk.

"Get settled in," said Professor Collins, "and everyone meet at 11 a.m. at the main tent."

I looked at my watch. "I have thirty minutes," I said to James. I lay down on my cot and went to sleep. When I woke up again it was night. I darted upright in a panic, thirsty and needing desperately to pee. James was unpacking next to me.

"What happened?" I asked.

"You missed everything, and Professor Collins is annoyed with you, but go back to sleep."

"What? Fuck." I started to sit up.

"It's 11 p.m., dude. It's too late. Just go back to sleep and be fit for tomorrow."

"Why didn't you wake me?" I asked.

"We tried!" he said emphatically. "You were out, almost comatose. Seriously, go back to sleep. You'll fix everything in the morning."

I slept the rest of the night and woke up at 6 a.m. the next day feeling back to normal. I found Professor Collins in his tent and apologized. He seemed incredibly gracious about the whole thing.

"Don't worry about it," he said. "I know that you're not like this. It's your first time in a foreign country, and you got carried away. Don't do it again. Have James fill you in on what you missed."

The archaeologists' camp looked like something from *M*A*S*H*, a series of large olive-green army tents. Aside from the student tents, Professor Collins had his own quarters. The main project area was a large, open canopy with work tables, one covered with maps and charts, another for cleaning and analyzing our finds. We had a few plastic buckets of saltwater for holding items discovered underwater. This was to prevent them from deteriorating when brought to the surface after being submerged for 2,000 years.

Caesarea Maritima was built by Herod the Great from 25 to 13 BC. The notable thing about the city was its harbor. It is located on a straight coastline with no natural inlet from which a harbor could be constructed. The nearest major harbors were Piraeus in Greece and Alexandria in Egypt. To build the harbor, they sunk boats filled with concrete, forming strong harbor walls. The method was incredibly effective, as the harbor withstood the forces of the sea for hundreds of years, becoming a major port and commercial center for the area. It was a focal point for the rise of Christianity until it was abandoned following the Muslim takeover in 638. It was later recaptured by Christian crusaders and then again by the Muslims until it was abandoned again in 1800, finally settling into a quiet fishing village in 1884. It once more developed into a proper city in 1940, formally being incorporated in 1977. Much of ancient Caesarea still stands. The theatre and hippodrome are impressive. The theatre has been partially restored and is currently in use.

Professor Collins's project was studying the harbor. His focus, and our focus, was underwater archaeology. We spent most of our days in scuba gear at shallow depths looking for artifacts such as coins, pottery, etc. Many city structures with intricate tile floors, columns, and fixtures remained submerged. This stuff was too large to be recovered or moved and was studied in situ. Underwater areas were sectioned off using a system developed by Professor Collins. Each area was then photographed and mapped. Each of us was given a section to cover. I spent hours scuba diving. In the shallow depths, my air lasted a long time and there was little risk of the bends. Surface time was spent cataloging and analyzing the recoverable items. Each was photographed, labeled, and organized. Ancient coins were an interesting find and more common than you would expect. Professor Collins made this his specialty.

I settled into a routine. My mild iniquity on the first day was quickly forgotten as I got back to my old nerdy and dependable self. We would start work at dawn and go until lunch, when it got really hot in the Israeli summer. There would be a long break following lunch for napping through the heat of the day, and then back to work in the late afternoon. We spent our evenings hanging out on the beach drinking beer. As mentioned before, there were six students in the group, all from CU. There were James and I. Holly, who was this hyperactive, tall, freckled, auburn-haired volleyball player and bossy, but she was cool once you got to know her. Still, it rankled me whenever she tried to order me around. Latrell was an African-American guy whom I had used to see in class but never knew until this trip. He was another of those all-around Renaissance-man types. He had ridden motorbikes in the past, loved music, and played bass. Yet he was easy to talk to, read voraciously, and could give a knowledgeable opinion on most any subject. Carrie was a quiet girl, very nerdy but with a cute face and extremely focused on her work in Caesarea, keeping everything organized. At some point during the summer, she got a tattoo and dyed her hair purple. Lastly, there was Derek, a short guy with cropped hair who wanted to become a doctor someday. He was somehow always missing, and the common refrain in the group was "Have you seen Derek?"

I emailed Elena, the Israeli girl whom I'd met in Boulder. She lived in Haifa, about a thirty-minute train ride away. We began dating almost immediately. What struck me was the ease with which the relationship began, no games. I was told this was common amongst non-American women. You met, and if you liked each other, you were together. None of this waiting two days to call someone back, trying not to appear too eager. She was very sweet and often cooked me dinner at her apartment. Because she had a private room in a shared flat and I lived in a tent with two other dudes, I would often go up to her place for the weekend. Occasionally she came down for a visit. The girls in our group got to know and like Elena and were cool letting her roll out a sleeping bag in the girls' tent. But there was little time for us to be alone in Caesarea. We could, however, wander alone at night, amongst the ruins, finding an ancient, secluded spot in the warm Mediterranean nights.

By the campfire, Professor Collins regaled the group with stories of Caesarea. His passion for history shone through, holding us rapt, just as he did in his lectures.

"Where would the world be without egotistic megalomaniacs?" he said one night. "Don't be surprised. I mean. How many of the tourist attractions we hold to be great accomplishments of mankind were built by megalomaniacs as tributes to themselves? The Great Pyramid in Egypt was built as a tomb for Cheops. Louis XIV built Versailles. King Herod founded Caesarea as a location for his lavish palace that featured an Olympic-sized swimming pool.

"Think about it. These monuments to ego sometimes had civic value to the people, like the harbor here. One could argue that the Great Wall of China was built to protect the people, even though it was really to protect the emperor's power. But many people suffered and died to build these, not to mention that they were a major drain on the economy when that money could have been spent on more beneficial civic projects. But who, for instance, in France 300 years ago would have imagined that Versailles, built at such expense, would be such a source of tourist revenue today?"

"But it's so beautiful!" said Holly.

"Of course it is, but it was not built for the people of France. It was built for Louis XIV. Louis's father, Louis XIII, began it as a relatively modest hunting lodge in 1623. Historians estimate that what Louis XIV built would, in today's money, cost $200 to $300 billion dollars. Imagine the uproar if the French government tried to develop such a project now. You think the French strike a lot currently? France is a democracy today and people have a choice, but in the eighteenth century they didn't. Money that could have gone to other infrastructure—developing the overall economy, for example, or helping the poor—instead went to this lavish palace for one person's pleasure."

"But there isn't a Frenchman who doesn't take pride in Versailles. Or the other châteaux," Holly said.

"My point exactly. Now, Versailles is a point of pride, but originally it was an obnoxious extravagance. This extravagance led to the eventual overthrow of the nobility during the French Revolution. At least the construction of Versailles didn't cause the deaths of thousands of laborers. One of the most glaring examples of that is the Great Pyramid in Egypt, built by slaves and costing the treasury the equivalent of $5 billion in today's money, all so one guy would have a better chance of getting to the afterlife. Now millions of tourists flock to see it, collect mini replicas, and have their pictures taken on a camel. Its true history of slavery and death are told as an interesting footnote.

"Look around the world at the manmade tourist attractions. Most were built at the expense of others for one person's glory, even religious monuments. Rich patrons sponsored churches, temples, mosques, etc. for their own desire to gain favor from their deity of choice.

"But it's okay with me as an archaeologist. I have interesting things to look at and explore. These monuments to ego tend to be built solidly in order to withstand the test of time. They are preserved now because of the economy they create as tourist attractions. Common houses and household items are rarely preserved because no one cares. Think about your own lives. You save the family jewels, the valuable furniture, the keepsakes. But the stuff you use every day like the television, your pair of jeans, the eating utensils are just thrown away. But it is these common items that would best tell archaeologists two thousand years from now how your life really was, not your grandfather's expensive pocket watch.

"That's why the common structures are often destroyed to make room for new structures. Look around us now." Professor Collins gestured to the entirety of Caesarea. "This place is incredible. Thank you to King Herod and his self-aggrandizement, which has given us something interesting to do this summer. Are any of you interested in walking a hundred meters inland to dig up some common homes from 2,000 years ago? There are some right over there, but there's no intricate tile work, no pottery, no friezes, no murals, just a normal home. Why aren't we archaeologists more interested in the everyday lives of Caesarean residents back then? Because commoners are boring compared to the grandeur of King Herod. Here's to egomaniacs!" Professor Collins concluded, raising his beer in a toast.

"Hear, hear," we all said.

10

While Walking Home Late at Night

James and I often went into modern Caesarea to have a few beers and some time away from the group. We felt safe walking the twenty minutes down the quiet and somewhat dark road to reach the main area, where there were a few decent pubs. While the threat of terrorism was a definite concern in Israel, crime was nearly nonexistent. And that's why what happened this night was so unusual. Not only that, I found something out about myself that I hadn't known.

James, Elena, and I went out for some food, a few drinks, and dancing. Israelis love to party. Americans watching the news think that Israelis spend all their time huddled in bomb shelters. Israelis are inured to the threat and party despite it. Maybe it's defiance. Maybe it's a release. Maybe it's both. Popular dance music, what we call techno in America, becomes popular first in Israel and Europe and ends up two years later in the United States.

We didn't have to work the next day and so we stayed out late that night. It was 2 a.m. We were walking down the dark road when a group of five guys in their late teens approached. They came up quickly from the side, and we thought at first that they were also just coming back from partying, like so many other people we had seen out and about that night. But they stood in front of us and, in some sort of accent, asked for our money. They had no weapons. We looked at them in disbelief, none of us knowing what to do.

"Money, give us your money!" said one, shoving James.

"Okay, Okay!" James looked at both me and Elena.

I was frozen and didn't know what to do. I stared at James.

"Just give it to them," he said. "It's not worth it."

I reached into my pocket and took out the equivalent of $20. One of the teens snatched it from my hand. James pulled about $5 worth of shekels from his pocket. But Elena was wearing tight jeans and was having a little trouble getting her money out.

"Hurry up!" one screamed at her.

"Just a sec. I'm hurrying. It's stuck," she said, nearly crying while tugging at her pocket.

The muggers were shifting on their feet and looking around impatiently. Another guy said something in a foreign language, maybe saying to forget Elena and to just leave. The teen harassing her became more anxious and shoved Elena. Not too hard, but she must have tripped over a rock or something. She tumbled backward, hitting her head on the ground and passing out. She stopped moving.

"Fuck!" I heard the muggers say in English and run off, while the guy who had pushed stood there in shock. I saw Elena out cold and the idiot guy standing there with his mouth gaping, and, in what must have been an instant, something in me tripped. My vision jumped, and I literally saw red.

"You fucking son of a bitch," came out of my mouth. I pushed the guy to the ground, jumped on top of him, and began pummeling his head with my fist. I pounded away with my fist. With each punch his face became more distorted, blood pouring out his nose and eyes, the back of his head hitting the ground with each punch. He went unconscious, but I kept going. Hitting him, repeatedly, for I don't know how long. Anger coursed through my arms. Through the fog of rage, I didn't hear James saying "Stop, stop, stop." He tried to grab my fist but couldn't stop me, so he instead wrapped himself around me and said calmly, "Joe, stop. He's out. Elena's hurt. We need to get her to a hospital." I stopped and stared.

"Come on," James said.

I stood up slowly and looked at Elena. She was awake, sitting up and leaning on one arm, rubbing the back of her head with the other hand. Her eyes focused on me sitting on top of her assailant, now out cold and a bloody mess. "Oh my god, Joe," she said.

The hospital wasn't far away. We slowly walked Elena there, she constantly saying, "I'm all right. I'm all right. I just hit my head." The doctor diagnosed her with a minor concussion and wanted to watch her overnight. The hospital called the police. An officer showed up and took a report. He was professional and polite, unlike most officers in the States. I told him the whole story, even what I had done to the assailant.

"You should probably send someone out there," I said. "See if the guy needs help." I didn't really mean it. I just wanted to sound altruistic to prevent any trouble with the cops. The cop radioed in the report.

A few minutes later the cop got a call on his radio. "My partner found no one at the spot you mentioned, but there was blood. We'll keep looking for him. This has been happening more lately," he said. "These teens come across the border, and they have no money. They have no weapons and just intimidate their victims by approaching in groups. They don't want any trouble and usually run away at the slightest resistance. It's unusual what happened to your friend. The assailant probably got carried away."

"Do you think he's okay?" I asked.

"Probably. I mean, I don't know for sure. But there was no one there at the spot. If he were seriously hurt, he'd have gone to a hospital, and if he was dead, we'd have definitely heard about it."

"What happens next?" I asked.

"If we catch the guys, we'll let you know, and you and your girlfriend can press charges. Chances are we won't find them."

"And what happens to me?" I asked.

The cop looked me straight in the eye and said, "Nothing. Sounds like self-defense to me."

James went back to camp to tell Professor Collins what happened. I stayed with Elena in the hospital. They just sat her down in a room. A nurse came by every hour or so to check on her. Otherwise, they told her not to sleep because of the concussion. I sat next to her, keeping her awake. She leaned on my shoulder. There was a bandage on the back of her head covering a small cut. She lifted her eyes toward me. "What happened to you back there?" she asked.

"I don't know. I lost it. When I saw you on the ground, I just—"

"I've never seen you like that. You don't have a temper."

I said, "I've never even been in a fight."

"Not even playing hockey?"

"When I played hockey in college I was always the calm one. There were some guys who wanted to fight. I thought it was silly. They were usually the bad players who watched hockey on TV and thought being tough made up for their lack of skill. These guys would try to intimidate me in front of the net, but I never bit. I just didn't like to fight."

"You did try to protect me."

"But I didn't protect you. You got hurt, and then I reacted."

Elena was silent for a while and then said, "What happened afterward. How you kept hitting that guy. You just kept going."

"What about it?" I said.

"It was scary."

11

Where's My Last Meal?

"This was the first time you did anything like this?" asked Chris Billings.

"It was. It caught me completely off guard."

"Do you feel good about what happened?"

"You mean beating up the guy who knocked my girlfriend down?"

Chris nodded.

"Yes and no. It felt good, but mostly I felt guilty. That night I was out of control. Civilization and justice is supposed to be a path from pure animalistic revenge to the higher values of due process and trial by one's peers, rather than the victim or victim's loved ones taking action into their own hands."

"On the other hand, you may have meted out the only justice that mugger ever received."

"I've often thought about that. After it happened, I thought, *Maybe he and his friends learned a lesson that night and went out and got proper jobs.* But I was naïve. These people were desperate refugees who needed our money to survive. They couldn't just go out and get a job. And there were too few people helping them. It doesn't make their actions right, but I am not sure what I would have done in their place. That's where my thinking began to change. We need to help desperate people, so they don't have to resort to violence."

"I guess the naysayers who'd scared you off from your dream of vagabonding around the world because it was too dangerous were proven right. You got mugged."

"No, they're still wrong. Problems happen. But I found that avoiding robbery meant just being smarter. Don't walk around at night. Robbery is a real problem. In Africa. In Asia. In South America. Even cities in North America. Pretty much anywhere but the South of France, if you get what I mean. I never got robbed again. From then on, I didn't walk around at night unless it was in a large group or in well-lit major areas. Otherwise, when I went out at night, I took taxis at night or didn't go out at all. This became easier as I got older, got married, and had less desire to be hanging out at bars in foreign countries after midnight. So, no, mugging is not just a travel problem. It's just common sense anywhere in the world. I mean, would you walk around LA, Chicago, or New York alone at night?"

"I guess not."

"By the way. Where's my last meal? I'm getting hungry."

"What happened after that? When did you go to Africa? The summer must've been ruined after that."

"No, not really..."

12

The Summer Ends

Elena healed and things quickly returned to normal. From that night on, we took a better-lit route to town or even spent the small amount of money we had for a taxi. Except for that night, it had been an amazing summer. Working on the project at Caesarea had taught me a lot. At some point, I had spoken to Professor Collins about options following the year. This experience of living in a foreign country for a few months had made me more comfortable traveling, but—I am embarrassed to admit this now—I still wasn't ready to go vagabonding around the world on my own. Through one of the guys in my group, Latrell, I had heard about a program volunteering in West Africa. Not wanting to go home and still looking for adventure, I figured I'd ask him about it and see what it was about.

"It's very different from Israel," Latrell told me. "There's not much in West Africa to see. There are some wildlife parks, some culturally interesting sights, but better versions of all those things can be found in other parts of Africa. It's nothing like there is to see here or in Europe."

"I know, but we wouldn't be sightseeing. I'm interested in volunteering, helping people, and seeing a part of the world I ordinarily wouldn't be traveling to on my own."

"They need a lot of help there. My older brother runs the program in Mali. Do you know where Mali is?"

"Timbuktu."

"Correct. This part of the world is like hell. During colonial times they called it the White Man's Graveyard. It's perpetually hot, humid, full of disease, unsanitary conditions, unstable governments, ongoing conflicts, food shortages, and unclean drinking water."

"But that's why they need us."

"I'm trying to give you a realistic picture of working there. They need us badly. The NGO's mission is clean water and sanitation. We dig sustainable wells, show people how to treat water and keep it clean and how to dispose of waste. It's tough, disgusting work but extremely necessary. Why do you want to do this?"

"To be honest, I've lived a middle-class life of privilege, and I want to help out. Plus, I'm interested in adventure. It's hard, if not impossible, to see West Africa without being in a group. And if these people living there can benefit from my ambition, all the better."

"Oh, you'll find adventure," said Latrell. "A few French tourists fly into Timbuktu just to say they've been there, but otherwise we're in the boonies. This will be an experience for you."

* * *

"West Africa?" Elena asked when I told her my plan.

"Probably," I said.

"Aren't you worried about getting in over your head?"

"Nah, I'll be with an organization."

"I don't mean that," said Elena. "It's just that you have this ambition to travel. Israel was a good start for you, and now you're jumping into the deep end. How about doing some traveling through Europe and Asia first? You can visit me in France. Then you can move on to places like Africa."

"That brings me to another reason for going. I figure that after being in Africa, even if it's with a group, I can travel anywhere."

"That's not a sincere motivation."

"So? I want to help people. And if this NGO's goals align with my search for adventure, I'm sure the people I am helping won't mind."

"True."

"You're making me sound so selfish. Imagine if those immigrants who'd attacked us had had help and were not desperate. They may have never needed to resort to robbery."

"And what about us?" asked Elena.

Elena was a great girlfriend and one of the sweetest girls I met. Looking back, I could see we were just twenty-two years old, and she was the soundtrack to the best summer of my life, but she had been accepted to grad school in France that fall, and I was going in the opposite direction. I could have gone with her to France, and I did think about it, but more of me wanted to venture out and see things. It's the arrogance of youth when you can throw away a great person who cares about you, thinking there would always be another. But she was too nice, too sweet. I knew I'd never fall in love with her. I learned later that I like girls with an edge.

On our last night in camp, I had that sad but hopeful feeling one gets before something good comes to a close. The archaeological group would disperse forever. It was one of those warm Mediterranean nights that I just loved. The sun was setting over the old city of Caesarea. James had been accepted to Army OCS and was going back to the U.S. to begin his training. For Professor Collins, it had been another dear summer of research before returning to the beautiful but completely different climate in Boulder. As we drank our beers, we couldn't help but turn our well-deserved admiration toward Professor Collins, who had made all this possible. The next morning, Latrell and I took the bus to the Ben Gurion Airport to catch our flight to Bamako, Mali.

13

Mali

The NGO for which Latrell's brother, Mike, worked was sponsored by the UN and was part of their larger clean-water initiative for the world. Mike was the head of the NGO for West Africa. Apparently, few people were willing to volunteer in West Africa. He was happy to have someone recommended by his younger brother, someone whom he could trust.

Bamako, Mali, straddles the banks of the Niger River. Its location near the rapids separating the upper and middle Niger valleys makes it an ideal trading port. It grew rich through the movement of gold, ivory, kola nuts, and salt. As the French colonized West Africa in the nineteenth century, it became the capital of French Sudan in 1908 until it was absorbed into the French West Africa federation. The French left in 1959, and Mali was granted independence in 1960. French was the lingua franca, although more and more Malians were reverting to their indigenous languages.

Bamako's airport was a smallish affair. It had been built with great things in mind, but the government had failed to maintain it. It was dirty, and the air conditioning and lights were turned off to save power. Two border control officers were stationed in booths made from pressed wood, the glass missing from the windowpanes. A long line formed of disembarking passengers, the government unconcerned about needing more officers to speed up the process. I was required to fill out an arrival card, which, in addition to asking my name, birthdate, nationality, etc., wanted to know which tribe I belonged to. I was definitely in Africa. I wrote "Colorado Buffaloes." The border control officer checked my visa and passport but failed to remark on my tribal affiliation.

It was hot and extremely humid, the kind of weather where after five minutes you needed another shower and a laundry. But this was Africa, and everyone was in the same stinky boat.

Mike met us at the airport in a new-model white Toyota Land Cruiser, paid for by the NGO. Toyotas are the workhorses of Africa. They are the taxi vans, the pickup trucks, the SUVs, the cars. Toyotas were reliable and simple to fix. Africans are great mechanics and could keep these cars running for years. Many of the cars I got into were wrecks on wheels, the upholstery torn, the speedometers and odometers long disconnected, the gear sticks shaking uncontrollably, and yet the engines still ran. Road conditions in Africa were bad, even in the cities. Cars that were in no way designed to drive off the pavement were treated like 4x4s.

Mike met his little brother with a big hug, and then Latrell introduced me, "This is Joe."

"Nice to meet you, Joe," he said. Mike was a tall African-American gentleman, full of wit and personality. He had the strong presence of benevolence, of someone wiser than his age. He was in his mid-thirties.

We got in the blessedly air-conditioned Land Cruiser. Bamako was aspiring to be something more than a backwater African capital. Several new buildings had gone up or were going up, including the impressive Bank of Africa on the banks of the Niger River. The streets were unkempt, with a lot of motorbike traffic. Women, dressed in a mix of traditional West African garb and modern clothes, walked along the street, which was mostly dirt and open sewers with no paved sidewalks. The women's African dresses were beautiful, clean, and elegant, especially when compared to the dress of the men, who mostly wore modern, nondescript t-shirts and jeans.

We drove to the Novotel, a chain of French hotels designed for business travelers and often found in exotic spots around the world. The complex was gated, with security guards at the entrance. They let our Land Cruiser right through. Latrell and I shared a room. And even though Novotels were known for being quality middle-class business establishments, this was still clearly a hotel in Africa. The toilet wouldn't stop running. The sheets were too short for the bed. The television channels came in fuzzy. Yet the place probably cost a hundred dollars a night. I looked out the window at the city.

"What time do we have to meet for dinner?" I asked.

"Not till 9 p.m.," said Latrell.

"I'm going out. Want to come with?"

"Nah, I'll stay here. Careful out there. Be back by nightfall."

"No worries about that," I said, putting on my CU cap, sunscreen, and walking out the door. Several Westerners and Chinese people sat in the hotel lobby talking business. I walked from the frigidly air-conditioned lobby into the baking heat and humidity of Bamako. Beyond the gate was the real, unsheltered city. I was walking in Africa all alone for the first time, and I was nervous.

But people went about their business just like in any other city. I walked to the main road and saw a derelict small plane parked in front of an office building. The sign, in French, advertised mail couriers, who were needed to make deliveries outside the city because the country roads were poorly maintained, made from dirt, and often washed out during the rainy season. Goods could also go by river, but it was much slower.

I noticed a lack of any restaurants as we know them. In other words, there were no places with tables and chairs, where you would go in, sit down, and order. Instead, there were street vendors on the side of the street selling all kinds of food, like brochettes of meat on wooden skewers. My program materials told me to be wary of street food, but these looked so good, and I could see them being cooked right in front of me, so I bought one for the equivalent of twenty-five cents. It was delicious: meaty, fatty, flavored with local spices. I couldn't tell if I was eating beef or goat, but I guessed goat from the toughness and slight chewiness. Into the market I went, finding stalls selling common modern items: plugs, fans, brooms, mops, soap, laundry detergent, razors, toothbrushes, etc. There were stalls selling colorful spices in what was clearly the spice section of the market, which led into the fabric section. I wondered why merchants of similar products all congregated in the same section. Wouldn't they cannibalize each other's business? The narrow walkways in the markets were crowded with shoppers, moving about and stopping to examine items. Some people were boldly trying to get through on motorbikes or with wheelbarrows. Nobody minded bumping into each other, offering no apology like they would in America.

Few people took notice of me, the white foreigner against this sea of Africans. For all the horror stories I had heard about traveling in Africa, these were just normal people, going to work, to school, and making a living. They bore no ill intent against me. Within an hour, I felt comfortable. What had I been so worried about? I bought a Fanta, sat under a tree, and watched the world go by.

14

The Sahel

We met Mike for dinner in the hotel. Twenty other volunteers joined us at a table in a private conference room. Mike stood at the front of the room before a PowerPoint presentation projected onto a screen behind him.

"The purpose of this NGO is clean water and sanitation for underserved villages," began Mike. "Eighty percent of illnesses are caused by poor water and sanitary conditions. One out of five deaths before the age of five is due to water-related diseases. Dirty water is filled with bacteria and parasites. We believe that clean water and sanitation is the first step to development. A healthy populace can farm, raise cattle, and become educated. Water is a fundamental right.

"If you guys haven't noticed, it's pretty hot out there. Imagine living out there and not having consistently clean water to drink. Every glass of water could kill you or make you very sick. This has got to end.

"Our goals are to dig wells, keep the water in the wells clean, teach the villagers how to maintain those wells, and properly dispose of their waste.

"Tomorrow morning, we go to the airport, where a C-5 is bringing supplies. These include shovels, drills, piping, concrete, pumping mechanisms, filters, water purification tabs, etc. We will be loading these onto trucks and taking them to a town 230 kilometers from here, to a warehouse. At the warehouse, you'll be trained on the equipment. We've hired local translators to help you explain everything to the villagers. For now, enjoy your dinners and be packed up and ready in the lobby after breakfast at 9 a.m."

Dinner was served by hotel staff, who provided us steak, potatoes, and wine.

"This is pretty nice," I said to Latrell.

"My brother eats well here. NGOs pull out all the stops for their volunteers in Africa. I think they're just glad to have us."

I slept well that night. My first time in an air-conditioned room in a long time, after a summer in a tent in Caesarea.

The next day I was up early and found a delicious continental breakfast buffet in the hotel restaurant. They had bacon, but it was European style, which is a gross, soggy version, not crispy and delicious like American bacon.

Then, with my bags packed, I met everyone in the lobby, where we were taken in a convoy of Toyota Land Cruisers to the airport. The C-5 had already landed. Airport workers unloaded the crates and crates of content. Mike stood close by with a clipboard, checking off various items on his ledger. The crates were loaded onto trucks hired by the NGO. A few hours later, the convoy was on the move.

I rode in the truck with Mike. "How long have you been doing this?" I asked.

"About ten years," he said. "I came here, like you, as a volunteer just out of school. I worked here in Mali for two years and then went back to get my master's degree. They offered me a job after graduation, and I've been here ever since."

"Do you like it here?"

"I love it! The NGO treats its employees well. It's a sweet deal. I get to help people, work in an interesting place, and they provide us decent accommodation. If you enjoy your time here, after a couple years, you should think about following a similar path."

"Don't you miss home?" I asked.

"Not really. I miss watching American sports, and I miss some of the holidays, like the Fourth of July and Thanksgiving. But I can still get sports scores on my shortwave."

"Shortwave? What's that?"

"You've never heard of shortwave?"

"No," I said.

"They're radio signals that travel along the curvature of the Earth. Most nations have stations broadcasting to the world as a free service. I listen to the BBC or Voice of America. They have music, news, documentaries, sometimes live sports. I'll show you later."

Bamako's urban sprawl was limited, and we found ourselves almost immediately in the country. We traveled a road along the Niger River to Segou, a town located about 230 kilometers away. Near the river, the landscape was a mix of semitropical and desert. This region of Africa is known as the Sahel, a transition zone between the Sahara Desert in the north and the tropical climates to the south. The landscape was a contrasting mix of red clay dirt and lush green grass and trees. As one got close to the river, the thickness of the vegetation increased.

The road was mostly dirt, but attempts to pave it in some areas had done more harm than good. When a paved road is not maintained, it devolves into potholes and large chunks of asphalt. A dirt road, on the other hand, will develop ruts but avoids the problems of jagged concrete. Cars and trucks weaved from one side of the road to the other, looking for the way that would do the least amount of damage to the car, often driving on the opposite side. Ideas of safety were viewed differently here.

Villages scattered along the road were made up of a combination of traditional grass huts and modern buildings. The modern buildings were simply cinder blocks and concrete with either a traditional straw roof or sheets of corrugated metal. Metal was preferred because it didn't leak and would last years without maintenance, but it was also more expensive. I noticed a theme in Africa: building things but not maintaining them. None of these buildings had ever received a fresh coat of paint. They had been built, and that was that. As such, it was hard to tell the age of the buildings. There were many half-built buildings with concrete and rebar skeletons, maybe a couple floors, some bricks, no walls, no doors, sometimes staircases leading between stories. Were these new buildings being built or old buildings being torn down?

If something was no longer needed, it was abandoned and left to dete-riorate—same with cars, boats, farm equipment. No one felt the need to remove anything and perhaps clean up a place, which returns us to my theory of a lack of maintaining anything.

Few of the buildings had any sense of style or design, except for some remnants of the colonial French, usually administrative offices. The nineteenth-century French design was evident, and some of these towns had beautiful hotels de ville or old theatres. I even saw an art deco post office. Their faded elegance fired my imagination about what things used to be like. This region was known for its traditional mud construction. The locals mixed red clay with dung and molded it around wood skeletons, creating some magnificent structures. The eighteenth- and nineteenth-century explorers drew sketches to show them to the world back home. The area is known for several impressive mud mosques (more on that later), which are built well enough to stand for decades in this region of minimal rain.

Every village we passed had a small market of vendors selling local produce. It was always women and their very young children hawking goods by the roads, barely sheltered from the tropical sun. They sold baskets of fruit, brochettes of meats, packaged biscuits, and drinking water in plastic bags, something I had never seen before. Around mid-morning, we stopped in a small village to stretch our legs and use the bathroom, which meant simply going into the bushes. I know that a "bush toilet" at first sounds unpleasant to most Westerners, until they see what a "regular" bathroom is like. It is much cleaner being out in the grass and fresh air than going inside a smelly and dirty outhouse (more on this later too). While I was waiting for the convoy to get going, I stood feasting on brochettes sold to me by a charming girl of about thirteen. The meat had been sitting in the sun for god knows how long and tasted quite nice when Mike ran over, snatching away the brochette and screaming, "You'll get sick."

"I ate some yesterday," I said, "and the locals eat them."

"Their stomachs are used to it."

He made me nervous, and the other volunteers looked disapprovingly at me. Nothing, of course, happened. Thus began my love affair with trying different foods in local markets all over the world. You really get to know a culture walking through local markets and trying the food. I found the people always interested in showing me new foods and having me try things. Many times, I never knew what I was eating. And it was cheaper eating in local markets. Did I ever have a problem? Sometimes I got the runs and just dealt with it. But trying all those delicious foods was worth the risk.

We reached the NGO's warehouse in the town of Segou. Segou was a medium-sized town that had once been a conglomeration of four villages called Ségou-Koro (Old Ségou), Ségou-Bougou, Ségou-Koura, and Ségou-Sikoro, the last being the modern name for the town. The NGO's warehouse was an impressive affair, a brand-spanking-new, blue-and-white corrugated-metal building set on a solid and clean concrete foundation, surrounded by a chain-link fence with curls of razor wire on top. An electric motor slid the large doors open, revealing crates full of concrete mix.

We backed the trucks up to the door and unloaded half the payload. The rest would go to the warehouse farther north in Mopti. The NGO volunteers were housed in a nearby dorm, another newish building. On the inside, my new home was indistinguishable from my freshman college dorm, complete with bunk beds. The bathroom consisted of a couple of clean and well-run outhouses in the back with Western-style sit toilets, instead of the local-style squat toilets. Because sanitation was a large part of the NGO's mission, we had to set a good example. We had electricity most evenings, but not consistently.

The NGO employed a local woman who cooked for us and served us in a common mess. Malian meals consisted of some kind of meat and starch. The meat was either beef or goat in a sauce, served with rice or millet. I discovered later that this meat and starch combination was common throughout Africa, the type of starch, the type of meat, and the spices varying from region to region. To an American, the portions were small and left me feeling hungry. The first few nights, I approached the server and asked for "more meat." He shook his head no, even though I could see the pot full of meat and sauce. One of the other volunteers figured out the trick to getting seconds: the locals didn't know what we meant by "meat." To them, it was called "sauce." From then on, we asked for more "sauce," which came with more meat.

I soon learned a new lesson. My American habit of overfilling my belly didn't go over well in West Africa. First, I was getting a little fat on all that starch. But more importantly, a full stomach felt awful in the oppressive heat. Lighter meals left me feeling much better and had the added benefit of reducing my trips to the "bush toilet" when out in the field. But most importantly, what my naïve mind didn't realize at first was that any food we didn't eat would be given to our cooks and servants to be brought home to their families. The servers always politely gave us more when we asked for it, even though we were literally taking food out of their families' mouths to overfill our Western stomachs. I felt awful when I learned this and cut down on my portions, taking another step toward living lightly on this planet. Another crack opened in my sheltered and privileged worldview.

15

Clean Water

The day after our arrival, Mike took me, Latrell, and the other newbies out to show us the ropes. We drove along a little track in the bush in a convoy of two SUVs and a utility truck. Locals herded cattle along the road, pushing the animals to the side to let us pass. After three hours, we reached a village, nothing more than a patch of dirt with a few huts scattered about the sparse vegetation. It was more primitive than the villages we had seen along the main road. There were no concrete buildings with corrugated metal roofs, and no electricity. The mud-brick huts were either square or round with conical straw roofs. The entirety of the village came out to stare at us.

Mike approached a man who appeared to be the leader of the village and spoke to him in his local language, Bambara. Bambarans are the most populous ethnic group in the area and are known to be farmers and cattle herders. Bambarans either speak Bambara or Dyula.

The second-largest ethnic group are called the Bozos, initially causing immature clown jokes. The Bozos are mostly fishermen who live along the banks of the river.

After a couple minutes of conversation with the villagers, Mike turned to us and said, "We are very lucky today because you will see the reason for our mission. Come this way."

We followed the chief away from the huts, with the entire village curiously and silently in tow. Suddenly, we were hit by a wave of unbelievable stench, amplified by the heat. This was the place the villagers came to do their business. Shit covered the ground. There were only a few places to step without putting your foot in something.

"Do you see this?" Mike said. "We're less than thirty meters from the village. It's disgusting and unhealthy. But why are we lucky today?"

No one responded, everyone covering their noses futilely with their shirts.

"Does anyone know why they are shitting all over the ground instead of using a latrine?"

Still no one responded.

"There is a latrine. It was put here a few years ago by the local government, but it was poorly built and difficult to maintain. Now, it has become full and unusable. That's why they go outside of it. Today we are lucky because there is someone here working it. Come, I want to show you."

A little further on was a broken-down outhouse. Five men stood around the small wooden structure. Three were doing nothing. The other two were busy passing buckets from inside the outhouse and dumping them in a wheelbarrow.

"They're emptying the latrine," Mike said. "Want to see how they empty it? Come closer."

We cautiously approached and peered inside. The floor had been removed, revealing a hole. In the pit was a man, an actual man, wearing a t-shirt and shorts, standing up to his waist in waste, no protective gear whatsoever. The men from above handed him empty buckets. He scooped the defecation from around him and passed it back up, in exchange for an empty bucket.

"Oh my god," one of the girls in our group gasped.

I really wanted to throw up and backed away into the fresher air. "How does he work in there? I mean, why?" I asked.

"It's a job, and work is scarce," Mike said. "We want to make this job obsolete. Today, we are going to build a proper latrine, an adequate distance from the village, and one that'll last ten years with easy upkeep."

Mike told the guy in the pit to get out. Because we would build a new latrine, this one no longer needed to be emptied. Unbelievably, the man in the pit looked unhappy about this, asking, I found out later, if he'd still be paid for a full day's work. Mike promised the guy that he would.

"Now let's talk about water," Mike said. We walked half a mile from the village to a small river. In the river were kids bathing naked and women doing the laundry, along with cattle drinking and cooling off. "This is where the village gets its water from," he said, gesturing to the shore. "They're drinking the same water where these kids are bathing, the laundry is done, and the cattle are swimming, and I'm sure defecating. Do any of you want to drink from this?" said Mike as if he were admonishing us.

"Is none of this water treated?" someone asked.

"It's too expensive to buy chlorine tablets, and there is very little firewood to boil it clean. The firewood is used for other things, not boiling water. This is why people get sick. Moreover, it's the women who have to carry buckets of water to and from this river multiple times a day. It's hard on their knees, their backs, and ankles. Today, we are going to dig a proper well in the village to provide clean water."

We returned to the village to find the utility truck already drilling, right in the middle of the circle of huts. Dirt and mud were ground to the surface by the corkscrew drill bit. Once they had reached groundwater, concrete was poured around the well, forming a cover. A block with a sturdy metal pump was installed.

After a period for the concrete to set, magic happened. Mike approached a woman in the village and said something to her in Bambara, gesturing toward the pump. She looked skeptical, but Mike urged her forward. She hesitantly pushed down on the lever a couple times. Clean water poured out of the spout. The villagers gasped. The chief put his mouth under the faucet to taste it. He smiled and said something excitedly to the rest of the village. Everyone came over to drink, smiling, laughing, and splashing each other. A few women had just returned from the river with full buckets. They were told the news and witnessed the fresh water pouring from the well. They dumped their buckets of brown, muddy liquid.

Elsewhere, behind the village, our rig had dug a nice deep hole for the drop toilet. A concrete floor was installed with a metal hatch for upkeep. Mike instructed us on how the toilet was built. He told us to grab some wood, a saw, a hammer, and some nails. We got to work on building the wooden outhouse over the newly dug pit.

When we finished, Mike said proudly, "This will last for ten years."

Exhausted from the heat and hard work, I returned to the newly dug well. It was getting late. The joy I felt as the sun set on that day, seeing the villagers rejoicing at their good fortune, sent chills up my spine. They smiled at us, at me, and were incredibly welcoming and warm. The look in their eyes of people so grateful, of people being helped, gave me a euphoria I'd never felt before. It was like a drug, a good drug. I was addicted. I wanted more. This was both an adventure and helping people. I'd found my purpose in life.

I sat next to Mike on the drive back. "Why isn't the Malian government providing clean water and sanitation?" I asked.

"They're just not at that level yet," he said. "They provide some money, but there's still the usual problems of bureaucratic inefficiency, corruption, and a lack of will. Most of it is short-term thinking."

"What do you mean?" I asked.

"Clean water and good health are fundamental to building a modern economy. In America, we are so used to proper infrastructure that we forget its importance. Do you ever think why we have roads, bridges, sewers, plumbing, electricity? Because people in America's past knew that providing these fundamental services meant that Americans could instead spend their time building businesses instead of on bare survival. These businesses created jobs. These workers spent their wages, which created more jobs, which grew the economy, and made America rich. Investors want to put their money into places that have clean water, reliable electricity, and roads to move whatever they're manufacturing. Did you ever think about infrastructure? Probably not because it's considered a given. In Mali, they are shortsighted. A road costs money. Sewage costs money. Clean water costs money. They view these things as expenses, not long-term investments that ultimately make the country richer. Get it?"

"I see."

Mike continued, "We're trying to change the mindset of the government

85

through education. In the meantime, these people on the ground need our help. And just maybe, like priming a pump, getting these basic services to the people will get the government going in the right direction once they see the economic benefits. Clean water and sanitation will become standard."

16

Liz

Six months working for the NGO had gone by. I loved being in Africa. I loved the food, the people, the different cultures, and the work. Yes, there were the normal frustrations of Africa: the bureaucratic incompetence, the infrastructure that rarely worked, the missing of some stuff from home (football season had come and gone). The electricity was sporadic. Every place you went in Segou, candles and matches were on standby. I enjoyed the power outages. The town would go dark, candles would be lit, and everyone would sit around in the glow, just like the old days. It became noticeably quiet. Machines that whirred in the background all day went unnoticed until they became silent. New sounds emerged: people talking, birds, insects chirping. Existence was natural.

However, no electricity meant no evening movie. Because there were no movie theatres, video dens were the substitute. A video den was a local proprietor who would set up chairs in front of a TV and video cassette and charge customers the equivalent of a nickel to watch movies. Aside from bars, video dens were the center of social activity most evenings, full of locals talking, eating, and joking during the films. Watching a movie in a video den was an interactive experience. Action movies were the most popular, especially Schwarzenegger. Hong Kong and other Chinese action films, like Jackie Chan, were a close second. Everyone got into the over-the-top fight scenes. Many were action-comedies or slapstick comedies.

Africans are natural-born capitalists, amazing at starting businesses and making money where they could, but they were untrained and missed obvious opportunities. For instance, the video dens never sold food and drink. People brought them in from the outside. But why not sell soda, beer, candy, even brochettes? They had a captive audience. They'd make a killing. I mentioned this to one of the video den owners, and he just shrugged. Maybe he didn't understand my French. Heck, I didn't understand my French most of the time.

I split my time hanging out with the locals and the other volunteers in the NGO. I certainly did more drinking than I was used to. In college, I drank occasionally, mostly at those post-hockey celebrations, preferring to focus on studying. There was more drinking in Caesarea with the group around the campfire at the end of the day. But Africa was a different story. Apart from the video dens, there was little to do in Africa at night. As such, us NGOers met and drank at night, and that's what we did. We drank, played cards, bullshitted, and complained. I became quite good at card games: euchre, hearts, spades, crazy eights. It was very social and fun. It's what I imagined life was like before television. The morning hangovers made the heat of the day less tolerable, but it was worth it.

There were a couple of cute girls in the group who were nice, but for whatever reason, I simply wasn't interested in dating at this time. Nights that I wasn't drinking or watching movies, I read. Books in English were hard to come by. People in the group shared whatever we had, and soon all of the dog-eared books had been read by everyone in the group.

As to the work itself, I had become proficient at the different methods of building wells and proper toilets. The NGO did a good job expanding throughout the area, helping more and more villages. Each time we finished a project, the people's joy felt just as fresh as the first time. Life was good. I was happy.

This was when I met Liz.

Mike had grown to trust me with larger responsibilities. One day he sent me up to Mopti for a few weeks with a convoy of trucks to restock the warehouse and familiarize myself with the operations. Mopti was an interesting town about two hundred kilometers up the Niger River at its confluence with the Bani River. The town was squeezed into a small area. During the rainy season, it became a group of small islands connected by elevated causeways.

We had eaten lunch at an eatery on the second floor of a two-story restaurant near a bridge crossing the river. After lunch, I was standing outside under the shade of our truck, waiting for our guys and watching the river go by, when I saw a white person ride up on a wreck of a 250cc Chinese motorbike. The rider wore light blue jeans, beat up sneakers, a loose white t-shirt, and a red crash helmet. It looked like a girl, but how could it be? Yet strands of sandy blonde hair fell out the back of the helmet. She parked the bike in front of the truck, got off, and took off her helmet, her matted hair dropping in waves around her head. She squinted her eyes at the sun. She was beautiful, about medium height and in her mid-twenties. I stared unabashedly, wondering who the fuck she was. All the white people in the area generally knew each other. I'd surely have heard about a blonde girl riding around on a motorbike.

It was customary for foreigners in Africa to acknowledge one another. We stood out like sore thumbs, but mostly there was a sense of camaraderie, helping each other in this foreign place. However, despite my standing less than ten yards away next to a rather large truck, she took no notice of me and strode directly into the restaurant, grasping her red helmet in her hand. I was just about to follow her in when one of my workers approached me, asking about some issue. I barely focused on what he was telling me, instead wishing he'd just go away. He kept repeating his question until I realized that it was something important. I refocused on him, trying to resolve a problem about the delivery of some items.

Five minutes later, the girl walked out of the restaurant toward the river and behind our truck, where I couldn't see her anymore. I figured she would emerge from the side, but she didn't. She must have been standing behind the truck. But why? I couldn't concentrate anymore.

"Excuse me," I said to the worker. "You work this out. I'll be right back." I walked to the other side of the truck to find the girl standing in a sliver of truck shade, smoking a cigarette and staring across the river.

"Hi," I said. "Where are you from?"

She was beautiful but raw. Brown eyes. Skin naturally tanned by the African sun. Toned muscles in her arms, strong from work, not from a gym. Her hair was matted and dirty with bits of burrs stuck in it, as though it hadn't been washed in a while. Her jeans were ratty and dirt stained, her dusty white t-shirt frayed at the edges.

She glared at me resentfully for intruding upon her reverie. "I'm British," she said, drawing in a puff and exhaling it forcefully from her lips and then returning to stare at the river.

"What are you doing here in Africa?" I asked.

"Working," she said, staring into the distance. Something about her was off, very weird.

I struggled for more conversation. "What kind of work?"

Without answering my question, she said, "I'm meeting some people and just using the shade of your truck for a smoke." She threw the cigarette on the ground and walked off, back into the restaurant.

I was astonished by her rudeness. Didn't she wonder who I was? Didn't she want to know what I was doing in Africa, like everyone else you meet?

My translator came around the truck. "Are you ready?" he asked. We all piled into the truck and continued down the road.

"Do you know who that girl was?" I asked my translator.

"No," he said without elaboration.

"I thought you guys knew what all the foreigners were up to."

"I'm not from here," my translator said.

"Can you ask about her?"

"Sure," he said uninterestedly.

At our station in Mopti, I asked a few of the volunteers about her. None of them knew anything. "She might be a trader," offered one of the cooks. He couldn't elaborate or explain what he meant by "trader."

Two weeks went by, and each day I found an excuse to go into town, always stopping by that restaurant, for lunch, for a beer, for just a bottle of water. They really liked me, as I was becoming their best customer. I asked the staff about the girl. They had just seen her that one time and knew nothing. It was very strange for everyone not to know what was going on. This was because for millennia, gossip in Africa passed by word of mouth. Modernly, this was called the "African Telephone." Foreigners were often the subject of this gossip, and I found it spooky to show up in a village only to have them expecting me. So why didn't they know this girl?

One afternoon, I was sitting in the restaurant drinking a Coke and reading, keeping vigil as any good stalker would, when I heard a motorbike pull up and saw, through the open door, the girl get off her bike, wearing the same outfit. She walked in.

"Hi," I said. "I figured I'd run into you again."

"Oh, hi," she said indifferently.

"What is your name?" I asked.

"It's Liz," she said in a thick British accent, without emotion. She looked over my shoulder and around the restaurant as though looking for someone and then back at me. "And you?" she asked as an afterthought, maybe trying to be polite.

"It's Joe. Nice to meet you." I extended my hand. She shook it but then immediately turned around and looked out the door.

"Would you like to sit down?" I asked to the back of her head. My question was interrupted by three Chinese guys who walked through the door. The Chinese were investing in Africa, setting up mines and taking advantage of its resources, needed for China's booming economy. I had been seeing more and more of them but hadn't met any yet, mostly because they didn't speak English, and I didn't speak Chinese.

"Can you excuse me?" she said fleetingly without waiting for my answer. She left me and approached the Chinese guys. Dumbfounded, I watched her greet them in Chinese! They spoke at a conversational rate, Liz perfectly using the Chinese tonal inflections, completely at odds with this disheveled blonde Brit. From her gestures, she seemed upset about something. It became apparent that they were negotiating a business transaction. There were nods of heads, and then they departed from the restaurant.

I followed, curious to see what was going on. A truck was parked by the river. The discussion continued, someone occasionally gesturing in the truck's direction. After five minutes, she shook hands with the Chinese men. The scene concluded with the men getting in the truck and driving off, with Liz following on her motorbike.

17

Learning to Ride

From then on, I saw her more and more around the area, always riding her motorbike. I smiled and waved like an idiot. This was generally ignored as she sped by. The other volunteers found this extremely funny. I was never able to catch her in the restaurant again. I had no idea where she was staying or even where she hung out. I became more obsessed with the mystery of Liz. But I was getting nowhere.

"Hey, Latrell, could you show me how to ride a motorbike?" I said one day.

"You don't want to get involved with motorbikes. You know my story."

"Everyone else is riding them. I see whole families of five on one bike."

"That's because they have to, man. Most people never wear helmets either. I don't even think Mike would let you. You might have noticed that everyone around here has scars. You know where those scars come from? They're not there by accident; they're there by accident."

"Whatever. I'm buying a motorbike, and I'll pay you to teach me how to ride it well."

"You don't have to pay me. Why do you want to learn?"

"I need it to get around. It's easy and efficient. I'm getting tired of being stuck riding around in our SUVs or taking moto-taxis."

"It's that weird girl, isn't it?" Latrell asked.

I was silent.

"The blonde one with the disheveled hair, who always wears the same outfit," continued Latrell.

"You've noticed her too?"

"No, I haven't seen your mysterious ghost white girl, but you've been talking about her constantly. I agree, the mystery is interesting, but she sounds like a mess from what you've said. She's probably involved in something illegal. Maybe she's a former Russian prostitute who escaped and is now trading drugs with the Chinese in Africa."

"She's British."

"So what? It's weird. You don't want to get involved with anyone like that. Here in Africa, if they suspect anyone of being involved in drugs, they throw you in jail forever. And there's no way out. You've seen the government buildings here, imagine how bad the prisons would be. Heck, they might even have the death penalty for drugs in Mali. The death penalty is probably a better option than prison."

"You've seen too many movies, Latrell. I'm getting the motorbike. I need your help. Please."

Latrell sighed. "Okay. Only because I don't want to see you kill yourself."

The next day we asked among the NGO local staff if anyone knew of a motorbike for sale. Finding one was easy, as they knew that they could get a better price from a foreigner. The cook mentioned that his cousin was selling his Chinese motorbike. In less than an hour, the cousin brought it by. The motorbike looked like every other bike around: dusty, dented, a little run down, no paint job, black seat, and grimy engine parts. Latrell looked it over, tugged at the chains, and started her up.

"It runs decently," Latrell said. "Go ahead and ride it a bit. I want to see how it moves," he said to the cook's cousin.

"You don't want to ride it yourself?" asked the cousin.

"I'd rather not," said Latrell.

The cook's cousin hopped on and rode it up and down the street a couple times, skidding to a stop in front of us.

"That'll do," said Latrell.

We worked out a price, which I'm sure was way more than the locals would have paid. Still, I didn't feel too guilty paying the higher, foreigner price because the guy selling us the bike got a little extra money and the satisfaction of besting a foreigner, and I got a motorbike cheaper than I would have in the States.

That afternoon, Latrell explained everything about motorbikes. First, buying fuel for motorbikes in Africa was interesting. For the first few months I was there, I had wondered why shopkeepers kept shelves of reused water bottles filled with tan-colored liquid. This was gasoline, and every store selling these bottles was a de facto gas station. You pulled up to one, and the storekeeper, usually an eight-year-old boy or an older woman, would pour the gas into the tank from the plastic bottle and tell you how much it cost, which was very little.

Latrell took me to the dirt patch where the kids usually played soccer.

He couldn't hide his enthusiasm for motorbikes. "You're going to love this," he said. "They're dangerous, but motorbikes are practically life, freedom, possibility."

"You haven't ridden since your accident, have you?" I asked.

"No, I haven't."

"You clearly miss it."

"I do, but..."

"Want to ride again?" I asked.

"It's not a hard and fast rule why I am not riding, but...let's get to teaching you."

He showed me how to shift, how to start from a dead stop. "Let out the clutch slowly till it starts to move, and then add gas in a smooth motion, pick up your feet, and you're off."

He continued with turning: slow-speed turning, counter steering, leaning into turns, not to brake on turns, emergency stopping, etc. My poor motorcycle got dropped numerous times, but the rugged Chinese bike took it like a pro. The clutch smoked from my constantly stalling, but after a couple hours, I got the hang of it. He took me down to the riverbank to show me how to start on a hill. This was challenging, and at one point the bike nearly ended up rolling backward into the Niger River.

I found that a lot of motorbike riding involved faith and just going for it: "Lean into the turn and look around the curve, you won't fall over," said Latrell. "When you're going up the hill on the riverbank, suppress your fear. The bike will make it. Let out the clutch, add the gas, and keep going through all the bumps. As soon as you get scared, try to stop, or put your foot down, you're toast."

"Dude, you've been such an amazing help," I said to him at the end of the day.

"It was fun."

"You wanna ride it? I wanna see what you can do."

He looked at the bike in silence. "It's been a while. Bikes really changed things for me..." He paused for a long moment, thinking about his lost football career. "Okay," he finally said.

Latrell hopped on the bike, started her up, and rode around, gingerly at first. Then came a growl from the small engine. He kicked the bike up to speed, going up and down the lot. He did a couple donuts, skidding around the dirt expertly, and finally popping a wheelie.

He stopped in front of me and got off. "That's enough, man. Thanks for the memories. Now buy me some beer."

18

Finally!

Motorbikes had never entered my mind until that day. I had viewed them negatively, dangerous and associated with gangs. But this was fun. The freedom was intoxicating. It burned almost no gas, could take me anywhere, and it was a piece of junk, so there was no pretense to it. I loved the feeling of the wind in my hair, but I wisely invested in a crash helmet, a minimal affair like the type they wore in the 1960s, with no faceplate and held on by a chin strap.

I had two favorite things about riding: First, the acceleration from a stop to full speed. It felt like I was escaping from somewhere. It went like this: you're at a full stop, you look around to see if it's clear, then let out the clutch, hit the gas, and go. The acceleration pulls me back on the seat, my arms extended, hands gripped tightly to the handlebars, the wind blowing passed me, feeling the bumps of the dirt road, the scenery disappearing behind me.

The second thing was turns. Now, I'm not talking about crazy racing turns with the bike leaned way over, knee nearly touching the ground. I'm talking about leaning into normal turns on a winding road. "S"-turns were the best. I'd lean one way, then up, and then the other way.

Few of the roads were paved, so I'd only reach speeds of thirty-five to fifty miles per hour, but it felt faster. One thing I figured out quickly was that hitting soft sand, a rut, or a deep pothole (things all too common in

Africa) were bad. I ate it more than once. Not seriously, but it was common for me, especially early on, to return from riding covered in dirt, scrapes, and bruises. This taught me to slow down, watch the road, and anticipate what was coming.

I rode my motorbike everywhere, hoping to run into Liz. One day I saw her riding into town. As nonchalantly as possible, I drove up next to her. "Hey," I said, nodding my head upward, as one did in the nineties.

"Hey," she said back, quickly turning a corner and speeding off, me continuing straight ahead stupidly.

* * *

"You need to give up, man," Latrell said to me later. "She's not interested, or she's got other things going on, and she's weird."

"But I'm curious! Aren't you?"

Latrell, by this time, had seen her around too. "Of course I am. It's a little odd to see a white girl riding around in West Africa by herself, doing business with the Chinese, but I am not as curious as you are. Let it go. I'm sure we'll eventually hear what she's up to. We always do."

"But I want to know now. I mean. Don't you think it's pretty awesome? Here we are, all coddled and taken care of by this NGO. What she's doing is pretty cool. I want to meet this girl."

"She's not cute."

"Yes, she is."

"I've never seen her in another outfit. Her hair is matted and dirty."

"I love the rawness," I said.

"I doubt she shaves anything," said Latrell.

"Yuck, let's leave out that imagery for now."

"You have weird tastes, man. Why not hook up with one of the girls here? I think Julie is cute."

"Everyone has hooked up with everyone here. Speaking of gross, you've hooked up with Julie."

"Just once."

"I don't want your sloppy seconds."

"All right, man. Keep going after Tarzan girl. You're going to be disappointed. She's going to be trouble. I'll lay ten to one odds that there's some horrible issue in her past."

* * *

The next day, I saw Liz riding out of town into the country. I kicked my bike into gear and sped after her, pulling alongside. She looked at me briefly, slightly acknowledging my existence, and then stared straight ahead.

"Where are you off to?" I yelled over the wind.

"Just back to my camp," she said matter-of-factly.

"Your camp? Where is that?"

"That way." She pointed dismissively.

"What do you—" My voice trailed off as I wasn't watching the road. I hit a patch of soft sand, my bike's front wheel sticking and then wobbling. I tried to regain control but couldn't. Barely avoiding a tree, I instead crashed into a bush. My bike lay next to me, its wheels still spinning.

I was okay, just bruised and incredibly humiliated. I looked up to see Liz stopped just ahead. She looked back at me from her bike, saw me sitting up, then turned again forward, hit the gas, and was gone, disappearing around a bend, the noise of her engine fading with her. I remained sitting in the bush in the relative silence of the countryside, listening now to some birds and insects. I had scraped my elbow. It was bleeding, but this had been a normal occurrence since purchasing the bike. I stood up and realized that I had hurt my ankle too, not horribly, but I limped a bit to walk it off and then sat down on a tree stump to rest for a bit. I couldn't believe she saw me crash and took off. I swore that was the end of my pursuit of her. She was not nice at all.

But then I heard the whine of a motorcycle engine from a distance and saw a cloud of dust. It was she. She was coming back. She pulled to a stop in front of me and took off her helmet, her dirty blonde hair dropping over her shoulders, awesome in its unkemptness.

"Are you okay?" she asked.

"Yeah," I said, smiling embarrassedly but also happy that she had come back. "Just a scrape and my ankle is sore, but I am okay."

"That was rude of me," she said.

"It was, kind of."

"What do you want from me?" she said.

"Can we get a beer?"

She sighed. "What do you want besides that?"

"I'm just curious about you."

She hesitated. "One beer. But then I really need to go."

We rode back to the restaurant in town, finding it cooler inside. I approached the guy at the bar and ordered a couple beers. The guy reached under the shelf to grab some bottles when Liz stepped in and said something to him in French. He nodded and disappeared into the back.

"What'd you ask him?"

"They sometimes have beer cooling in the river. I asked him for that."

"You speak French too?"

"Yeah," she said nonchalantly and then added, "Don't you? This was French West Africa."

"A little, but I really should learn. I'm an American. We only speak one language." She didn't acknowledge my comment. "And you? You speak Chinese? Anything else?"

"Spanish. And a little bit of the local language."

"Wow," I said stupidly. We sat down at one of the tables. She lit up a cigarette. The guy returned with the beers. They were dripping with river water, their labels nearly washed off. They were cool to the touch, not cold, but cool, a treat when refrigeration wasn't all that common. The guy popped off the tops and slid them in front of us.

"What do you want to know?" she asked.

"Where are you from?"

"I'm British, I told you."

"But from where?"

"All over, I guess. I'm a British subject, but I was raised by my aunt, who's a diplomat with the Foreign Office, so I grew up in Zimbabwe, France, and Singapore."

"That's why you speak Chinese and French?"

"Yep."

"What are you doing here?"

"The same thing you're doing here."

"How do you know what I'm doing here?" I asked.

"I saw you driving around in those brand-new air-conditioned NGO trucks," she said with derision. "You're digging wells and building toilets."

"You're with an NGO? Which one?"

"No, I'm with my own NGO. If you can call it that."

"You have your own NGO?" I asked.

"Your NGO is bullshit. You waste so much money on new Toyota SUVs, comfortable housing for you and the other volunteers, and you're corrupt too."

I was taken aback. "Corrupt? How so?"

"Do you know where all your materials to build the wells and toilets are coming from? The concrete, the trucks, the drills, the pumps, etc."

"I hadn't really thought about it."

"You're overpaying for all this stuff from companies owned by government cronies. It's a scam."

"Are you sure? Really?"

"I'm sure. I used to work for an NGO. But then I got tired of that bullshit. I wanted to actually help people, not feed into the corrupt bureaucracy. I buy all the same materials at a fraction of the price from the Chinese. Then, instead of using Western volunteers like yourself, who need to be air-conditioned and coddled, I hire locals who actually need the money and jobs. By operating at a fraction of the price, I get more stuff done."

"I don't know what to say."

"Most people don't. That's why I am doing this alone."

"Where do you get money?"

"The internet."

"The internet? How does that work?"

"I built a website to promote my project, and I take donations by wire. I don't need much."

"How come we haven't run into you before?"

"I've been working mostly in Burkina Faso. I came to Mali because my Chinese supplier had to reroute his trucks through here. The Chinese are here building mines. I glean off that by buying their concrete and drilling equipment. By the way, your NGO does a crappy job too."

"What do you mean 'crappy'? This is one part I am proud of. We're helping people."

"You're not helping them as well as you could be. Neither your wells nor your toilets are dug deep enough, and you're not lining them with concrete. A well that's not lined with concrete eventually becomes contaminated with the same waste that was contaminating the river. Oftentimes, this is because you didn't line the pit of the toilet either."

"So, we're doing a lousy job, at too much cost, while enabling corruption?"

"You said it."

"Are you working with other people?"

"I hired some locals. I told you."

"I mean other foreigners. Friends? Boyfriend?"

She frowned. "I'm the only one. It's all me."

"Aren't you worried about being a foreign girl all alone in Africa?"

"No, should I be?" She took a smoke and then held her cigarette out casually at length, letting it rest between her fingers. "Look, I need to go." She went from relaxed to snuffing out the smoke right on the surface of the table, and then she stood up.

"Wait. Where are you going? This is Africa. No one is in a hurry here. Even if you have an appointment, you can show up an hour late and be fine."

"I don't like being like that."

"Don't you want to ask me some questions? To know anything about me?"

"Not really."

"Why are you like this?"

"It's a long story. Look, I don't know what you want, but I really don't

102

want to date right now."

"How about some company? Maybe you miss having someone to talk to in English at normal speed and discuss culture and pop references."

She thought for a moment. "Look, I really do need to go. But..." She paused. "Why don't I show you what I do? Meet me here tomorrow morning at 7 a.m."

"Sure! I'll be there."

She put on her red crash helmet, started up her bike, and rode off.

19

A Day in the Village

"She's running an NGO?" said Latrell.

"Not an NGO, so to speak. She's doing the same sorts of things, just by herself." I spared Latrell from telling him Liz's criticisms of his older brother's operation. "Can you cover for me tomorrow?"

"It's my day off," said Latrell.

"So what? You don't have plans. We're in West Africa. Come on, dude. She wants to hang out."

"Fine, what'll you do for me?"

"I'll pay in beer, and I'll cover for you sometime."

"Fine."

The next day, I was up at dawn, showered, shaved, and rode my bike to the restaurant. Liz was already there waiting on her motorbike, five minutes before our meeting time. She didn't smile as I approached but simply said, "Let's go," right away starting the bike and hitting the gas before I could respond.

We drove in silence along the road, me three lengths behind her. The Africans were busy starting their day, carrying goods to town for sale, opening shops, kids going to school. I appreciated the rare times I was up this early to experience the beautiful light and the coolish weather before the scorching heat set in.

Ninety minutes in, we turned onto a lesser road that was essentially a dirt path. I didn't know where we were or where we were going. I was just following, happy to be doing something with Liz, even if it was three motorcycle lengths behind her. It was then another hour of me trying to keep the bike upright through uneven ruts, puddles, sand, and patches that were more brush than path. Eventually we reached a village. It was very primitive. No electricity, no metal roofs, all traditional clothing. Maybe I saw a couple plastic items, but certainly very little civilization was getting here. Liz stopped in the center.

All the villagers emerged from the huts when they heard our approaching motorcycles. A flood of children came out and embraced Liz before she could even get off the bike. A few gentlemen approached to shake her hand and say hello. For the first time, I saw Liz smiling. She had a beautiful, glowing smile. I wondered why she didn't smile more.

Almost forgetting me, she woke up to my presence and introduced me in the local language. I shook hands with the men.

"Do you know why I brought you all the way here?" said Liz in her first words to me in hours.

"I don't know. I'm here at your behest."

"I want to show you what's possible, so that maybe you can show your boss."

"Okay?"

"It's pretty remote out here, right?"

"Yeah."

"You've probably noticed how little of the outside world is here. I mean, these people go to the market, but it's far."

"Yeah," I said.

"We had a tough, long ride. Neither trucks nor the drilling rigs can get out here, right?"

I nodded dumbly.

"However, look what we've done." Liz gestured to the area between the huts. There was a pump stuck in some concrete.

"How'd you build that out here?" I asked.

Ignoring my question, she said, "Come with me." We walked on, the entire village in tow, to behind the huts, where a latrine was located. Liz unscrewed the access panel on the back. "Take a look in."

"It's all concrete lined," I said.

"Yup, and so is the well."

"That's amazing, but you told me all this in town yesterday."

"Joe," she said, saying my name for the first time. "I wanted to bring you all the way out here to make a point about what's possible. We're on the same side. I want to see your organization succeed. We're both trying to help the people. We just need the grit and determination to make things happen in a tough environment. Your NGO has a good heart, but it's not putting in the time, money, or effort to be truly great. It's not getting to these remote towns, nor is it building these facilities correctly. A good-quality facility is more important in the bush, where upkeep is even more difficult. Your organization has been helping only where there are accessible roads for its supply trucks and drill rigs to get in. In many towns, there is only a footpath. They need help too."

"How did you solve this problem?"

"I bring in supplies via animal cart and then pay the locals to dig the wells by hand. It's more effort than using a truck and drilling rig but necessary. My point is that we don't give up helping these people because it is too far or too difficult. We deal with the hassle and simply make it happen."

"But why isn't my NGO helping these smaller towns?"

"Ask your boss, but I think you're too lazy."

"*Lazy?* There seem to be plenty of towns to help where there is road access. Maybe we plan on getting to the rest later."

"Whatever you say," said Liz. "I just brought you out here to share my ideas."

"Fair enough, but why aren't we lining our wells and pits entirely with concrete?"

"You're cheap."

"*Cheap?*"

"Cheap. More concrete means more money. Of course, you're paying way more for concrete than I am due to corruption. It's worth it to pay the extra cost for lining the wells and latrines with concrete."

I just stood silently, not knowing what to say.

"Oops, I nearly forgot the main reason why I came out here," Liz said. She reached into a bag on the side of her bike and pulled out a washer and a few bolts, along with some tools. "These Chinese pumps are good, but for some reason, the washers leak. I can fix it by putting in good, strong washers. Somehow this one got missed."

Liz unscrewed a few bolts on the pump, removed the head, and took out a weak little rubber donut. It was half as thick as the new one. She confidently inserted the new one and bolted everything tight. "There. That'll hold a long time."

One of the little boys in the village ran up and took her hand, indicating that he wanted to say something in Liz's ear. Liz bent down to the boy, who looked up sweetly, cupping his hand over his mouth to protect his secret while whispering in Liz's ear. I watched this scene, realizing that I was falling hard for this girl.

Liz looked up at me. "We've been invited to lunch. Do you want to stay?"

"Do they have enough food?" I asked.

"They do now," said Liz. "The main problem was a lack of clean water." She smiled again, each time like a new miracle.

The little boy led Liz by the hand. I followed them into the hut and out of the sun where we sat down on the earth floor. Liz comfortably sat cross-legged on the ground. Being less flexible, I sat on my butt.

The woman and Liz spoke in Bambara.

"What's she saying?" I asked.

"She asked if you were my husband. I said definitely not."

The discussion continued. "She says that you're very handsome," Liz translated. I smiled. Liz saw my smile and frowned. "Don't let it go to your head," she said. "Unless you're looking for a Bambaran woman. In which case, that could be arranged."

"Humor?" I said. "From the cold, English girl. What's going on?"

"Don't expect it to happen again," she said. "I'm not English. I'm British. I have Irish blood, Scottish blood, and Gypsy blood thrown in for good measure. On my mum's side, that is. That's why I am always wandering about and never settled."

"What's your full name?"

"It's Elizabeth Erin O'Rourke."

"That's so Irish. But part Scottish and part Gypsy, an interesting mix."

"What about you?" she asked.

"This is your first question to me," I said.

"Don't expect it to happen again," she said.

"Joseph Levy. I'm American, so I guess my family comes from all over too, but we're not concerned with heritage too much. We're Jewish. I think my great-grandparents came over from different parts of Europe in the mid-to-late nineteenth century, after one of the many pogroms, way before the Nazis."

"Where are you from?" asked Liz.

"Denver, Colorado. Ever been?"

"Never, but I'd love to ski there. I went to school in Switzerland and got into skiing, downhill and cross country. How'd your family end up in Denver?"

"In the early twentieth century, my grandparents arrived when the town was still growing from mining and ranching. Denver was still very much the Wild West at that time."

"Were they miners or ranchers?"

"Jews? No, they ran businesses in Denver. Jewelry, insurance, banking, that kind of thing. Pretty stereotypical, I guess."

In the middle of the hut was a small pit where the residents placed hot coals and an iron pot for cooking. While we waited for lunch, a woman poured a cloudy liquid from a pitcher into two cups and handed one to each of us.

"What is this?" I asked Liz.

"Ginger beer," she said.

"It's a little early in the day for me."

"You'll be fine."

"Is it safe?"

"You'll be fine."

It was sour, not too strong. The woman brought us a pitcher of water and held it in front of me, saying something in Bambara.

"It's to wash your hands," said Liz. I must've looked confused because she added, "Put your hands out." I put my hands out and the woman poured the water over them. Once my hands were wet, she waited for me, but I didn't know what for.

"Use the soap," said Liz, gesturing to a little white bar on the ground. I picked up soap, scrubbed my hands to a lather, and then put the bar back down. The woman poured more water, rinsing off the suds. She did the same for Liz. The woman served us a plate full of meat stew and rice, which we ate with our hands, the food so piping hot that it burned my fingers.

"This is delicious," I said.

"I love Bambara food," Liz said. "Mmm. The spices they use. Actually, I love West African food in general. You rarely get a bad meal here, unless I get stuck in a Western-style restaurant, which is almost never."

"I remember you said that you were raised all over the world. How come you lived with your aunt?" I asked, as I stuffed a bit of rice and goat in my mouth.

"It's a long story. My parents died when I was very young. I don't remember them much."

"I'm sorry," I said nearly choking on my food as I realized that I asked a sensitive question.

"No, don't. It's fine. I don't want anyone feeling sorry for me."

"Saying 'I'm sorry' is just being polite, ya know."

"Sorry. My aunt, she is the most amazing person ever. She never married and served a long career in the Foreign Office. From ages two to ten, I was a little girl in Zimbabwe, formerly Southern Rhodesia, then ten to fourteen in Hong Kong, then France for high school, then Switzerland for more of the same, and back to England for college at Oxford."

"That's quite a childhood. How did you make friends, form a life?"

"I didn't really. I never was good at making friends. My aunt was my best friend. I always felt more comfortable around adults than kids my age. I was considered odd. I felt judged. I don't like people judging me."

"Who does?" I said. "I'm an only child. I know that feeling of preferring adults to kids. There weren't many kids in my neighborhood, so I found adults to hang out with. I didn't know how to relate to kids my age. I was considered weird. Meeting someone who gets me is rare."

"Exactly. It's rare. I moved around too much to form real friendships."

"I learned to be more social in college," I said. "Maybe it was the freedom. I kind of learned to hide my weird side at first, to not give the wrong impression. People are turned off by weirdness, even if it's a good weirdness. But I found that once I'd made the friendship, I could open up. I have a couple close friends. However, I've formed a number of surface friendships, which is fine for what they are. I mostly prefer my own company."

"I can't do the surface thing. Fuck it. I'd rather be alone," responded Liz. "I get along with these Africans better than anyone in the places I've lived. I don't fit into English society. I am a natural ex-pat, an outsider wherever I go, so being an actual outsider in a foreign country suits me. Here, I am not 'strange,' I'm a foreigner."

"I know what you mean. In the same way, I prefer the company of the dead over the living. Sorry, I know that sounds weird."

"No, it's okay," Liz said. "Keep going."

"I listen to old jazz from the twenties, thirties, and forties, and watch old movies, where most of the cast is long gone. In a sense I am watching ghosts. I grew up with these people as my 'friends.' They don't judge me. They just are, Humphrey Bogart, Dorothy Lamour, Richard Widmark. They're always there for me."

"Me too!" she said. I caught the first signs of excitement in her voice. Then she settled back down and focused on her food glumly.

"You okay?" I asked. "You looked happy for a moment and then suddenly changed."

"I'm fine." She then changed the subject by talking to the woman in Bambara.

Trying to bring back the vibe, I asked, "What brought you back to Africa?"

Liz just looked at me. "Let's save that for another time."

110

The afternoon heat had set in. Inside the hut, we were both full and sleepy from the ginger beer. Like the villagers, we lay on the ground and had a little nap. That little nap lasted a couple hours until I felt Liz shaking me awake.

"You ready to go?" she said.

It was just past four and a bit cooler. We said goodbye to the villagers, who were sad to see her go but at the same time happy at her having been there.

Liz and I rode out via the dirt track. Once on the road, she was more talkative, pointing out different trees and birds. About thirty minutes before we reached Mopti, she stopped alongside the road by a turnoff to a dirt track. "This is where I am staying, so I am going to say goodbye. Do you know your way?"

"Of course I do, no problem. Thank you for inviting me out. It was a nice day. And it was nice getting to know you."

"Yeah," she said reservedly.

"Would you like to hang out again tomorrow?" I asked.

"Tomorrow, I have to meet the Chinese miners for supplies again."

"The next day?"

"That day we're doing a village."

"When are you free?"

"I don't really know."

"I have to go Djenné on Friday for a few days, so I might not see you for a while."

"Djenné. That's where they have the mud mosque?"

"You haven't been?" I asked.

"No, not yet."

"It's like the main tourist thing to see in the area. It's amazing. Why don't you ride up to Djenné this weekend? It's not far from here. You can just come for the day. I'll show it to you."

"I'm not sure."

"Come on, Liz. We had a good day."

"I guess it is nice talking to someone in English at normal speed."

"So, you'll come?"

"Maybe."

20

No Thanks, I'm Not Hungry

I traveled to Djenné regularly. We had an operations facility there along with a small storage space for equipment, because it was close to several areas that needed our help. Djenné was unlike other places in the area in that there was something to see, which attracted the small number of tourists who came to West Africa. This meant a few hotels and a couple decent Western-style restaurants for when I needed a respite from the local food. For this reason, the NGO put me up in a hotel while I was there. Liz snickered when I told her where to find me.

I left Mopti on Friday morning for the short ride to Djenné, checked in to my hotel, and then spent the day working in various villages, fixing a few wells, installing new ones, and teaching the locals to maintain them. I finished my work late Friday afternoon and returned to the hotel.

"Any messages?" I asked the receptionist.

"Still nothing, sir."

"You'll let me know if anything comes in?"

"You've already left us instructions."

I changed into my swimsuit, sat by the pool, and read for hours, before going down to the hotel dining room for a dinner of ill-prepared French food.

Saturday was more of the same. My work kept me away from the hotel all day. I didn't get back until sunset. Again, no messages for me. Sunday was my last day. I had just a couple errands to run in town before returning to Mopti, so I figured I'd sleep in and get a late start. Around 8 a.m., someone was knocking at my door. I couldn't imagine who'd be bothering me in Africa that early on a Sunday.

I was wearing only my boxers and so cracked the hotel room door open just a tad. "Oh my, Liz. What are you doing here?"

"You invited me."

"I know but, uh, I didn't think you'd come this late and this early."

"Is it not okay?"

"It's fine. Come in," I said, starting to open the door. "Oh, give me a sec. I'm in my underwear," I said, accidentally slamming the door in her face. "Sorry about that," I yelled through the door. I scrambled into my pants and a t-shirt, and then opened the door. She looked amused. "Hi again, you must've left Mopti pretty early. Come in."

"Not too early. I came from a village nearby where I spent the night. I had stuff to do here and figured I'd accept your invite...while I was in the area," she added, entering the room and looking around. "Wow, this is nice. A/C, a TV, and a fridge. The NGO pays for all this?"

"I guess. It's a perk of being out here."

"It doesn't bother you?" asked Liz. "People are donating their money to build clean water and wells for poor people, and you're staying in a comfortable hotel?"

"I hadn't really thought of it," I said. "The NGO considers it a necessary expense to attract volunteers to this area of the world. Otherwise no one will come and help."

"I don't believe it," said Liz. "People will come because they want to help."

"So, umm," I began, trying to change the subject. "Would you like me to show you around? I have a few errands to run in the morning, and then I have the whole day for you."

"Sure. I came to be shown around."

"Let's get some breakfast first. I think I can sneak you into the hotel buffet."

"As long as no donors are paying for it," said Liz.

We went down to the continental buffet breakfast, where Liz feasted on a large plate of eggs, bacon, fruit, croissant, cheese, and tomatoes.

"You certainly aren't shy," I said.

"This is nice," she said. "I haven't been in a place like this for ages. I don't mind making the hotel pay for my big breakfast." Liz devoured everything and then went back for her third cup of coffee. "I haven't had real coffee in so long. It's actually coffee, not instant. It's rich and smooth. If I didn't feel so guilty, I'd join your NGO."

"You do miss Western culture?" I asked.

"Hell yes. I never said I didn't. I didn't come here to live as an ascetic. I just have higher ideals of what to do with money from people who want me to use it to build wells. I miss tons of things from back home. I'll go back someday, but right now I have things I want to do. I don't want to be home right now."

"Why is that?"

Her expression turned sour. "I'm just not in the mood to be there. Home, I mean." She finished her coffee. Suddenly shifting moods, she said, "All right, I am ready."

Liz accompanied me while I went to pay the NGO's local suppliers in cash. "All right, my chores are done," I said. "Let me show you the main attraction in Djenné." I led Liz a short distance through the market till we emerged in a square in front of a large, light-brown adobe building.

"This is the Great Mosque of Djenné, also known as the Great Mud Mosque."

"Wow," said Liz. "That really is pretty amazing and better than I expected. It is actually entirely made of mud and wooden sticks."

"It is kind of impressive. You can see why it is West Africa's main tourist attraction. It measures 250 feet by 250 feet and is placed on a mount ten feet high, making it that much more imposing."

"I have no idea what that means. America needs to switch to the metric system."

"I'm just using the system your people invented."

Liz smirked again; I was noticing that she did that a lot. "How did they build it?"

"It's the same building process as the mud huts we see in the villages, just on a larger scale. It's river mud mixed with straw, dried into bricks, and stacked into walls and roofs around a scaffolding of *toron*. Toron are—"

"—I know, toron are those sticks pushing out of the building and holding it up. I speak Bambara."

"Right," I said. "It's also covered with plaster to give it a smooth look."

"When was it built? It actually looks a bit French."

"It's funny you should notice that," I said. "There have been mud mosques here since the thirteenth and fourteenth centuries. Many have been destroyed. The most famous incident was by a local conqueror, Seku Amadu, in the early nineteenth century. He built his own mosque on a much different, flatter design. When the French took over, they decided to rebuild the mud mosque in 1907, using forced labor. The design incorporates French architectural ideas such as arches. In fact, one French journalist visited and was horrified by the French influence, calling it a cross between a hedgehog and a church organ. He said something like, 'it's a baroque temple dedicated to the god of suppositories.'"

Liz covered her mouth, laughing.

"Sorry, I'm totally nerding out on you," I said.

"How do you know so much?" she asked.

"I love history," I said. "Since I've been here, I've been reading up on this stuff and asking around. It's really interesting."

Liz looked at me intently as if wondering what to make of me and then said, "Why aren't non-Muslims allowed?" A sign in front of the entrance said "*Interdit Aux Non-Musulmans.*"

"That's a funny story. It's nothing discriminatory on the locals' part. It's about Westerners not showing respect, as usual," I said. "*Vogue* magazine did a shoot here without permission. The conservative locals didn't like pictures of scantily clad women taken in their venerable mosque."

"I can imagine," said Liz.

"Non-Muslims have been banned ever since. Too bad because I hear it's amazing inside. Somebody always has to ruin it for the rest of us."

"Western influence ruins everything cultural. I mean, why couldn't they just have used an original all-African design?"

"There is a positive side," I said. "Think about this: every culture in the world is a mix. This style of building actually comes from Sudan. African design has influenced Europe, like Moorish architecture in Spain, for example. You're just offended because of the European influence."

"Fair enough," said Liz.

"You have to admit that it's pretty cool. The town is proud of it. Every year there's a festival in which the whole town gets together for its care and maintenance. Since it's mud, the weathering and rain damage have to be repaired."

We admired the mosque in silence.

"Come, I'll show you old Djenné."

"Sure," she said.

"We'll go on my bike."

"I'm not sure about getting on your bike with you. Your skills aren't exactly developed."

"Come on," I said. "You're a risk taker." Liz got on the back of my motorbike. We rode two miles to a place called Djenné-Djenno, or Old Djenné. There was an archaeological dig taking place at the site. It is suspected that early occupants of West Africa lived there from 250 BC to 900 AD. I had befriended an Australian archaeologist named Bruce, who had been working on the site for a few years. I had met him a couple months earlier and started chatting with him about our common interest in history. He had actually heard of Professor Collins. I did not know if he would be there on a Sunday, but I was hoping to get lucky so that I could impress Liz with my connections.

Fate was on my side because as we pulled up, there was Bruce standing inside one of the holes swinging a pickaxe at the sidewall, a few terra-cotta figures next to him in a basket. Bruce was a short and loud Australian guy in his sixties with nearly white blond hair down to his shoulders in the back and combed over in the front.

He stopped his work once he saw that it was me on the motorbike.

116

"What brings you here, mate?" he asked, crawling out of the hole.

"Bruce, this is Liz. She's been working in the area for...gee, I don't know how long. How long you been here, Liz?"

"A couple years," she answered.

"After two years here, and she had never been to Djenné to see the mud mosque, so I took her there and then brought her here to see Old Djenné. I was hoping you'd give her a little tour."

"I'd be happy to give the pretty girl a tour."

Bruce, like Professor Collins, could tell great stories for hours. He described the history of the site and what he had found there, and then took us into the tent to show us a number of artifacts he had found.

While Liz focused on him, intently listening, I stared at Liz. She asked Bruce several insightful questions, to which Bruce responded by saying "That's an interesting thought" or "No one has asked me that before."

After a couple hours, I thanked Bruce for his time.

"The pleasure's all mine," he said. "I love talking about this, and it's nice to have an interested listener. Take good care of her, Joe."

I knew Liz wouldn't like that, but she responded somewhat politely, "I can take care of myself."

We rode back to town, where I dropped her off at her bike near the hotel.

"Did you enjoy that?"

"I guess you could say that the afternoon was pretty interesting."

"I guess I'll take that as a compliment."

"It is. I hadn't been paying much attention to the history of the region. I've just been focused on my work, focused on the right now. But this does give me insight into the culture and the people I'm helping."

"I'm really happy you enjoyed it. Bruce is fascinating."

"I have to say that I took you for one of those dumb volunteers when I met you, just here to pad their resume and drink."

"What do you think about me now?" I asked.

Liz examined me a bit. "You're an interesting guy. I guess." Then she added, "And kind of sweet."

On that I blurted out, "Can I buy you dinner?"

Liz started to answer with what, by the look on her face, appeared to be a no, but before she could form the words, I said, "I'm paying."

"You're nice, but I don't want to eat at one of those tourist places. The free breakfast is enough, but I don't want to give them any money."

"Why?"

"They're ruining the region. I hate the principle. These tourists flying in just to say they have been to West Africa and Timbuktu, as though they're some intrepid explorer, when in fact they're completely coddled. Not my crowd."

"Stop being such a snob. There is one place right on the river that is really good. You sit on a balcony overlooking the water, they have candles, and excellent sauces."

"I'm not hungry, really. And I don't want you to pay. Nor can I afford to pay."

"Just sit with me, then."

"I was going to go back to Mopti tonight, but I guess I could stay in that village again."

"Is that a yes?"

"I'll join you for a little while."

Liz followed me on her bike to the Djenné Hotel, located right on the Niger River. There were a bunch of older French tourists emerging from a bus, obnoxiously covered head to toe in clothing, despite the heat, to protect against mosquitoes and malaria. We parked our bikes and walked into the lobby, both of us dressed in our dingy clothes, Liz with her tangled hair. Anywhere else in the world, we'd be tossed out of a hotel of this caliber, but in Africa, it was okay because we were white.

We approached the maître d', who led us to a wooden deck built on stilts over the river. He seated us at a table for two right next to the water. The sun was setting, creating that orange-red glow that is perfect for photography. Canoes slid by, their handlers silhouetted in the fading light. On each table sat a metal and glass lamp with a candle inside.

Liz gazed at the scene as though visiting an alien planet. "This is amazing. But what a waste of money when there is so much poverty around. All these people here at the hotel being spoon-fed Africa."

"You have no problem speaking your mind. Do you?"

"What's the point of holding back?" she said. "I'll just disappoint people later."

"Being pliable at first is a way to make friends, and then if you find someone you connect with you can get deeper," I said.

"That's so fake."

"It's not necessarily fake; it's polite. If I don't like someone, I don't hang out with them."

"I just don't hang out with them to begin with."

"Liz," I said. "This is a nice night. Let go of whatever's bothering you and enjoy yourself."

Liz stared at me a moment with her examining look that had become her wont. Her face softened. "This is nice."

"Are you sure you don't want anything?"

"I'm not hungry."

"Not even some wine?"

"No, thank you. I'll just watch you."

"I'm going to have some wine."

I ordered a bottle of wine from the waiter.

"You're ordering a whole bottle?" Liz asked.

"It's cheaper than by the glass, and I usually bring the rest back to the room."

The waiter brought the bottle out, chilled. Poured me a small amount to taste. And once I gave the okay, started to pour some into Liz's glass.

"No thanks," she said, holding up her hand. The waiter paused.

"Are you sure you don't want some?" I asked.

"It is a bit weird letting you drink alone. Just a little," she said to the waiter.

"Cheers," I said, holding up my glass.

"Cheers," she said, clinking glasses but not looking me in the eye.

"Wait, you have to look me in the eye."

"Why?" she said.

"You're cursed with seven years' bad sex."

"I've never heard that."

"It's a fact. Let's do this again. Cheers," I said, clinking her glass and staring purposefully into her eyes.

"Cheers," she said, opening her eyes overly wide and staring into mine. She sipped. "Mmm, not bad."

The waiter returned. "Have you decided what you want for dinner?"

"Liz?" I asked.

"I'm not hungry. I don't want anything."

"If you're sure," I said. "I'm going to eat. I'm hungry. What's your soup of the day?"

"It's potato and leek."

"I'll have that," I said. "And the salad too."

"You want both the soup and the salad?"

"Yes," I said.

"All right, sir." He began taking the menus.

"Wait, I want to order a main course too."

He said, "Sorry, sir. What would you like?"

"I'll have the steak au poivre, *à point*. Does that come with *frites*?"

"Yes, sir."

"And the chocolate soufflé for dessert. I see on the menu it says to order it early because it takes forty-five minutes."

"Yes, sir. Anything else?"

"That's it."

The waiter took the menu and left.

"You must be really hungry," said Liz.

"Yep."

The buzz from the wine took hold, and soon we were talking about how we both liked foreign films.

The salad arrived, a healthy mixture of lettuce, tomatoes, bell peppers, cucumbers, and a blue cheese dressing.

"Looks delicious," I said.

"It does," said Liz. "I haven't seen a salad that good looking in a while."

"Do you want some?" I asked.

Liz hesitated. "Maybe a little."

I scooped some onto her bread plate, which she ate up hungrily. "Have some more," I said. Without waiting for her response, I added more to her dish.

We then discussed our mutual love of sports. For her it was soccer, for me American football, or simply "football," as I didn't see the point of inserting the word "American" before it. Liz disputed this.

"People don't know which sport you're talking about if you just call it 'football,'" said Liz.

"Not true, you tell by the context. Like, if I say, 'That football game was so boring, no one scored,' you know that I meant soccer. And if I say, 'What an exciting football game with lots of action!' then you know I mean American football."

To my surprise, she laughed at this.

The soup arrived. "My god, that smells good," I said.

"What'd you order again?" asked Liz.

"Potato and leek soup."

"Mmm, I loved potage parmentier when I was going to school in France."

"Waiter, can you bring us another bowl?" I asked.

"No, it's okay," said Liz, but the waiter had already left and returned with another bowl.

"Just a little, please. I'm not hungry." She sipped a few spoonfuls. "It is really good!"

Next, we talked about literature. She apparently read a lot, and we spent the soup course describing book we both have read and then recommending books others.

Alas, the pepper steak arrived, steaming hot, crisscrossed grill marks, and a sprig of parsley. Juicy French fries on the side. The scent of pepper wafted off the plate. "Mmm," I said. "Smells delicious."

Liz leaned over and took a whiff. "It does look good."

"Another plate," I said to the waiter.

Liz savored her portion. Finally, the waiter delivered the chocolate soufflé with vanilla ice cream on the side. This time he brought two plates and two spoons without my having to ask.

"I haven't had chilled wine or food like this in years."

"We're not out here to torture ourselves. It's a sacrifice, but there's no reason to be a martyr about it."

Liz sat sullenly, her mood suddenly changed.

"Something wrong?" I asked.

"I don't know about all this."

"What do you mean?"

"I mean hanging out. Having this kind of dinner. I don't want to get involved with anyone. I'm not even sure I want anyone around right now."

"Why? What is it that happened to you?"

"I don't want to talk about it."

"If you ever do want to talk about it, I will listen." Liz took a few more sips of her wine. The bottle was nearly finished. "Do you want to get another?" I asked.

"This one is enough." She looked out over the river. "If I tell you, do you promise not to judge me?"

"I swear."

"This stays between us."

"I promise."

"I don't know if you'll want to hear it," Liz began.

"Tell me."

"A few years ago, I was working in Sharm El-Sheik, the beach resort on the Red Sea."

"I've heard of it."

"I went with some friends. We rented a house. It was very much a party scene, a bunch of us just out of school. I was working at a dive resort as a scuba master. It was a great life. Scuba dive all day and then party at night."

"So, you did party?"

"A bit," said Liz. "As you might expect by this point, I got involved with one of the guys in the house. It was just for fun at first. But then..." She paused. "I got pregnant. I'm not sure how it happened. It certainly wasn't planned. Upon talking about it, we discovered that we cared for one another and decided to keep the baby."

"Were you guys going to get married?" I asked.

"It wasn't discussed. We just decided that we were going to be together and raise the child."

"You're so young, though."

"Do you want me to continue? You said you wouldn't judge."

"I'm not judging. I'm curious. You don't seem like the type who'd want to settle down so soon. That's why I am asking."

"I don't know, but when I found out I was pregnant, it just felt right."

"Then what happened?"

Liz took a sip of wine. "A few months in we were making plans to move to Germany. He was German. We'd told everyone. Our friends were shocked but trying to be supportive. We were actually happy. At least, I was. He seemed to be too. But then we both came down with typhoid. I'm not exactly sure how. It happens in these parts of the world. I got very sick. I was put in the hospital and...and I lost the baby." Liz's voice cracked. She smiled uncomfortably and then finished off the glass of wine. "That was it. It was so easy. The baby was gone. My ex was devastated. I don't know even how to describe it. He completely shut down. We tried to talk about it, but he just refused. Not long after, he said that he was going back to Germany. He got on a flight and left. I tried to contact him a few times but got no response."

I watched her the whole time she was telling me the story, her eyes becoming glassy. "What did you do?" I asked.

"I left as well. I couldn't stay in Sharm. It was a resort for partying. My friends were nice, but they ultimately had other things to do. I was a damper on everyone's fun. My boyfriend had left and was uncommunicative. I couldn't face anyone and needed to get away. My aunt was on assignment, and I didn't want be trouble for her. I'd never been to West Africa. It seemed about as far away as I could get. I'd heard about the need for wells and clean water. I just showed up here and spoke to a couple NGOs about working for them. One was weirded out by my just showing up. The other showed me the ropes and wanted me to hang around, but the NGO turned out to be just another scene of twenty-year-olds living together. I couldn't deal with it. Then I saw a better way. I had the website built to raise money, arranged for money by wire transfer, and got started. It was ridiculously easy. Best of all, I was alone. I avoided Westerners who would ask questions. That is, until you and your persistence. To be honest with you, I was ready for someone to speak English to at a normal speed. That's the story." Liz tried to read my reaction.

It was like a punch in the gut. To hear about her pregnancy with another guy and imagine all that's associated with it, the intimacy, their connection. Additionally, when you're as young as I was then, there's an illusion of purity that still exists. I knew no women at this point in my life who'd had to deal with issues of pregnancy and certainly not who had had to grapple with a tragedy of this magnitude. This left me with a sickening feeling. Yet this was a girl whom I cared about, and beyond that, a damaged individual who had just opened up to me with a painful secret. She was looking for understanding. I had to rally. I had to suck it up and push aside whatever repelling feelings I had.

I reached my hand across the table put it tenderly on hers. "It's okay," I said. She turned her hand over and held mine tightly. "I've never been through anything like this, and I hope that I'm able to say the right things here, but you seem like an incredible person. I can only imagine what it's like to lose a child and then be abandoned by someone whom you care about, left to deal with this all by yourself. It explains a lot."

"I thought you were just going to run away when I told you the story," Liz said.

"No, I'm here. Look, whatever you need right now, I am available. You can talk to me any time. And if you're ready to rejoin people, I can introduce you to my friends in the NGO. And if not, that's cool too."

"Thank you," she said. "It's late. I have to be getting back. I'm tired."

"Are you all right to ride back to the village?" I said, a bit shocked.

"I'll be fine."

"You've been drinking. I mean, you can crash with me in the hotel. I won't do anything. I promise."

She smiled. "I'd rather get back."

"I won't push, but if you change your mind."

I paid the bill. It was more than I was used to in West Africa but still far cheaper than a similar meal in Europe. I walked Liz to her bike. I hugged her good night. "Thank you for manipulating me into eating dinner," she said.

I laughed. "You figured out my plan."

"And thanks for listening," she said, pausing, just gazing at me. I saw my moment, and so I leaned in and kissed her. Her lips fit just perfectly with mine. I didn't know how far to pursue the kiss, but we just kept kissing. I went with it. The kiss continued for a few minutes. I put my arms around her, holding her tight until she gently pulled away. "I'm leaving now," she said abruptly, putting on her helmet and fastening the strap. She got on her bike, started the motor, waved goodbye, and drove off.

I remained, listening to her engine fade into the distance and watching the red taillight disappear between the trees, until it was dark and silent.

21

For Whom the Bell Tolls

I returned to Mopti the next day. Latrell was in our room listening to music on his headphones. I waved hi. He continued listening. I gestured to take off his headphones. He tapped them to tell me that he was listening to a good song and not to bother him. About a minute later, he switched them off.

"What is it, man?" he asked.

"I kissed Liz."

"You did. Wow. How was it? All dirty?"

"Please stop. She's hot. I betcha she cleans up really well."

"You saw her in Djenné?"

"I asked her to come visit me so that I could show her around, and she did. I took her to dinner at the Djenné Hotel, softened her up, and went in for the kill."

"As long as you're happy. How far did you get?"

"Whatever," I said.

"When are you seeing her again?"

"I dunno. Now that I think about it, we haven't made any plans. Wait. I never found out where she was staying or how to reach her. Oh, shoot."

"This girl is drama, I tell ya."

"Damn it. I can't believe I didn't ask how to get ahold of her. By the way, you were right."

"About what?"

"Her past."

"What happened?"

"I can't tell you. Just sayin'."

"Run, man, run."

A few days passed. I hadn't seen or run into Liz. It was strange after the connection we had in Djenné. I didn't know what to do except what I had done before, which was stalk the restaurant into Mopti and hope she showed. I asked around the restaurant and at some of the shops in town if they had seen her. No one had.

Maybe I had pushed things too far in Djenné. Maybe I had scared her off. If she didn't want to be found, I should respect that. Then there was a part of me, let's call it the Latrell voice, that told me this girl was trouble and to run.

After a week, I rode my motorbike outside of town, looking for the dirt track where she had turned off that one day we had gone to the village. There were many dirt tracks leading off into the bush in Mali, and they all looked the same. I wasn't familiar enough with the landscape to determine which one was hers. I only remembered that it was thirty minutes from Mopti. I drove out that far and began looking around. Nothing struck me. I realized that I was facing the other way. We had been going back when she had turned off, so things would look different to me. I turned around and tried the opposite direction.

Even if I found the right track, I didn't know how far she was down the track, or even if she turned off on another trail. It felt like an impossible task. All the choices made me hesitate until I finally picked one.

There were various motorcycle tracks in the dirt, but no way to know if they were hers. I needed to get lucky. There was not much out there, just bushes and fields, not even huts. I then worried about getting lost and running out of gas and water. I considered turning back. Finally, I reached a village. In the little Bambara language I knew, I tried to convey that I was looking for a white girl. The woman just looked at me, confused. Then I simply said, "Liz," and the women pointed in a direction. I didn't know how to ask how far I needed to go. "I should have filled up with gas before leaving and brought extra water," I said to myself.

Up ahead, I saw a small lake with a large solitary tree next to it. Under the tree was Liz's motorbike, a Western-style tent, a small table, and other items lying about. I pulled up, stopped the motor, and called Liz's name. There was some rustling and moaning from within the tent.

"Liz, are you in there?"

"Go away," came a weak voice.

"It's Joe. Were you sleeping?"

"I'm not feeling too well. Come back another time."

I unzipped the flap of her tent and looked in. "I didn't know how to get in touch with you, and we didn't make plans, so I...." Liz was a ghastly white, lying on a sleeping pad with no camping sheet. "Oh my, you really aren't well."

"I'm fine. Just let me be. I'll be fine in a few days." She started to sit up but didn't have the strength. She lay back down.

"You look terrible," I said.

"Shut the fuck up," she said.

I crawled in. She was soaked with sweat. I put my hand on her forehead. "You're burning up. What are your symptoms?"

"I already know what it is. It's malaria. I've had it before."

"Don't you take malaria pills?"

"Just leave me be."

"I won't leave you be. You could die. Where's your water?"

Liz pointed at the 1.5-liter bottle.

"Is that it?"

"I have to get more."

"You can barely move," I said. "Do you have food?"

"I have some biscuits."

"I'm not going to stand by while you commit slow suicide in West Africa. This is ridiculous, Liz. Just rest," I said.

I went outside, zipped up the tent, got on my bike, and then remembered my gas situation. I looked in the tank to find it nearly empty. "Liz, I'm taking your bike. Mine's out of gas." There was no response.

In town, I found Dr. Ouologuem in his office, reading a magazine. The NGO contracted with this doctor for us volunteers. He was a genial man, a local guy with a huge family of twelve kids, educated at the medical school in Bamako. He was in his forties and rather overweight for a doctor. He dressed in black slacks, a white oxford shirt with the top buttons undone, and polished black leather wingtips. I told him about Liz. Initially, he was unwilling to travel all the way out into the bush. He was even less inclined when I told him that it was impossible for him to go by car and that he would have to go by moto taxi. I finally convinced him after reminding him of his Hippocratic oath but more importantly paying him a moderate sum in U.S. dollars. I then loaded up my bike, or I should say Liz's bike, with water, food, and gas and then hired a moto taxi for the doctor. I led the doctor on his moto taxi out to see Liz.

She was not happy at all to find three people invading her tent, but she had too little energy to protest effectively. I eventually kicked out the moto-taxi driver. The doctor looked her over, took her vitals, and quickly determined, "Malaria."

"I told you," mumbled Liz.

He gave me some medicine and instructed me to make sure that she had plenty of water, rest, and food. "It was good you came along," he added. "She was severely dehydrated and too weak to get herself food and water. Keep an eye on her for the next two or three days at least. Either that or bring her to the hospital."

"I'm not going to a fucking hospital," came a mumbling from Liz's tent.

The doctor looked at me and whispered, "If the fever isn't gone in two days, bring her to the hospital."

The doctor departed on the moto taxi. I stayed until Liz fell asleep and then rode back to town to get my stuff and see about work. Mike happened to be in Mopti this week. I found him in the warehouse taking inventory.

"Hey, Mike. Do you have a sec?"

"What's up, Joe?"

"I need a few days off. I don't know if you heard, but there's a British girl who's been doing the same sort of stuff we are. She and I have become friends, and in any case, she's come down with malaria. I got the doctor to see her, and he says I should look after her for a few days."

Mike laughed. "Latrell told me about you and her. I also heard that Latrell covered for you a couple times so you could see her. Why don't you bring her into town, so we can watch over her?"

"She's really weak. You've had malaria. You know how awful it is to be moved at this point. Besides, I already asked her, and she got pretty ornery."

"Where is she?"

"She's living in a tent, under a tree, by a lake about fifty kilometers from here."

"You're kidding."

"She's the rugged type. I figured I'd grab my camping stuff and stay with her."

"You should bring her to town. It doesn't sound healthy."

"Dr. Ouologuem said she's best where she is unless the fever doesn't break in the next couple days. I just got to make sure she has food, water, and someone to look after her until she gets better. I don't know about you, but when I'm sick, I like to be at home, not moving about."

"It just doesn't sound right to me."

"Because she's a Westerner?"

"Not just that. The NGO needs you right now. We have that big shipment coming this week, and we're in a transition period between old volunteers leaving and new ones coming in. We're short staffed, and the new guys need to be trained. I'd rather you brought her here."

"Are you serious? I've barely taken any time off since I've been here. Can't you give me a few days? Especially since I am doing this to help a friend, not just goofing around."

Mike sighed. "Fine. You can have a couple days."

"I might need more than that. She's not going to be better in two days. I've been here for over six months. Give me a break."

"Three days."

"Wow, Mike. Fine."

I stormed off to my room and threw together my tent, sleeping bag, other sleeping stuff, and books. Latrell walked in.

"Your brother's being a dick," I said straight off.

"He can be like that," said Latrell.

On my way out of town, I stocked up with food and water-purification equipment. When I returned to Liz's camp, it was nearly dark. Liz was still sleeping.

I realized that her camp site was actually quite nice. The sounds of the town were replaced by the chirping of insects and birds. It was clean and smelled fresh, like nature. I lit the lantern and sat on Liz's makeshift chair, which was a tree stump. The sunset was gorgeous, and I understood why Liz had chosen this spot.

I heated up the canned food and crawled into Liz's tent to gently wake her up.

"Leave me alone," she said in her deep British accent.

"The doctor says you need to eat."

"Fucking go away." Her voice was muffled and actually kind of cute.

It took a few minutes of poking and prodding before I managed to get Liz awake and sitting up. She was so weak that I had to prop her up on my rolled-up sleeping bag. She sat there placidly trying to eat, food dropping onto her chest. I tried to spoon-feed her, to which she said, "I can feed my fucking self." And she did. She made a face. "This is awful. What is this shit?"

"Canned meat of some sort," I said.

"God awful," she said, now looking somewhat alive. She continued eating until she had finished the can.

"I brought a couple books. Want me to read to you?"

She stared at me in her examining way. "What do you have?"

"I have *For Whom the Bell Tolls*, by Heming—"

"I know it's by Hemingway."

"...and *Ethan Frome*, by..." I waited for Liz to fill in the blank.

"Edith Wharton."

"Which one do you want?"

"Not *Ethan Frome*. The ending is way too depressing. How about *For Whom the Bell Tolls*, still depressing but more heroic."

"Thanks for spoiling the endings of both books for me."

"Oh, god. *Everyone* knows the endings of those books. Let me guess, you found them in the market?"

"All they have in markets here is classic literature."

"That's because these books are sent to the schools for educational purposes, but people just sell them in the markets to suckers like you. Read me Hemingway."

"Yes, ma'am. Since you've already read it, I'll start where I last left off..." I read her the part where Robert Jordan first meets the guerrilla fighters and follows them into the mountains to the camp for the first time. Liz lay back, closed her eyes, and listened.

After half an hour, she stopped me. "Joe, you've been really nice to me. About the other night in Djenné..."

"Yeah?"

"It still holds what I said. I don't want to get involved with anyone. It was a nice night and maybe I got carried away with the wine, the view, and just having someone pay attention to me. I didn't want that to happen. The kiss, I mean. I'm just trying to be honest. I don't want you doing all this for me, expecting that it may lead to something."

"I understand," I said. "You went through a lot and are not ready. I would do what I am doing now for any friend," I lied.

She looked at me skeptically, but I just continued reading. Thirty minutes later, I stopped, thinking she had fallen asleep.

"Keep going," she murmured, but then went to sleep.

22

The Chinese

er fever broke the next day, but she was still very weak. The doctor said that it would take her a week to recover her strength. After a couple days, I started nudging her to get up and move around. "There's a point in every illness where you're passed the rest period and you just got to get moving again," I said. As you might imagine, she was quite ornery about this. But I slowly got her up and walking.

Liz had a bit more energy, but she still needed my help. The three days that Mike had given me were up. I went to see him again at the warehouse about getting more time. "If she's better, you can leave her during the day and see her at night," Mike said.

"I can't believe you're being so heartless about this."

"I got an NGO to run here. We're helping a lot of people, not just one. Don't you get it? Liz is one person. There are many more people in worse shape."

"If you got sick, you'd be okay us leaving you alone all day?"

"Watch your mouth," Mike shot back. "You're not the one in charge here. Get back to work today, and you can see your girlfriend in the evening. She's going to be fine," he said, walking off.

I was too stunned to respond. I was never good in these situations. I told Latrell what happened.

"He's a total control freak," said Latrell. "I mean, he's my brother, and I love him and all, but, man, he can be a dick. I'll cover for you."

I got my errands done and went out to camp to see Liz. She had managed to get herself to the tree-stump seat and was soaking up the sun.

"Good job. This is the farthest you've gotten," I said.

"It was a struggle," she said. "I just want to sit here a few hours. I was going stir-crazy in the tent." Then she asked, "What day is today?"

I looked at my watch. "It's Wednesday."

"Wednesday." She pondered the idea of Wednesday. "Oh fuck, tomorrow is Thursday."

"That's usually how it works."

"The Chinese are coming tomorrow. I have to go to town to meet them."

"Too bad. You're not up for it."

"If I don't show, I'll lose that supplier. They're shipping this stuff in for me specifically. They won't know what happened to me, and they'll think I welched on the deal."

"It's not happening, Liz."

"Let's see how I feel in the morning."

The next morning, I asked Liz how she was feeling.

"Much better," she said. "I think I can make it to town." But when she tried to sit up, she put her hand on her forehead, and then plopped back down.

"You're weaker than yesterday," I said.

"I'm fine," she said. "Just give me a few minutes." She tried again but could barely sit up.

"That's seals it," I said. "You're not going."

"I am."

"Go ahead," I said. "Get up and go."

"Fuck you," she said.

"That answers that."

Suddenly she smiled sweetly at me. "Joe, you've already been so nice, and I wouldn't ask this but... "

"Oh my god, no, Liz."

"Please, Joe. This is a large deal with the Chinese. Lots of people are depending on me."

"I don't speak Chinese."

"It's not a problem. I'll write everything down and give you the money."

"What if something goes wrong? How will I communicate?"

"Nothing will go wrong," she said.

I sighed. "I guess I have to go to town anyway."

"Thank you. Thank you. Thank you. Get me my pen and paper, and then go out to my bike and unscrew the seat. My money is in there."

I got the pen and paper and then unscrewed the seat on her bike to find quite a wad of brand-new hundred-dollar bills. "I can't believe you keep this much money on you," I said.

"I haven't had any problems."

She wrote out a note in Chinese and then dealt off a few hundred-dollar bills. "This will cover the shipment. They may try to take advantage of you, since it's not me. Don't let them. This is all the supplies cost. No more than this. Okay?"

"What? I can't bargain in Chinese."

"You can handle this. Just fold your arms if they start to argue with you. They need to make this sale too after driving the supplies all the way here."

"What happens after I pay them?"

"They know where to take the truck, but if not, the instructions are in the note."

"All right," I said. Hesitantly, I put the money in my pocket, got on my bike, and rode into Mopti to the restaurant and waited.

I was a little early, so I asked for a coffee. The coffee relaxed me. I was just starting to feel comfortable when I saw Mike walking around outside, shopping for something from the various vendors. *What's he doing here? Please don't see me, please don't see me,* I thought. *It's going to be okay,* I said to myself. *It's bright outside and it would be difficult to see me through the door into the dark of the restaurant.* He passed before the door a couple of times and then moved on out of sight. *Phew!*

I sat back and relaxed, letting out a sigh. Then I heard, "Hey, Joe!" in a friendly voice.

I turned around quickly and looked at the other entrance. "Hi, Mike," I said nervously.

"What are you doing here? I thought you were going down with Latrell to set up some new wells today."

"Umm," I said, trying to think of something. "He said he could do it himself and instead wanted me to handle some stuff in town."

"He said that he could take care of it alone?" said Mike. "I didn't realize he was now in charge and making personnel decisions."

"He's not," I stuttered. "You are, but we just thought this would be a better use of resources to split the work."

"I told you both to go down there. Workers have been siphoning off our supplies at the village, so I wanted one of you to watch the supplies while the other set up the well, remember?"

"That's right. I forgot."

"You forgot?"

"Sorry, it won't happen again."

"Something doesn't seem right." Mike paused. "He's covering for you, isn't he? You're not working today because you're taking care of the girl, aren't you?"

"Mike, I'm sorry. It's just that—"

"—This is way out of line. You are flaunting my authority at this point."

"Mike, let me explain."

"There's no excuse. But wait. If you're taking care of the girl, why are you here in the restaurant drinking coffee?"

Just then three Chinese gentlemen walked in the door. I could see them looking for Liz. I just sat there, afraid to do anything. Not seeing her, they walked back outside.

"Are you listening to me?" asked Mike. "What are you looking at?"

I could see through the door that the Chinese guys were impatient and about to get back in the truck and leave.

"Excuse me. I, uh, have to take care of something." I got up, walking right passed Mike, leaving an incredulous look on his face. I waved down the Chinese guys just before they left and handed them Liz's note. They seemed a bit confused at first, but then they read the note and made a gesture asking for the money. I took out the wad of bills and handed them to the main guy. I sensed Mike glaring at me over my shoulder.

"What the fuck is going on here?" Mike asked. "Who are these people?"

"Mike, just a second," I said. The guy finished counting the money, then gestured that he wanted more. I didn't have time to argue, so I just peeled off another bill from my own money. That satisfied him. He shook my hand and then hopped in the truck, hopefully driving it to wherever Liz had instructed.

"Don't tell me to wait a second. What are you doing?" Mike said, approaching me as the truck drove away. "You're buying supplies for that girl, aren't you? I cannot believe this. You're having my little brother cover for you, and instead of working for me, which is the whole reason the NGO is paying for you to be in Africa, you are working for that girl."

"Mike..."

"In my office tomorrow morning at 9 a.m. You're done." Mike stormed off.

I returned to camp and told Liz that everything had gone fine with the deal. She seemed relieved, but she could tell that I was distracted. "Everything okay?" she asked.

"I'm fine." I didn't want to burden her with my problem while she was sick, and I was afraid she would blame herself. But she slept a lot that day, so I didn't have to explain further. I knew that I would eventually have to tell her what happened.

* * *

The next day I went to town to meet Mike. He didn't actually have an office in Mopti, but I knew he meant the warehouse. I found him sitting at the desk, waiting for me.

Without greeting me, he started right into his statement. "Since the organization has a responsibility to get you in and out of here, we have booked you a flight home. The soonest we could find one at a reasonable price is a week from now. Until then, you can stay in the dorm, but get your own meals."

"Mike, would you please let me explain?"

"I don't want to hear it. You lied and disobeyed my authority."

"Mike—"

"Stop. It's too bad because you were a good employee till you met that girl. You could have gone far in this organization."

I went back to the dorm and found Latrell there.

"Did you get in trouble?" I asked him.

"A little bit. He chewed me out, but I'm his little brother, so he's not going to fire me. My mom would kill him."

"I'm sorry, dude. I didn't mean to get you involved. I never imagined—"

"—Seriously, dude. What were you thinking doing work for her?"

"She had to complete that deal, or she'd lose the Chinese supplier. She was sick and couldn't make it. I had to come to town anyway to get supplies. It took five minutes. It's just bad timing that your brother showed up. That's all."

"I told you that girl was trouble."

"Do you think you could explain things and smooth things over with your brother?"

Latrell laughed. "He ain't going back now that he's fired you. He'd lose face. Trust me, I know him. There's nothing I can do. But I'm going to miss having you around," he added.

"Yeah, me too."

23

One Good Turn...

iz gradually got her strength back over the next few days, and it was time to tell her that I was leaving. However, something happened to me which didn't allow me to make it.

It was the day before I was supposed to fly out, and with Liz well enough, I had stayed the night in the dorm to say goodbye to everyone and pack up. The next day, I would go out to see Liz, tell her that I'm leaving, and hopefully see if she would like to meet me again, somewhere in the world. My co-workers took me out in town for a few drinks. Well, more than a few. I had started to feel unwell in the middle of the night, a pounding headache, nausea, not entirely different from what you'd feel after a night of drinking, but something about this felt off.

As I was packing up, I kept having to sit on the bed and rest. Much of the pain of hangovers is due to dehydration, so I kept downing bottles of water. Each bottle made me more and more nauseous. Latrell came in to find me sitting on the bed. "You all right, man? You looked a little peaked."

"Just a bit hungover. I just need to rest—" But I didn't finish getting the sentence out. Instead what came out was last night's dinner, beer, and all the water I had drunk. Latrell jumped out of the way. I crashed down a steep descent into misery. Strength left my limbs. I barely carried myself to the bathroom, where I continued to be sick out of both ends. It would not stop. All I wanted to do was sleep, but I couldn't leave the bathroom. The headache pounded even harder than before. I was burning up and shaking uncontrollably.

When I thought everything had come out, I crawled out of the bathroom and into bed. Latrell brought me a bucket and placed it on the floor next to me. He piled blankets on top of me. I faded into fever dreams, coming in and out of reality. I don't remember Dr. Ouologuem showing up. He was just suddenly there, examining me and saying that he thought it was typhoid. He gave me a bunch of medications and then gave some instructions to Latrell.

I woke again. It was dark out. Hours must have passed, even days. I was alone in the room. I remembered Liz, worried about what she must be thinking when I didn't show up. But then I got sick again. I couldn't move. I only wanted to stop being sick and sleep. I hoped Liz would figure out what had happened. Part of me wondered if she'd think I took off on her. How could she possibly think that now? I'd built trust with her, right?

There was no way to contact her. I'd just have to hope that she had faith in me and realized that something had gone wrong. On top of that, I was supposed to fly out but hadn't told her yet. There was no way I could leave before seeing her.

I woke up again to find that it was daytime. I had no idea what time it was, but it felt like morning. Again Dr. Ouologuem appeared out of nowhere.

"Doctor," I said, my voice weaker than I could imagine. "That girl, Liz, out by the lake. You have to tell her that I am sick. You have to tell her before I fly out today."

"You aren't flying anywhere today."

"I have to. I've been fired. Mike won't let me stay."

"I'll talk to Mike," said the doctor.

"And you'll get a message to Liz?"

"I'll send someone out there."

I slipped off to sleep without warning. The runs and the vomiting slowed, but I still was running a fever. It was afternoon when I woke to find Mike standing over me.

"Get up," he said. "You're out of here."

In my feverish haze, I didn't quite comprehend what he was telling me.

"What?"

"I don't believe this bullshit about typhoid. You've missed your flight, which cost the NGO money. You're no longer an employee, and you're not staying here."

Latrell, who'd been nearby, walked in. "Mike, why are you being such a dick, bro?"

"Stay out of this," said Mike.

"He's clearly sick. Talk to Dr. Ouologuem."

"I don't care what the doctor thinks. Joe's on his own time here. Let his weird girlfriend come take care of him."

"What weird girlfriend?" asked Liz, walking in the door.

Everyone turned and looked at her. She examined the room, directing her gaze at me in my awful condition and then scanning the room like a Terminator, figuring out who everyone was and then focusing in on Mike like a laser, her eyes narrowing, her lips constricting. What came next sounded like it had been running through her mind for a long time, a discourse aimed at all the corrupt NGOs in Africa, but she had never had the right outlet. Mike had given her justification and become the perfect target. "You piece of shit bureaucrat are just like every corrupt leader in Africa, more in love with himself and his fucking power than actually helping people, hiding behind the guise of your NGO to make it look like you're a holy person working for the good of the people, when in fact you're just a narcissist interested in his own power. You build shitty wells and do the minimum to help people, while paying bribes to government employees, condoning and supporting their corrupt kleptocracy. The evidence of your depravity is right in front of you: you fire Joe, a volunteer who was trying to help me out and bring clean water to Africa, and when he becomes sick, sick with fucking typhoid, you kick him out, because your stupid ego was bruised because he didn't follow your orders. I've run into so many helpful volunteers in Africa who cannot connect with real people and attempt to cover up their assholiness in their personal lives by working for NGOs. Why not focus on the real problems here? And enough of your perks and air conditioning and fancy dinners with officials. Look in the mirror. You're part of the problem."

Mike stood in stunned silence. Apart from his mother, he'd likely never been dressed down by a woman like that. Liz's withering attack reduced him to a burnt-out ember of a man, because he knew it was all true, and because Liz was right. The evidence of his moral emptiness lay right in front of him in the form of a sick volunteer whom he was booting out into the street. Even his little brother had defied him. Mike looked around the room, everyone staring at him, and simply walked out the door without a word.

No one said anything until Latrell finally broke the silence. "Your girlfriend's cool!"

"You must be Latrell," Liz said. "Help me get Joe out of here."

"But you just said—" began Latrell.

"—He's not staying here with that wanker around. We'll take him to a hotel, where he can recover in peace."

Liz and Latrell dressed me. I was ashamed to be this feeble in front of Liz, but she handled it like a professional, helping me put on my pants and shoes and holding me up as we walked out. But then I threw up again.

"Come on. It's not far," said Liz.

Latrell and Liz walked me slowly out of the room, where all the other volunteers were standing, having heard Liz's diatribe. She waved everyone out of the way, saying, "Move if you're not going to help." The other volunteers parted like the Red Sea to let us through. The short block and a half to the hotel was the longest journey of my life, the hot sun more oppressive than usual. The hotel was owned by some Persians who were known for keeping clean, inexpensive hotels for businessmen. Liz got us a room with a clean bed, air conditioning, and even satellite TV.

Liz looked at Latrell and said, "Thank you for your help. I'm sorry about your brother."

"He had it coming. That was amazing. It was even better that all the volunteers heard you. We're not going to see him for days. He was getting such a big head, acting holier than thou because he ran an NGO. He's always been a dick. He's still my brother, and I love him, but he needed that."

Latrell returned to the dorm to retrieve the rest of my stuff.

"Thanks for coming, Liz," I said.

"You did it for me. At least this way, I won't owe you anything."

"I was so worried you'd think I abandoned you when I didn't show yesterday."

"Not for a moment. After you stood by me when I was sick...after what I told you? I knew you wouldn't do that. But I wished you told me that you were fired."

"How'd you find out?"

"I came looking for you. Dr. Ouologuem explained everything to me. It was big news around town."

"I was going to tell you but not while you were sick. I knew you'd feel responsible."

"But it was my fault. I'm sorry I got you fired. I was selfish, making you do the deal with the Chinese. I got too caught up in my work and stopped thinking about others. Maybe I'm as bad as Mike."

"No, it was important to get those supplies. As you said to Mike, we have bigger worries than my job. You couldn't lose the Chinese as suppliers."

"Are you really leaving?"

"Not anymore, I guess."

"Do you want to leave?" Liz asked.

"Right now, I don't feel like even existing."

"I mean..." Liz paused. "Because maybe I can use your help. Why don't you stay? We can work together, doing our own thing. If you want to, that is. As friends, I mean. I don't want you to get the wrong idea."

I smiled at her. "As soon as I'm better, I'm all yours."

24

On the Niger River

For the next few days Liz and I stayed at the hotel. She brought me food and water, just like I did for her. When she left for work, I watched the satellite TV. My favorite channel was MDC2, a Saudi station that showed movies all day. I called my parents and had a long, expensive talk. Clearly, they were not happy about my health and now being without the support of the NGO, but my mom was cautiously supportive. My father liked the idea that I would be working on my own with another person. He saw this as my "entrepreneurial side coming out." Gradually, I got my strength back and began to venture out and about. When I was strong enough, I left the hotel and relocated to the lake to stay with Liz.

Despite everything that had happened, Liz and I never talked about our relationship. Things were push and pull with us, characterized by moments of closeness, then a pulling back on her part. She slept in her tent, and I slept in mine. There was no kissing or any hint of it since that one night in Djenné. She wouldn't look me in the eye, and I didn't try to kiss her again for fear of ruining something.

One day she said to me, "Ever been to Timbuktu?"

"No, but I've been wanting to go. I mean, it's Timbuktu. Have you?"

"I haven't. Do you want to go? We have an opportunity."

"What's up?"

"There's a boat parked on the Niger River with a bunch of pumps on it.

It was supposed to supply one of the Chinese mines in the area, but the company changed its mind. So, they just sit there. We can get them for cheap, so long as we get the barge back to Timbuktu. There are a number of villages in that area that need help. I figured we could move the pumps there, rent a warehouse, and work around there. Are you up for it?"

"Sounds incredible. It might be good for us to get away from here for a bit. When do we leave?"

"Tomorrow. It's a three-day boat trip. We'll be sleeping on sandbars along the way. We can hire a couple boatmen."

The next day, we woke early, packed up our camping materials, and rode our bikes to the shores of the Niger River. There we found a medium-sized barge tied up to the shore with about forty water pumps on it. One of Liz's Chinese contacts met us there and accepted the money. I kept my eye on the barge while Liz hired a couple boatmen, one of whom could cook. We then went to the market to buy food for the next three days, including vegetables, and live chickens that would serve as dinner the next couple nights. As there was no refrigeration, the chickens would have to be kept alive until we were ready to eat them.

By late morning we were off, the barge's diesel engine putting up the river. We passed villages along the shore. Men in canoes waved to us as they drifted by. They were either fishing or carrying produce to market. By midday, the sun beat down on all of us. Neither the river nor the boat offered any protection. I put on my baseball cap and Liz put on her straw hat that she often wore for extended periods in the sun. We sat in silence for hours, just bearing the heat.

Around sunset, it began to cool off. Liz took off her hat. I stared at her, watching her look at the shore and the passing villages, she propped up on her tan and toned arms.

"Where did you get that scar on your chin?" I said, grabbing Liz's attention. She rubbed it with her finger.

"That? Oh, I crashed my motorbike."

"How'd you do that?"

"I don't remember."

"Was it bad?"

"Not the worst," she said. "I've crashed a few times."

"How many times?" I asked.

"Seven."

"Seven times?" I said.

"You've crashed a few times yourself, as I recall. It's normal when you have a motorbike." Then Liz began rolling up her sleeve to expose her golden shoulder. "I have a scar here from road rash," she said, pointing to a discolored spot. "And here on my arm." She showed me her elbow. "This one was the worst." She turned her head and lifted the hair above her ear, revealing stitch marks. "I split my scalp on this one, had a concussion, and couldn't remember my name for a week."

"What?"

"That's why I wear a helmet now. My aunt insisted after that. Otherwise, I wouldn't deal with that bullshit."

"You're beautiful," I said suddenly.

Liz looked away and went silent.

"I am falling in love with you," I said.

She said nothing. I felt stupid. A few minutes later she said, "Don't say things like."

"It's how I feel."

"We're just friends. I don't want to get involved."

"Come on, Liz. You don't feel anything back. All this time together. All that's happened."

"No," she said. "I don't want to talk about this." She returned to staring at the landscape.

For camp that night, we beached the boat on a little island, more like a sandbar with a few bushes and a couple trees. We set up our tents on the shore while one of the boatmen slaughtered the chicken and plucked the feathers from its carcass, throwing them in the river. He did this expertly and without remorse. He had been doing it his whole life. It was still jarring to me, as a Westerner, to see where my food comes from. Not too much later, the chicken was stewing in the metal pot, the smell of the commonly used local spices wafting over the beach. The chicken was served with rice on plastic plates. This chicken had not been raised on a poultry farm like in the West. It had grown up simply living about the grounds of the village, eating whatever it could find: bugs, seeds, etc. It was not plump like American supermarket chickens but lean and gamey. The result was a tough but absolutely delicious meat, full of rich flavors.

After dinner, the boatmen scrubbed the pot in the river while Liz and I sat on the beach watching the moon rise over the Niger River.

"For all its disease and poverty, Africa is a beautiful place," I said.

"Let's subtract the disease and poverty and just leave the beauty," Liz said.

"Is that possible?"

"They can both improve the economy and keep the beauty. Preserving the environment is about being healthy, happy, and poverty-free. Anything else is a short-term solution."

"I am not sure if that's possible. Countries like ours destroyed their environments building their economies: cutting down forests, polluting lakes and rivers, smogging the skies, only later figuring out how precious their natural environments were and too late trying to protect them."

"How about these developing countries learn from our mistakes and build their economies in a sustainable way?" Liz said.

"That's not what China's thinking," I said, "building their economy at any cost."

"China feels like they were left out and now it's their turn."

"China was left out by their own choice. They're the ones who wanted to be Communists for fifty years. We'd have been glad to have them be part of the market economy. They're like the guy who shows up to the party at 2 a.m. You know, people are passed out, a couple is making out on the couch, the music is turned low, the beer is finished, but the Chinese are like 'let's party! Come on, what's wrong with you all? I had to work earlier, so I want to party now.'"

"You're nuts," said Liz.

"Pot calling the kettle black," said I.

147

"This is a nice night for a swim," she said, apropos of nothing.

"In the Niger?"

"Why not? Let's do it after the boatmen go to sleep."

"What about bilharzia?" Bilharzia is a parasite found in freshwater tropical lakes and rivers. It burrows into your skin and lays eggs in your liver. It can be dormant for years, and then the host suddenly finds himself feeling lethargic. It leads to liver damage. This was why I had not done much swimming in West Africa.

"Supposedly if you're in the water for less than fifteen minutes, they don't have time to get into your skin."

"I've heard that, but it sounds phony."

"Let it go," said Liz. "Stop analyzing every risk."

"Only if it's a skinny dip," I said.

Liz snorted an "as if," and then said, "I'll meet you out here at ten."

The boatmen, oblivious to our swimming plans, cleaned up, drank a little of the local palm wine, talked, and then went to sleep in the boat around 9 p.m. I slipped into my tent and put on some boxers for swimming. Then, at around 10 p.m., I emerged to find a bright full moon illuminating the riverscape and hearing the soughing of water going by. Liz exited her tent with a towel wrapped around her. She put her finger to her lips, whispering "shhh." She beckoned me to the other side of the island with a wave of her hand, away from the sleeping boatmen. She dipped her toe in the water, removed her towel, and threw it on the sand away from the water. She was completely naked. She slid into the water, her firm, heart-shaped calf muscles first, then her knees, then up to her strong curvy thighs, and finally over her wide hips and shapely ass. I felt like a dork standing there in my boxer shorts, my mouth agape like a moron.

"Are you coming in?" she said.

Without a word, I dropped my boxers and joined her in the water, embracing her without hesitation. We kissed for the first time since that night in Djenné. I may be a dork, but I know an opportunity when I see one. And thus, we began, first on the beach and then in the tent, making love all night.

25

Timbuktu

At some point before dawn, I returned to my tent so as not to offend the sensibilities of our boatmen. The sun climbed out of the river, foreshadowing the warmth of the day. Liz was already out of the tent and packing up. I walked up to her and kissed her on the lips. She gave me a quick peck. "Not in front of the boatmen," she said.

"Who cares?" I responded.

I packed up my tent and joined everyone on the shore by the water for some bread and instant coffee. Thirty minutes later we were cruising along, the diesel engine droning away. Liz was silent and distant again, staring at the landscape without looking at me. I decided to let her be. A quiet morning passed without a word between us. We pulled the boat ashore to eat a quick lunch of canned tuna with the leftover bread. Then back to the boat and another hot afternoon. That night we camped ashore again, on an island similar to the one from the night before. I tried a few times to begin a conversation with Liz, but she was nonresponsive. After dinner, she simply said "I'm going to sleep" and disappeared into her tent.

The following morning was much the same. We had only a few hours more till arriving at the port of Timbuktu. It was then she finally spoke up. "I want to talk about the other night," she began.

"Okay..." I said.

"It was nice. I enjoyed it. I can't promise it will happen again."

An hour later, we arrived at the port of Timbuktu. Timbuktu used to be right on the shore of the Niger River, but rivers tend to wander, so the port and the city of Timbuktu are now separated by ten miles. Liz hired a truck to carry the supplies from the boat to the warehouse in town. We hopped in the cab of the truck with the driver and drove the dusty road into town.

The entrance to Timbuktu was marked by an arch and a gate. Police manned a checkpoint there, checking permits, IDs, et cetera. These checkpoints were common in Africa under the pretense of security.

"They're going to want a bribe," said Liz. "They see two white people in the front of the truck as a money-making opportunity."

As expected, this officer pulled us aside and ordered us to open the back of the truck. The officer climbed in to inspect the pumps. He then asked if we had a permit. We did not, and it wasn't even clear what kind of permit was required. Liz offered to apply for a permit, but to our surprise he wasn't interested and instead asked us to come with him to the police station. He ordered us to get in the truck and follow them to the station, an old French colonial building.

Our driver parked outside. The officer climbed on the truck, reached in the window, and took the keys from the ignition. This was more serious than we had thought. We were led into the chief's office. The chief was an overweight African in a comically baggy official uniform, unkempt, with the shirt's top two buttons undone because of the heat. An electric fan blew air over his bald head. He was occupying himself by chatting with his assistant, a young lady who seemed amused by what he had to say. She regained her professional composure when we walked into the room and dismissed herself to her desk, stationed just outside the chief's door. The office was sweltering, built with too few windows, and painted a pale green, much of which had chipped off over the decades since the French had been here.

Liz addressed him in French. I could only gather bits and pieces of the conversation. Liz got pretty intense, but much to my surprise, she wasn't tearing the officer a new one – more pleading with him.

"What's going on?" I finally asked her.

"He says that we don't have the proper permits for the pumps, nor the customs forms, nor the certificate to transport the pumps. I've never needed these before."

"Will he let us pay the fine and fill out the necessary papers?"

"I've offered him fifty dollars, but he doesn't want it. He says he's confiscating the pumps."

"He doesn't want a bribe?"

"It's not a bribe. We don't pay bribes. But we will pay the legally sanctioned fee for a permit."

The chief said something to Liz. "What?" I said, wanting to understand. Now she got very upset and began speaking rapidly in French. The chief shrugged and motioned to one of his officers, who quickly approached Liz and put her in handcuffs.

"What are you doing?" I said in English. Another officer cuffed me as well. "Liz, what's going on?"

"We're being arrested."

"I can see that, but why?"

Liz was spitting mad, screaming at the guy in French. Her hands in cuffs, she yanked herself away from the officer and leaned over the chief's desk, yelling in his face.

"Liz, knock it off," I said. "You're going to make things worse."

But she just continued till the officer pulled her off the chief's desk, literally kicking and screaming as they dragged her out of the room, which caused me to yell at the officers in English to let her go and to stop treating her that way. Another two officers yanked me in a separate direction away from her, until I found myself also kicking and screaming and being dragged out of the room. Eventually, they put me to a jail cell, where the officers took everything out of my pockets, passport, money, etc. It was my first time in prison. The walls of the ten-foot by ten-foot cell had a two-toned paint scheme with a light grayish-green color on the bottom half, sharply delineated from a dark, grayish-green for the upper half of the cell. The door was made of metal bars, like a jail in the Old West. Once the door was slammed shut, I calmed down. I examined my situation. There were no other occupants, and the only piece of furniture was a sad-looking metal toilet in the corner with an open window above it. I stood on the toilet and looked out the window into the courtyard. There were several other windows.

"Liz!" I yelled.

"I'm here," came a reply.

"Are you okay?" I asked.

"Just angry."

"What happened?" I asked.

"I don't know," she said.

"Liz, stay cool. They'll eventually tell us what's going on. The more you get pissed, the more trouble we'll have."

"I'm not going to stay calm. This is bullshit. BULLSHIT!" she yelled for everyone to hear.

About an hour later, an officer came by and got me. I was brought back into the chief's office. Liz was there too, handcuffed to one of the chairs. The officer spoke in French. Liz was calmer than before but still visibly irritated.

"What's he saying?" I asked.

"He said that we are charged with illegally importing and transporting those pumps. Moreover, he says that I am here on a tourist visa and that I should not be conducting business."

"Did you explain what you were doing? That we're helping people."

"He doesn't care."

"Does he want some money?"

"Nope."

"What does he want?"

"I'm trying to find out." Liz continued in French. Getting angrier and angrier.

"Liz, calm down," I said. "What's going on?"

"They want us to spend six months in jail and then we have to leave the country and are never allowed to come back. All the pumps will be confiscated." Liz was mystified. "Something is wrong here. It smells funny. This is a setup. I bet Mike had something to do with this."

"Mike? He can't be that vindictive."

Liz started in on the chief again. The chief just shrugged and leaned back, listening. Then he waved his hand and two officers came and took her away.

"Wait, you can't do this," I said. "Where are you taking her?"

"To jail," said the chief in English. "Six months in prison. You too."

"But what about a trial?" I said.

The chief shrugged.

"I want to contact my embassy."

Again, the chief shrugged and waved for the officers to take me away. I worried about Liz. She and I would be separated. I didn't know what they would do with a Western girl in prison for six months or even a night. I couldn't let anything happen to Liz. I didn't even want to imagine what that would be.

"Wait!" I said. "A thousand dollars. I can give you a thousand dollars." The chief motioned for the officers to stop carrying me out.

"What did you say?" he asked.

"Let us go. We leave the country in twenty-four hours. I promise."

The chief considered the offer. "Ten thousand."

"What? I don't have ten thousand dollars."

The chief signaled for the officers to resume.

"Wait! Three thousand," I offered.

"Eight."

"Five," I said.

"Six,"

"Five," I repeated.

"Six," said the chief. "Get it today, and we let her go tomorrow."

"No, not tomorrow. Today. People know us and will be looking for us. If we disappear, two Westerners, people will notice, and you will be in big trouble. Take five thousand dollars. I'll get it wired, just get me to the bank while it's still open, and we will leave tonight."

The chief thought about that. "Okay, it's a deal." He smiled.

"And if you hurt her, I will make sure that you get what's coming. Britain doesn't take well to its subjects being harmed by police officers. Don't even touch her. Got it?"

"Don't worry about it. I'm more interested in your bail money. Hurry.

The bank's going to close soon." He laughed.

I wanted to get this done before he changed his mind, but in the rush to get the deal done, I didn't fully consider the ramifications of the phone call I needed to make and the conversation I was about to have. The two police officers escorted me in handcuffs to the bank and treated me as though I was the greatest threat to the people of Timbuktu, but I guess they had nothing better to do. They didn't speak English, but through the power of pantomime, I managed to explain that I had to go to the telephone shop first. The cops gave me back some money to buy a telephone card to call the United States. They weren't expensive, but it would give me only five minutes to explain to my parents why I needed them to wire me $5,000 immediately.

I dialed the number and heard a far-off American-style ringtone. Given the time difference, my parents would just be waking up.

"Hello," my mom said. It wasn't unusual for me to call.

"Hi Ma—"

"Let me get your dad on the line," she said quickly.

"Wait, I don't have much time—" But I could already hear her yelling for Dad. He clicked onto the extension.

"Hey, kid," he said. "How are ya?"

"I don't have much time. I have to explain quickly. Don't worry. I am okay. I am in Timbuktu. Yes, that Timbuktu. It's kind of a long story, but just trust me. We've been arrested. It's nothing horrible. We bought some Chinese pumps for a village but didn't get the right permits, so now we're considered smugglers, but I think there's also some corruption. In any case, they want to put us in jail for six months unless we pay them five thousand dollars and then leave the country tonight."

"What? Tell us what happened first," my mom said.

"I don't have time. There are two cops here, I have a five-minute phone card, and the banks are closing soon."

"Who's 'we'?" my dad asked.

"My girlfriend and I," I said.

"You have a girlfriend?" asked my mom.

"Not now, Mom."

"This is a lot of money. Give us some details first," said my dad.

"What do you want to know? Ask away."

"Who is she? Where's she from?"

"She's British. She was raised by her aunt, a British diplomat. She's legit. I met her through the NGO. The charges are bullshit, but that's the way things work here. They were going to keep us in prison for six months, but I worked out this deal to leave tonight. Mom, Dad, I am really worried about her in prison. She's a very pretty Western girl. I don't know what will happen to her in prison in this part of the word. I really need to get her out tonight. Please."

There was a pause on the other end of the line.

"Give us the wire instructions," my dad said. "Then call us as soon as you're in a safe place."

I gave them the wire instructions for the bank. The cops took me down to the Bank of Africa, where I showed them my passport and waited. The bank was about to close but stayed open long enough to receive the cash. My parents actually sent $6,000, a little extra I guess for me to get out of the country. Good thing, too, because the bank took a hefty service charge. The cops didn't notice while I separated the $5,000 for the chief and secreted the rest.

I returned to the police station to find a very happy police chief. He counted out $5,000 like he'd won the lottery. And then gave orders to his officers. A few minutes later, a confused-looking Liz was brought out to me.

"What's going on?" she asked.

"I got us out."

She started to say something in French to the chief.

"Liz, don't. Let's just go," I said.

She ignored me and carried on, her voice becoming more pitched.

"Stop, Liz. We're out. Don't make it worse."

"I want to know what happened. This isn't right."

"Liz, let's just go."

Then the chief added a thought, saying to me, "If you can't keep your woman under control, I'll put her back in jail."

"Fuck you!" she said.

The chief signaled to his officers to carry her back to prison.

"Wait," I said to Liz. "Seriously, you need to stop. Realize where we are and how they treat women. We're in a bad spot. We are out, now be quiet so we can leave."

"Not after that," said the chief.

"Look, we're sorry," I said.

"Have her apologize," he said.

"No way in hell," said Liz.

"Liz, enough!" I said. "You want to rot here?" I walked over to the chief. "Here's another five hundred dollars. Don't listen to her. We're gone. Okay?"

"What?" said Liz. "Don't you dare give that—"

"Just get them out of here," said the chief, interrupting her and taking the $500.

They took us both outside and uncuffed Liz, who continued to shout insults at the officers. They handed back our passports, credit cards, and nothing else. "*Con!*" was her last word to them as they walked inside.

I still had some of the extra funds my parents had sent, which I used to get us to the airport. The only flight that night with available seats was to Dakar, Senegal. I bought us two tickets with my credit card. While we were waiting in the terminal, Liz asked me, "What about the rest of our stuff?"

"Leave it," I said. "We have to leave the country."

"This is bullshit. You totally wimped out. They would have let us go. They wouldn't have held two Westerners like that. Our embassies would have had a fit. I could have called my aunt. How much did you pay them?"

"Five thousand dollars."

"Are you serious? That's a fortune here. The chief can now retire to a villa in the countryside. You totally got ripped off—"

Liz was silent the entire plane ride to Dakar. There we hailed a cab to a hotel. As soon as we got to our room, Liz started up again. "I guess I'll sleep in my underwear, since I have no stuff."

I was silent.

"You got royally ripped off. I could have done much better," she continued.

"It's not like you were doing any better, Liz," I fired back. "You screaming and yelling insults. I didn't see you employing any master negotiating skills."

"I didn't have a chance. You don't need to help me. I can take care of myself."

"I didn't know what they were going to do to you. I just wanted to get you out of there."

"Stop getting involved!"

"Enough, Liz!" I yelled. "I'm sorry I'm not as experienced in world affairs as you are. All I know is that the girl I am in love with is in jail in Mali, by herself with a bunch of seedy guys. I couldn't bear to have anything happen to you. I love you, okay? I wanted to help and take care of you. That's what people do for each other. I'm sorry about what happened to your parents and with your ex-boyfriend. But you need to stop treating me like the enemy. Stop yelling at me. I just might have saved you from spending the night with Abdul and his ten friends. You know what's going on between us, yet you resist and resist, always giving me a hard time. It's time for you to stop treating me this way and accept that there's another person in your life. I don't deserve to be treated this way."

Liz gave me one of her examining looks. Then she left the room without a word and slammed the door. I looked out the window and saw her light a cigarette and walk off. I remained in the room and turned on the TV – a few channels in French and little else. I switched it off. I couldn't focus. I kept thinking about what I had said, repeating in my head my words over and over again. I contemplated my situation: sitting in a hotel room in Dakar, fired, arrested, banished from Mali, lost all my stuff, and then ripped off for $5,500. I thought about Latrell's words. He was right. She was trouble. *Good riddance*, I thought, wondering if she had left forever.

An hour passed, and Liz had not come back. Now, my anger turned to worry about her walking around Dakar at night. I thought about looking for her but remembered that she said she could take care of herself. Two hours passed since she left, and I was really worried about her. Then I started to get mad. Would she really disappear on me like this after all that had happened?

After three hours, there was a knock at the door. I opened it to find Liz standing there irritated, looking down at her feet, lightly kicking the door jam. "I love you too," she said.

I grabbed her and kissed her on the lips, then led her inside the hotel and closed the door. We sat on the bed. She wiped the tears from her eyes and began to laugh, holding my hand. "Thank you for rescuing me from prison. But I could have gotten a better deal," she said.

"Whatever. You gotta learn to step back sometimes and be diplomatic in tough situations. Otherwise, it'll be your undoing."

She was smiling now. "We have no clothes, and my NGO has been killed by the corrupt Malian government. What do we do now?" she asked.

"Do you want to travel the world with me?"

26

Joe's Last Meal

"So that was how you met the famous Liz?" asked Chris.

"That's the story. It's all true."

"I'd never heard any of these details in the press. I just knew that you two met working in Africa. What happened with your folks?"

"I had a long conversation with them the following day. Once I explained, my mom and dad backed my plan, though they did agree with Liz that maybe I could have gotten a better deal than fifty-five hundred dollars and probably should have tried to reach the U.S. Embassy, but still, in retrospect, it was better not to have left Liz alone in jail. Despite my parents' understanding, I did have to pay them back the money. The good news was that apparently, I had that much money. They informed me that my grandfather had given me a ten-thousand-dollar bearer bond, which had matured. They withdrew the six thousand and sent the rest to me."

"What happened to Liz's well-digging operation?"

"Liz was able to return the operation's remaining funds to the donors. I asked her if she wanted to instead turn the funds over to another NGO. Her response ran something along the lines of 'I'm not enabling those corrupt assholes.' She left her donors free to choose what to do with their returned funds."

There was a knock on the cell door. "Dinner," said the guard from outside.

"Oh, good. My last meal is here. I hope it's as good as I hear last meals are supposed to be," said Joe.

The door opened. Two guards entered, one carrying a tray with a single bowl on it. The other appeared unsure what to do with Joe's handcuffs.

"Usually I am locked in here without handcuffs and the meal is slipped through the door," said Joe. "But because I have a guest, I am required to be restrained."

"I'll be fine if you want to take them off," said Chris to the guard.

"I can't do that," said the guard.

"No worries," said Joe. "I can do this with the cuffs on."

The guard placed the tray on the table in front of Joe.

"What is that?" asked Chris.

"It's Japanese ramen."

"You mean like Top Ramen?"

"Yes, it's a double portion, and I asked them to throw in a boiled egg."

"Didn't you want something more elaborate for your last meal?"

"I thought about it. Like maybe prime rib, foie gras, veal scaloppini, or something like that, but they'd probably just screw it up. Top Ramen is something I've loved my whole life and much of what I ate when I couldn't afford anything more."

With both hands in cuffs, Joe picked up the chopsticks awkwardly and removed them from the paper packaging using his teeth. He then separated the two wooden sticks by sliding his finger between them until they split apart.

He precariously perched the chopsticks in his fingers and, after a few unsuccessful attempts, caught some noodles and managed them to his mouth.

"Tastes delicious. I hope the ramen spilling from my guts isn't too difficult to clean up after my execution."

"You seem rather at ease with this."

"Why shouldn't I be? There's nothing I can do about it, and I've made my point."

"Did you ever find out if Mike was responsible for having you arrested in Timbuktu?"

"I never did. But I am pretty sure that's what happened."

"And the police chief?"

"That story turned out pretty well. Liz contacted her aunt in the Foreign Service, who had a fit. She wanted to know the name of the police chief and wanted to know everything that transpired. She reported it through the proper channels to the British Embassy in Mali. The British Embassy made a big deal of it. The guy was canned. But there was no trace of the fifty-five hundred dollars. I can guarantee that once his superiors heard he got fifty-five thousand, they took their piece of it. He ended up without a job. At least he got his comeuppance."

"Is that what you want? People to get their comeuppance?"

"I want justice through due process. A proper 'comeuppance' is only appropriate punishment if done under the law."

"But that's not what you did."

"Not ultimately." Joe slurped away at his noodles. And then he went after the boiled egg, the egg successfully evading his attempts to grasp it with the chopsticks. "This might take me a while."

"And this began your years-long period of seeing the world?"

"Yep…"

27

Around the World

In Dakar, I checked email and found one from James.

Dear Joe,

Congratulations on the new girlfriend. I can totally see you with that type. You need someone who'll challenge you. But man, getting her to come around sounded like climbing Everest.

The trip around the world is a great idea! Do you realize that you finally are ready to do your vagabond thing? You cut your teeth in some of the hardest parts of the world, going from being too chicken to travel anywhere to working in West Africa. Even better, you now have your ideal travel companion.

It's best to travel like a vagabond when you are young. Go to the difficult places first. Then you will appreciate the relative comfort of the developed places at the end. Don't do it the other way around or you'll be unhappy. Trust me on this.

I got some good news too. My application to the Special Forces was approved. Now I move on to the next steps. Training will be hell, and I'll have to go through all sorts of background checks. I'll try not to mention my friend who got arrested in Mali and beat up a guy in Israel. Haha

I hope all is well. Say hi to Liz and tell her that I look forward to meeting her someday.

James

"Where do you want to go?" Liz asked me one day. She had been to a lot of places for a girl in her mid–twenties, but I had been only to the unusual combination of Israel, Mali, and now Senegal. Liz and I decided that James's advice was good and that we would get the hard places out of the way first.

We would fly to India and go east from there to Japan. And then fly back to Europe. But this was all flexible, as we did not have any concrete plans, nor any idea how long we'd be gone. Buying proper traveling equipment, like backpacks, travel towels, good hiking shoes, etc. was difficult in Dakar, but we bought what we could in the local market and made do with cheap stuff. And thus, we left Africa. I peered over Liz's shoulder out the window of the plane, saying goodbye to the continent that had been so challenging to me, but which I had grown to love deeply.

The next few years were incredible, just Liz and me traveling the world. Our remaining money took us pretty far. We stayed in hostels. India, Pakistan, and Central Asia were pretty cheap, so we were often able to afford our own room and have some privacy. We were three months in India. There was so much to see. In expensive places like Japan and Korea, we had to be stingy, cooking in the hostels and eating as much street food as possible. We went through most of Southeast Asia, such as Thailand, Laos, Myanmar, Cambodia. We explored Nepal and other countries in the Himalayas, doing quite a lot of trekking. We spent a long time in China, as there was a lot there too. Robert Ripley called it the most interesting country in the world. We explored parts of Russia, Turkey, Central Asia, Iran, Greece, and Italy.

But we were far from being lazy bums. This wasn't in Liz's nature, nor increasingly in mine. Everywhere we went, Liz wanted to help. Everywhere we'd do some sort of volunteer work. It was never just giving away money or food. Liz went by the "teach a man to fish" theory. Physical things were ephemeral. We helped by teaching or building something, something with which our presence would have an impact years after we left.

It wasn't unusual for us to be in some remote village and suddenly Liz would switch from tourist to NGO coordinator. For instance, we were trekking in the Laotian countryside, chatting with a local while we stopped for lunch, when he mentioned that the village could produce more crops if they just had more water. Liz said, "But there's a stream right there. Why don't you just channel the water over?" Apparently, no one had thought of that, which seemed incredible. And the next thing I knew, Liz was using our guide as a translator to gather people to dig a trench. At first, the villagers were incredulous, this young blonde girl spouting orders, but soon everyone was on board when they saw her plan. By the afternoon, an irrigation canal was bringing fresh water into the fields.

"We need to do more of this," said Liz to me.

Nor was our trip just work and self-sacrifice. Far from it; we indulged ourselves and had a wonderful time. For instance, in India we stayed in a houseboat on Lake Dal in the Kashmir province for a month. It was a huge, elegant affair that cost almost nothing. We rented a canoe and spent our days exploring the lake. A couple renting the boat next door were big into meditation. Liz wanted to learn. I resisted at first, thinking it was hokey, but then I tried it. Meditation became a big part of my life and added to this period of peace and contentment.

I saw meditation bring a wonderful change over her. She was able to better control her emotions and be more open. The hard, resistant girl receded and transformed into a woman who learned to trust others. Inside her I found a soft, warm heart that the other men in her past had never taken the time to break through the hard shell to find. To me, she was worth it. Her strength, which had been directed against herself in many ways, was instead refocused in positive directions. She began drawing, adding to her many skills. Sketching, like everything to this gifted woman, came easy, and soon she was turning out pencil sketches that looked like she had been an art student for years.

Eventually the money ran out, and when it did, we'd find ourselves work. Often this was teaching English or working in a resort. These jobs didn't pay much, but that didn't matter to us. It was all about sustaining the travel. We lived frugally, and that made it all possible. Most of the work we found was under the table in places that hired backpackers. The owners often took advantage of this, paying us very little, but the atmosphere amongst the other travelers was a lot of fun. When one travels, you meet people who are different from your average person at home. People who are more curious, open-minded, worldly, and intelligent. I know that I am being snotty here, in that I am a traveler myself, but this is my opinion.

It was while working at one of these resorts in Fiji that events turned our lives in a new direction. Fiji is an island nation in the Pacific, often a destination for Australians looking to get away. Overpriced beach resorts with fancy drinks were not our scene. If we did go to the beach, it was to do something cultural or an activity, such as hiking, spelunking, or scuba diving, not just lying in the sun drinking a cocktail. While scuba diving in Borneo, we met an Australian couple, Sandra and Roger. They were taking a break before the high season began from a resort that they were just about to open in Fiji. They were fellow wanderers who never wanted to return home and so opened a resort. We'd hit it off with them, and soon they were asking us if we would like to work for them during the three-month high season. The pay was better than usual, and even though we would be stuck at a resort, the money we'd be earning would sustain us for longer. Fiji wasn't so bad in that there was plenty of hiking and kayaking. Plus, we got along with Sandra and Roger like peas in a pod.

Liz and I couldn't believe the opulence of the Degei Beach Hotel when we arrived. It was unclear where Sandra and Roger got the money to build this place. From the main road, it was a drive up a sand track toward the beach, and at the end was a circular driveway and the hotel. The hotel was set in a wide-open space amongst the jungle and adjacent to the beach. The lobby had a slanted wooden roof built to withstand the daily tropical rainstorms, but with no walls so that the reception was technically outside. The floors were a polished brown-reddish wood, the furniture tropical wicker with white cushions, and ceiling fans that looked like they had been imported from Rick's Café in Casablanca. Reception was behind a teak counter. There was a welcome table with an unlimited coffee, tea, and tropical juices. In the center of the lobby were several couches and chairs where guests could meet and talk, along with an upright piano. A greeter opened the door to our taxi and welcomed us as if we were guests.

We approached reception and told the woman behind the desk that we were there to see Sandra. A minute later, Sandra came out and gave us a hug, plus a kiss on both cheeks.

"You both are going to like working here."

"I had no idea this place was so opulent," said Liz. "Especially compared to the places we've been staying."

"This is not opulence," said Sandra. "You should see some of the higher-priced resorts around here. Beach hotels on the island need to look like exotic jungle retreats, regardless of class or price. Competition is stiff here, and it's what the travelers expect. We get upper-middle-class guests here, those who want an all-inclusive vacation in a place that makes them feel like they're royalty, but not the ridiculous standards of, say, a five-star resort. Come, let me show you where you'll be staying."

Sandra took us behind the lobby to the guestrooms, located in two buildings, each three stories tall with balconies. The buildings opened up into a V shape toward the beach. There was a large pool in the middle surrounded by chaise lounges, featuring a diving board, a water slide, and a swim-up bar. Already at 10 a.m., several guests were in the pool drinking colorful drinks.

"You guys own all this?" I asked.

"Us and our investors."

"It's a hell of a place."

"It's a great place to look at. We just need to make it work. It's our first season in operation. Roger and I put all our money into this thing, along with a bunch of our friends and family. Here," said Sandra, pointing to a cabin. "This one didn't get finished in time, so we can't rent it out to guests. The construction company said they had other projects to finish and can't get to it till after the tourist season. You know how things go in these countries. Anyways, you two are welcome to stay here. The floor's concrete and there's no wall between the bedroom and the bathroom, but I think you'll find it more comfortable than the workers' dorms you've been staying in."

Liz and I walked in to find a large room, a big bed, a desk, and a couple chairs. It was missing most of the wood paneling that would eventually cover the walls. And, yes, there was no wall for the bathroom.

This became our home for the next three months. When one of us needed to use the bathroom, the other looked away. Eventually we put up some cardboard, but it didn't prevent noises from escaping. One gets very comfortable with each other's bodily functions traveling together.

Our jobs were to help manage the workers and work the front desk. At this point we'd had quite a lot of experience working in hostels, but this was a better class of accommodation. Before starting work, we had to tidy up a bit from years of vagabond travel. I'd let my hair grow out and had developed a beard, only because I didn't feel like shaving. Liz washed her hair for the first time in a while, and I actually saw her combing it. I had never seen her in a skirt. She wore that with a white blouse. I liked her rawness, but she was stunning when girled up.

Fiji is the embodiment of paradise for many people, especially the tourists, but the money rarely trickled down to the local population, leading to a large wealth disparity. The rich were very rich, and the poor very poor. A middle class was almost nonexistent. The result was instability within the government. People vied for power. Power meant access to the tourist money. This had led to several coups in the last few years. One night, we got to be part of one.

There was a pounding at our door in the middle of the night. It was not unusual for us to be disturbed by a guest issue, but it didn't sound like that kind of pounding. Liz put on her bathrobe. I asked who it was.

"Open up," said a man with a local accent.

I cracked the door open to find two soldiers in camouflage with machine guns. "Get dressed and come to the lobby. Hurry up. We will wait for you here."

"What's going on?" Liz asked.

"You will find out," said the soldier.

Liz and I put on our hotel staff uniforms and then walked out of our cabin.

"Follow me," said the soldier. He walked ahead of us, the second soldier behind. We arrived at the lobby to find several guests.

"What's going on?" asked an older woman guest who was there with her husband. More guests arrived, escorted by soldiers, sitting around, looking afraid.

"Quiet," said one of the soldiers. I shrugged at her. Roger and Sandra came in talking with one of the soldiers, who appeared to be in charge.

"Is everyone here?" a soldier asked.

Roger and Sandra looked around. "I think so. Did you check all the rooms?"

"All the guest rooms are empty," said a soldier.

The man surveyed everyone in the room; sleepy and scared guests in an array of bathrobes or clothes thrown on in the last minute were sitting on the floor or on the couches. The hotel employees woken from their rest were seemingly out of character in their casual clothes. Then there were the on-duty hotel staff, prim in their uniforms but now deposed of their control of the resort. "I am Captain Raikuna, part of the forces currently trying to rid the country of the thief, President Samo. You will not be hurt as long as you cooperate. Other members of our movement are currently in the capital and have arrested President Samo. Once we have taken back control of our country, you will be released. Thank you."

Everyone looked at one another. A guest in her late fifties, probably just there to relax and spend some time on the beach with her husband, started crying.

I turned to Liz. "They're holding the tourists because they know it's the whole economy. We're their bargaining chip."

"I wonder how their coup is going in the capital?" said Liz.

"Who knows? We'll get no real information out of them."

"This is, like, the fourth coup in twenty years. Governments change here like the weather," said Liz.

"I don't think they're going to harm us."

"I don't think so either. There'd be hell to pay internationally," she said.

"In the meantime, we've got a hotel full of scared and upset guests."

I scanned the room and saw several women crying. A few kids sat in the laps of their parents, fear in their eyes. There was no way to explain to them that this was just a stunt, and they'd more than likely be fine.

"I'm going to do something," said Liz, getting up before I could ask what that was and hoping she wouldn't lose her shit. Instead she approached Captain Raikuna and said, "We have a lot of scared guests here. Can we serve them refreshments? Food, coffee."

"No, just sit down."

But Liz continued, "These were families just here on vacation who suddenly found themselves part of a hostage situation. They're scared, upset. You are less likely to have problems if we keep them happy."

The captain thought about this.

"You know that if anyone gets hurt, you'll be in big trouble with your superiors," Liz added.

"Where is it?" he asked.

"Just there." Liz pointed. "In the kitchen. Let me send a couple employees in to make coffee and other stuff."

The captain looked at Sandra and Roger. Roger nodded and said, "It'd be easy. Send one of your soldiers along with us if you don't trust us."

The captain acceded, and soon Liz had organized a couple employees to serve the guests. But few seemed like they had any stomach for snacks. Guests continued to get more upset. Crying was the main sound we heard. The nervous tension in the room was palpable. One of the guests began complaining to the captain, losing her temper. The captain ordered us to calm her down. A few more people started arguing with the soldiers.

"Everyone, please, calm down," said Sandra. "They're not here to hurt us."

"You have to do something," yelled a man at Sandra. "They're threatening my family. Don't you have security? I didn't come here for this."

"Please, sir, everything will be okay as long as we cooperate. This just makes it worse," said Roger.

Another man with his family said, "Please just let the women and kids go. You can keep the rest of us."

"No one is leaving," said the captain.

Angry voices rose up from the guests – the captain was losing control of the room. I was scared what he might do if people didn't comply. He might make a rash decision that would have serious consequences.

It was then that I heard the opening notes from "The Promise" by the band When in Rome being played on the piano. Everyone shut up and looked over at the piano. Liz was sitting at the keyboard. "Come on, everyone," she said, continuing to play and singing, "*If you need a friend, don't look to a stranger. You know in the end, I'll always be there.*" She was smiling like we were at a party. I rolled my eyes, but I could see what she was doing.

I walked over to the piano and joined her in my terrible singing voice, accompanying her, "*And when you're in doubt, and when you're in danger. Take a look all around, and I'll be there.*" Some of our guests actually appeared even angrier at us, incredulous that we were singing an eighties song at this moment. I waved at Sandra and Roger to join us. They jumped at the opportunity. "*I'm sorry, but I'm just thinking of the right words to say. I know they don't sound the way I planned them to be.*" The four us were beckoning the rest of the guests to join in, and some actually began to sing. "*But if you wait around a while, I'll make you fall for me. I promise. I promise you I will.*"

In those few verses, the vibe in the room went from imminent danger to ridiculousness, a sing-a-long. Liz went through an array of popular songs from the Beatles to David Bowie. John Lennon's "Imagine" was a must, then Elton John. By this point, everyone was on board. Well, maybe a few people were still resistant, but the potential mob had been quelled. I even saw one of the soldiers humming along to "Ruby Tuesday." Dawn arrived, and Liz was still playing. Some of the guests had passed out asleep. But Liz kept belting out the hits.

An hour after dawn, Captain Raikuna's radio crackled. He put his ear to the receiver and his face fell. From outside the hotel complex, a bullhorn rang out orders in the local language. Liz paused her playing. The soldiers who'd been holding us hostage dropped their weapons, fell to their knees, and put their hands behind their heads. The captain turned to everyone in the room and said, "I'm sorry." Fijian soldiers rolled in and arrested the rebel soldiers.

The wife of the father who had threatened the soldiers approached Liz, who was sitting quietly at the piano, and gave her a hug. She said, "Thank you." Liz just smiled at her. "Yes, thank you," another person said.

"It's okay," said Liz. "It was kind of fun."

The guests began shuffling back to their rooms. "I'm exhausted," I said.

"Want to go back to the room?"

"We have to work soon," said Liz. "It's already almost eight a.m. We might as well just stay up."

"Liz," I said, "will you marry me?"

She gave me her examining look, her eyes darting back and forth. "Yes, I will."

28

Aunt Julia

We found out that later why the coup had been a failure. They had hoped to arrest the president while he was dining at a fancy club in the capital, but they couldn't find him. Apparently, instead of going to the club, he was instead patronizing his favorite house of ill repute. The revolutionaries' plan was to hold a few tourist resorts hostage to force the government to step down, but getting tourists involved did not go over well internationally. The British, U.S., Australian, and other embassies stepped in and made clear, in no uncertain terms, that this wouldn't be tolerated. And so, with the president still at large, the government refusing to step down, and international pressure, the revolutionaries were offered leniency if they surrendered with no one harmed.

The guests at the resort that night had nothing but good things to say about the resort and how the staff had handled the hostage situation. Word spread amongst the travel agencies in Australia, guests posted rave online reviews, and suddenly Roger and Sandra had more business than they could handle. Their first season had been a success.

One interesting thing for me about this incident was finding out that Liz could play the piano – something I had never known in the now years of traveling with her.

"I am not that good," she said dismissively. "My parents had started me when I was very young, and when they died, my aunt made me continue. I hated the lessons, I hated my teacher, I hated the piano, I hated the songs. Once I was free, I never wanted to play again."

"But you're so good!"

"Meh," Liz said. "Those were easy pop songs."

"Why did you choose 'The Promise'?" I asked.

"I had to choose pop songs. I wasn't going to sit there playing Chopin! All they play at this resort is eighties music. I kept hearing the Muzak version of 'The Promise' over and over. The damned thing was stuck in my head."

After five years of traveling, we decided it was time to go back to civilization and pretend to act like adults. Liz didn't really have a place she called home, and so we decided to get married in Colorado. Neither of us wanted a big wedding. But before we could go to Denver for that, Liz informed me, "You're going to have to meet my aunt."

"I'm ready."

"No, you're not."

"Is she like you?"

"Worse."

"That can't be possible," I said.

"She's one of the top diplomats in the Foreign Office. Her specialty is shuttle diplomacy. Whenever the British government is trying to negotiate a deal between two obstinate leaders, they send her in. You know the type of leader I mean. These guys with huge egos, surrounded by yes men and used to getting their way. She straightens them out. They hate being told what to do by a woman, but my theory is that she acts like their mother by telling them what to do like they're five-year-olds. It strikes at their inner child, and they become scared of getting in trouble and disappointing 'mommy.' This leaves them pliable to being told what to do. The result is these big, bad dictators kiss and make up with the other side."

"Sounds a lot like Richard Holbrooke."

"Richard Holbrooke is a lot nicer than she is."

"You've met him?"

"Of course."

When the season came to a close in Fiji, Liz and I hopped on a plane to

London, our first time visiting Western civilization in years. It was also my first time in London. The huge city was overwhelming. I recognized sights that I'd known only from TV and movies. I was like a kid, pointing out Big Ben, Parliament, London taxis, and Piccadilly Circus.

"I know what those are," said Liz. "It's not necessary to explain them to me."

When she wasn't traveling on diplomatic affairs, Liz's aunt lived in an apartment in central London. Apparently, there was no room for us to stay comfortably with her, but she had another apartment nearby where she put up guests. Liz and I really didn't discuss these things, but I got the sense that there was some old family money here that allowed Liz's aunt the luxury of living life as a public servant and gave Liz the ability to have a proper upbringing, attending all the best schools. And by "old family money," I don't mean they were nobility or extremely rich, just well off, established.

This became more apparent to me as the doorman greeted us at the apartment building where we would be staying. I found out later that the building itself, located near Piccadilly Circus, was 350 years old and had been built as the London home to a nobleman and his family. About a hundred years ago, someone had cut the home into separate apartments and installed an elevator. The elevator was one of those art nouveau metal cages that rose through the previously empty center staircase. The guest apartment was on the top floor. Liz and I, being who we were, chose to take the stairs instead of the lift.

"What time are we meeting your aunt?"

"Three o'clock for tea," said Liz.

"That's so British. I love it."

"Are you sure you're ready?"

"Why do you keep asking that? She can't be that bad."

"You don't know her."

"She raised you, so I have an idea."

"I'm just nervous and hope that everything goes well."

The truth was that I wasn't really nervous at all. I wasn't the type of boyfriend whom rebellious girls brought home to upset their parents.

Parents liked me. They would note my good manners. By the end of the first meeting, the parents would be saying what a nice young man I was. In high school and college, when I met the parents of my friends who were girls, I would hear later that they asked, "How come you're not dating Joe?" Meeting Liz's aunt would be easy.

Shortly before three p.m., we walked a couple blocks to Liz's aunt's apartment, or "flat," as they say. It was a properly drizzly afternoon in London. Liz greeted the doorman by name, who was excited to see Liz "after all these years" and remarked how she had "grown up." We were let up to Liz's aunt's flat. Four flights of steps. Liz rang the bell, and I heard a "come in."

Liz turned the handle excitedly and ran in to her aunt, wrapping her arms around this diminutive woman in her mid-fifties, maybe no larger than five feet tall, smothering her with kisses, saying, "Aunty, I missed you so much."

Liz's aunt suppressed a bit of a smile. "That's enough, Elizabeth. We have a guest." Liz withdrew, revealing the tiny woman, wearing a smart power suit with shoulder pads, the style at the time, neatly done curly hair, sensible earrings, and shoes. Her eyes were intense beams, and she had a presence that filled the room, despite her size.

"Is this your young man?" she asked.

"Yes," said Liz happily. "This is Joe."

I walked forward to shake her hand. "Nice to—"

"—Would you mind removing your shoes?" Liz's aunt interrupted. "It's wet outside, and these rugs were just cleaned."

"I'm sorry," I said, fumbling my way back a few steps back and pulling off my hiking boots, beat up from months of travel. I was now in my white, American-style sport socks. I shuffled forward, extending my arm to shake hands. But Liz's aunt just kept her hands at her side. I was confused and then looked at my hands, which were now muddy from having taken off the boots. "I'm sorry," I said again.

"Let me get you something to wipe off with," said Liz, scrambling into the kitchen. I wondered why her aunt hadn't asked Liz to take off her shoes as well. Liz strode back into the room with a towel. I wiped my hands until they were clean and saw that the nice linen was now soiled with mud. I looked around the room for a place to dispose of it. "Just put it there," said Liz.

"Where?"

"There. By the umbrella stand." I put it on the edge of the umbrella stand, but it just slipped onto the floor. I shrugged.

I extended my hand once again to greet Liz's aunt, and she still kept her hands at her side and said, "The moment passed. Have a seat." I walked over and sat down on the very uncomfortable sofa. A maid entered carrying a tea tray and set it on the table.

"Nice place," I said, making the pretense of looking around admiringly.

"Thank you," said Liz's aunt.

"I'm sorry," I said again, "but what should I call you?"

"Aunt Julia or Julia is just fine." She examined me from head to toe. "Is this how you usually dress?"

Liz stepped in. "We've been traveling the world for five years. We haven't had time for a proper wardrobe."

"I see," said Aunt Julia. "You're going to marry my niece?" she said, jumping right in.

"We got engaged a few weeks ago. I love her very much," I said.

"I hope so," said Aunt Julia. "And what are your plans for the future?"

"Uh, future? I hadn't thought of it," I said. "I assume that I'll find a job. We want to start a family."

"What did you study in school?"

"I studied computer science and history."

"Where?"

"At the University of Colorado, Boulder."

"I'm not sure I'm familiar with their reputation," said Aunt Julia.

"It's the state-run university in Colorado," I offered.

"I figured that out," said Julia. "How do you expect to support my niece?"

"Aunty!" admonished Liz.

"I want someone who is good enough for you, my dear."

"Excuse me," I said, getting a bit irritated. "I've taken pretty good care of your niece over the last four years." Now Liz gave me a dirty look. "I mean, we took good care of each other. We're a team."

"Taking good care of her while bumming around the world is different from being in society, where you'll have to get a job to support a family."

Liz grabbed my hand as a signal not to get upset.

I took a deep breath. "I plan to find a good job. I haven't started looking yet. We have been traveling, and—"

"Where do you plan to live?" interrupted Aunt Julia.

"We don't know," Liz jumped in. "We'll figure out those plans later."

"We can live wherever. We thought we'd check out a few places first," I said. This was followed by a look of disapproval from Aunty Julia. "Can I have some tea?" I asked, trying to change the subject. This was met with silence.

Then Liz said, "You're supposed to wait till it's offered."

"Sorry."

"It's okay, young man," said Aunt Julia, this being the friendliest she had been to me. "Help yourself."

"All right," I said with trepidation. I picked up the teapot, not realizing how hot it was and that I was supposed to use the cloth, so I burnt my fingers, dropping the container, spilling hot water all over the tray and the wooden table, streaks of white stains spreading throughout the wood.

"What is this thing you bring me, Liz?"

I looked up in astonishment. "Excuse me?" I asked.

"This man has no prospects, went to some state university, has spent the last five years living as a bum, and has no means to support you. He has no manners, dirtying my floor and ruining my new table. And you...I haven't even seen you in five years. After all the best schools and education, you spend your time being a bum in Africa and then you come home with this. Is this some kind of rebellion against me?"

"That's enough," I said. "I may not have gone to Oxford or the Sorbonne, but I have a good education, and have striven to educate myself in the real world. Don't get Liz involved. I have taken good care of her...I mean, each other... She is everything to me, and I will work my ass off being the best husband and father to our children." I could feel Liz tugging at my sleeve, urging me to stop. "No one speaks to my future wife that way. I don't care if you brought her up. I don't care if you're her mother, father, aunt, or the top diplomat in the Foreign Office. I won't take this from anyone, you old bitch!" Liz dropped her teacup, smashing it to bits on the floor. Then she put her hand in front of her mouth. I knew I'd gone too far as soon as I uttered the "B" word.

Liz's aunt, who might have been used to this stuff, narrowed her eyes like a cat and said, "Get out."

I grabbed Liz's hand, and without saying a word, stomped to the front door, grabbing my shoes with my other hand and kick-slamming the door behind me. I led Liz down the steps and out of the building until we were on the sidewalk out front. I peered down at my stockinged feet, now soaked with rain. I looked at Liz, who was staring at me sympathetically.

"I thought that went well," said Liz.

29

Joe's Parents

We decided it was best not to stay in Aunt Julia's guesthouse and found a cheap hotel near Paddington Station. The next day Liz tried to call her aunt and got no response. I could tell this really hurt her.

"I'm sorry about this," I said.

"It's not your fault. She set you up from the start. I should have done a better job preparing both of you. She's really protective of me since I lost my parents. Also, I have been gone five years with minimal contact. She's mad at me. There was nothing you could do."

"What are you going to do about her? Can you make up?"

"It'll be okay," Liz said. "She just needs to cool off. I'll give her some time."

"Was she like this when you were growing up?"

"Yes and no. She's a good person. She did a great job raising me, given the circumstances, but she was always a career woman who never wanted to marry or have kids. When her brother – that is, my father – died, along with my mother, she truly stepped up, despite it not being the life she wanted, but she raised me her way. In other words, how a tough diplomat would raise a child. She cared a lot but showed it through sending me to the best schools, teaching me piano, languages, preparing for my future, et cetera. She doesn't show it through normal parental methods, like hugs and ice cream."

"In other words, her ordering me to get out was like her saying she loves you."

"You could say that."

"You'll find my parents a little different," I said.

We had planned to spend a few days with Liz's aunt before flying to the U.S., but understandably, our plans changed. Instead, Liz showed me around London and the places she had used to hang out when she lived there. I loved seeing real parts of Liz's life that I'd only heard about.

We caught a direct flight from London to Denver International Airport, otherwise known as DIA. There, my father and mother greeted us at the arrivals area, my mom hugging me and my dad giving me one of his great big bear hugs that squeezed the life out of me.

As if they couldn't figure out who the wild-looking blonde was next to me, I said, "This is Liz."

"Nice to meet you," said Liz, extending her hand for my dad to shake. My dad blew passed her extended hand and grabbed her for a big hug. Liz was not prepared for American-style affection and looked like a pet lizard being squeezed by an overly adoring child. My mother followed up with a warm embrace.

"You're part of the family now," said my mom. "We don't shake hands."

On the drive home, my mom and dad peppered her with questions, my dad driving and peering back at her through the rearview mirror whenever he talked to her, my mom twisting around from the passenger seat. What was her background? How had she liked growing up around the world? What kind of food did she like to snack on, so they could have some around the house for her? Is she allergic to anything? Did she prefer a soft bed or a hard bed? Was there anything in Denver she wanted to see? Did she want to go skiing – everyone wants to go skiing in Colorado? Etc.

Liz was mystified by the attention but went along with it. When we got home, my mom immediately took her out back to show her the garden: "The tomatoes were bigger last year." "I figured out these flowers do better in the shade." "This tree is finally large enough to block the neighbors from looking in." Liz took it all in stride, as if being given a tour of a museum.

My dad and I sat at the kitchen table, catching up. "So, she's the one?"

"Yep," I said.

"She is very pretty. Very raw."

"Makeup and nice clothes aren't Liz's thing."

"She seems like a wonderful girl. Very bright."

"She is both."

"I'm very happy for you. It's been too long, Joe."

"It has. I think Liz and I are going to settle here, in Denver. At least for now."

We were a bit jet lagged, being seven hours ahead of Denver, but Liz and I put up a good show while my parents made us a huge American-style feast on the patio in the backyard. My father barbecued steak, chicken wings, and sausage while my mother made a huge salad and attempted English bread pudding for dessert, which didn't turn out as well as expected, but I could tell that Liz was touched by the gesture.

We ate dinner on the patio as the stars rose in the clear Rocky Mountain night. We talked about everything happening in America, Britain, the rest of the world, some of the stories of our travels, and most importantly got caught up on American sports, which I'd been following sporadically whenever I could find an internet café.

Because my parents tended to be old-fashioned, I thought we'd be relegated to separate bedrooms, but to my surprise, my mom had us both share the guest room. When the evening ended, I closed the door to the guest room and stood in front of it, my back to the door as though barricading it, relieved that we were finally alone.

"They are nice people," said Liz.

"I was afraid you'd be worn out by their constant questioning and attention."

"They're sweet. They love you. You are lucky. This is the family life I always wanted. I wish...well... Things would have been different if my parents hadn't...you know." I walked over and held her head against my shoulder.

"You have that now. You're part of my family. I promise to always look after you."

30

I Don't Want to Make a Mess

Joe finished up the ramen noodles and wiped his mouth with the napkin. "No matter how many times you eat it, it always tastes good. I'm finished," Joe shouted out to the guard.

The sound of a metal key in a lock clanked and the cell door reopened. The guard came in and took the tray. "You sure that's all you want, Joe?"

"That's all. I don't want to leave too much of a mess for you to clean up after you shoot me."

"You're not funny, Joe."

"I think I am...and I'm the one being shot, so I get to make the jokes."

"It's not pleasant for us either."

Joe laughed. "I'm awfully sorry about inconveniencing you."

The guard just took the tray and left.

"From what I've researched, this began some tough years for you and Liz," said Chris.

"They were difficult but formative. Life was ideal traveling the world, but that wouldn't last forever, especially since we both wanted to start a family, which, at the time, required us to get 'real jobs.'"

"How did the idea for your business come about? How did you make your fortune?"

31

EasyData

James and I kept up a steady correspondence by email over the years, despite my not having seen him during that period. There is a part of downtown Denver that used to be full of unused warehouses surrounding the railway station. Like most downtowns, this was being repurposed into lofts, bars, restaurants, and art galleries. This area, previously referred to as "Lower Downtown" became "LoDo." This is where they built Coors Field, the stadium where the Colorado Rockies played when the franchise was awarded to Denver. James and I met for drinks at this art deco bar in LoDo called the Cruise Room. It was weird because he looked so much older. I guess I was too. He suddenly looked like a professional man in his late twenties, instead of a college kid. We hugged, as straight men do, waists apart like an A-frame.

"You've been working out," I said to James.

"I have to, dude. The Green Berets like us to be in shape."

"I know you always wanted this, but you always seemed so artsy. What's it like killing people?"

James laughed. "The downside is everything you would expect: paperwork, bureaucracy, suck-up and kick-down superiors, but the upside is we get to torture people for information."

"What?"

"I'm kidding. Don't worry. The upside is everything you'd expect too: the field work is really cool. We go on interesting missions around the world."

"And kill people?" I said.

"All the time. It's fun."

"Do you miss art and traveling?"

"The art I still do on my own. I still get to travel but for different reasons. I want to get involved more in intelligence, counterterrorism, that kind of thing. I'm learning some languages to make me more likely to be qualified for such positions."

"Now that sounds interesting," I said. "I'll tell you, man. You should get the U.S. Army to do something about corruption around the world."

"Trust me, that would be great, but it's not our jurisdiction. We often turn a blind eye to corrupt leaders because they provide us information and resources to help with counterterrorism."

"I know. It'll never happen."

"Enough about that. Let's talk about you and Liz. When do I get to meet her?"

"Soon – she had a thing tonight. We've had to deal with a shitload of paperwork in order to get married. Technically, she's not allowed to work in the U.S. yet, so she's volunteer teaching underprivileged kids how to read in the local library."

"Always volunteering."

"Sometimes I think Liz wants to save the world all by herself."

"And what are you doing?" James asked. "For work, I mean."

I sighed. "I just got a job. It's my first real job, an office job."

"Eww."

"It reminds me of that miserable job I almost took out of college."

"Why'd you do it?"

"I don't know. I thought I should. I mean, Liz and I are getting married, and we want to have a family. Plus, this way I can get an apartment and not have us live with my parents."

"True, but didn't you learn anything? You're not built for an office job. What does Liz think?"

"She hates the idea. She didn't want me to take it at all, saying that she'd rather we figure something out that's not an office job."

"You and she are born entrepreneurs."

"This is hopefully just temporary."

"It'd better be," said James.

"Say, I have a question for you. I'm looking for a best man for my wedding, preferably a Green Beret with a rifle. Know anyone?"

"Will he have to shoot anyone?"

"Probably."

"I can volunteer myself, then."

"I was hoping you'd say that."

* * *

Through a rather lengthy process, Liz and I managed to complete the paperwork to get married. Liz never wanted a big wedding. We simply went down to city hall and got married. After, we had a faux ceremony in my parents' backyard. Since we couldn't go to Vegas, James hired an Elvis impersonator to marry us. It was only my parents, James, and of course, Liz and me.

We got an apartment in downtown Denver. It wasn't lovely or large but was sufficient for then. Liz could now work and got a job as a translator. We were both happy but were looking for something more substantial in our careers. My job stank. James was right. How does one work in a cubicle after five years of traveling the world? I got a job with Datacorp, the world's largest database software maker. Basically, their software stored and organized data. People would enter data into their system and the system stored it, organized it, and allowed other people to retrieve it, manipulate it, and update it. The data were things like financial records, medical records, any information that needed to be kept and indexed.

My job was IT support. I took phone calls from clients who needed help with their software. This was the mid-2000s, and Datacorp was the most popular database system in the world, but they still used a text- and menu-based system. By this time, most PCs and Macs ran GUIs – basically, a

Windows-type system. To explain better, a GUI system is what we all know now. You can point and click on anything, open icons, menus, move the pointer anywhere, or the computer can accept keyboard shortcuts. There were a million ways to make the computer do something.

By contrast, major corporations used large computers to store their data, but these systems still ran Datacorp's menu-driven text systems. In other words, instead of a Windows-like system, there was a text menu. The user selected the menu item by typing its corresponding number to take them to the next screen. You could go back and forth, but that was it. Data was entered or retrieved from the appropriate screen. It was just like the DOS systems that I remembered from the mid-1980s. It was crazy and not at all user-friendly. Many of the tools that are available on a GUI system, like cut and paste, could not be used on this system. The reason for this antiquated user interface, I was told, was that it enabled access by multiple users, because no one could type over someone else's work. In other words, two people could not edit the same record at the same time. I did not understand why you couldn't do the same in a GUI system.

At home, I'd constantly complain to Liz about this. I can't say she found it interesting.

"Develop your own system," she said one day.

"Huh? Me, nah. It's too complicated."

"You were a computer science major. You can do it."

"Do you know how much work that would take?"

"Why don't you find out? I think you're scared."

"Scared?"

"It's just like the story you told me about vagabonding. You chickened out. You were afraid. It turned out you could do it after all."

"I traveled around the world because I had you to go with me."

"You would have done it anyway, especially after West Africa. Besides, you have me with you now. Don't be chicken. Do you want to work in an office the rest of your life? Have you not learned anything from our travels?"

"That's what James said too."

"There you go."

"But we're trying to start a family."

"You'll always have an excuse, Joe. And then time will pass, and you'll be unhappy that you never tried this. Remember the old Nike slogan 'Just do it'? Well, just do it."

"I'll have to work nights and weekends in my free time to get this done."

"So? I got things to keep me occupied. Just as long as I get to see you at night, so we can keep working on having a family."

"Okay, then."

I began building a new system on my home computer. Datacorp had me working long hours. In addition, I had a cell phone on which they could reach me in case someone needed IT help in the middle of the night. But when I got home, I would go into the bedroom, sit down at the computer, and start coding. My coding from college was a bit rusty, and there had been several updates to the programming languages I knew, plus the addition of a few more. My first objective was to figure out what language I wanted to program in and then learn it inside and out.

"I'm going to take a programming class," I said to Liz one day.

"Don't you know how to program?"

"I do. I mean, I did, but things have changed."

"Get a book and figure it out."

"That's why I want to take the class."

"That's not the reason. You're just fucking around. The class is an excuse. You're chickening out again. It's like those people who want to be writers but feel the need to buy every book on writing there is and take every class instead of just sitting down to write."

"But I don't know everything."

"You'll figure it out. Go back to the computer and start coding."

After a few days of googling programming languages, I figured out which one would be best for me to develop my software. Then I ordered a couple books on it for reference and just started coding. I made mistake after mistake and went down dead end after dead end. I referenced the books when I needed to. But Liz was right, I was learning by actually programming and making mistakes. I didn't need the class. It would just have been a waste of my time.

Liz did her own thing while I worked away during nights and weekends. The further I went, the more wrapped up in it I got, to the point that the program owned me. It was all I could think about to the extent that I stopped watching a CU game at halftime to get back to coding. I was barely sleeping and kept myself going with coffee. I was burning myself out and Liz saw it. She convinced me to get a little more sleep and instead wake up early to code before going to work.

Slowly the database software took shape to where I had a simple user interface screen. I showed it to Liz, who said it looked too boring and overly functional.

"That's good," I said. "It's supposed to be functional."

"It needs to be pretty, or people won't use it."

I made the interface modern and sleek. As I tinkered, the interface went from simple to complex. With each iteration, I thought through the process and the complications I faced with the old system at my job. This inspired me to add more tools to make the user's life easier and more productive. I was trying to think of what the user would want and need before they did. As I went, I found a lot of bugs – so many bugs. One bug drove me completely nuts. The screen would suddenly go blank for no reason. It took days of frustration before I finally found the problem. If it had gone on another minute, I would have thrown the computer out the window.

Finally, after months and months of sacrifice, in front of me was a beautiful product. It was a masterpiece. In creating it, I'd missed nights out, football games, time with Liz and other friends. But here it was. I called the new software EasyData.

"It's ready," I said to Liz one day as she sat on the couch of the living room reading, legs folded underneath her. This was her usual position.

"Congratulations," she said and gave me a high five. "Now quit your job."

"What?"

"Quit your job."

"But we haven't made any money off it yet."

"The software is ready. Right?"

"Right."

"What's the next step?" Liz asked.

"Marketing and selling it."

"How are you going to do that being at work all day?"

"I guess, umm...I can work around it. Sell it in my free time."

"No, you can't. It was possible to program at nights and weekends, but if you're going to go out and sell your software, you need to do it during business hours. You're at work during business hours."

"Money will be tight if I quit. We could only rarely go out and will have to eat a lot of Top Ramen," I said.

"I like Top Ramen, and besides, we never go out anyways. I've saved a bit. We'll be fine. The goal of this is financial security and independence. It's an investment."

The next day, I walked into work and gave my two weeks' notice. They didn't care. They neither liked me nor hated me. I was just another one of their IT guys in a huge company. My mind had been so elsewhere anyway that I hadn't bothered to make any friends.

The next few weeks were a blur to me and required a major change in my personality because I was an introvert. Sales required pressing the flesh and putting myself out there. I couldn't be bothered. I'd much rather be home watching the Avalanche play hockey than working a room full of people. But I did it. I asked James to reconnect with his design skills and create a logo for me, flyers, and brochures for the software. With the money Liz and I had saved, I printed up a ton of marketing material. Then it was cold calling, knocking on doors, going to business networking events. I got a lot of no's. It was depressing, and getting turned down was hard on my confidence. But Liz was there to pick me up at the end of each day.

Months passed, and little was happening. Liz and I were getting more creative with the ramen, putting in eggs, tofu, sometimes chicken or ground beef. Most of the weekends were spent reading library books or taking long walks around town. Our savings were being eaten away, and I started to take on credit card debt.

"Maybe I could work part time and market the other days?" I said to Liz one day while walking through Cheesman Park.

"You have a good system, right?"

"It's a great system!"

"Then keep going."

Still nothing was happening, until one day I had a breakthrough.

I was being booted from the lobby of a medical records company when one of the guys who'd been hanging out near reception grabbed me as I left the building.

"Did I hear you say that you have a GUI data-entry system for multi-users?"

"That's right."

"Can I see it?" he asked.

We went to a coffee shop around the corner, where I took out my laptop and gave him the demonstration. He sat quietly sipping his coffee as I went through all the screens and available tools. When I was finished, he said, "Can I try it?"

"Of course," I said. "I even have sample medical records for you to input."

"That's not necessary," he said. I watched as he flipped through a bunch of screens. "...And this can be used by multiple users at the same time."

"As many users as you like. Individual records are locked while they're being edited to prevent conflicts. There's even access through the internet, so people can work remotely on a simplified system, even where the software is not installed."

"What?" said the man. "Are you serious? You can input remotely through the internet?"

"Yep."

"Data can be input anywhere in the world?"

"Of course."

"Do you store the data too?"

"For extra, we provide storage space. Or you can buy your own server. It's up to you."

"And what did you say the cost was?"

I told him.

"Why so cheap?" he asked.

"Small overheard. It's my software. I'm the only employee. And the upkeep is pretty small."

"Let me get back to you," he said.

The next day, I got a call from him wanting me to come into the office that afternoon to demonstrate my system to the board. When I returned to the office, the receptionist who had booted me the previous day appeared a bit peeved that I had been allowed back. I was shown to a glass conference room where I was left alone to set up my computer. The board of directors entered the room, each member carrying a yellow pad. They shook my hand and sat down. I ran through the demonstration for them.

"Can your system be accessed from Mexico?" a board member asked.

"Of course," I said.

"Do you have a Spanish version?"

"Yes," I lied. "You can choose your own language. Data can be entered into the Spanish version of the software and be read by anyone in the English version."

I got a good vibe from the board, but I didn't hear anything for a couple days, so I called to follow up with the first guy. He told me that he liked the system but that the board was thinking it over. A week later, the guy called me.

"We want to install your system. The board was impressed. With your software, they can cut the number of data-entry personnel in half here in the U.S. and move some of the operations to Mexico. How soon can you implement it?"

I immediately ran out and hired myself a Spanish translator to make a Spanish version. I paid him a ton to work for forty-eight hours straight. By Monday, I was back at their office. I already had a program that would automatically transition all their records from Datacorp's software to my system. I prepped their system for the transfer. With management standing behind me watching, I crossed my fingers and hit the command to begin. The percent complete bar ran from left to right across the screen till it read "100% Complete." I clicked open my software, and there it was: all their data that had previously been in the outdated menu-driven Datacorp software was sitting there, perfectly placed, in my sleek new system.

"Amazing!" said one of the board members. They gave me my first payment, which I immediately deposited and used to pay off our credit card debt; the rest, Liz and I used to celebrate that night. But instead of going to the nicest restaurant, we went to the best ramen place in Denver.

For the next week, I hosted seminars on how to use the new system. The company seemed very happy. The satisfaction was palpable amongst management and those who actually did the data entry. Moreover, they loved all the new tools I developed, including a means to build their own reports to analyze the data.

It wasn't long after that I got a second client, recommended by the first, then a third, then a fourth. Word was spreading. People liked my system. Companies liked the price. There were almost no bugs. My nights of going through the software over and over had paid off.

With all these new clients, I could no longer handle all the work myself.

"I can't believe this," I said one day to Liz. "I actually have to hire employees. I guess that means renting office space for them to work."

"Don't do that," Liz said to me.

"Don't hire employees?"

"Definitely hire employees but forget the office space. You didn't want to work in a cubicle and neither does anyone else, so why inflict it on them? You don't need a place for them to work."

"You mean, have everyone work remotely?"

"They can do it, and you'll have happier employees. All the software demonstrations take place on site, not in your corporate headquarters. Otherwise, your employees can work at home or anywhere. You don't need to rent space, buy furniture, or anything else."

"I don't know. How do I know my employees will actually be working?"

"Trust," said Liz. "Simple as that. Did your bosses ever trust that you could work outside an office?"

"No."

"And you hated it. You have to extend that trust to your employees. If they do a crappy job, they're gone, just like any job, office or not. But if you trust your employees and give them the freedom to work on their own schedule, you'll have happier employees and a more successful company. Treat people like responsible adults, and they'll act like responsible adults."

I hired an employment attorney to work out all the kinks. Then I interviewed candidates. I needed to hire ten people to be both sales and support. Most IT companies hired good-looking young people, just out of school. They were cheap and decent salesmen. But I had three goals in hiring:

First, I wanted people of all backgrounds – kids out of school, yes, but also long-time older professionals, middle-aged professionals, men, women, minorities. I separated my resumes into piles to make sure I interviewed people from each category, which wasn't quite legal, but whatever.

Second, my employees had to be qualified.

Lastly, they had to be nice, and by this I don't mean that I wanted to hire my best friend. I discovered in my own job searches that companies were overly concerned with "fit," which seemed more like they were looking to hire someone to be their next best friend whom they could have a beer with. I didn't care about that. By "nice" I meant were they approachable, someone whom my customers would be happy to call and chat with. Sometimes, this was a nerdy introvert who had no interest in chatting over beer, but so long as they were engaging to my clients, that's what I wanted.

I spent hours interviewing people until I had my first ten employees. They reflected everything I was looking for. I hired a conference room at a hotel for training, bought ten laptops, and then held my first course. Looking around the room, the new employees represented various ages and backgrounds. And having selected them well, I found the classes were a pleasure. The new hires soaked up the information with little effort and were fun to have around.

Over the next few months, my company grew. My team was flying all over the country closing deals and giving support. Employees who brought in new business were given a bonus. I expanded the team with another set of ten employees, then another set. Before long, I was running a fairly large company. Money was pouring in. Liz and I left the dinky apartment and moved to a house in Western Denver, near the foothills. Our diet was much healthier now, with ramen mostly replaced by fruits, vegetables, and lean meat.

Liz and I were continuing to try for a family, and while that was fun, we were having little success. I could see that it was bothering Liz, the memory of losing her first pregnancy to typhoid haunting her. Then one day, I came home, and Liz leapt into my arms.

"You knocked me up," she said.

"How do you know?" I asked.

"A morning spent over the toilet and then a store-bought test. I'm going to start working on that mural for the nursery."

"You know what this means," I said.

"I know. I know. One more cigarette tonight, and then I'm quitting."

Everything had come together for us. I couldn't be happier. That is, until the next day, when there was a knock at my door. A man stood at the door with a messenger bag. "Joseph Levy?" he asked.

"That is me," I said curiously.

He handed me a thick envelope. "You've been served."

32

Memories of West Africa

The law offices of Cuvier, Larchmont, and Reims sat atop the highest three floors of the tallest building in downtown Denver. I had wanted to hire a smaller firm, someone who was part of the new economy. But given the now-large size of my business and the size of this case, I bent to pressure from my parents and corporate attorney to go with a large law firm. Liz and I sat in their glass-walled boardroom overlooking the city of Denver and the Rocky Mountains.

A middle-aged gentleman with graying hair entered the boardroom wearing a suit and tie, followed by a man in his thirties and a girl in her late twenties who was not far from our age.

"I'm Robert Cuvier. This is our associate who will be in charge of your case, Eric Sawyer, and our new associate, Catherine Best." We shook hands, and all sat down.

"I don't understand how the fuck Datacorp could do this, basically steal my husband's hard work and ingenuity," Liz jumped right in.

Mr. Cuvier winced at the curse word. "We, uh, are going to fight this for you. Datacorp has a good case against you, but I think that the facts are on our side."

"To paraphrase my wife," I said, "how can do they do this?"

Mr. Cuvier began, "When you worked for Datacorp, your contract stated a few things. One, that you worked exclusively for Datacorp, and two, that any innovations done in the scope of your employment are the property of Datacorp. Datacorp's lawsuit claims that you developed the EasyData software during your employment with them and therefore that it's their intellectual property."

"What are the consequences if we lose?" I asked.

"In a worst-case scenario, Datacorp would own your business, all its intellectual property, all profits earned to date, and a penalty for using their intellectual property."

"That's fucking bullshit," said Liz. "This can't possibly be right or the purpose of the law. That my husband develops this brilliant software, a better product than their shitty software, and we could lose everything and more."

"That's exactly the problem," said Mr. Cuvier. "Datacorp is getting their clock cleaned by your company. They've been the largest data-entry software provider in the U.S. few years, but you're gaining market share from them quickly. Let's face it. They never adapted their software to the modern age. It's terribly outdated, and now you've developed something better. For years they lived off this cash cow. They had entrenched clients. It was like the Detroit automakers. And now they find themselves fighting a losing battle. However, if they can prove that your software is technically their software, then they've neutralized your threat, plus they get your software for nothing."

"But I never did any work on EasyData at their office. I worked at home on my own computer. I had an inkling that this might be the case, and I wanted to protect my innovation from exactly this. Plus, it's not moral to work on my own business on their time."

"You're absolutely sure you didn't do any work on their computers?" asked Mr. Cuvier.

"Definitely not."

"Did you use your company cell phone to make calls on behalf of EasyData, marketing it, et cetera?"

"Definitely not," I said.

"Those are facts in your favor. Since it's their lawsuit, the burden is on them to prove their case. It's up to us to refute their evidence."

"How much will all this cost me?" I asked.

"Our rates are five hundred dollars per hour for me, three hundred dollars for Mr. Sawyer, and two hundred dollars for Miss Best. We're going to need a fifty-thousand-dollar deposit to start."

I took out my checkbook and wrote a check for $50,000.

"The next step is to find out what their evidence is against you," said Mr. Cuvier. "To do that, we serve discovery requests, which is basically serving the other side with questions and requests for copies of their evidence. They are required to provide it under the law."

Datacorp had thirty days to respond to Mr. Cuvier's discovery requests, but they turned over the evidence much quicker.

Mr. Cuvier called me one afternoon to explain what he had found. "Their case is based on a couple things: first, the exclusivity clause in your contract was violated for working on your own business during your employment, even if it was outside of their office."

"So what?" I said. "Even if I did violate that part of my contract, it doesn't mean that my company is theirs."

"That's what we're going to argue. The second part is a little more damning. They have evidence that you used the company's computers and BlackBerry to check your personal email."

"So? Everyone does that."

"Not everyone has started a hugely successful business that is also the competition. They don't care about everyone else."

"Just because I checked my personal email on their computer, that means my business is theirs, even though I didn't actually use their computers to build my business."

"That's what they're arguing."

"Sounds pretty weak to me. How does that affect my case?"

"It does leave you vulnerable," said Mr. Cuvier.

"What do you suggest we should do?"

"They've made a settlement offer."

"I'm not interested," I said.

"Just listen to their offer," Mr. Cuvier said. "I'm required to tell it to you."

"Go ahead."

"It's not as bad as you think," Mr. Cuvier said. "They are offering a deal where you own part of the business with Datacorp. They need you to continue to develop and support the software. This way you might be able to hold on to some ownership, avoid expensive and lengthy litigation, and avoid the penalty for using their intellectual property."

"Again, no way," I said. "They're getting something for nothing. It's not fair."

"Joe, do you want me to be honest with you?"

"Go ahead."

"You did work for them and got the idea from their software. You saw what they were doing wrong and how to make it better. You wouldn't have got the idea if you hadn't worked for them."

"You know that is bullshit, Robert."

"You should at least think about it. Their offer is a start, I can negotiate something better for you. At least think about it."

I told Liz.

"No fucking way," she said. "Fight this thing to the end. I don't care if we lose everything. We're not letting them get away with this. It's just like the bullshit we dealt with in all those third-world countries that we hate so much."

I called Mr. Cuvier back. "Let's go to trial," I said. "We're not settling."

"It's going to be expensive," he said. "And if you lose, you won't have the means to pay. I'm going to have to ask for a one-million-dollar deposit up front."

In the meantime, it was necessary for me to continue to run the business as if nothing was going on. The stress of the lawsuit on me and Liz took a toll. We tried to remain optimistic. Friends were supportive. I wasn't sleeping much, and neither was Liz.

Focusing on becoming parents and enjoying the moments we were supposed to be enjoying was difficult. In our new home, we had converted one of the rooms into a nursery. Liz had already begun painting a mural of a

West African landscape. We hadn't yet put in a crib or a mobile, as the birth was still months away. There was just a blanket that my mom had given us for the baby.

Then one day I returned from a weekend business trip. I walked into the nursery to find Liz with the mural halfway finished. There were beautifully drawn trees, rivers, animals, straw huts, native Bambara, and of course a well and an outhouse. Liz was just putting the finishing touches on a lake.

I walked in, put my arms around her, and kissed her on the cheek. She didn't really move and just kept painting.

"Everything okay, babe?" I asked.

"I lost the baby," she said.

"What? How can you be sure?"

"I'm sure. It happened this morning."

My heart crashed. I wanted to know more details but didn't ask. Liz was clearly holding her emotions back. If I pressed her more, I was afraid the dam would break, letting loose a torrent of everything she felt inside.

"Did you call the doctor?"

"I'm seeing him this afternoon."

"Liz, why are you still painting this?" I said.

She was silent and then said, "I have to finish. I just have to finish. There's got to be another chance. Things will be as they were before."

I turned Liz away from the painting and looked her in the eyes. "I'm not leaving," I said. "I'm not going anywhere." She lay her head on my shoulder and clutched my shirt in her hands, pulling it tightly, and began to cry.

That afternoon I went with Liz to the doctor. He did an examination and ordered a number of tests. We came back home that evening where Liz continued to work on the mural. It became more beautiful and more complete every day.

A few days later, we returned to the doctor for him to deliver the results of the tests. "What I have to say is not good news. Unfortunately, because of complications with what happened with your wife's first pregnancy years ago that was terminated due to typhoid, your wife was rendered unable to have children."

Liz and I looked at each other. She was silent. I asked, "Is it possible to fix this?"

"There is no way," the doctor said. "She could get pregnant again, but she will never be able to carry a child to term due to the damage. Future pregnancies might also be a threat to her health." He looked at Liz. She was nonresponsive.

My heart was broken that Liz and I wouldn't be able to have a family, but my immediate concern was for Liz herself. I'd never seen her like this before. She was silent the entire car ride home, staring first out the front window, then the side window, then the front window again. Whenever I asked her if she was okay or tired, she just nodded.

"We could always adopt," I said.

She continued to stare silently. When we got home, she returned to the nursery and continued painting. She started work on the last wall. I stood in the doorway and watched her as she dipped her paintbrush in the green paint and drew a blade of grass. I watched for as long as I could handle before walking to another part of the home to be alone. My cell phone rang. It was our lawyer. I ignored it. Liz continued to paint into the evening, the scene of a hut somewhere in the fields of Mali taking shape. I offered her dinner, but she politely said no. When I told her that it was time to go to bed, she just said, "I'm going to work on this a little longer."

I got into bed and looked at the ceiling, nodded off for a bit, but then couldn't sleep. I got up at 2 a.m. to find Liz still painting, the final wall nearly complete. She was just putting in a few flowers and trees. I sat down against the door jam and just watched her. She had become such an amazing artist. How much our child would have loved growing up in a room like this with such a beautiful landscape. By 4 a.m., Liz had finished the mural.

"Are you going to bed now?" I asked, finally getting sleepy.

"In a little bit," she said. "I have one more thing to do."

"I'm going to bed. Come join me when you're ready."

I got into bed and finally slept. I awoke around 9 a.m. to the heat of the late-morning sun pouring through the white blinds. Liz's side of the bed was still empty. I got up and walked to the nursery, not prepared for what I found there.

The mural of West Africa was gone. Liz had painted over everything in white. Where there had been a beautiful African scene, there were just blank walls. All that remained was Liz, curled up on the floor asleep, her head resting on the blanket my mother had given us for the baby.

33

Free Spirits Come Together

L iz never spoke about what happened. I never pressed it. Life continued rather painfully. Every effort was now focused on preparing for trial. Depositions were taken. Dates were set. Finally, the trial date arrived. Datacorp's attorney presented their side, their evidence, their witnesses. Mr. Cuvier presented our side. After two weeks of back and forth, showing up to court each day in a suit and tie, the matter went to the jury. We were told to wait at the courthouse throughout the afternoon, but when no verdict was reached, Mr. Cuvier told us to go home and wait.

A second day passed. "This jury is taking unusually long," Mr. Cuvier told us in a call.

"What does this mean?" I asked.

"It's hard to tell," he said.

On the third day, my phone rang. Mr. Cuvier said, "They've reached a verdict. Come to the courthouse."

Liz and I got in the car and drove the fifteen minutes to the courthouse. The judge took the bench.

"Has the jury reached a verdict?" asked the judge.

"We have, your honor," said the foreman.

"Please read the verdict."

"The jury finds in favor of Datacorp on all claims." The attorneys on the other side smiled and shook hands with their clients in congratulations. Liz and I held hands. "That's everything," I said to her. "I guess we'll have to start all over again."

"Fuck that. It's not over," said Liz. "They're getting something for nothing. This is not going to stand. These attorneys are wankers. We shouldn't have gone with a big bullshit firm. Let's find someone who is at our own speed."

Mr. Cuvier took us aside into a courthouse conference room to soothe us, but then the asshole said something along the lines of "We told you that you should have settled." The law firm sent us a final bill. They had run through our $1 million deposit and then claimed to be owed about $100,000 more.

"You'll get it," I told them.

"I recommend that you appeal," he said.

"We're not going to need your services any longer," I said.

* * *

Liz and I met Ben Juarez for lunch at the Bistro Vendome French restaurant in downtown Denver. The décor was very French and looked nothing like the Western frontier style that characterized many of Denver's buildings. We sat in a leather-lined booth with tall, dark, wood-paneled walls. Ben had brown hair parted on the side, in his mid-thirties, wearing a shirt with no tie.

"It's great to finally meet you guys," said Ben. "I've been following this case for months. I'm glad you called me."

"We should have called you before," I said. "You came highly recommended, but we got bad advice that we needed to go with a big, expensive firm."

"Those big firms are a rip-off," said Ben. "They have the name and hire all the best graduates from the best schools, but they do a shitty job. Everyone thinks they are so worth the extra money. The partners do very little legal work. They basically go out and look for new business and sometimes try cases. The young associates do all the heavy lifting. And despite being bright kids from good schools, they are so overworked with so many cases that they're incapable of providing the quality and personal service necessary."

"I feel like they gave us a lot of lip service," said Liz.

"Did you read over the pleadings I sent you?" I asked Ben.

"This a bunch of crap," said Ben. "Your attorneys, for all their big money, incorrectly cited the law, missed cases that would have helped you, failed to make obvious arguments, and dropped the ball on several issues. It's typical."

"What do you want for paying them a million dollars?" I said.

"So often," Ben said, "I'm the second guy coming onto one of these cases after the big firm messed up. I'm just by myself. I have no office. I meet clients here, at this restaurant, and I do a good job. I have to. Being alone, I'm working without a net. I do all this at about half the price. You get much better service from small firms or solos."

"What did you find in the pleadings? Is there anything we can do about the appeal?"

"Tons! The court and the jury made errors in the law. They basically found that you violated the noncompete in your contract, giving Datacorp ownership of your business. It's true that working on your business while being their employee, even in your own time, was a breach of contract, but the penalty is not that EasyData becomes theirs. They incorrectly applied the law. Moreover, your checking personal email on your work BlackBerry is insufficient to show that you used company resources to create EasyData. I have case law on that. Your previous attorneys should have made this clearer."

"Do we have a chance on appeal?" I asked.

"Hell, yeah!" Ben said.

"What's your fee? We may not have any money right now."

"I don't usually do this," Ben said, "but I'll just take twenty thousand dollars up front. Do you have that much?"

"We can swing it."

"Good."

I borrowed some money from my parents and hired Ben. He filed our appeal. The judgment turning EasyData over to Datacorp was stayed. This meant I had to continue running this business that was no longer mine.

Briefing schedules were ordered for each side to present their arguments. Then a hearing date was set before the appeals court. Ben stayed on top of everything. He was easy to deal with and kept us well informed. It was better that we were dealing with someone of our own kind, another free-spirit entrepreneur. Hearing day arrived. Ben did a great job laying out our argument, going point by point through everything the judge and jury had done wrong, backing each contention with evidence. Datacorp's attorneys were on their heels. It became clear very quickly that we were right, and the trial court had incorrectly applied the law.

Following the hearing, a few nervous weeks passed while we waited. Then finally, the result came in. The appeals court had ruled in our favor: reversed and remanded. We got a new trial. We then had to go through the whole ordeal over again. Ben expertly handled the retrial, citing the appropriate law and submitting damning evidence. This time the jury found in our favor. But Datacorp appealed.

We had to wait some more, until one day I got a call from Ben. I put him on speakerphone for Liz to hear. "It's over. Datacorp lost their appeal. The business is yours again."

Ben Juarez had won our case for about $90,000 total in legal bills. Another lesson that we should have already learned was learned again.

34

The Feel of Your Last Night on Earth

"That was quite a rollercoaster ride you and Liz went through. How did you guys get through all that stress?" asked Chris.

"We had each other. I know it sounds corny, but with us, we were a team. I supported her whenever she was down, and she supported me when I was down."

"How was life different after the verdict?"

"Life was good again. We were now worth a few hundred million dollars, a big change from living in tents in West Africa, vagabonding around the world, working in bars and hotels, and eating ramen while building EasyData."

"And what happened to Datacorp?"

"EasyData usurped Datacorp's market share. Datacorp made no effort to build a better system. Instead, their strategy was to steal our system. When their case was ultimately lost, they belatedly tried to create a GUI system, but it was chintzy and flawed. It was over for them. About six months later, Datacorp filed for bankruptcy. The rest of their customers switched to us."

"They got their comeuppance."

"They sure did," said Joe, looking out his cell window. "This is my last night on earth. Funny how I notice everything now. The temperature on my skin, the feel of the seat, the handcuffs, my clothes, things I never paid much attention to before."

"Is this when the business took off?"

Joe pulled his attention away from the window. "The business had already taken off. It was time for us to go public and expand worldwide. Shortly after we won our case, we filed for an IPO and had a massive first day on the market. I was suddenly a billionaire. The business expanded quickly, and within a few years, EasyData became the largest provider of data-management software."

"Is this when you began your first organization to help the world?"

35

NewWays

We were in our late thirties now. Liz and I had reached a level of acceptance about not being able to have our own kids. One day I asked Liz, "Now that we're settled financially – what do you think about adopting?"

"I've been thinking about that," said Liz. "Maybe I wasn't meant to have a family. Maybe there is a higher purpose here."

"What do you mean?"

"Twice I lost babies. But we are massively wealthy. We now have the opportunity to help *a lot* of people, not just raise a child or two. Remember my idealistic younger self? I wanted to save everyone in the world, but I could only do it one person or one village at a time. Do you realize that we could now literally help millions of people? Or develop ideas that could help a billion people. Let's create an organization to help a lot of people instead of adopting."

"There's no reason we couldn't adopt and run such an organization."

"Having children would be a distraction from our bigger project. Parents are busy people."

"Liz, we deserve things for ourselves too. We want a family. I want a family."

"Joe, I'm sorry. I don't want to adopt anymore. I know it's wrong, and I hate to say this because adoption is great, but for me, it's just too devastating to think of the two children I lost. Other parents do this magnificently and adopt after such tragedies, but I cannot. I'm sorry. I've thought about it and tried to deal with it. But unlike those other parents who adopt, we are billionaires. We can help a world full of people."

"All right," I sighed. "Let's do it."

And that was the creation of our first organization...well, second organization, if you count Liz's well and sanitation project in West Africa when we first met. One night at home, Liz and I drew up the plan on a yellow pad. I hired a lawyer to draft the legal aspects, and then we went out and hired experienced people to be on the board. One day, Liz and I sat in a rented boardroom with our assembled board for the first time.

"Ladies, gentlemen," Liz began. "We're going to save the world. I don't mean that in a Doctor Who or James Bond sort of way. I mean we're going to save the world in the way that only real people can. We don't just want to throw money at problems. I've always believed in the 'teach a man to fish' method. Yes, we plan to provide food, and yes, we will give money in a productive way. But this organization is not for giveaways. We will provide equipment for farms to produce food, we will provide books for classrooms, and we will provide pumps for wells. The more people are educated, fed, and healthy, the less they will accept living a life of poverty. And the more they will want governments that provide basic services and not just kleptocracies that concentrate wealth amongst an elite few. Our job is to avoid corruption and greed. Other organizations who help people are content paying bribes to operate in third-world countries. We will not, and those who request those bribes will be exposed publicly. We have enough money behind us that people cannot ignore us. It's a new way of thinking about international aid, and that's why our organization will be called NewWays."

Liz and I wanted to be personally involved. There's a selfish aspect to altruism. For us it was interacting with the people whom we were helping. It gave us joy. It's that feeling I first felt in West Africa bringing fresh water to a remote village. This was going to be a worldwide operation.

Years passed, and the organization grew quickly and grew large. We kept Liz's vision. And soon, the organization expanded into South America and

Asia. Africa was our main focus. We loved Africa because we had met in Africa. "Those people are amazing," Liz would say. "They're natural-born capitalists and innovators. All they need is a little education and to be pointed in the right direction. With their resources, Africa will rule the world. It's time for them to control their own destiny instead of people deciding for them and taking advantage of their disarray to steal their natural wealth. First it was the European colonials and now it's the big corporations."

"We operate almost everywhere in Africa but Zimbabwe," I said.

"Zimbabwe is the big one," said Liz. "I want our organization in there."

"We've been trying for years, but they are insistent that we pay tributes to the government. They are really anti-American and anti-British. The government holds power through sustained hatred for the former colonial powers who ruled there. There's no sense of trying to move forward by working with the international community."

"Let's see if Aunty Julia can help." Liz placed a call to her aunt to see if she could work her channels to get a meeting with Zimbabwe's ambassador to the U.S. We didn't use Aunt Julia much because we didn't want to take advantage of her connections. She was an important person, and it was a source we didn't want to tap too often. However, by this point, Aunt Julia was retired, and she was a restless retiree, as you might imagine. "She's been begging for something to do," said Liz.

Aunt Julia came through. Liz and I boarded a plane to DC. We strode into the distinguished Jefferson Hotel to meet with Mr. Zengeni, the Zimbabwean ambassador to the United States. He was a man in his late fifties, wearing a suit without a tie, drinking a martini at the elegant bar and talking to the twenty-year-old blonde next to him. I recognized him from his picture. Liz and I were dressed in casual business clothes. "Remember, Liz, be diplomatic," I said to her before meeting him.

"Don't worry. I will."

"Mr. Zengeni," I said, approaching him. "Nice to meet you."

"Mr. and Mrs. Levy, nice to meet you."

We all shook hands.

"I made us a reservation for dinner," Mr. Zengeni said. "Come with me.

You'll love this place." We followed him into the restaurant.

"Welcome, Mr. Zengeni," said the host.

"Thank you, Alex," said Mr. Zengeni.

"I have your regular table ready. Follow me." The host led the three of us to the table, Mr. Zengeni first, followed by Liz and me holding hands.

We sat down. The menu was quite pricey. Of course, we could afford it at this point. Mr. Zengeni ordered the duck confit and what I believe was an expensive bottle of wine. Not knowing much about good wine, I couldn't immediately tell.

"Now, what is it I can do for you?" asked Mr. Zengeni.

"You're aware of our organization?" said Liz.

"Of course," said Mr. Zengeni. "Everyone has heard of Joe Levy, EasyData, and his new organization to save the world."

"The organization belongs to both my wife and me," I added.

"That's what I meant," said Mr. Zengeni.

"Great," said Liz, smiling. "We would like to help Zimbabwe. As you're aware, Zimbabwe used to be the breadbasket of Africa. You had more food than you knew what to do with and were a net exporter. But now your people are starving. When Land Reform was implemented—"

"—There's nothing wrong with Land Reform," Mr. Zengeni interrupted. "It was implemented to right many colonial wrongs. Those farms illegally belonged to white farmers. That is African land, and that land belongs to Africans."

"If you had let me finish," said Liz sternly, "I was going to say that we have no opinion on Land Reform or the politics of Zimbabwe. All we know is that Zimbabweans are starving because the land is not being properly farmed. All we want to do is teach *whomever* owns the farm how to do it properly."

"We have no need for a Brit and an American telling us how to farm."

"Clearly you do," said Liz. "Because your people are starving."

"The Zimbabwean government has implemented several programs to help teach people how to farm. Your organization is welcome to contribute to those programs."

At this, I knew that Liz's diplomatic side had come to an end. "I've seen your programs, and they're rubbish. There's no money being put into them. Few of the farmers even show up because they don't care. The farms are just given to government cronies as rewards for their loyalty. If you want Zimbabwe to be wealthy again, then let our organization in, and for whomever owns the farms, we'll make sure there's a competent local manager in place."

"Mrs. Levy, if you want to come to Zimbabwe and teach, then you must fill out the proper applications, pay a foreign operations fee to the government, and we'll let you know what we can work out."

"Our organization does not pay bribes. You ought to know that by now."

"It's not a bribe," Mr. Zengeni said. "Even here in America you have to register as a foreign corporation, which requires that you pay a fee and taxes. You call that a bribe?"

"Don't even start. That's an administrative fee written into the law that is charged equally to any company who applies. Is there a fee schedule you can show us that is applied equally to all applicants?"

Bypassing Liz's question, Mr. Zengeni said, "I'm simply telling you how things work. Put in the papers, and we'll let you know the fee. I'm also willing to help you, pursuant to a 'fee schedule.' It all depends on how badly you want to be in Zimbabwe."

"And you don't care that people are suffering and dying?"

"Zimbabwe does its best to help our people. It's colonial powers like yours that caused all the problems."

"Bullshit!" Liz said. People at the neighboring tables turned around to look. Liz adjusted her napkin and recovered her composure. Then she looked over everyone's shoulders, across the room. "Oh good, my friend Diane is here. Diane, over here." We all turned to see a middle-aged woman walking powerfully across the room in a business suit. "So nice to see you," Liz said.

"Hello, Liz," said Diane, hugging Liz and kissing her on each cheek.

"This is my husband, Joe. And this here is Mr. Zengeni," said Liz.

Mr. Zengeni stood to shake her hand, confused as to what was going on. "Nice to meet you," he said.

"Diane is a reporter for the *Washington Post*," Liz said. "When I told her that NewWays was going to reach an agreement over dinner to operate in Zimbabwe, she said that it was a big story that the *Post* would want to cover."

"Definitely," said Diane. "Zimbabwe has been reluctant to let in organizations without them paying massive bribes. It's a major step that Zimbabwe has agreed to let your organization in, given NewWays' no-corruption policy."

Mr. Zengeni looked like he been punched in the face. He turned to Liz, finding her smiling at him smartly, and then turned back to Diane. "Diane, if I can call you that, Zimbabwe never requires bribes. I—"

"—Mr. Zengeni has told us that NewWays can operate schools to teach farmers how to properly farm and grow crops," I interrupted. "It'll make Zimbabwe rich again. The government is very happy that we will be there to help, right, Mr. Zengeni?"

"Right," he said, patting his napkin on his mouth.

"Let me tell you about the plan we've reached..." Liz then spent the next hour telling Diane everything that our organization planned to do: the schools we were going to open, the new irrigation canals, the new markets for distribution of food to the locals, and the independent accountants who would monitor the food supplies and the money earned from their sale. Diane took notes while Mr. Zengeni just nodded.

At the end of dinner, we had chocolate mousse for dessert. When the waiter brought the bill, Liz turned toward Mr. Zengeni and said, "Shall we split it?"

"Split it?" Mr. Zengeni said incredulously. "But you invited me to dinner."

"It was government business," said Liz. "We couldn't buy you dinner. It would look bad, like we were bribing you or paying you for your time, especially in front of a *Washington Post* reporter. I mean, it's your job as ambassador to meet with us."

"That's right," said Diane. "I'm paying for the two drinks I had and the dessert. I'm a reporter. I have to be neutral."

I threw in my credit card for me and Liz. Diane dug out some cash. The waiter stood by, waiting to take the tray, while Mr. Zengeni fished through his pockets. "I seem to have forgotten my wallet," he said.

"Don't worry," I said. "You come here a lot. Certainly, the waiter can add it to your tab."

"Of course, Mr. Zengeni. We'd be happy to do that," the waiter said.

* * *

Liz and I laughed the whole cab ride back to the hotel. "Did you see that look on his face when you asked him to split the bill?"

"My god, I wish we had videoed it and uploaded it to YouTube."

Two days later, the *Washington Post* had a large story about NewWays' agreement with Zimbabwe, along with a picture of Liz, me, and Mr. Zengeni at dinner.

36

Monsters

The organization moved quickly into Zimbabwe before the effects of the *Washington Post* story had faded. We rented an office in Harare and set up several warehouse dumps for equipment in locations around the country.

Liz and I flew in a week later. It was not easy to get a foothold there. Many of the local police and soldiers hadn't gotten the message that we weren't going to pay any bribes. Liz was brilliant. We met the first shipment of supplies at the airport. A C5 flew in with several crates. We hired trucks to meet us there. Zimbabwean customs officers inspected our paperwork.

We watched as an officer read the paperwork and examined the cargo. Finally, he said, "Your paperwork is not accurate."

"What's not accurate about it?" asked Liz.

"That crate of shovels is not listed here."

Liz snatched the paperwork from his hand. The inspector couldn't believe the insolence of this woman. She ran her finger down the paper. "Here, it's right here," Liz said, leaning into his personal space, poking at the paper.

"I see. But those containers are not allowed."

"Containers? Which containers?"

The inspector led us over to a crate of metal containers. "These," he said.

"These?" Liz asked. "That's insecticide."

"That chemical is not allowed."

"Show us the regulation that says that," Liz said.

"It's not allowed."

"Prove it."

"I know my job."

"He wants some money," I said.

"I know," said Liz. Liz dropped on her butt, right on the tarmac, like a petulant child, and just waited.

"Ma'am, you can't sit there," he said.

"Let the crates go, and we'll move."

The inspector went into his office. Liz continued sitting on the tarmac of the Harare airport. Every so often, the inspector looked out of his office to see if Liz was still there. After an hour, he came out, exasperated, and just waved for us to leave. We finished loading the crates onto the trucks and drove away.

"I betcha someone called him and told him to get that plane off the tarmac," I told Liz.

"He had no choice but to let us go," laughed Liz. "This is just the beginning. Remember, none of us are giving in to these bribes. We just need to teach them the right way of doing things."

We leased a warehouse in Zimbabwe's farm country near the town of Banket. We also rented a building where we could establish our first school for farm management. The plan for getting the farms back in order was twofold. First, a little history of agriculture in Zimbabwe. Don't worry, it's more interesting than it at first sounds. Zimbabwe used to be Rhodesia, a British colony named after Cecil Rhodes, the man who would "civilize" Africa. The capital was Salisbury, named after Lord Salisbury. Like most of the British colonies, they treated the locals pretty poorly, underpaying them for hard work, taking the resources from the country without payment. But colonialism also left a positive legacy, which one hesitates to talk about given the horrific nature of the negatives. The British left railways, roads, bridges, dams, and other infrastructure, along with courts, government, and administrative bureaucracy. The Zimbabweans were bequeathed this infrastructure to start their own country. However, what the British didn't leave the Zimbabweans was the proper education, skills, and culture to use all this infrastructure. When you treat the locals as second-class citizens, the result is in-fighting and corruption, which led in Zimbabwe to a deterioration of government functions.

Zimbabwe got off to a good start. Robert Mugabe became president of the country through its first democratic election after its apartheid. Mugabe was a hero at first. He was the leader of the ZANU-PF, a rebel group seeking equality in Zimbabwe. During his time in prison he earned six degrees through long-distance learning, including two law degrees.

Around the year 2000, Mugabe implemented Land Reform. The country had not healed from the harms of colonialism, but instead of implementing a policy of truth and reconciliation like the one that had worked so well in South Africa, which brought together whites and blacks to work together to form one country and forgive the transgressions of the past in the hope of a better future, Mugabe wanted to correct past wrongs by taking farmland from the white farmers and giving it to the black Africans. The white farmers had been extremely successful, and, as previously mentioned, Zimbabwe had become the breadbasket of Africa. To the poorer locals, taking farmland from the rich white farmers seemed like a good idea and fair, given the history. The problem was that those white farmers had been well established for generations, skillfully operating these modern farms, which were driving the economy of Zimbabwe. While the original sins of the British were terrible, taking the land from the white farmers suddenly seemed unfair in the other direction. Worse still, the "locals" being given the land were just cronies of Mugabe and his government. It was a reward for their loyalty. In reality, it was stealing land to give to his friends. Many white farmers defended their land to the death. Some of the new owners couldn't be bothered to actually work the land and just enjoyed living on the large estates, leaving the farms fallow. Those who did work the land didn't have the knowledge to run it properly.

When agriculture fell apart, the rest of the economy soon followed. Rapid inflation struck Zimbabwe. Poverty hit everyone. The former breadbasket of Africa now had people starving in the streets. Crime skyrocketed. Mugabe responded by pushing for more land reform. Those who turned against Mugabe's government were violently put down – taken to prison, beaten, or even killed.

Mugabe's pride prevented him from admitting that his policies had destroyed the country. He ignored orders from the international community and banned the BBC for reporting truthfully on the situation. The World Bank refused to do business with him. As a result, the country remains in self-imposed misery. In 2017, the army ousted Mugabe and replaced him with a deputy, who wasn't much better. After a succession of corrupt leaders, President Shaw took over and continued the same policies.

This brings us back to our twofold plan. Part one, our organization would establish schools to train farmers. For those who wouldn't or couldn't come to the schools, we sent personnel out to the farms to show them how to properly run them. Part two, we provided seed, farming equipment, and any necessary items. These were not loans but gifts to get people started. We put GPS trackers on the equipment to make sure they remained on the farm to which they had been given and were not sold.

Liz and I had our own opinions of Mugabe, and now the Shaw government. But we were here to help people. We stayed out of politics. The official policy of the organization was to help whomever owned the farm without debating who should own the farm.

To execute our plan, we needed to establish a network of equipment-supply stations and buildings to house our classrooms. The local authorities had initially resisted, so we weren't too surprised to arrive to bad news.

"The warehouse was robbed last night," said Anthony, our local contact in the area.

"What happened?" I asked.

"We had it all locked up. Someone cut the locks and took everything."

"Did you inform the police?" asked Liz.

"They don't care," said Anthony. "It was probably the cops who did it."

"What happened when you saw the police?"

"The desk sergeant said he'd look into it."

"And that's it?" I asked.

"That's all."

"Did he take a written report?" asked Liz.

"Nope."

"We'll talk to the police," said Liz. "Unload the trucks into the warehouse, replace the locks, and put on a night watchman."

Liz and I drove to the police station. It was a little building on a mud street, with a couple motorbikes parked out front. Inside, the station badly needed painting. Papers were pinned to the wall, and a hallway led to a back area with more offices and presumably a holding cell. There were a couple cops at ancient metal desks. One was messing with some paperwork, and the other was talking on his cell phone.

"Hello," I said, greeting the intake officer. "I'm Joe Levy. Who is in charge?"

"Sergeant Ndlovu," said the cop, not looking up from his paperwork.

"Can you tell him that we'd like to see him?" asked Liz, tapping her finger on his paperwork in front of his face.

The officer looked up like a dog whose food bowl had been taken away. He probably wondered why this white woman was tapping her finger in front of him. He didn't seem to like it. But he slowly got up from his important work and walked down the hallway as though wandering to the bathroom after waking up. About a minute later, Sergeant Ndlovu strolled out, followed by the intake officer. Sergeant Ndlovu looked like a baby and was maybe twenty-five years old. He walked with a false sense of importance, as though trying to live up to the authority of his position.

"This guy's father probably knows somebody who knows somebody," I whispered to Liz.

"What can I do for you?" Sergeant Ndlovu asked in a thick accent.

"I'm Elizabeth Levy and this is my husband, Joe. We run NewWays. Perhaps you're familiar?"

"I'm not familiar."

"You should be, because we have a rather large warehouse nearby that stores farming equipment. It was robbed last night."

"We know about that. Someone reported it this morning."

220

"We've heard that the police may have been behind it themselves," said Liz.

I poked Liz, reminding her to be diplomatic.

"Will your office be investigating?" I asked.

"Most definitely," the sergeant said.

"Good," continued Liz. "Because we're here with permission of President Shaw, and he doesn't want there to be any problems for us."

This was kind of a lie. While Liz had wrangled the Shaw government into letting us be here, I can't say they had been all that cooperative.

"If we have any problems," Liz continued, "I'll call the president's office and tell him. Can you tell us what's being done about the robbery?"

"I said we're investigating, Mrs. Levy."

"We just got a shipment of plows and stored them in the warehouse. I'm telling you this not so you can steal them, but so that you can protect them."

"We don't have the money to send officers out there to protect your equipment, but you may hire some if you like."

"I don't want your officers. That's like asking the wolf to guard the hen-house. I'm sure you'd find some excuse why all my equipment disappeared in the morning."

"I'm in charge of the police and am not going to take this from a woman. Mr. Levy, you need to control your woman."

"Don't speak to my wife that way, sergeant. I don't 'control my woman,' she is her own self. She can do and say what she likes."

"Not to me. I am in charge here, and I don't take orders from a woman, especially not a British one. The British are gone. If you don't like how things work here, you can leave, and we will take care of our people."

"Corrupt police officers like you can't take care of themselves," said Liz.

The sergeant's face turned red. "Get out. I don't want to see you. Don't expect help from the police around here."

"Just so long as you stay away from our warehouse," said Liz as I was tugging her out the door.

We got out of the police station and into the car. I turned to Liz. "You have to be careful with these guys. These young guys who are put in charge due to their connections are often too young, too inexperienced, and unqualified. They can act irrationally to demonstrate their authority."

"I'm not scared."

"Liz, be careful. I don't know what these guys might do."

"Rubbish. I'm the wife of a well-known billionaire. They wouldn't dare."

We got to the warehouse. Liz made a phone call to our main office in Harare. The woman we had in charge there had recently contracted a private security company to watch over our warehouses. Using outside security was not unusual. But the security company wouldn't be able to send someone to the warehouse outside Banket until tomorrow, which meant we had to spend the night guarding it ourselves.

There were five of us: me, Liz, Anthony, and a couple local workers. Liz and I set up a tent behind the warehouse. The other workers had a hut in which to sleep that was fairly comfortable by local standards.

We bought a chicken from one of the local farms, slaughtered it, and stewed it with some African spices and sadza, a white, starchy cornmeal that is a staple of the Zimbabwean diet. We ate dinner together outside, all of us sitting in our shorts and t-shirts, our bare limbs thick with mosquito repellent. We listened to the insects buzzing around us and watched them circle the lantern.

"What are you going to do if the police come back to rob the warehouse?" asked Anthony.

"They won't come back," Liz said. "They don't want any resistance or trouble. Our presence is enough until the private security company arrives tomorrow."

"Why are you and Mr. Levy doing this?" Anthony asked. "You're the bosses and rich people. Let us do it."

"It's not your job either. If you have to watch the warehouse, it's only fair that we do it too."

Just then a couple police vehicles drove by. The officers stared out the window at our little camp as they passed.

"There they go," I said.

"They're just scoping us out," Liz said.

Not ten minutes later, two pickup trucks filled with armed men abruptly turned the corner and stopped in front of us. The men jumped off the back of the truck and spread out, approaching us. Liz and I stood up, along with the rest of our party. They were locals, rifles slung over their shoulders. I was scared shitless. We were completely unarmed.

"You need to leave," said a man of about twenty-five. "No more white people here. Colonialism is over."

"We're not leaving," said Liz, folding her arms.

"Liz, let's just go," I said.

"I'm not letting them take our stuff again."

"Liz, come on. We're not looking for trouble. We were going to simply watch over the site, not fight an armed battle over it."

"What's the point if we're always going to back down?" said Liz. "There's just going to be more corruption and more people are going to suffer."

"We don't want to hurt you," said the armed man. "But we will if you don't go."

"We're not leaving," said Liz.

"Liz, come on."

"Stop taking their side and undermining me," Liz yelled at me. Then turning back to the armed leader, she said, "I am not leaving. We're here with the permission of President Shaw. There'll be hell to pay if you don't take your rifles and get out of here."

"I mean it," said the man.

"No, you don't. You're just a kid pretending like you're in the army fighting for freedom. Well, you're not, you're just a little punk part of a corrupt system." I wanted to stop Liz. I did. I knew her and knew that she could lose her temper and go too far. Maybe if she hadn't made that comment to me about undermining her, I would have stopped her. I should have just put my hand over her mouth and pulled her away. But that's not how I treated her. That's not the relationship I had with my wife. Before I could do anything, the man had lowered his rifle from his shoulder and fired, sending a bullet through Liz's chest, throwing her to the ground.

"Liz!" I shouted, running over to her. She was on her back, writhing. I could see her choking on her own blood. She couldn't breathe. Blood spread quickly on her shirt and sputtered out of her mouth.

The armed men got scared, jumped back in the truck, and sped off.

Anthony and the other two stood behind me watching, too shocked to act. "Call someone," I screamed. "Please call someone. Quickly."

Liz continued choking. I didn't know what to do. I took out my handkerchief and tried to stop the flow of blood. Blood poured out of her mouth and into her lungs. The choking became more violent. She was trying to say something. Her eyes rolled toward me. Nothing but horror in them. I'd never seen Liz so scared. She reached toward me, clutching my shirt, pulling me near her. Then, the choking slowed and finally stopped. Her grip on my shirt released and fell limp. Her mouth opened and her eyes went blank, staring at me.

"Liz?" I cried. "Liz. Please. No. Liz. Not now. Liz!"

II

He Who Fights with Monsters

37

The Year After

A buzzer sounded. I struggled to figure out what it was. Nothing made sense to me. The grogginess cleared, and I realized there was someone at the door. I lifted my head off the pillow. It was pounding. My mouth tasted like garlic and onion and vodka. I smacked my lips, sat up, and grabbed the glass of water next to my bed and drank it down. My stomach felt queasy, and I wanted to throw up.

The buzzer continued to ring. I stood up shakily. My legs were stiff and heavy. I rubbed my head. I had stood up too quickly. I fell back onto the mattress, and then made a second attempt to get to my feet. This time I was up. I grabbed my jeans and put them on over the underwear that I had worn to sleep. I grabbed my t-shirt off the chair and put it on. I stumbled across the room over an empty glass vodka bottle, accidentally kicking it into another one. They made a clink. As I walked through the door, I looked back at the large, empty bed.

"What is it?" I said to whomever was at the door. I peered through the peephole. And then opened the door ajar to bright daylight. I squinted.

"It's Wayne," said the man.

"What do you want?"

"I'm sorry to bother you."

"Just go away. If you need something, call my assistant."

"It's about EasyData," said Wayne. "I need to see you personally. You need to sign something."

"Email it to me."

"I can't. Look, Joe, just open up."

I lowered my head and sighed. I unlatched the door and opened it. Light poured in, making me squint. There stood Wayne, looking subservient, yet persistent at the same time. "Come in," I said.

Wayne stepped through the door and looked around my foyer. "It's so dark in here. Why don't you open the shades?" He sniffed the air, making a face. "And a window too."

"What do you want, Wayne?"

"Your company that you own, EasyData, well – we'd better sit down. Is there a place we can talk?"

"I really don't care about EasyData. You can just leave."

"Joe," insisted Wayne. "I've been trying for weeks to talk to you about this. We need to have a conversation. You are in charge of a multi-billion-dollar company, and you can't just leave it."

"Let's go in the kitchen." We walked into the kitchen, finding an array of cookware, copper pots hanging from a rack over the cooking island, a knife set on the wall, glasses turned upside down hanging above the sink. Below, dishes sat unwashed in the basin, crumbs and juice stained the floor, empty ramen packages were scattered about the room.

"Geez, Joe. When was the last time you had the maid come?"

"I got rid of her. I don't want people bothering me."

"Joe, someone's got to clean this up. You can't live in this mess."

"Enough with the commentary. Let's sit here," I said, gesturing toward the table, pushing a bunch of papers and empty food packages to the floor.

I pulled back the chair and sat down. Wayne sat opposite me, taking the briefcase off his shoulder, removing some papers, and placing them on the table.

"I'm sorry to be the one telling you this. The board of directors has voted you out as CEO and president."

"I figured."

"We waited long enough for you to recover. It's been a year since Liz's death—"

I winced.

"—I'm sorry," said Wayne, seeing my reaction. "I won't mention—"

"—Just go on," I said.

"We had hoped that you would get better and come back. Christine's been running the company in your absence."

"I know."

"And she's been doing a good job. We kept your position open, but now we have to move on. I've been trying to get ahold of you for a long time, hoping to get you back involved, but you won't take my calls or answer my emails—"

"—I know. Enough. I don't care. Christine is more than capable. Let her be CEO and president. It doesn't bother me at all."

Wayne was silent and then said, "And that's what happened. I just need you to sign these documents so that she can take over. Of course, you are still the majority shareholder and—"

"—Let's just get this over with." I grabbed the papers from across the table. They were marked with "sign here" tabs. "Do you have a pen?"

Wayne reached into his bag. "Here," he said, handing one over to me. I scribbled my signature on all the "sign here" tabs, not looking at what I was signing.

"Done," I said, flipping the pen back onto the table and folding my arms.

Wayne stared at me for a few seconds.

"Is there something else?" I asked.

"No, but, Joe – look, I'm not exactly a friend, but this company is your baby and you need to—"

"Out!" I yelled. "I don't want to hear it. Just leave."

Wayne collected the papers, stuffed them in his briefcase, walked to the door, opened it, again letting in the too-bright daylight. Wayne took one last look at me, walked out, and shut the door behind him.

I put my head in my hands and wanted to cry but nothing came out. I walked to the freezer and opened the door to find nothing inside. I then checked the pantry behind the kitchen and grabbed another bottle of Ketel

One from the large carton I'd had delivered. It wasn't ice cold as I liked it because I had forgotten to put it in the freezer. I grabbed two more bottles and carried them over to the freezer. I unscrewed the top and took a shot from the bottle, wincing at the taste. Vodka tasted terrible when warm. I took a Budweiser from the fridge to chase away the harsh flavor. I looked at my wrist to find no watch. I didn't know what time it was, but I guessed morning. I didn't know what day it was, but it didn't matter.

I remembered my cell phone for some reason and decided to check it. I went to the living room and fished through a bunch of papers till I found it, turned off. I hit the lock button till the white Apple logo appeared. The screen came on, along with a low-battery warning. Five percent. A number of alerts popped up: emails, news, sports, texts, voicemails. Most of the voicemails were from unknown numbers. There was one from my folks. I didn't want to listen but felt too guilty not to. "Joe," it began. "It's your mom. Please call me. We're worried about you. We heard on the news about EasyData. That's your baby. Liz wouldn't have wanted this. Please talk to us. Your dad and I—" I switched off the phone.

I went to the kitchen, vodka bottle still in hand, looking for a package of ramen in the cabinet. None were left. "Guess I'll have to order some," I said to no one. I looked around all the cabinets for something to eat. Ketchup, some flour, dried spaghetti. I found a clean pot and poured in some water, put it on the stove till it reached a boil, threw in the spaghetti, and waited until it was ready. I couldn't find the colander, so I simply used a towel that I thought was clean and poured the water and spaghetti through it until I had a towel full of cooked noodles. I put them on a plate and poured some ketchup on top. I put it on the table and ate. It was disgusting. I took two bites and ran to the sink to throw up. Along with the spaghetti, out came last night's ramen dinner. I sat down at the table and drank some more vodka. In the beginning, the vodka had made the pain go away, temporarily. Now it just made it worse. I stared across the table at my copies of the papers I had signed that turned over control of EasyData. I threw the vodka bottle across the room, smashing it against the wall. I put my head in my hands again, but this time the tears came, for the first time since Liz died.

A few hours later, I entered the closet, looking for a box where I could throw everything that had belonged or was related to Liz. I pulled the box out, removing a photo. There we were, twenty years ago, in Mali, so young, next to our Chinese motorbikes. "You were so hot," I said aloud. I hadn't looked at these pictures since Liz died. Now I found comfort in the images. There we were on our wedding day, James with the Elvis impersonator. There was our dumpy first apartment in Denver. Pictures from India, Laos, Myanmar, Thailand, Russia, Tajikistan, France, and Fiji. A picture of us ringing the bell at the New York Stock Exchange on the day of EasyData's IPO. Night had fallen without me realizing it. When I had been through the whole box, I fell asleep on the floor, lying amongst all the pictures of Liz.

38

Rifle Systems

The next day, I woke up sober. I took the near-empty bottle of vodka and carried it to the giant carton in the kitchen. I grabbed the two bottles from the freezer and threw them in the carton as well. Then I carried the thing from my house, opening the door and walking outside for the first time in weeks. I took the box to a dumpster in front of the house across the street, where they had been doing construction, and dropped it in.

I went into the garage and found a box of trash bags. I went through the house, picking up every wrapper, food package, liquor bottle, beer can, and piece of trash. I carried bag after bag across the street to the dumpster. Soon the dumpster was full. Four hours later, the house was empty of trash. I stripped my bed and gathered up all my laundry, taking it to the pantry. I dropped it in the washer, found the soap, and put it on the extra clean/extra hot cycle.

Then I put fresh sheets on the bed, seeing it made for the first time in months. I got out the vacuum, figured out how to empty the filter, and vacuumed all the carpets. I swept the hardwood floors, then mopped the tiled kitchen and bathroom floors. I scrubbed the toilet, the shower, the sink, and then Windexed all the mirrors and windows.

Ten hours, three loads of laundry, and twenty trash bags later, my house was clean. I shaved off my scraggly beard, ruining three razors and cutting my face. I got out my trimmer and shaved my head to a "number two" length. I looked in the mirror at the tubby, pale, man with rings under his eyes that I had become. I got in the shower and washed from head to toe, then put on some clean, loose cotton clothes. I went to the living room, grabbed a cushion from my couch, and placed it on the now-clean floor. I sat on it, struggling to fold my legs Indian style. I put my hands on my knees, and for the first time in years, since Liz and I were in India, in fact, I began to meditate. Following my breath, in and out, from the diaphragm. My mind whirred, always going back to Liz. I struggled, eventually bringing my mind back to my breath. Hours passed. The evening came and went. I went to bed that night more at peace. I knew what I needed to do.

The next morning, I woke up at dawn and, went into the garage, finding my car, a Prius. The engine started right up. The tires were a little soft, so I drove to the gas station and filled them with air. The world looked different, as though I'd been away a long time. I drove west from Denver into the foothills off I-70, eventually turning off the road into a little canyon where there were some ranches and a steak restaurant. There, I arrived at the Front Range Shooting Range. I parked and walked through the door, entering a lobby and shop.

The lobby was a large, open area with glass cases filled with boxes of bullets and shotgun shells. Behind them were racks of rifles and shotguns. In the middle of the room were displayed an array of hunting clothes, neon-colored vests, camouflage, pants, jackets, flannel shirts. A few customers browsed through the items, mostly men. One gruff-looking woman stood behind the counter, talking to what seemed like a longtime customer.

I approached the woman and asked, "Do you offer classes? I want to learn how to use a sniper rifle."

"To shoot a long-range rifle, you mean?"

"Sure," I said casually.

"Classes just began. You missed the last session, but our next class for long-range hunting starts in six weeks."

"How about private lessons?" I asked.

"We'd be happy to. It'll be more expensive, though."

"That's not a problem," I said.

"What is your objective?"

"Objective?"

"I mean, what are your reasons for learning to shoot? Hunting? Competition? Your Second Amendment rights?"

"None, actually. I'm looking for a new hobby."

"Long-range shooting is more than a hobby. It's a lifestyle. At least in my philosophy. You'll find that I take a different approach to shooting than most people. I'm a Zen-focused shooting instructor."

"A Zen-focused shooting instructor? Shooting doesn't seem very nonviolent."

"That's where you are wrong. I apply the same philosophy of discipline, self-defense, and strength to avoid violence that you find in any of the martial arts, such as karate, kung fu, or jiujitsu. It's about inner strength and inner peace, concentration, mental focus, joining your thoughts and emotions with the physical body."

"I see, but with guns?"

"Rifles," she corrected me. "The martial arts have incorporated weapons into their philosophy for millennia: swords, nunchaku, kendo. Rifles are no different. We teach you first to do everything to avoid confrontation, but to have the strength to defend yourself when it's absolutely necessary."

"You fit right in in Colorado, especially in Boulder."

"In fact, that's where I am from and went to school."

"A fellow Buffalo. It sounds like you're exactly what I am looking for. What's your name?"

"Kate, and yours?"

"Joe. Do you give the lessons yourself?"

"I do, if you're the right person."

"How do you know that?"

"Let's start and see what happens."

"When can we begin?"

"Right now, if you like."

"What's your rate?"

"A hundred dollars per hour. It's a little more than most places, but we're offering a different type of service."

"Fine with me."

"Let's begin with rifle systems."

"Systems?"

"A rifle is not just one thing. It's a package of things. The barrel, the stock, the cartridge, the scope. And this is where we will begin. All these must fit you, be a part of you, an extension of you. It's like a professional musician with her exquisitely tuned instrument. We're going to need most of today. Do you have time?"

"I have all the time in the world."

Kate showed me a number of rifles. For each one, she had me hold it, balance it, feel it as a part of me, making sure it was the right size. Together we selected three rifles. She picked up a box of ammunition and took me to the range. This was followed by an hour of gun safety. "Before we even fire a round," Kate said, "I'm going to give you some basic gun safety. That is the first and most important thing we learn. Safety will be a continuous theme throughout your training. Today, I am going to give you some basics, so you can test fire these three rifles and choose the one that fits you best."

Gun safety was followed by learning how to hold the rifle and position my body. "The rifle must fit perfectly into your shoulder. It's another appendage. It's part of you. To be consistent, the same thing has to happen every time you fire. You're going to be completely comfortable with your rifle."

I fired the three types of off-the-shelf rifle.

"How'd I do?"

"You did fine for the first day, but your mind appears to be elsewhere."

"That's been my problem lately."

"But you're a good listener and you are open to what I am teaching you."

"Does that mean you'll take me as a student?" I asked.

"If you're ready to work hard."

"I always am."

"Good. Let's get you outfitted."

The Remington 700 long action fit me like a glove. From there we ran through different customizations, me trying out different accessories and equipment seemingly hundreds of times. Ultimately, I ended up with a Lilja Precision 26.5" 1:10 barrel, McMillan A-2 tactical stock with saddle-type adjustable cheek piece, McCann Industries Integrated Rail System rifle mount, Remington factory trigger, M16 extractor bolt modification, Nightforce 20 MOA Picatinny rail, Nightforce high rings, Nightforce NXS 8-32×56 scope, Knight's Armament Mk11 suppressor, and a Harris 6-9" swivel bipod.

I set the trigger pressure to two pounds. "When you pull the trigger," Kate said, "you should be surprised every time the rifle fires, so you don't jerk the gun. Squeezing the trigger is about applying even pressure at a steady rate. Once the rifle fires, you are not done, and must continue the pressure through to the end."

Over the next few months, Kate turned me into a marksman.

Like the "wax on, wax off" of *The Karate Kid*, Kate put me through a number of exercises seemingly unrelated to long-range firing. Kate was right about her focus as an instructor. First and foremost was safety, followed by maintaining my rifle system. She instructed me on proper care and maintenance. I kept my rifle system sparkling clean and in perfect firing order. Inspecting my rifle system was the first thing Kate did every day. When I made a mistake, she never got mad, never castigated me. She simply instructed me on the correct method, even if it was a mistake that I had made three times before. Then she made me do it multiple times until it had become rote. This was all before I got into position to begin shooting.

"It's all about the focus, being in the present. You are here right now: you, your rifle, the target. Nothing else matters. Feel your heartbeat. Feel your breath. Focus your mind. All work together to create the shot."

Little by little, I improved. Not just my shooting, but the process of learning this discipline. It calmed my mind, focused my emotions, and renewed my sense of purpose. The uncontrolled state of Joe that I was in following Liz's murder became the focused, disciplined Joe. I was now ready to return to the real world and take my next step in life.

39

A New Charitable Organization

My plane landed at Charles de Gaulle airport in Paris. I passed through immigration into the Schengen zone. I took the RER into central Paris, checking into my hotel in the fifth arrondissement, St. Germain area, near the Fontaine Saint-Michel. I looked out the window from my room overlooking the Seine, Notre Dame, and the Île de la Cité. I closed the blinds, sat in the chair, and performed my now-daily two-hour meditation. When I'd finished, I walked out and got myself a café crème, better than any I could have found in America.

After enjoying my coffee, I checked my watch. I walked down the Boulevard Saint-Michel and then took a detour through the Jardin du Luxembourg, observing the fountain, the flowers, and the students sitting in the metal chairs that were set out for the public. They were relaxing and chatting. At the southern end of the park, I arrived at the Closerie des Lilas, an old-fashioned brasserie frequented by Hemingway, among other artists. There I found James sitting at the bar, drinking a beer.

He stood up as I walked through the door, shook my hand, and gave me a huge hug, clutching me tightly.

"You look good. It's great to see you, James," I said.

"You look good too. I'd heard you were in bad shape."

"I was, but I came around a few months ago. I work out every day, running thirty miles a week, swimming three miles a week, yoga, plus two hours of meditation every day and a healthy diet."

"Good for you, picking yourself up after what happened to Liz. Oh, I'm sorry," said James, catching himself.

"It's okay. I don't mind. I like hearing her name. When people talk about her, it makes me feel like she's still alive."

"I'm sorry I wasn't there, Joe. The government had me doing all sorts of weird things. I couldn't just leave and come to Denver. Otherwise, I would have."

"I know," I said. "Let's sit down and get something to eat."

"Do you want a beer first?" asked James.

"I don't drink anymore. I'm happier sober."

"Good for you," said James. "I seem to enjoy beer more and more."

I signaled to a waiter, asking for a table for two. He sat us at a private booth in the corner. James ordered another beer, and I got some sparkling water.

"So, James," I began, "what's been happening the last few years? I know a bit. Can you talk about it?"

"I'll tell you anything you want to know."

"You sound bitter."

"I *am* bitter," James said.

"What happened? You were U.S. Army Special Forces, right?"

"Green Berets. It was awesome, a dream job."

"You were fighting terrorists, as I recall. What'd you do specifically?"

"Just that. Taking out terrorists."

"How do you mean?" I asked.

"You know how you hear on TV about drone strikes killing terrorist leaders? A lot of that was also done by people on the ground. I'm one of those people."

"You killed terrorists."

"Or those who supported them."

"You mean that if it wasn't possible to kill the terrorists from the air, you went down and did it by hand?"

"You could say that. High-profile targets are usually well hidden or protected. Too hard to strike from the air. But mainly, we went after the less sexy targets: the operatives, the planners, the bomb makers, the businessmen raising money for terrorist groups. Those who needed to be killed discreetly."

"Businessmen?"

"Terrorist organizations fund themselves through the sale of oil from captured fields and even from selling antiquities. They have businessmen who execute these transactions. We eliminated them and tried to discourage others from taking their place. It didn't work, though. There was always another."

"Why were you kicked out?"

"I didn't agree with our targets."

"Why not?" I asked.

"The Green Berets and other Special Forces recruit intelligent people. The problem with intelligent people is they tend to think and have opinions. Many of us began to question the 'why' and 'who.'"

"Meaning?"

"We didn't agree with the target selection. Some businessmen were left in place simply because they favored U.S. business interests."

"You only shot bad guys who were not associated with a U.S. company or other economic benefit."

"Some of the other guys and I felt that U.S. national security came first, economic interests second. We should get rid of anyone who threatened the United States, regardless of economics."

"Wouldn't terrorist deal makers then want to align themselves with U.S. economic interests to protect themselves?"

"And that's what began happening. These businessmen would offer sweet deals on oil and other commodities to U.S. interests so they wouldn't be killed. It was a giant protection racket. To make things more complicated, Russia was doing the same thing but with fewer scruples, creating competition. For instance, there was this really nasty guy, let's call him Bill. Bill is actually why I got fired. He was in control of one of the captured oil fields in Syria. Oh my, did he take advantage. He made himself very wealthy. Had people killed at will. He captured a whole harem of young girls. His money from oil sales went right into the pockets of terrorists. Seems like a prime target for us to take out, right?"

"Right."

"But we couldn't touch him. Through nefarious channels, that oil was making its way to U.S. oil companies. If we killed him, then his successor might sell that oil to Russia."

"Why not just destroy the oil field?"

"Ha, yeah right."

"I mean at least destroy their means of extracting the oil, leaving it safe for after the war."

"Again, yeah right."

"I see. How'd Bill get you fired? What'd you do?"

"I killed Bill."

"Seriously?"

"Seriously."

"And what happened to you?"

"Me? I enjoyed every second of it."

"I mean discipline-wise."

"I was kicked out. I got a dishonorable discharge. They said I was embezzling money. It wasn't true. They just couldn't say the real reason."

"What are you doing now?"

"I am semi-retired. I am a training consultant to private security agencies. Mercenaries. But it's tough financially. Jobs are scarce, and I lost my U.S. Army retirement because of my dishonorable discharge."

"Any regrets?"

"None."

"Interesting," I said. "I have an idea for you."

"Oh?" said James.

"I've been thinking a lot over the last year."

"I can imagine," said James sympathetically. "Are you okay?"

"I wasn't," I said. "You probably heard that I was holed up for a while, drinking too much, never leaving home."

"You were like Howard Hughes. I'm sorry, again, that I couldn't—"

"—It's okay," I said. "I needed to get through it myself."

"You seem better."

"I am better. And it's because of my idea. I want your help, but you have to make me a promise before I tell you."

"Anything. What is it?"

"That once I tell you this idea, if you're not interested in helping me, that you will keep silent about it and do nothing to stop me."

"Depends on what your idea is. If it's going to harm you..." said James.

"Come on, give me some credit. I need an unconditional promise."

"Okay, I promise."

"Good. I was doing pretty badly after...uh, you know. I drowned myself in alcohol and watched eighties music videos all the time, which you'd appreciate. For some reason, they reminded me of Liz."

"Eighties music solves all problems."

"I disappeared into a black hole of despair. I thought about suicide. Then my mom said the most cliché thing in the world to me that everyone says in this situation: 'Liz wouldn't have wanted this.'"

"Everyone told you that, dude."

"I know. But then I thought, 'What would she have wanted?' Liz was a tough, smart girl."

"I'll say," said James.

"She'd have done something. She wouldn't have just expected me to move on and marry someone else or whatever. At first, I channeled my energy in an unhealthy way. I wanted revenge. I cleaned myself up and started taking sniper rifle lessons."

"Really? Wow. How are you doing?"

"I've gotten pretty good."

"Whom were you going to shoot? They never found the person who killed Liz."

"No, they never did. But that individual who shot Liz is beside the point. It was President Shaw and his corruption that created the environment for that to happen. He encourages these armed gunmen to steal farms and equipment on behalf of the government. These men are paid. It's the corruption we see all over the world. People like President Shaw are the problem."

"You're going to kill the president of Zimbabwe?" James paused. "I like it, but—"

"—I know what you're going to say. Just let me finish. As I was learning to shoot, I realized that I was just seeking revenge. As they say, 'Those who seek revenge must first dig two graves.' I'd be killing myself too. Liz wouldn't want that either. Remember, Liz wanted to save the world. Killing one corrupt leader would do nothing but satisfy my bloodlust. Ultimately, it was not what I wanted and wouldn't help me, Liz, or anyone else."

"I agree completely. What's your idea, then?"

"You actually had a lot to do with it."

"Me?"

"Yes, what you were doing in the army. You told me a few years ago how you were eliminating terrorists, basically bad guys, trying to make the world better. Think about it. For years, when we thought about people starving in the third world, there would be TV campaigns to send them money, food, or clothes. Remember 'We Are the World' and Band Aid?"

"Of course," said James. "I remember Sally Struthers and her commercials in Ethiopia – 'for the same price as a cup of coffee, you can help a starving child.' People raised money, clothes, canned food to send to Africa."

"That commercial's been parodied a million times," I said. "But it's all bullshit! Most of that money and food never got to those who needed it. It just went into the hands of the same corrupt governments who caused the problem in the first place. And it was literally a 'band-aid' solution. In other words, not attacking the cause of the problem. Corrupt governments get rich from all that aid and are still in power. You've seen it."

"Oh, have I seen it!"

"Zimbabwe is the best example of this. It was the breadbasket of Africa, producing more food than they knew what to do with, the second-largest economy in Africa. Then Mugabe comes along with his corruption, premised on the lie of righting past wrongs, and now the people are starving. Those who aren't starving to death are mired in economic hardship. Meanwhile, those loyal to the government get richer. Zimbabwe doesn't need food. They don't need money. They need a new government.

"Look at every suffering country in the world and you find a corrupt government. Kleptocracies making themselves richer instead of building roads, sewers, clean water systems, airports – things that would help the people make money on their own. Liz and I spent so much time and effort digging wells for poor villages in Mali. That's great, but it was supposed to be their government's job to do that. That's what our tax dollars go to in the U.S. or here in France. There is corruption in the first world too, but stuff gets done, and yes people suffer, but not like in the third world. Do you see what I'm getting at?" I asked.

"I do."

"And there is something even more important: the environment. Corrupt leaders sell out their natural resources to their cronies. They roll back or ignore environmental protections without a thought of future generations. Many of these countries are stewards of vast forests, rivers, and oceans. Rainforests are allowed to be burned for mining, farming, and development. Factories pollute air and water without restriction. And no efforts are made to curb greenhouse gasses. This affects not just the populations of these unfortunate countries, but all of us on planet Earth. Global warming has reached a crisis and will only get worse as a result of this corruption, making the need to address this problem even more urgent."

"What is your idea to solve this?"

"I want to start a charitable organization – an NGO, if you will – to assassinate corrupt world leaders."

James leaned back in his seat and let out a sigh. "I am behind you one hundred percent. But, for instance, if you kill President Shaw, another of his cronies will take over and be just as bad, if not worse."

"Aha, you are right. That's why there needs to be a diplomatic side to our NGO. In almost every country there is a democratic opposition party, usually being persecuted, which seeks to run a functioning government. We will set up the democratic opposition to take control once we've taken out the corrupt government."

"I like the idea, but I have a few concerns. First, how do we know the new democratic opposition won't turn corrupt once in power? That often happens."

"I am willing to take that risk. We will tell them that we kill them too if they don't comply. We will literally be vigilantes. *Vigilante* comes from the word "vigilant," meaning 'carefully attentive and looking out for danger.' Our organization will watch over them, and we will make clear that they better stay straight."

"And what if the country descends into chaos or civil war?"

"Again, a risk that I am willing to take. These countries are in bad shape anyway. How much worse can it get?"

"Civil war is pretty bad."

"I agree that I'd rather avoid it, but the situation in Zimbabwe is already pretty bad. It's worth trying to make something good happen."

"I don't know, can democracy spring from violence?"

"Democracy, law, and order are able to exist for a couple reasons. First, we willingly submit to such laws. We hate getting speeding tickets, but none of us wish for the chaos of no traffic laws. We want rules to protect our lifestyles, property, businesses, and loved ones, but we want them to apply fairly to everyone. The second reason is the threat of violence to enforce the law. This means law enforcement, like the police. If you break a law, no matter how minor, a cop with a gun will eventually show up to enforce it. If you commit a minor crime, say trespassing, you will receive a summons from the court, charging you with misdemeanor trespassing. If you ignore the summons and don't show up to your hearing date, a warrant will be issued for your arrest. A giant manhunt for you as a trespasser will not ensue due to the minor nature of the crime, but if you get pulled over or have a run-in with law enforcement, the warrant will come up on their system, and they will arrest you. If you resist, they will use force. Resist enough that you threaten the safety of the officer or the public, and you will be shot. Every law is backed up by the threat of violence."

"True."

"Plus, how many democracies have sprung from violent revolutions against their oppressors? How about the U.S. Revolutionary War or the French Revolution here?"

"I'm on board with this so far," said James. "When I look around the world and see these corrupt leaders living lives of luxury while their people suffer, it makes me angry. I want to do something. I don't know how they can do it without guilt or a conscience. I like money like everyone else, and I haven't always been perfect, but I could never cause the suffering that these corrupt world leaders blithely ignore from their wealthy residences."

"That's it exactly. So—"

"But wait. I don't mean to interrupt, but I worry that your ambition derives from your emotions. Where does law and order come into your plan? Aren't we just exacting revenge? What about justice? Due process? Who made you god?"

"You are not wrong. I realized this the hard way. At first, I just wanted to kill President Shaw. I blamed him for... Anyways, I wasn't thinking clearly. There needs to be rules. Part of the mission of my 'NGO' is to push for the World Court to take action. In other words, to move toward justice and due process. Take President Shaw, for instance. His corruption has led to the death and suffering of thousands of people. Isn't that murder? The World Court should indict him, just like any murderer, and issue a summons. If he doesn't show, they issue a warrant for his arrest. If he shows up in a country willing to enforce that warrant, he would be arrested and brought to trial. If he doesn't comply with the warrant or is never arrested, he will be tried in absentia. The court determines his guilt and weighs the severity of his punishment. If his crimes merit the death penalty, an "*arrêt de mort*" or execution warrant is issued. Law enforcement is then given the green light to go get him. Anywhere in the world. Imagine the chilling effect that would have on these corrupt bastards around the planet."

"If they can get him."

"That's true of any criminal."

"There's another consideration: assassinating a country's leader is an act of war."

"Unfortunately, this where the reality of world politics becomes a factor. Clearly, if the president of Russia is found guilty of corruption, we can't assassinate him, or we would start World War Three. We are limited to countries that can't start such wars. If we assassinate President Shaw, Zimbabwe doesn't have the means to fight a war against us."

"Then your first target is indeed President Shaw?"

"Could you think of a situation more suitable? Let's send a message by showing the world what happens when we remove a corrupt, vicious leader. We must use decisive force before taking the diplomatic approach in seeking a more-powerful World Court. It'll take years to get the world community to see the benefit of law and order. I want to show the world what happens when you eliminate one corrupt leader and replace him with a democratic government. Will you help me?"

"Are you sure you want me for the job?"

"There's no one else I would want. I trust you. You've got the skills I need. In a sense, your job gave me the idea."

"What do you need from me?"

"You'll be the muscle. You'll head up the military wing of my 'NGO,' basically do what you were doing in the Green Berets. Hire a bunch of soldiers of fortune, capable men and women whom we can trust. Outfit them with the proper equipment. And plan the removal of President Shaw and his government. Once that's done, we'll plan future missions. Can you do that?"

"A mission of this size will require a lot of money. How much is my budget?"

I laughed. "Don't even worry about that. I'm a billionaire! This is just a repurposing of the mission of my old NGO, originally started by me and Liz. Except this time, we're not giving money, food, equipment, and education, we're going to save the world through good governance. Are you in?"

"You bet."

"You realize this is highly illegal?"

"Yep."

"You realize that we could go to jail?"

"Yep."

"You realize that we could be sentenced to death ourselves?"

"Just another day at the office."

"Let's do it," I said.

"Who's going to handle the diplomatic side?" asked James.

"I got just the person."

40

Back to London

R ain poured down as I rode the Eurostar train from Paris to London, a leather shoulder bag containing all I needed sat on the seat beside me. I read the *Economist* on my iPad, occasionally staring out the window at the passing landscape. In the row behind, a twenty-year-old English girl sat talking to her friend. She had a strong British accent, her voice mellifluous and young but with a smoky edge. I pretended to read, staring at the page, but instead just listened to her, imagining that the Liz I had known twenty years ago was sitting behind me, alive, accessible, only an arm's length away.

The train pulled into St. Pancras International station, where I switched to the Piccadilly Line destined for Piccadilly Circus station. I emerged from the Underground onto the rainy London streets and walked the short distance I remembered so well from my last visit, almost fifteen years before. I stood on the same wet spot on the sidewalk where I had been kicked out in my stockinged feet. I rang the bell. A servant answered.

"Joe Levy to see Julia O'Rourke," I said.

"Just a moment," said the man.

Rain continued to fall on me.

"She's not in," crackled the speaker.

"Come on," I said. "I know she's in. Tell her I need to talk to her. It's important. It's about Liz."

The telecom crackled off.

I waited silently. The door buzzed. I pushed it open and went inside, bypassing the ancient elevator and climbing the steps up to Aunt Julia's flat. The door was already open, her butler waiting for me.

"I'd be careful if I were you," he said to me.

I entered the apartment, unchanged in fifteen years.

"This way," said the butler, leading me into the room where I had spilled the tea. Aunt Julia remained enthroned in her chair, looking older but still a large presence despite her even more diminutive stature.

"What the fuck do you want?" were the first words out of her mouth.

"I see that nothing has changed," I said.

"You're lucky I even let you in, and I can easily have you removed. The only reason I agreed to see you is because you said this was about Liz, so let's get this over with."

My polite continence fell quickly to confrontation. "Why have you always been against me?"

"Liz could have done better. You coming in here with your ragged hair and clothes."

"That was fifteen years ago. I'm a successful businessman now."

"You're just a punk."

"The organization Liz and I started has helped tens of thousands of people."

"You piggy-backed off her intelligence."

"Damn right," I said. "She was a brilliant woman. But she believed in me. She supported me. In return I loved her. I took good care of her."

"You got her killed!"

I lowered my head, walked silently to the window, and looked out at all the people and cars passing by. It felt like the people in those cars had no problems.

"You're right," I said. "I should have done better."

There was silence in the room. "I'm sorry," said Aunt Julia in a soft voice. It was the first time I'd heard such a tone from her. "I know how much you loved her. Liz was Liz. She did what she wanted. You did your best. I know what she was like. I raised her, or tried to. My only hope was to channel all her strength and energy, but I wanted her to be free. You were the best person for her, because you let Liz be Liz and accepted her for what she was."

I smiled.

"She was worth all the trouble, wasn't she?" Aunt Julia asked.

"She was," I said. "She absolutely was. For as difficult as she was, the rewards came back a millionfold."

"What do you need from me?" asked Julia.

"I'm starting a new NGO to help the world, in honor of Liz's. And I want you to help."

"Whatever for? I'm retired, all washed up. They forced me out of the Foreign Office because of age."

"That's why I want you. I'm going to tell you something, and I hope you will keep my confidence." I paused, hoping for an affirmative answer, but Julia just looked at me, so I continued. "I'm starting an organization to assassinate corrupt world leaders." I looked at Julia, waiting for her reaction. She continued to stare at me. "I've learned over the years that bad governance and corruption cause all the problems of poverty, hunger, and disease. All this stuff is preventable with proper democratic governments. My plan is to take out the corrupt leaders and their main cronies and replace them with the democratic opposition. I have a buddy, ex–U.S. Army Special Forces, who'll handle the military side. I need someone to handle the diplomatic side. In other words, to line up the democratic opposition to take power once the government is removed, to guide them and steer them toward democracy. That's why I need you. The first government we will take out is President Shaw in Zimbabwe."

Julia leaned back in her seat and exhaled. "What you're proposing is illegal. It's also murder."

"I know."

"You want to avenge Liz's death."

I paused. "At first that was my goal, but that's not what Liz would have wanted. She wanted to help people. Part of the punishment aspect of crime is to provide justice for the victim. Liz is the victim. I am the victim too because I lost my wife. Unfortunately, the way international justice is set up, I have to provide my own justice."

"That's not the way it's supposed to work."

"But that's why I need you. I want you to join us. You've got the diplomatic experience I need. You've got the connections I need. You're as tough as nails. And...you loved Liz, just like I did."

"And what would a washed-up diplomat do in your organization?"

"Two things: First, you're the one in charge of getting the democratic opposition on board with our plan and setting them up for power, democratic power. Let's face it. This is initially a coup. We don't want a power vacuum that leads to more violence and disarray. We must ensure that there is someone to take control. Once they take power, we expect new elections and a new constitution within six months."

"Or else what? We kill them too?"

"Possibly. At least that's what we'll tell them. Once we've taken out the corrupt government, there will be no doubt of our capabilities."

"And if you fail?"

"We won't fail."

"What's the second thing?"

"This is the part you'll like. Once President Shaw is gone, I want to lobby for a stronger World Court. One that actually goes and arrests corrupt politicians. Or if they don't show up, tries them in absentia and issues an execution warrant."

"You know the world has been steadily moving away from the death penalty?" asked Julia.

"I have a theory on why on the death penalty has gone out of favor in Europe while still remaining popular in the U.S. It's because it was abused in Europe. Look at the French Revolution, with royal beheadings by guillotine. Or here in England, where the death penalty seemed to be applied to almost any crime in the past, including theft. Then there was the Holocaust, and frequent massacring of government enemies in Eastern Europe under the communists. We've gone from one extreme to the other, and now people just view any sort of death penalty as government overreach. But in the U.S., it's only for serious, horrible murders."

"Even though I am British, I don't disagree with you. It's going to be challenging, if not impossible, to convince the World Court to issue execution warrants. The European nations who give the court its power will be against it."

"They may not realize it, but the death penalty is issued all the time. What do you think we're doing with these drones? Those guys we're taking out from the sky don't even get a trial or due process. Yet most of these Western governments are fine with that."

"But that's war."

"It's semantics. Look at how the U.S. killed Osama bin Laden. There's a term for it. I'm sure you know it. 'Extra-judicial killings.' What I am proposing is even more civil because at least these men, or women, will get their due process. Jail time for most crimes. The death penalty is for the serious offenders only. Corrupt leaders are responsible for thousands of deaths and much suffering. That doesn't deserve execution? It would be an incentive for these corrupt leaders to show up for trial, in the hopes that they'll just get life in prison if convicted. If they don't show up and are found guilty, we'd have to go after them, and that may be by assassination."

"And what about the right to democracy? Many of these leaders are duly elected by their people. It's true that these elections are mostly rigged. But there are corrupt leaders who get elected and reelected with immense popular support despite their horrific regimes. Don't people have an absolute right to elect their own leaders?"

"No right is absolute. We have a right to free speech, but you can't use hate speech, or speech that provokes violence, or yell 'fire' in a crowded movie theater. In the U.S., we have a right to bear arms, but that is tempered with gun control laws and regulations and limits on who can get those guns. It's the same with elected leaders. Populations of democratic countries often make bad decisions. Often those elections are based on lies. There should be no absolute right to elect anyone you want. Hitler was elected democratically. Do you think that a democratic result should be absolutely protected? That some outside body shouldn't have had a check on that right to say, 'No, you cannot elect a leader like that'? There should be no absolute right to democratically elect whomever you want. The totality of the circumstances should be examined. Was the person elected on lies? Or is he or she a nationalist appealing to the basest instincts of the uneducated population, such as hatred toward an ethnic group? Is this person going to start a war? Starve their people? Perpetuate severe corruption? Be destructive toward the world community? Are they populist conmen who are patently unfit for office? That may have been the original point of America's electoral college, to be a check on the people."

Aunt Julia took a sip of her tea and leaned back, tapping her fingers against the teacup.

"What do you think? Are you in?" I asked.

"They booted me out of the Foreign Office because they said I was too old. I had a forty-five-year career in which I chose diplomacy as a means to make the world better, but I learned that diplomacy means little unless there's some force backing it up. Joe, have you seen the movie *The Man Who Shot Liberty Valance*?"

"You watch westerns?"

"For heaven's sake, I've seen every movie with Jimmy Stewart. I'm not that stodgy."

"I saw it when I was a kid, but I don't remember it well."

"The point of that movie is that Jimmy Stewart, the budding lawyer, shows up in the Wild West trying to establish law and order, but John Wayne tells him that will never happen because the gun rules the West. It turns out they were both right – Jimmy Stewart more than John Wayne, though. Because Jimmy Stewart attempts to bring the outlaw Liberty Valance to justice, but he's only able to do so because John Wayne is the muscle who enforces the law when the criminals don't comply. Law and order only exist when people respect it. People respect the law because peace officers, operating within the rules, enforce those laws. You are not operating within the rules."

"Not yet," I said. "That's why I need you."

41

Back to Salisbury

"**Y**ou know this used to be a Best Western," I said to Julia.

"It certainly seems like it would have been," said Julia. "Did you and Liz ever stay here?"

"We did. When we first arrived here in Harare on our last trip. Now it's the Jameson Hotel. It's a lot nicer now. This is a decent-looking conference room."

"If you say so," said Julia.

It was a typical hotel conference room, but this one was in Harare, the capital of Zimbabwe. Businessmen stayed here all the time, except that business in Zimbabwe was almost nonexistent because the economy was in shambles. International sanctions had been in place for years, and there was no trusting that the Shaw government wouldn't steal a company's investment once established here, and thus nobody dared try.

"It amazes me that Jameson bought this place and fixed it up. They must be hoping for better times. I bet Best Western was glad to leave," I said.

"Maybe they had to leave as a result of the sanctions," Aunt Julia said. She checked her fashionable watch. "Always late in this part of the world, even the good guys."

Just then there was a knock at the door, and a hotel servant popped in and in a thick Zimbabwean accent said, "Mr. Enati is here."

"Instruct him that will see him now," said Julia.

We both stood up as a dignified African man in his fifties walked in, wearing a business suit. He had the bright smile of any politician. "Good evening, Mr. Levy. I am Tinashe Enati."

"A pleasure to meet you," I said. "This is Julia O'Rourke, a former British diplomat."

"Nice to meet you as well," said Mr. Enati.

"Would you like some tea or coffee?" I asked.

"Coffee would be nice," said Mr. Enati.

I asked the servant to fetch some coffee.

"Thank you for coming back to Zimbabwe, Mr. Levy. I'm sorry about what happened to your wife," offered Mr. Enati. "As you know, I lost my wife as well, in a car accident."

"Thank you," I said. "I'm sorry for your loss. We just have to keep pressing on."

"We do," Mr. Enati agreed.

"How are things in Zimbabwe right now, Mr. Enati?" asked Julia.

"You know the story," said Mr. Enati. "Pretty poor. People are starving. The economy is in shambles. The current government of President Shaw refuses to relinquish power, nor admit its mistakes. But we continue to fight. I think we will be able to force a democratic change eventually. The people are behind us. We're happy that your organization wants to provide aid and education. I'll do anything I can to help."

Julia and I looked at each other.

"How long has your party, the MDC, been working to establish democracy in Zimbabwe?" asked Julia.

"Probably twenty years now."

"Have you had any success?"

Mr. Enati's face became defensive. "We've had some. We forced a change in the government to allow power-sharing with first Mugabe and then President Shaw."

"But that's just nominal, isn't it?" Julia asked. "You don't really control anything, do you? In fact, the situation has gotten worse. The government continues to rule without any checks. Land and money continue to go to loyalists, while your people suffer."

Mr. Enati glared at Julia and then me, asking, "Is she the one handling this meeting?"

"She's the one in charge here," I said. "I am just the pocketbook."

"What's this about?" asked Mr. Enati. "My secretary said that your organization wished to return to Zimbabwe to continue to educate our people on proper farming techniques."

The waiter returned with a French press full of coffee, pouring out three cups, and placing one in front of each person. He then placed a cup of tea in front of Julia. "Do you need anything else?" the waiter asked.

"No, thank you," I said. "Please leave us. We don't want to be disturbed."
The waiter nodded and left.

"Mr. Enati," said Julia, "would you be interested in removing President Shaw and his government from power?"

Mr. Enati looked confused. "That's our goal."

"As part of that, would you then be interested in installing your party, on the premise that your party will hold elections within six months, establish a new constitution with term limits, and then continue to adhere to the new constitution and democratic institutions?"

"Yes, of course. But—"

"—We're prepared to offer you that opportunity," Julia said. She picked up her teacup and saucer, took a sip, and placed it gently back on the table, before adding, "Conditionally."

"You mean the British government will remove President Shaw from power?"

"We don't work for the British government," I said.

"You work for the American government?" Mr. Enati asked.

"Not the American government either. We are our own organization," I said.

"But you're an NGO dedicated to education, clean water, sanitation, and entrepreneurship. You don't get involved in politics," said Mr. Enati.

"We're expanding," I said.

Julia jumped back in. "You've been trying to rid Zimbabwe of the ZANU-PF government of Mugabe and President Shaw for decades through peaceful means: protests, international sanctions, foreign leverage. Nothing is working. The situation grows worse. The people of Zimbabwe are proud. At one time they had the second-largest economy in Africa. There were no shortages of food or fuel. There were plenty of jobs. This country is gorgeous and full of resources. Ninety percent of the country is literate. The current dire situation exists only because of the ZANU-PF. How many people have suffered?"

"The whole country has suffered," said Mr. Enati.

"And how many people have died as a direct or indirect result of ZANU-PF's policies?" asked Julia.

"We couldn't even estimate it," said Mr. Enati.

"Then President Shaw and his government are murderers, aren't they?"

"There's no doubt," said Mr. Enati. "What are you suggesting?"

"Our organization," said Julia, "will eliminate President Shaw and his top five advisors. Then you will immediately take power, under the condition of pledging to hold elections in six months and establish a new constitution."

"Eliminate how?" asked Mr. Enati.

Julia and I were silent.

"Oh no," said Mr. Enati. "What you're proposing is a coup? Is this for real? You're a well-known businessman!"

"This is very real," I said.

"The MDC party has never advocated violence," Mr. Enati continued. "If we do that, we'll be just as bad as they are. No, no, no. I will not be part of this. We will continue to push our democratic movement through peaceful means."

"And how is that proceeding?" asked Julia.

Mr. Enati looked askance at Julia. "I'm leaving. This is crazy. I won't be a part of this. And I'm going to report this. Goodbye." Mr. Enati rose brusquely, buttoned his coat, and headed to the door of the conference room.

Quicker than I thought a seventy-five-year-old woman was capable of moving, Julia stepped in front of the door. "The fuck you will," she said, arms folded, head tilted back to stare up from her 5'1" frame to Mr. Enati's

6'2" build. "You're not going anywhere. Was it not President Shaw who caused your wife to die in a mysterious car crash? Or jailed you for five years, torturing and beating you, taking your property, jailing your family? The same thing happened to other members of your party. People have disappeared never to be seen again because they fought for democracy. How many Zimbabweans are starving? How many continue to die today while President Shaw and other members of his ZANU-PF party live in luxury on their large estates, unconcerned with the misery they have caused? We'd all like to be the next Gandhi, seeking democracy through nonviolence. But the India situation was different. The British government could be reasoned with. In another era, the United States had to fight a war for its independence. President Shaw and others like him understand nothing but strength. Sometimes strength is necessary to create law and order. Face it, your party's peaceful efforts at democracy have failed. Don't let your ego get in the way. You can't be the next Nelson Mandela. We offer you an effective alternative. Your party could flounder for decades trying to achieve democracy while the people continue to suffer. You need to end the Shaw regime. Sit down!"

Mr. Enati's jaw dropped. For a moment, it looked like he was about to mutter something.

"Sit down!" Aunt Julia said again.

Mr. Enati took an uneasy step back to his chair, reached for it without looking, and dropped sheepishly into place.

Julia returned to her seat, picked up her teacup and saucer, took a sip with her eyes lowered, and then looked directly at Mr. Enati. "Now. Let me tell you how this is going to go..."

42

The Traveling Wilburys

J ames and I sat in the bar atop the ZB Life Towers in downtown Harare, overlooking Africa Unity Square.

"Nice view from here," said James, taking a drink from a bottle of Zambezi, Zimbabwe's national beer.

"Lovely," I said. "Harare's not a bad place, I guess. Imagine how nice it must've been before all these buildings fell into disrepair."

"I had some great times here," James said. "For the first few years after land reform, there were still great bars and restaurants at cheap prices, much better than the ex-pat or white Zimbabwean places. They have so much more atmosphere. The beers are cheaper, and they are more likely to play eighties music."

"It's time to move your musical tastes beyond the eighties."

"The eighties saved Africa."

"How's that?" I asked.

"'We Are the World' and Band Aid. The most popular musicians of the eighties came together to write a song and sell records to help starving children in Africa. Eighties music saved Africa."

"As I recall, 'We Are the World' featured many sixties artists as well, like Bob Dylan."

"That's true. And 'We Are the World' wasn't even that great of a song. Band Aid's was much better. It featured the real artists of the eighties, Duran

Duran, Culture Club, Madness, the Thompson Twins, Heaven Seventeen, and Spandau Ballet, among others. And it was a pretty cool song too. They saved Africa."

"They didn't entirely save Africa, and that's why we are here," I said. The bar was empty but for a couple drinking at the next table.

"That reminds me. I think we need a name for our organization," said James.

"What for? We're not marketing our secret organization."

"Even secret organizations need a name. We need a name to refer to ourselves."

"What'd you have in mind?"

"Something that's not obvious, a name we could use freely without anyone having any idea what we're talking about."

"Clearly."

"It must be something scary. Something awful."

"And that is?" I asked.

"The Traveling Wilburys," James offered.

"Pardon?"

"The Traveling Wilburys."

"They were pretty awful and scary, I do agree," I said.

"That group was kind of amazing in that all these great musicians came together and made such terrible music."

"It was indeed terrible. Who was it? Bob Dylan, Roy Orbison, Tom Petty. Who else?"

"Jeff Lynne and George Harrison."

"That was some major talent. How'd that go wrong?"

"It's unclear."

"'That song, 'Handle Me with Care.'" I shivered with disgust.

"Don't forget 'End of the Line.'"

"Who'd want to remember it? Why are you picking that name?"

"No one would suspect it. We are indeed traveling. But I'm not sure what a Wilbury is. We will handle our missions with care, and it will be the end of the line for corrupt politicians."

"It's true that nobody would suspect anything. And it's time that the name Traveling Wilburys was associated with something positive in the world. It's a stupid name, but okay, fine by me. We are the Traveling Wilburys."

The two people who were drinking cocktails at the next table got up and left, leaving us alone in the bar. James and I turned our heads to watch them leave.

"They're gone now," I said. "Tell me the final plan."

"A week from today," James began, "President Shaw will be celebrating his birthday publicly in the plaza below. This will be accompanied by a rally in support of the government. President Shaw and his ministers, who are our other five targets, will be there too. It's the perfect opportunity for us. President Shaw will appear there with his wife," said James, pointing at the gazebo area. "It's going to be his usual giant birthday cake. After he blows out the candles, they will have fireworks. This has the effect of creating a lot of smoke. Our guy will replace the fireworks with ones that are more smoky than usual. In addition to the fireworks, we're going to plant smoke bombs, there, there, and there." James pointed to various spots around the park. "If everything goes according to plan, it should get pretty smoky down there, obscuring everyone's view. The crowd will think that it is just part of the show."

"We'll have six sharpshooters," James continued. "One there—" He pointed at a tall office building. "Two there"—pointing at a separate building—"and three there"—the rooftop of a third building.

"What about using that cell tower?" I said.

"Too obvious. He'd be seen. Our man would have to get up there and then back down afterward. They'd be looking for a man climbing down. Shooting from office buildings, our men simply dispose of the guns and act like they're just working there."

"That makes sense," I said. "And where will I be?"

"You?" asked James. "Out of the country, I imagine. What do you mean?"

"I told you that I wanted to be involved. I want to be the man who shoots President Shaw."

"No," said James. "Not happening."

"This is nonnegotiable," I said. "I'm the one shooting President Shaw."

"Sorry, pal, I know this is personal to you. But your few months of training is no match for the men I've hired. I have professional, military-trained sharpshooters. You're a guy who programs computers with a shooting hobby."

"I can do it. I've gotten pretty good."

"It's not just the shooting. You have to get in the building clandestinely, prepare for the shot, dispose of the gun, and then get out without being caught. My men, and one woman, have done things like this before. You haven't."

"Show me how."

"It's not happening. Just leave and go back to Denver. You'll read about it in the news. It's better you're out of the country anyway. We don't want any suspicion falling on you."

"How would suspicion fall on me?"

"Because of what happened to Liz."

"Pshaw. Again, this is nonnegotiable."

"Joe, with all due respect—"

"—which always means the opposite," I interrupted.

"Joe, come on. This is too important. Leave it up to us, the professionals. You put me in charge of military operations for a reason. Let me do my job. Your personal feelings will jeopardize this mission."

"I'm the boss. This is my money and organization. Either I shoot President Shaw, or the operation is off."

"Look who's now putting people at risk to service his own needs. If your mission is to help people against those who are only concerned with their own desires, then you're setting a bad example."

"I don't care."

"Neither do those corrupt politicians. Find another military operative. I'm walking." James slammed his beer on the table and got up.

"James, wait," I said.

James stopped.

"You're right," I said. "It is personal. Please let me have this moment.

262

I realize the greater good of our organization. But I gotta be the one who shoots the person I hold responsible for Liz's death. This organization exists because of Liz, because I care for Liz, because Julia cared for Liz. Let me do this. I'll make you a deal. Take me out and watch me shoot, see what I can do. If it's not good enough for the mission, I'll step aside and let your professionals handle it."

James stood at the door of the bar, his back toward me. He turned to face me. "You promise?"

"I do."

"I have the final word on whether your shooting is up to par?"

"Yes."

"And if you're not good enough, you'll accept my order to have one of my professionals take over?"

"Absolutely."

"And any instructions and orders I give you during the mission, you'll follow to a tee?"

"Without hesitation."

"It's a deal, then." James walked back and sat down. "Look me in the eye."

I looked him in the eye.

He offered me his hand. I shook it. "Good," James said.

"Where will I be positioned?" I asked.

"There in the Old Mutual Centre," said James, pointing. "You'll be all alone in an empty office. It's probably a two-hundred-thirty-yard shot. Can you handle that?"

"I can," I said.

"Let me dig up a rifle for you, and we'll go out shooting."

"No need," I said. "I have my Remington here with me in my hotel room."

"You do? How'd you get it into the country?"

"I have my ways too. You think I was married to Liz all these years without learning how to get things done?"

* * *

263

James and I drove a few miles outside of town to a field with a small hill.

"This'll work," said James. "Grab your rifle."

I pulled my rifle case from the backseat.

"Go up to that hill and set up. I'll walk to those trees and create some targets for you," said James.

I hiked 300 feet up the hill, approximately the height of the building from which I'd be shooting. I took my scope out of the case and watched James pinning some homemade targets to the trees, the same distance from which my shot of President Shaw would be. I took out the rest of the rifle, assembled it, inserted five bullets into the magazine, and chambered a round.

James finished setting up and hiked back to me on top of the hill, all while holding a Zambezi beer in his hand. He approached and examined my rifle. "Hmm, this is the civilian version, the Remington 700. The military uses the M24, which is based on this version. It has a heavier contour barrel and a long-action bolt face."

"Is that bad?" I asked.

"Nah, it's important you use the rifle that you're most comfortable with," said James. "Your rifle is in exceptional condition. It's beautifully cleaned and oiled. You've also nicely outfitted it to your specifications. Clearly, whoever trained you did an excellent job. Let's see what you can do. Are you ready?"

"All set," I said.

"Look through the scope. See the white target on the tree to the far left?"

"Yeah."

"Three shots to that one."

I inhaled, felt my heart rate slow, and then fired three shots at the target. James peered through his binoculars. "Not bad. One bull's-eye, one on the target, and one off the target. Try the next."

I shot at the next couple targets, James looking through his binoculars and just humming acknowledgment of each shot. When I finished all three targets, he said, "Let's go take a look."

We hiked down the hill and across the field. We approached the second target. "Again, you've got a near bull's-eye. Another one on the target, and another off target," explained James. "You've clearly been practicing, and you know what you're doing, but you're not consistent."

"Is it good enough?"

"I thought this over and here's the deal: my guys will hit that bull's-eye every time. Let me ask you this – do you want to make sure President Shaw is dead on Wednesday with one of my pros, or do you want to leave it up to chance with you? This is personal, so I'm letting it be your call."

43

Taking the Shot

I walked out of the Jameson on the morning of President Shaw's birthday. The streets were quiet for the national holiday; just a few restaurants and coffee shops were open. Morning in Zimbabwe was a little cool, but the intensity of the sun could already be felt, promising a hotter day to come. I had dressed in slacks and an oxford shirt, the top buttons undone, and carried a leather satchel just as any businessman might. I strode down the street feeling relaxed and confident. I entered the first coffee shop I found open, bought a chocolate-chip muffin and a medium coffee to go, and deposited the muffin inside my satchel.

Bits of traffic passed on the street. Nobody took particular notice of me as I walked along, sipping my coffee. Ten minutes later, I arrived at the entrance to the Old Mutual Centre, a modern glass office building, and pulled open the door into the lobby. It was decorated inelegantly but professionally with faux marble. A man in a suit and tie stood behind the security desk. "Good morning," I said politely.

"Good morning," he replied as I passed into the elevator lobby and pressed the "up" button. I walked slowly in circles until one of the four doors dinged and the up arrow lighted. The door opened, and a man emerged without glancing in my direction. I stepped in and pressed the button for the sixteenth floor. The doors closed, the counter ticked off the passing levels. The elevator came to rest and the door opened onto my floor. I stepped out, and finding no one around, I reached into my satchel and pulled out two leather gloves, slipping them onto my hands.

Beyond the elevator lobby, the floor was entirely carpeted. Corridors led left and right, blank white walls on both sides, occasionally interrupted by a door to an office suite. No outside light entered the hallway. The neon bulbs remained constantly on for the few people who used the corridor throughout the day. Beyond the stifling silence, there was just the sound of the HVAC system blowing air softly into the space.

I proceeded down the hall, my feet making no sound, until I reached number 1604. I put the key in the lock, turned the handle, and entered the office suite. It was empty but for a neglected desk, an office chair, and a bookshelf. Scraps of paper and torn-open boxes were scattered all over the floor. Sunlight poured in through the floor-to-ceiling windows making up the entire far wall of the office behind the desk. A sliding glass door led to a small balcony on which sat a weathered chaise lounge.

I placed my bag on the desk and pressed my head against the glass. Below the balcony was a plaza containing an awning under which people worked busily, preparing for President Shaw's birthday celebration. Chairs for the audience were arranged into rows in front of the pavilion. On the pavilion was a banquet table covered with a tablecloth in Zimbabwe's national colors. A servant set the tables with plates and silverware, while another placed bouquets of flowers.

I checked my watch – still four hours to go. I reached into my satchel and pulled out a book. I sat down in the office chair to read but was having trouble focusing, reading the same paragraph over and over again. Instead, I put the book down, halfway closed my eyes and began to meditate. An hour passed without my knowing. My mind clear, I picked up my book again, this time able to focus on the story.

Between chapters, I peered out the window, noticing a progression of people arriving, saving their seats with coats, purses, and programs. The pavilion had taken shape, worthy of the arrival of a head of state. Still two hours to go. I returned to reading.

Through the soundproofing of the glass, the roar of a crowd reached me. I removed my gaze from the book and looked out the window. President Shaw had arrived. I checked my watch – an hour to go. I returned to my book. It was during a pivotal scene in the novel that my watch alarm went off. I put the book into my satchel and pulled out my long-range rifle, broken up into four parts. I attached the scope to the top and put the silencer on the barrel, turning it tight. I loaded four bullets into the magazine.

I slowly pulled open the sliding glass door, just enough for my body to slip through sideways. Keeping low, I got on my knees to be hidden behind the balcony wall. The hard floor of the balcony hurt my kneecaps, so I pulled over the dirty cushion from the chaise lounge, placing it on the floor and pushing it to the edge of the balcony. I lay flat on my stomach. The balcony wall had a slight gap of maybe four inches from the floor. It was through this space that I aimed my rifle. Looking through the scope, I could see President Shaw standing at the podium on the pavilion, giving his speech. Behind him, seated at the banquet table, were his wife and the members of his cabinet, including his chief of staff and the head of the Zimbabwean military. Near the president was an obnoxiously large birthday cake, one you'd expect to see at the birthday of a dictator. The cake too was decorated in Zimbabwe's national colors, with a flag drawn into the icing on one side and an image of President Shaw's face on the other.

Three minutes to go. President Shaw wound up his speech to a standing ovation from the crowd. He stood bowing, first to the left and then to the right, absorbing their adulation. An attractive woman strode onto the stage in a beautifully gaudy sequined dress, carrying a handheld microphone, further arousing the crowd's applause. She smiled and waved at the crowd, blowing kisses to everyone. She signaled to the crowd to quiet down. At that point she put the microphone to her mouth and said, "Today we wish a very happy birthday to a very special man. President Shaw has led this country out of difficult times, bringing back its full power and wealth. He is one of our greatest leaders who cares for the people of Zimbabwe. We owe our undying love and respect to this wonderful man on this day, his birthday." The crowd again stood and applauded. "And now I want to give him my gift." The crowd oohed. And then she began singing. *"Happy birthday to you..."*

I pulled the bolt on my rifle, chambering the round and cocking the mechanism for firing.

"*Happy birthday to you...*"

I peered through the scope, putting the crosshairs right on President Shaw's head.

"*Happy birthday, dear Mr. President...*"

I placed my finger on the trigger and breathed deeply, feeling my heart slow, noticing at which point I would be between beats.

"*Happy birthday to you.*"

Fireworks shot into the air, and the scream of approaching air force jets passed overhead. Smoke covered the stage, obliterating President Shaw and the stage from sight. Through the infrared lens of my scope I saw President Shaw perfectly through the smoke, smiling and clapping. My watch alarm went off. I squeezed the trigger, feeling the rifle recoil against my shoulder.

But just as I did, President Shaw leaned forward to kiss the singer. Through the scope, I saw my bullet strike the ground behind President Shaw. Meanwhile, in the background, our other targets, seated behind the table, jolted as they were struck by the bullets from our other sharpshooters. They slumped in their seats. The chief of staff slid from his chair and fell under the table.

"Shit!" I said aloud and quickly pulled the bolt of my rifle, chambering another round. Because of the smoke, no one had yet noticed that there were five dead men behind the banquet table. My hands began to shake, which made holding the crosshairs on President Shaw's head difficult. I could feel myself breathing hard. I didn't have time to calm myself, instead envisioning this mission being a failure, and doing all this for nothing. I fired another shot, this one also skipping off the ground behind him. I must've just grazed President Shaw, because his face changed. Someone screamed, another person screamed. People were realizing what was happening. Before I could chamber another round, two security men grabbed President Shaw and ran him off the pavilion.

I lost the president in the crowd as people were now running everywhere. Soldiers had their guns drawn, looking upward but still having trouble seeing clearly through the dissipating smoke.

"Fuck, fuck, fuck!" I said.

"What do I do? What do I do? I have to do something." I was completely freaking out, all my discipline and training out the window, just a panicking child taking over. Then I took a deep breath. "Okay," I said to myself. "They'd take him to the motorcade and get him out of there, right? Or would they just shelter him in a building? No, it has to be the motorcade." I knew from the planning meetings that the motorcade was parked just off the plaza, on the north side of this building.

I backed off the cushion and off the balcony into the office, grabbed my satchel, and ran to the door with my rifle still in hand. I emerged into the hallway. "To the right," I said and ran until I reached three doors that led to office suites on the north side. I shook the handle of the first door. It was locked. Then I jiggled the handle of the next door. It too was locked. I turned the handle of the third door, finding it open and pushing into the office suite. This office was clearly used by someone, full of furniture, books, diplomas hanging on the wall, and a couch. It was unoccupied today due to the holiday. I ran to the sliding glass door and looked. Yes, there was the motorcade, waiting, security men with guns drawn. I pulled the handle of the sliding glass door, but it was locked. I moved the switch that should have unlocked it, but it wouldn't move. I scanned the sides and saw that it was bolted permanently shut for whatever reason. I put my bag and rifle down on the desk. I picked up the office chair and threw it at the glass, but it just bounced off. I groaned. I should have known this type of glass wouldn't break except with a special hammer.

I was running out of time. There was one option left, but I had to go quickly. I grabbed my rifle, leaving the bag, and jogged to the office door, and out into the hallway. I looked around. Spotting the exit sign, I followed it to the stairwell that said "Roof Access." I threw the door open, not caring if anyone heard the sound, and ran up the stairs. I knew I had three flights to the roof, but I was in shape. I barely felt the strain of sprinting up three floors, two steps at a time, awkwardly holding a rifle in my hand. I quickly reached the door to the roof and pushed down the handle, but the door was locked. "Oh my god, no," I said aloud to myself. "Don't these doors need to be open for firefighters?" I pushed again. It moved a bit. It wasn't locked, just jammed due to weathering and constant rain. Probably no one had been up there in ages – that, plus a lack of maintenance. I stood back and gave the door a good kick. It moved a little bit more. I took two steps back and kicked again. It moved a little bit more. "Come on." I took two steps back and gave one last kick. It popped open, exposing the roof and daylight but opening with such force that it swung around and banged the wall loudly.

I ran to the side of the building, looking down at the motorcade. I saw that President Shaw was approaching quickly, surrounded by security. I pulled back, afraid of being spotted by his security detail, who were now scanning the rooftops. I dropped to my knees and then onto my stomach. I positioned my rifle. I was breathing heavily from the run up the steps and couldn't hold the rifle steady. I chambered my third round and looked through the scope. President Shaw was now a moving target, but being older, he wasn't moving quickly. Further making the shot difficult was that he was surrounded by his security detail acting as shields. I put my finger on the trigger and squeezed it. My rifle again recoiled, my bullet missing President Shaw again but hitting one of his security men in the chest. The man dropped to the ground. It took the others in the security detail by surprise. They watched their man fall but left him there and continued without him.

I chambered my last round and looked through the scope. President Shaw was almost to the limo. I could try a shot now, but instead I decided to wait a second. I closed my eyes, took a deep breath, let it out, took another deep breath, let it out. I opened my eyes. President Shaw had arrived at the limo and was being pushed in the door. This was it. If I missed, he was gone. I had to time the bullet perfectly. I calculated that by the time I fired and the bullet reached him, his head should be in the small space between the open door of the car and the interior. I aimed for that spot, and then felt for the right moment. I squeezed the trigger for a last time. The bullet left my rifle, traveling through the air, perfectly threading the needle between the gap of the door and the car, penetrating the back of President Shaw's skull, sliding through his fucking brain, out his left eye, and into the cushion of the seat in front of him, splattering blood and brains with it.

"Yes!" I shouted. I crawled back and stood up once I was far enough from the edge not to be seen. I returned the way I came, down the staircase, and out onto the 16th floor. I returned to the office, where I retrieved my briefcase. I checked my watch. Two minutes behind schedule. Then I returned to the original office and approached the empty bookshelf, pushed it aside, and removed a loose board from the base of the wall, revealing a small hole. I disassembled my rifle, struggling to unscrew the scope that I had fixed too tightly. Finally, it came off. I pushed all the parts through the hole, hearing nothing, as they must have fallen hundreds of feet. Then I removed my shirt and pants, dirty from lying supine on the floor. I threw those down the hole, along with my gloves. I replaced the loose board and hammered in the nails with the hammer that had discreetly been left for me amongst the other junk in the empty office. I pushed the bookshelf back into place. I reached into my bag and removed a clean shirt and pants, putting them on quickly. I tucked my shirt into my trousers and fastened the belt.

I looked at my watch – still two minutes behind. I'd be okay. We had a contingency for this, right? I grabbed my satchel off the desk and looked out the window at the chaos below.

I exited the office, walked down the corridor, pressed the button on the elevator, and continued past the elevator bank. I took the stairs pursuant to the plan, as we couldn't risk that the elevators might be shut down with me in it. It was sixteen stories to the lobby, but at least it was down. I took the steps in stride, my knees aching after ten stories. Around and around the stairwell, meeting no one along the way. I reached the bottom and pushed the door open into the faux-marble lobby, where the security guard who had seemed so calm before was now distressed and talking furiously on the phone. When he saw me, he lowered the phone from his ear and was about to address me.

But before he could say anything, I said, "What the hell is going on here? Are the elevators not working? I had to walk down sixteen flights."

"There's been an emergency. Have you seen anyone suspicious?"

"Suspicious? What's going on?" I said indignantly.

"I was just told to look for anyone suspicious in the building and keep them here. Have you seen anyone at all, maybe someone carrying something?"

"I haven't seen anyone. But I will look out for someone."

"Okay, sir," said the security guard. I walked out. White privilege gets you pretty far in this world.

Outside, police and military were in disarray. People were running in opposite directions. Authorities had shoved a group of people to the ground. Locals were herded into paddy wagons. Sirens blared. A few shots rang out. Two cops seized my arm. "What's going on?" I said.

"Everyone is being rounded up." They pushed me into the back of a police car.

The police got in the front seat of the car and drove slowly through the crowd with their lights flashing. The cop in the passenger seat stuck his head out the window and yelled for people to move. A barricade had been set up by the police. It was opened to let our car pass through. On the street, military personnel vehicles were dropping troops off in spots around the city. The troops jumped from the personnel carriers and took positions on the corner. We passed the capitol building, where soldiers had already set up in front. We took a side street and drove passed the TV station, where more soldiers had set up barriers.

The police car pulled up outside the Jameson Hotel. The cop on the passenger side got out and opened the back door for me. "We're here, sir."

"Thank you for the escort, gentlemen," I said, getting out of the vehicle.

I walked from the police car and past the security cordon being set up at the Jameson Hotel and then into the lobby. I climbed the stairs into the conference room, now full of people talking on phones. James and Julia were running about, shouting instructions to people.

"Get someone on the newspaper. This was supposed to be covered, damn it!" said James to a staff member who was holding a phone away from his ear. He asked James a question, but I could not hear what he was saying. James replied, "Tell the editor that he's printing the edition we supplied to him on the thumb drive, and if he doesn't, he'll be shot. I mean, not really. Don't shoot anyone at the newspaper. But just have our guys threaten him a little bit."

James looked up and saw me. "Joe, thank god. You made it." He came over and gave me a big hug. Across the room, I saw Aunt Julia give me a nasty look.

"How's it going?" I asked.

"Mostly according to plan," James said. "The capitol building is secure. Most of the politicians from President Shaw's party have been rounded up and arrested. It was easy since they were all at the birthday party."

"Has there been much violence?"

"Not much. Government forces have generally been cowed. We caught them totally by surprise, and we were well organized. Our pro-democracy faction of the military was in place and ready to go, taking control of everything quickly."

"When is Mr. Enati going on television?"

"In one hour," said James.

"It looks like this is going to be a success, then?"

"So far it looks like we're going to avoid being shot as revolutionaries."

Aunt Julia stomped up to me. "I want to talk to you in private," she said to me. She turned to James. "You too."

"But we're in the middle of the—"

"Now!" shouted Julia.

She led us out of the conference room and into a private office, shutting the door behind us.

"What the fuck do you think you were doing?" Julia said to me.

"I had to do it, Julia."

"No one told me that you were going to be the one shooting President Shaw. I only found out when you fucked it up."

"Julia, I—"

"Shut up! You listen to me. Look around at this operation, this operation that you set up, that we set up, that was set up for Liz. Months of planning. Millions of dollars. Millions of lives at stake. And you insisted on being the one to shoot President Shaw?"

I stood silently.

"And you," she said, turning to James. "You let him. You are the military professional here. You should have known better. I know why you both didn't tell me, because you knew I'd disapprove."

"But I got him," I said.

"You fucked it up and then got lucky! We have hired professionals for this."

"Julia, I needed to be the one."

"Wake up, you fucking prick. You putting your need for revenge first defeats the whole purpose of what we're doing."

I lowered my head.

"Do you realize what would have happened if you'd failed? We'd have been shot as insurrectionists. All our employees would have been shot. Our allies would have been shot. There would have been a major crackdown by President Shaw, and things would be much worse for the people of Zimbabwe, the very people this organization is in place to help."

"Okay, Julia. I get it."

"No, you don't. The three of us make these decisions together. You go over my head one more time on something like this and not only am I going to resign, but I may consider turning you over to the police."

"I'm sorry," I said. "I wasn't thinking clearly. It's just, when it comes to Liz..." I paused in silence, not able to finish my sentence.

Julia softened. "Look, Joe, we're here because of Liz. This organization exists because of Liz, but let's stay focused on what Liz would have wanted and what we want from this organization. We want law and order and justice. Justice is blind. I miss Liz more than you can ever know. For a woman like me who never had anything more than a career, she was the one bright spot in my life. I lost my parents, I lost my brother, and I lost Liz. She was a bit of tenderness in a life filled with tough negotiations with tough people. I get it, Joe. But stay focused. You got it?"

"Got it," I said. I wanted to hug Julia, but I knew that wasn't going to happen.

"Now, let's finish this up and get out of here."

44

President Enati

Two days later, James, Julia, and I arrived in a car outside the presidential palace. A soldier opened the door. We got out and ascended the steps into the grand building. A valet led the three of us to a small room off the main office.

Mr. Enati was sitting at his desk working on a laptop when we walked in. "Ahh, hello," he said, smiling. "Thank you for coming." He stood to greet us, shaking hands with me first, then James, then Julia.

"Come sit down." Mr. Enati offered us seats on a couch around a small coffee table. James and I sat on the sofa, while Julia opted for a straight-backed chair.

"Would you like something to drink?"

"Coffee," we all agreed, after three days of little sleep. The valet who had shown us to the office nodded and walked out.

"Why are you working here in this small office?" I asked.

Mr. Enati laughed. "You mean instead of President's Shaw grand office? I thought you'd appreciate that. I am only here in this presidential palace to symbolically show that I'm in power. I don't intend to live in grandeur just because I am in charge. This office is all I need. Once things are settled, the government will decide what to do with this monstrosity. Maybe we make it into a museum. Who knows?"

"You know, after the American Revolution the founding fathers had the same thought and wanted a modest place for the president to live to show the country that he was one of the people. However, they realized the need for a leader to have some creditability on the world stage, and thus the White House was built. So maybe you do stay here," I said.

"This is too much for Zimbabwe. This is like a Versailles. Something modest along the lines of a Number 10 Downing Street would be more appropriate."

"How are we looking for the upcoming elections?" said Julia, interrupting the small talk.

"We make the announcement today that elections will be held in six months and giving the exact date," said Mr. Enati.

"And the constitution?" she asked.

"We're working on it," said Mr. Enati.

"I hope that I don't need to tell you this, Mr. Enati," said Julia, "but don't end up like a lot of leaders and get drunk with power, as Mr. Mugabe did. We expect you to carry out your democratic goals, or we will shoot you too."

Mr. Enati looked a little nervous.

"What Julia means," I said, "is that we know you'll keep your promise. Honestly, though, why would you want to stay forever in power? It seems like a lot of trouble. Realistically, if you complete your goals, then you will be forever viewed as a 'good guy' by the international community, and here in Zimbabwe, you'll be lauded. You'll be a hero, never wanting for money or comfort. Those are your selfish motives to stick to a plan of democracy."

"You are right," Mr. Enati said. "I wish more leaders would come to that realization."

"Good," I said. "Back to the constitution. You'll be using the draft we gave you, correct?"

"Yes," said Mr. Enati.

"Mr. Enati," said Julia, "we agree that you are now in charge of Zimbabwe. However, we insist that you use the perfectly good draft we gave you. You have some freedom to make some changes, but things like term limits and the length of office terms must remain. Moreover, we have designated a perfect equilibrium of checks and balances between the judicial, legislative, and executive branches of the new government, similar to what they have in the United States. We don't want any branch becoming too powerful, especially the executive. I think you understand our concerns, given what has happened here and in other countries."

"Ms. Julia, you have nothing to worry about. We will send you the final draft. Now, let's all go eat lunch."

45

One Rockefeller Plaza

"Just put the microphone right here, on your lapel, Mr. Levy," a production assistant was saying to me. She was a blonde in her mid-twenties wearing tight jeans and a green t-shirt, her hair in a ponytail. A walkie-talkie that was clipped to her belt squawked. She took her hands off my lapel and pulled the walkie-talkie to her mouth. "He's mic'd up and ready," she said to whomever was on the other end. Then she turned to me and said, "Just wait right here until you're introduced."

"Okay," I said. I was standing in the wings, just off the stage in One Rockefeller Plaza, New York City, noticing how different it was from where I'd just been. I was wearing a dark suit with a white oxford shirt and no tie.

From behind the curtain I could see the director, a young man wearing a headset, signaling to the on-air personalities that they were about to return from commercial break. *Three, two, one,* he counted down on his fingers.

"Welcome back," the on-air personality said. "In our next segment, we interview the software entrepreneur, billionaire, and former CEO of EasyData, who is just back from a recent trip to Africa. This will be his first interview since his terrible personal tragedy and the exit from his company. Please welcome Joseph Levy."

I emerged from off camera and walked confidently over to the host, an Asian woman of medium height wearing an excess of makeup. I shook her hand. She gestured for me to sit down. The arrangement was two chairs around a coffee table. I unbuttoned my coat, as a gentleman should do before sitting, and sat in the seat she pointed to.

"Welcome, Joe," she said.

"Thank you, Jane," I said. "It's incredible to be here. In college, I once came here to watch the show from outside that window."

Jane smiled. "It's better to be inside on a cold day like today."

Before I could reply with something friendly and clever, she simply continued, "I'm very sorry about what happened to your wife, Mrs. Levy."

"Thank you," I said quickly, hoping she wouldn't go too deeply into it.

"You were off the radar for a bit as a result."

"It was a tough time, as you can imagine. But Liz and I started NewWays, and the best way to preserve her memory is to focus on the organization and its goals."

"You just returned from Zimbabwe, the country in which your wife was murdered. Was it difficult going back?"

"A little bit, but the point of going back was to show defiance to what happened by returning to help the people of Zimbabwe rebuild their agricultural sector."

"You were there during the coup, when President Shaw was assassinated. What are your feelings about what happened?"

"I'm never for unruly violence, but President Shaw was extremely corrupt, and his people were suffering as a result of his policies. Only those in power were reaping the benefits of the wealth of Zimbabwe. The economy was in tatters, people were dying. Now things are better with Mr. Enati in charge. He is going to hold elections, push forward a new democratic constitution, and put the country on the right track."

"You're saying the coup was a good thing?"

"Liz and I had been hoping for years that President Shaw's opposition would effect change through nonviolent democratic policies, but that is difficult when you have someone like President Shaw who doesn't respect democratic institutions and is basically a thug who holds on to power through violence and corruption. Mr. Enati and his party had no choice but to act in the way they have. Now the people of Zimbabwe have a chance.

There has never been a famine in a democracy. So, yes, sometimes a coup can be a good thing. Call it a revolution, if you will."

"You've formed a new organization to focus on this mission."

"That's correct. I'm announcing today our new organization called Due Process, in conjunction with my wife's aunt Julia O'Rourke, a former British diplomat. It's basically pro-law, democracy, and due process. We're going to be lobbying governments and spreading the word that a more powerful World Court is needed to hold corrupt governments accountable under the law. We seek transparency from all governments and the ability to arrest and prosecute corrupt world leaders."

"Like the coup in Zimbabwe?"

"Not exactly. It will be like what happens if anyone commits a crime here in the United States. When there's probable cause of a crime, an arrest warrant is issued, and the police come get you. You are given your due process, a fair trial – a chance to confront your accusers, question the evidence, and have a decision rendered by a jury of your peers."

Jane looked at her notes and then said, "There are rumors that you were behind the coup in Zimbabwe to avenge your wife's death?"

I smiled. "I've heard those rumors. That's ridiculous. President Shaw's corrupt government may have been indirectly responsible for Liz's death, but I am a man who believes in working through a proper legal process. I was there to support my organization and promote good agricultural practices. As you know, NewWays, the aid organization, exists to avoid politics, hence why my new organization, Due Process, is a separate, political group, pushing for worldwide law enforcement. That said, I'm not sorry to see President Shaw go."

"Thank you, Joe. That's all the time we have. Best of luck to your organizations and good work."

"Thank you, Jane."

46

The Next Charitable Act

My plane touched down at Cointrin Airport in Geneva, Switzerland. I passed through border control and customs, then caught the airport train to the Geneva CFF station, where I transferred to the Zermatt train. I got a window seat, put on my headphones, and spent the three-hour journey staring out the window at the passing mountainous landscape. Nothing calmed me more than listening to music on a train. It was my personal soundtrack to the world around me. The train pulled into Zermatt station, where I caught the free shuttle to the Coeur des Alpes Hotel. My phone dinged with a text through WhatsApp. *You here yet?* read the message from James.

Just about, I replied. *Where are you?*

In the bar, duh.

Let me check in, and I'll be right there.

The Coeur de Alpes was the number-one hotel in Zermatt; its setting in the snow-covered skier's paradise could not be beaten.

"Good evening," said the man at the reception desk. "How may I help you?"

"I'm Joe Levy. I have a reservation."

"May I see your passport?" The man looked it over and typed a few things into a computer. "Here you go," he said, handing me back my passport along with a keycard. "You're in room 209. The bellboy will help you with your luggage, err, backpack."

"No thank you," I said. "I can carry it."

"As you wish. The elevator is around the corner to your left."

"Thank you," I said, picking up my backpack and walking past the elevator, and instead up the stairs to the second floor, and down the hall to my room. I slipped in the keycard until the light turned green; the lock clicked open. The room was a nice size with a coffee maker, flat-screen TV, and double bed. I put my backpack down on the rack reserved for suitcases, left the room, and walked downstairs. The Aussen Lounge looked out on a view of the Matterhorn. I found James talking to the bartender, a gentleman about our age.

"James," I said. "Good to see you."

"Hey, dude," James said, giving me a hug. "You look a mess. Did you fly coach again?"

"Of course," I said.

"You're a billionaire. Upgrading to first class for a long flight would be nothing for you."

"It's not my style," I said. "I'm not sure I like the people I meet there. Besides, I lucked out and had a whole row to myself in the back of the plane, so I was able to spread out."

"You got to admit that this place isn't so bad." James gestured to the luxurious bar in which we were sitting.

"Generally, this isn't my type of place, but this is where Julia likes to go skiing, and this is where she stays, and seeing as there are few inexpensive options around here, I figured I'd splurge a little and stay here. If it weren't for Julia, I'd be happy being elsewhere. The kind of people who come here are so stodgy. Give me the inexpensive hotel any day. It's a much better crowd."

"I think you're a reverse snob," said James.

"What do you mean?" I said.

"I mean that you're so intent on proving that you're just so down to earth that you are snobby against people who might enjoy comfort. Maybe there are interesting people here too. There are people who do cool things and also like the niceties of a resort. What makes you better because you are willing to stay in a cheaper place?"

"I just think... Okay, maybe you're right."

"Just relax. Don't be a reverse snob."

"Where is Julia?" I asked. "Have you seen her?"

"I saw her earlier. She wanted to do a few more runs before the day finished. She'll be meeting us here for après-ski."

"My god, that woman is incredible at her age. I see where Liz got her energy from. Liz's parents must've been the same way."

James took a sip of his whiskey.

"How are you doing?" I asked.

"Fine."

"You've been drinking a lot," I offered.

"I know." He said this matter-of-factly. "The real question is, how are you doing?"

"I'm well. You know. Meditating daily still, focusing on plans for the organization."

"No, I mean, how are you doing after Zimbabwe? It was your first time," said James, looking around to make sure no one could overhear our conversation.

"Just say it, James. You mean killing—"

"That's what I mean. Did it make you feel better?"

"Not really," I said. "Liz is still gone. I mean, initially, yes, it felt good to watch that bullet crash through the fucker's skull. But then the emptiness returned."

"Did I not tell you? What Julia said to you in Harare was correct. I hope this is the end of your personal vendetta."

"Who else is there to take vengeance on? President Shaw is gone, and I'll never find the guy who actually shot Liz. And, so what?" I added. "The result was positive. President Shaw is gone and Mr. Enati has already begun to turn things around. The election is next month, along with the referendum on the new constitution. Once a democratically elected government is in place, the sanctions against Zimbabwe will be dropped, international monetary aid will return, a new currency will be introduced, and the economy will stabilize and grow again."

"You are right that our result was positive. And I don't believe that there is such a thing as a completely altruistic motive. Even Mother Teresa, I'm sure, derived pleasure from her work."

"Then the subject is put to rest," I said just as Julia walked in stiffly wearing her ski boots and thick gloves, her diminutive frame bundled up from head to toe in ski gear, goggles propped atop her head. She looked like a child – an ornery and defiant child.

"Hello, Julia," I said.

"Good evening, Joe," she said formally.

"Your skis must be twice as tall as you," said James.

Julia glared at him. "Let's go over here and talk, away from everyone else. Bartender, Hennessy cognac, please. And bring it to that table in the corner." Julia trudged over to the table in the far corner without waiting for us. James grabbed his beer off the bar as we followed her over. She set her gloves on an empty chair and removed her jacket, leaving the ski goggles on her head as though forgetting them.

"Thank you for coming," I said. "Let's talk about which country our organization is going to help next."

"Traveling Wilburys," said James.

"Pardon?" said Julia.

"That's the name of our organization: the Traveling Wilburys," said James.

"In any case, I have a few suggestions," said Julia. "Clearly, I didn't bring any paperwork to show you, given the nature of our business. There are plenty of corrupt governments in the world, but I've focused on countries that I believe we can actually help. Countries small enough that we won't end up starting any wars. Countries where there is a reliable, democratic opposition or movements that can step in. In other words, countries where taking out the leader makes a difference and does not just allow the next corrupt guy to take over. I've narrowed it down to three prospects: Uzbekistan, Venezuela, and the Democratic Republic of the Congo, aka the

DRC."

"Forget the DRC for now," James said. "We just did a country in Africa. Let's mix it up a bit, so it doesn't seem like we're picking on Africa. We can get back to it later. We want to show that this kind of intervention is effective in other cultures and other parts of the world."

"I agree with James," said Julia. "It will look better when we lobby for a stronger World Court and law enforcement against corrupt world leaders if the examples come from a variety of places. Africa is singled out too often, quite frankly. Not that they don't have their problems, but there are plenty of other places in Asia, Central America, South America, and Europe too that are just as bad. The DRC can definitely use us, but later."

"That makes sense," I said. "As for the other two? I suggest Uzbekistan. Let me run through my thinking—"

"—No," said Aunt Julia, interrupting. "No one has heard of it and no one cares. Zimbabwe has been in the news. Everyone knew Mugabe and Shaw. That's why our first operation got so much attention."

"Julia's right," James added. "Many people don't even think Uzbekistan is a real country. A coup in Uzbekistan would barely make the evening news, and if the Kardashians did something that day, it wouldn't make the news at all."

"But they do need our help," I offered.

"The government there has been running it like the mafia for years," said Julia. "Political opponents are tortured and disappeared. Government cronies steal the wealth of the country's people. But there is good infras-tructure and a robust economy. The structures are in place. However, the culture of corruption needs to change."

"That's true of all our targets," I said. "These people have been living with corruption so long that it becomes ingrained in daily life. People play the system because they must to get by. It's tough changing minds, convincing them that following the rules is better. First, they have to see that other people are following the rules. It's similar to doping in sports. Do you want to be the one clean guy getting whooped in the hundred-meter dash by dirty players? Changing the culture of corruption is incremental. It's important to have an honorable person leading the country, setting the example. For instance, things started off well for us in the U.S. because we had George Washington as our first president. Many thought President George Washington would become a king and remain in power, but he stepped down after two terms and peacefully transferred power, setting the example. Imagine if he hadn't done that."

"That Mr. Enati is a good guy. So far, he's lived up to his stated principles," James said.

"He has done a fantastic job," said Julia, taking a sip of her cognac, which had been delivered. "Let's hope he continues."

"Have some faith, Julia," I said. "The change there is palpable already."

"I've just seen too many good men go corrupt with power," said Julia.

"Do you wish President Shaw was back?" James asked.

"Definitely not. That bastard had to go," said Julia.

"Guys, we're off track," I said. "Back to the business at hand."

"It sounds like we're left with Venezuela," said James.

"Hugo Chávez drove that country and its economy into the ground," began Julia. "Everyone's heard of it, mainly because there's oil there. Nicolás Maduro took over when Chávez died, and then he was ousted by José Juarez, which turned out to be just a power grab and not a step toward fixing the problems there. There have been protests, riots, mass inflation – unemployment is now at sixty percent. That country should be rich! They have oil and had a thriving tourist industry, which could easily be revived once stability returns. Meanwhile, the people are starving. It's a perfect target."

"Venezuela is supposed to be beautiful. Angel Falls, the highest waterfalls in the world, are there, named after Jimmie Angel, the pilot who first flew over them," I said.

"You'd be great on *Jeopardy!*" said James.

"Anyways," I continued, "there's an established opposition there whom we can approach to take over, the Democratic Unity Roundtable, or in Spanish, Mesa de la Unidad Democratica," I said, stumbling over each syllable.

"Your Spanish is terrible," said James.

"Boys, enough," said Julia.

"They're called MUD for short, which you gotta love. It's basically a coalition of opposition groups. They've been kept down for years, but their goals are our goals, which are human rights, democracy, and political pluralism. There are fifty parties within the coalition, so they've sometimes had fallings out. At first, they struggled to find a common message, but what makes this good for us is that in the last couple years, a leader has emerged. His name is Ramon Montoya. He's young, in his mid-thirties. He's extremely bright, educated at Oxford, and has been very active in pro-democracy movements his whole life. He's good-looking and married with a couple kids. The question is how open he will be to our plan. Julia, have you had any interactions with Señor Montoya?"

"None, but I can ask a few people without raising suspicions. I've mentally prepared a list of Juarez's people whom we would need to remove, just like we did in Zimbabwe."

"James, operationally, is José Juarez an accessible target?"

"I'll look into it and talk to my guys who have worked in South America. This is a different part of the world. The African mercenaries we used in Zimbabwe won't work there, as they wouldn't quite fit in in South America. I'll have to hire new guys from South America who speak Spanish, at least better than you."

"Shut up, dude."

"If you two are done fucking around," began Julia, "I have another suggestion other than assassinating the president and killing his ministers. The point of this organization is the removal of corrupt governments and replacing them with democratic institutions. What if, instead of killing these men, we kidnapped them? The World Court has already indicted Mr. Juarez and many of his cronies. This could be an arrest. It would make a hell of a statement to the world if we could nonviolently remove them and bring them to justice."

"Hmmm," I said. "James, is that possible?"

"I suppose. I mean, I haven't studied the logistics yet, but I can see if a kidnapping/arrest is feasible."

"Do that," I said. "Julia is right. Our aim is law enforcement. We could arrest and have these criminals tried, just like any police force does for any criminal in any country. Police first attempt to apprehend and arrest nonviolently before employing more forceful means."

"At least in theory," James said. "I'll see what I can do."

"Julia, you're brilliant. You must've picked that up from Liz."

Julia gave me her death glance before taking a sip of cognac.

"You guys look into your respective parts of the Venezuelan plan," I said. "I'm off this afternoon to meet with Senator Godfrey in Geneva."

"Horatio Godfrey from Utah?" asked Julia.

"Yes, that guy."

"He's a punk," said Julia.

"What do you mean?" I asked.

"He's a blowhard. I assume you're meeting with him because of his work in Africa."

"Exactly," I said. "He's been working for years as chair of the Senate Foreign Relations Committee in securing funding for NGOs in Africa. I want to meet with him to push our political agenda. He's the number-one senator responsible for raising money for aid organizations there. I want to see if I can get him to focus on pushing democracy."

"What's he doing in Geneva?" James asked.

"He's on vacation," I said. "I contacted his office for an appointment, and they said he was here on holiday and for some business in Switzerland. They didn't say if it was government work or personal. But since Julia wanted to meet in Switzerland anyway, it made sense for me to see him here, rather than wait till he returned to DC."

"I always thought there was something off about him," said Julia.

"He's fine," I said dismissively. "Not that U.S. senators are never corrupt, but their corruption is usually within acceptable parameters, such as appropriating funds for constituent projects. I can live with that. I'm mostly interested in his connections in Africa. He'd be a strong ally."

"Maybe I should go with you," said Julia.

"I'll be leaving here around late afternoon and meeting him for dinner. Come if you like."

47

Senator Godfrey

J ulia and I arrived at the Bistro de la Tour at 8 p.m. for our dinner reservation. It had a modern design with hardwood floors, black tables, white walls, and a wine rack in the back. Red glass candle holders decorated each table. It had been reported to me that Senator Godfrey liked to eat here. Getting a reservation for two was difficult, and when Julia decided to join us, it was hard changing the reservation to three, but I called my concierge service through my American Express Black Card and secured a table.

"Good evening," I said to the host, a lean, fit man wearing a tight black t-shirt and a pair of black slacks. "I have a reservation for three under Joe Levy."

The host looked down the reservation list. "Your table is ready." He grabbed three menus but then looked back up with concern. "Are you all here?"

"It looks like it's just two of us for the moment," I said, looking around.

"We can't seat you until your whole party is here," said the host. "We have a months-long waiting list, and if he is not here in fifteen minutes, we have to cancel your reservation."

I was about to speak, but then Julia, as I should have expected, stepped in. "Young man, this is Joseph Levy. I'm a former member of the British Foreign Service, and we are waiting for Senator Godfrey."

"You should have mentioned that," said the host. "Senator Godfrey is a regular. He's always late. I'll seat you."

The host led us to a table for three. "Would you like some drinks while you wait?" he asked.

"A Hennessy cognac for me," said Julia.

"Just sparkling water for me," I said.

The host left.

"What an asshole," I said. "Didn't even apologize."

"I hate these snobby places," Julia said.

I was about to point out that she was calling the kettle black but chose to just let it slide.

Half an hour passed, and Senator Godfrey still hadn't shown.

"This guy is running really late."

"Typical," said Julia. "He's a blowhard, just as I said."

"Should we wait?"

"He'll be here. He just has to make his entrance."

"I'd text him, but I don't have his number. I just made an appointment through his office."

A few minutes later, the host returned with a now-friendly manner. "Would you like another drink? Senator Godfrey is on his way. He's always late," he said again.

"No, thank you," I said, turning to Julia to see if she wanted more cognac. She shook her head.

It wasn't until 9 p.m. that the senator came rumbling through the door, an hour late. A white guy in his mid-fifties, obese, and wearing a suit with a bow tie, just like I'd seen him on TV. We stood to greet him. He flashed a big smile and extended his hand to me and Julia. "I'm so sorry," he said. "Senate business. It's business hours back in DC, and I got stuck on a few calls. This often happens. My office should have warned you."

"No problem. Julia and I were just enjoying a conversation about skiing," I said, immediately sucked in by his charm. My anger melted away, and I was surprised to find myself wanting this guy to like me. "I'd like to introduce Julia O'Rourke; she's my late wife's aunt and formerly of the British Foreign

Office. She is in charge of my new political organization. I thought it would be nice to have her along."

"So nice to meet you," he said, shaking hands with Julia. "I'm very sorry to hear about both your loss."

"Thank you," said Julia matter-of-factly.

We sat down. "Have you had a chance to look at the menu?" Senator Godfrey asked. "I'm starving."

"We've had plenty of time," said Julia.

Senator Godfrey beckoned the waiter, who responded immediately. "I'll have the usual with my usual. What would you two like?"

"I'll have the steak filet with garlic butter, medium-rare," said Julia, and the waiter took down the order on his iPad.

"I'll have the same thing," I said, not really feeling like eating.

"Good choices," said the senator. "This place is known for its wonderful wine selection. Do you have my favorite?" he said, turning toward the waiter.

"We saved a bottle just for you."

"Excellent, you all will like it," said the senator, turning to me and Julia. "How has your stay been in Switzerland? Where are you staying?"

"We're at the Coeur des Alpes Hotel. Julia picked it. She's the big skier in the family," I said.

"You're from Denver, right?" Senator Godfrey asked. "You never got into skiing living in the beautiful Colorado Rockies? Shoot, I ski in Utah any chance I get."

"When I was a poor, young student at the University of Colorado, I didn't have the funds to go skiing. The other students' parents must've given them money, because they all seemed to disappear into the mountains every weekend. My parents were not about to support a skiing lifestyle, so I took advantage of the free ice rink on campus and played hockey."

"But now you're a billionaire," said Senator Godfrey. "Surely, you can afford to ski. Indulge yourself."

"It's too late. I've been a couple times, and it was fine, but it's something I should have picked up as a kid. It doesn't interest me. And everyone I know who's a skier has blown out their knee. That's something I wish to avoid. Kids are indestructible and don't care about such things."

"I did that and was out for two seasons," Senator Godfrey said.

The waiter arrived with a bottle of 1996 Château Léoville-Las Cases, showing it first to the senator.

"Would the senator like to have the first taste?" asked the waiter.

"No, go ahead and pour."

The waiter poured first for Julia, then tried to pour for me. "No, thanks," I said. "I don't drink." He filled the senator's glass.

"Cheers," said the senator as we all clinked glasses, me with my sparkling water.

"Now that I have some wine in me, what is it you want to see me about?"

"As you know, since my wife passed—"

Julia interrupted. "In addition to our charitable organization, we've started a complementary political organization to promote good governance around the world. We've discovered that eliminating corruption and establishing proper institutions of law and government are more important in the long term than simply sending money and food aid into a black hole that usually just goes into the pockets of the corrupt leaders who are causing misery for their people in the first place."

"It's that exact situation," I added, "which existed in Zimbabwe with Mugabe and then President Shaw, that created the environment in which my wife was murdered. Now that President Shaw is gone and a proper democracy has been established, the situation has already improved."

"As such," interjected Julia, "we are pushing to give more power to the World Court to prosecute and enforce laws against corrupt world leaders." Julia then went on to explain to the senator our plans, minus our clandestine assassinations, of course. The senator listened attentively, his face remaining neutral but interested, him occasionally taking a sip of wine, and quickly finishing his glass before Julia and I finished ours. The waiter poured him another glass, which he also quickly consumed. He motioned to the waiter to bring another bottle of wine. Appetizers arrived, raw ahi tuna mixed with tomatoes, cucumbers, jalapeños, and lemon juice, served on a light rice cracker. He munched up most of the appetizers, leaving just two for me and Julia.

"...and the reason we are meeting with you, Senator," I said, "is because we know you've been involved in developing countries, providing money and resources. We're hoping to convince you to, in addition to the aid, focus on governance. If possible, we'd like to have hearings before the senate. As you are aware, there's a committee hearing next month about foreign aid programs, specifically corruption. Would you work with us to arrange for me or Julia to speak before that committee?"

After he had sat silently and listened to our argument, Julia and I both stared at the senator, awaiting his response, trying to read his body language. He finished chewing on a piece of bread, and then took a sip of wine to clear his palette. "What you say is very intriguing," he began. "I've actually thought for years that maybe we just need good governance. Of course, the aid I've arranged to have sent to these countries has helped quite a few people. I wouldn't just dismiss its benefits, despite it occasionally ending up in the wrong hands. I'm proud of my record and feel like my efforts have helped millions over the years."

"Senator, I didn't mean—" I interjected.

"—It's okay," interrupted the senator. "I understand what you're saying, and I agree. I just don't think it's as black and white as you think. Moreover, you've pointed out the obvious problems of trying to arrest and prosecute the heads of state of sovereign nations."

"We're trying to change people's mindsets," I said. "The world is connected now. We believe that criminal heads of state should no longer be viewed as unassailable gods acting with impunity. Technology and transport have made the world smaller, and with that has come a change in view that everyone is subject to the law. We want to continue to move the world's thinking in that direction. It won't happen right away, but we would like your help. You're the chairman of the Senate Foreign Relations Committee, and you have a stellar reputation throughout the developing world because of all you've done in the past. That's why we're coming to you."

The senator gave an uneasy smile, the first crack in his veneer of a larger-than-life, in-charge statesman. He seemed to be getting a little tipsy, a clear consequence of all the wine he had drunk. "I support a lot of what you said. I'm having a big fundraiser next month in Utah. Perhaps you could attend, and we could discuss the matter further."

The meal arrived, the waiter placing before me a large plate containing a small portion of steak with a dollop of garlic butter, partially melted and nearly sliding off the top, a smattering of sliced potatoes, and a radish cut into a flower at the top of the plate for garnish. The senator's usual meal was a rich portion of stewed oxtail over a bed of mashed potatoes, heavily buttered. He dug right in.

"Senator, as you know, none of my organizations give political contributions. I'm not implying anything; it's just that if we're pushing for good governance, it should be the elected representative's job to help our organization, and not in return for political contributions."

The senator finished his bite and wiped his mouth with the napkin. "The reality of being a senator or congressman nowadays in the United States is that it takes a lot of money to run an election campaign. I can help your cause, but if I don't get reelected, my opponent may not be as open to pushing your agenda. I know what you're thinking, but this is how things work."

"We don't think so," Julia replied. "As we said, we're trying to change mindsets. I realize that it's become conventional in the United States to accept campaign contributions in return for access. I'm fully aware that you're here talking to us because Joe is wealthy. But if you perpetuate the culture of pay-to-play, you end up with a system no different from a third-world country in which the wealthy get favorable policy in return for their money. You want what's best for America and the world, right? Therefore, if we have an idea that furthers that cause, you should do it regardless of whether we contribute to your campaign or not. Isn't that correct?"

The senator swallowed hard. "Of course!" he said. "That doesn't mean I don't need money for reelection. Don't hate the player; hate the game."

I had no response to this statement.

The senator read our expressions and caught himself, adding, "Look, Joe, Julia. What I would like is the credibility of an endorsement from you and your organization. Throughout the world, you and your organization have a stellar reputation, and pardon me for being direct, but you garnered a lot of sympathy after the tragic death of your wife. An endorsement from you would go a long way to helping my reelection campaign. I agree with many of your policies. If I work with your organization, would you endorse my reelection bid?"

"Certainly, if we consider you to be a worthy statesman and someone whom we feel is doing a good job, we absolutely would endorse you. That's not only proper but honorable. We just don't pay to play," I said.

"Excellent," said the senator.

* * *

"What'd you think?" I asked Julia on the train ride back to Zermatt.

"He's a prick, a typical politician prick. He's not going to do anything for us."

"You think so? I don't agree."

"He reeks of corruption. He's in Switzerland, drinking his usual expensive wine, having his usual expensive and rich meal, skiing. I wouldn't be surprised if he was getting some sort of kickback from all that aid he arranges to third-world countries."

"You don't know that. Have you run into him before in your diplomatic career?"

"Fortunately, not. He's clearly a big deal as chair of the Senate Foreign Relations Committee, but I never had the pleasure of dealing with him directly."

"Please ask your contacts. To an extent, I can deal with slimy politicians to get our way and further our goals. I mean, if we only dealt with completely clean and honorable politicians, we'd get nowhere. But I don't want to sell my soul just to get my agenda through. It's a deal with the devil that ultimately makes us look bad, especially if we're going to be endorsing him."

"He's charming, for sure. That's a politician, though. Good talkers with charisma make wonderful politicians. But do they use their powers for good or evil? I couldn't help liking him, despite his being an hour late, despite his arrogance, despite his eating most of our appetizers," said Julia.

"You noticed that too?" I asked.

"Not to mention all the wine he drank. And what is that 'don't hate the player; hate the game' bullshit?" said Julia.

"It's an American expression from hip-hop music about dating and hooking up. It's generally not about politics at its highest level, but I get his meaning, even though it was a bit ridiculous coming from him."

"'Hooking up'? What does that mean?"

"Oh, come on, Julia. You must be able to figure that out." I stared out the window at the passing landscape, eerily illuminated by a full moon reflecting off the fresh snow. Trees zoomed by in the foreground, while hills and mountains passed more slowly in the background. Occasionally, there was a home, a Swiss chalet, warm light glowing from the windows, smoke drifting from the chimney. I envisioned a cozy scene, a family and a couple children.

I broke the silence. "Find out more about Senator Godfrey."

"I'll ask some old colleagues in the Foreign Office."

48

A Nice Day for a Visit

I was breathing hard, running through a grassy meadow on a clear, sunny day. That was the great thing about Colorado. In the middle of winter, we would often get a few days like this, where the cold and snow went away, and it would suddenly be sixty-five degrees and sunny. It was a must for me to go running on days like this, and there was no better place than the foothills of the Colorado Rockies behind my home in Denver. A favorite route of mine followed a dirt path bounded by a wooden fence against an abutting pasture where horses grazed. I puffed away, pounding up the last big hill before descending back to the relative civilization of my neighborhood. I looked at my GPS watch; it read six miles. I was nearly finished.

The memory of Liz was with me all day, every day, and every night. There were only brief moments of peace when I could stop thinking about her and be at ease. One of those moments was running on days like today. The warm, nourishing sun made me feel alive, my muscles burning, my heart pumping, my breathing determined and focused as I pushed up that last hill.

I had reached the top of the hill and was now heading back down, a view of the city in the far distance and my neighborhood in the near distance. The sense of accomplishment turned back to sadness as I realized that the only good part of my day was nearly at an end. If I could have, I would have run all the time. Run to escape. But even though I was fit, I was in my forties, and my body could only take so much running each week. Rest days were needed to recover. Otherwise, there was the risk of injury, which meant there would be no running at all.

The end of my run was where the dirt path became the cul-de-sac to my street. I transitioned from my running pace into my cool-down, walking pace, pressing stop on my watch, which had been monitoring distance, time, speed, and heart rate. As I approached my house, a sinking feeling killed my runner's high. There were two black SUVs parked out front.

Two G-men got out of the first vehicle; other agents remained sitting in the second vehicle. The G-men were actually a man and a woman. The woman wore khakis and a short-sleeved polo shirt. She was squat with strong arms and legs, her dark brown hair set into a ponytail. She walked like a man and had one hand casually placed on the holster of the gun visible at her side. The man was a bit older, Hispanic, wearing an ill-fitting suit and tie, and had an academic look about him. He walked a couple paces ahead.

"Mr. Levy?" asked the gentleman.

"It is I."

"I'm Dr. Rios from the State Department. This is Agent Phelps. Can we speak with you for a few minutes?"

"What's it about?"

"Can we talk inside?"

"Come in. I just finished my run, so I don't know how presentable I am."

"It'll just be a few minutes."

Dr. Rios and Agent Phelps had the typical law enforcement attitude, or "coptude," as some called it. It was a sense of superiority, that they were the ones who were in control and could boss people around because they had the power of the state on their side. I'd always suspected that law enforcement attracted weak and insecure people who needed to feel the importance of the authority the job conveyed to them. In theory, they were there to protect and serve. They worked for us, enforcing our laws, not the other way around. But it was true that I was now a lawbreaker as well as a proponent. I was curious to see what they were here about.

I approached the front door and put my key in the lock. It was a single key on a soft keychain that was easy to carry while jogging. I turned the lock, opened the door, and ushered in the two agents.

"Is this your primary residence?" Dr. Rios asked.

"Yeah, why?" I said, knowing already what he was implying.

"Because you're a billionaire. We expected that you'd have a big mansion."

"This is the house I bought nearly ten years ago with Liz, my wife. But now that she's gone, it's enough for me. Maybe I'd have moved if we had had a family, but that's the way things go."

Dr. Rios accepted my response and looked around the entry.

"Come into the living room and sit down," I said, gesturing to the couch in the adjacent room. "Would either of you like anything to drink? Coffee? Water?"

"No, thank you," Agent Phelps said.

"Give me a second," I said. "I just finished my run and would like a glass of orange juice."

I went into the kitchen, grabbed a glass from the cabinet, pulled from the refrigerator the carton of 100% pure orange juice, no pulp, and poured it into the glass.

I carried it back into the living room and sat down in the chair opposite the agents. "I always treat myself to a glass of orange juice after a long run. I know it's full of sugar, but I feel like I've earned it."

"Mr. Levy, have you been to Venezuela lately?" asked Agent Phelps.

"I haven't ever been. It's kind of a mess there. I would like to see it someday, once it calms down. The tallest falls in the world are there."

"As you know, there was a coup there last month. President Juarez was overthrown by the opposition leader, Montoya."

"I read about it," I said. "It was great news. That Juarez was a bastard. Montoya has pledged to return the country to democracy and consequently, prosperity."

"Does your organization NewWays operate there?"

"It does," I said.

"What do they do?"

"The same thing we do in every country we operate in. We provide systems

301

for clean water, waste management, agriculture. Mostly we instruct people on how to use modern agricultural systems, to enable them to do things for themselves going forward."

"Does your organization ever get involved in politics?"

"Never. NewWays is apolitical."

"But publicly you oppose corrupt governments and have another organization, which is political, correct?"

"Those are my personal opinions. My other organization, Due Process, is separate from our charitable organization, NewWays. NewWays doesn't care who is in charge. We just want to help people. If we start inserting ourselves into these political systems, we lose the moral authority to operate effectively."

"You've said publicly that you don't like Mr. Juarez."

"That's no secret. I just said it again a minute ago."

"You also have been pushing for greater powers for law enforcement to arrest corrupt heads of state."

"I am. May I ask what this line of questioning is about?"

"It's just that we find it kind of funny the way the coup in Venezuela took place last month."

"What about it?"

"It seems that President Juarez and his entire administration disappeared in one night. That very same night, Mr. Montoya and his supporters took over and declared themselves in charge. It was all very organized. No one knew initially what happened to President Juarez and his cabinet. For the first few hours, Juarez supporters took to the streets. World leaders called for answers as to their whereabouts. Then, suddenly, President Juarez and his entire cabinet were found tied up and gagged just outside the World Court in The Hague."

I laughed.

"We found it funny too. And, off the record, while we didn't love President Juarez and while we do see Mr. Montoya as an improvement, we are interested in how such a revolution took place."

"President Juarez was under indictment by the World Court. Somebody went and arrested him, I imagine. Now I guess he'll be tried like any normal criminal."

"That's what's bothering us, Mr. Levy. It takes a lot of organization to perfectly arrange for twelve men to be kidnapped on a single night and then flown all the way to the Netherlands – surreptitiously, mind you. They weren't exactly put on a commercial flight, so it had to have been a charter. At the same time, Mr. Montoya and his supporters were put in a perfect position to take charge."

"Good for Mr. Montoya. He sounds brilliant!" I said, taking a sip of orange juice.

"We're skeptical that he has the skills, and more importantly the money, to execute something like this. We know you've been pushing for exactly this type of action."

"You're suggesting that I had something to do with this?" I asked.

"We're just asking if you know anything."

"I don't, but I'm very happy about it."

"Looking at the operation in Venezuela, there are earmarks similar to what took place in Zimbabwe last year. It's no surprise to you that there were rumors of your involvement in that assassination and coup."

"What kind of earmarks?" I asked.

"We can't really say."

"It's not a shock that I was happy – maybe 'happy' is the wrong word – that I was *in favor* of President Shaw's death, given what happened with my wife. But I think your agency is falling into the conspiracy theory trap put out there by the twenty-four-hour news cycle, which now sources mostly from rumors and innuendos to feed its viewers' insatiable thirst for intrigue."

"You have to admit that both the coup in Zimbabwe and now in Venezuela are pretty interesting. They'd make good movie plots."

"They would. But what makes you think that I'm involved? What evidence is there?"

"Nothing we can talk about."

"You guys are listening to the news too. This is silly, and you know it. Is coming here just checking off a box? Just to say that you spoke to me? I totally support what happened but had nothing to do with it. Mr. Enati has done a great job in Zimbabwe in just over a year. He's now the democratically elected president, presiding over a democratically elected legislature, with a duly appointed high court. They have a stable currency again. Businesses and jobs are returning. Now, let's see what happens in Venezuela. I hope these events make the points that I and my political organization are trying to make about good law and governance leading to prosperity, but to suggest that I had something to do with it? Come on, guys. Just be happy that those leaders are gone."

"Mr. Levy, I'm going to be frank. You've done a lot of good in this world and are a respected member of the U.S. business community. The State Department isn't exactly upset about what happened in Zimbabwe and Venezuela. But if you are involved, we would like you to stop. Keep advocating in public for your beliefs, but if you're working on something behind the scenes, cease and desist. Otherwise, the State Department will get involved. Got it?"

"You're giving me far too much credit."

"Have a good day, Mr. Levy." Dr. Rios stood up and gestured to Agent Phelps to leave. I walked to the front door to let them out and watched the black SUVs drive away.

I went to my bedroom, where I found my already-packed bag. It would be a quick shower and then off to the airport to fly to DC.

49

Julia in a Dive Bar

I arrived that evening and checked into the Hay-Adams Hotel in DC. It was a cold and clear night, the light pollution obliterating the stars. The monuments were lit spectacularly: the Washington Monument, the Lincoln Memorial. Coming to our capital made me feel patriotic, with our over-the-top monuments to liberty – some acknowledging the challenges of our past like discrimination, slavery, and the treatment of Native Americans; others glorifying the things we had done right, becoming the first democracy in nearly 2,000 years and setting an example for the rest of the world through the rule of law and not man.

I dropped my stuff upstairs and then walked down to the bar, where I found James having his third or fourth drink. Excessive drinking didn't affect him as much as you might expect. "Hey, dude," he said, shaking my hand and hugging me.

"Good to see you. Where's Julia?"

"In the restroom," said James.

Julia emerged from the restroom, her elegance filling the room. I tried to give her a hug hello, but she just offered me her hand.

"Hello, Julia," I said.

"Good to see you, Joe," she said.

"Shall we head out?" I said.

We put on our coats and left the elegance of the Hay-Adams and walked a few blocks down the street to where the neighborhood became residential. "This is the place," said James, stopping and pointing at a dive bar, the sound of a live band spilling out onto the street.

"Here?" I asked James.

"I used to come here all the time for private conversations. The loud music drowns out anyone who might be listening."

"This might work for us, but I don't think Julia fits in," I said as James and I turned to Julia, her hair neatly styled, sophisticated jade earrings, an amber necklace, high heels, a smart dress covered by a Burberry raincoat.

"She'll be fine," James said dismissively.

I shrugged. We walked passed the bouncer, who just waved us in without carding us. The band was a middle-aged group of men and women playing hit tunes from the sixties and seventies. Currently they were on Van Morrison's "Brown-Eyed Girl," which I always expected to hear from a band like this.

"Beer?" James offered me.

"While it seems appropriate for a place like this, no thanks. Just get me a nonalcoholic."

"Julia?" asked James.

Julia was examining the entire bar, unsure of her place here, probably never having been to a joint like this before. "I'll have a gin and tonic," she said.

James plopped some money on the bar to cover the tab. We got our drinks and sat down on some stools away from the band.

"I think we're clear now," James said.

"They really bug all the hotel bars and lobbies in DC?" I asked.

"Wouldn't you if you were the CIA? All these diplomats and foreign businessmen coming to the capital."

"It's done all the time," Julia said. "That's why it's better that we meet in person."

"You're probably right, but I feel like we're too paranoid," I said.

James interrupted his sip of beer and looked at me. "You don't get the gravity of what we're doing, do you? We are controlling world events, taking out world leaders. We're playing a dangerous game."

"Things seemed much simpler when Liz was alive and I was just a businessman."

"A billionaire businessman," said James.

"Great job with Mr. Angel," I said, referring to our code word for the Venezuela operation. "I haven't seen you since then, so I didn't have a chance to congratulate you."

"Thank you! I know you don't like to use our encrypted network," said James.

"It's best that I don't," I said. "I know you have to use it to communicate with our operatives and organize the operations, but I need as much distance as possible. Agents from the State Department came to my house this morning."

"Good god, what happened?" asked Julia.

"They asked about Venezuela and Zimbabwe…" I related the conversation. "I got the feeling that it was all based on innuendo and not so much on hard evidence."

"But they told you to stop?" asked Julia.

"They did, but they weren't exactly upset either."

"It's likely they know something. We're too large of an operation not to have things leak out," said James.

"What do you think they'll do?" I asked Julia.

"Nothing. I suspect that they're going to let us keep operating," she said. "We're pushing U.S. interests, in a sense. The U.S. government is not involved at all. We're taking out corrupt world leaders for them."

"You think they probably just came by so that they could be on record as having warned me and therefore deny any involvement should we be caught?"

"Possibly," said Julia.

"Did you find out anything on Senator Godfrey?" I asked Julia.

"Nothing horrible," she said. "He's a politician. He gets campaign contributions from companies that the U.S. and other aid organizations use to supply developing countries."

"Corruption is everywhere, ain't it?" James said.

"NewWays needs to create a policy on which politicians we deal with. How much corruption do we consider normal politics, and when is that line crossed? Senator Godfrey arranged to have me testify before the committee on Wednesday," I said.

"What time is the hearing?" asked James.

"10 a.m.," I said. "Julia, what are you up to in Washington?"

"After your hearing, I'm meeting with some former contacts in the U.S. Department of State to push our agenda. I want to get as many people on board as possible."

"And how is everything going with our next target?" I asked both Julia and James.

"It's moving along," said James. "On the operational side, this one will be more difficult. Uzbekistan is a police state. Security is everywhere. It's the post-Soviet model of a big brother. Venezuela was in disarray, so security was less stable there, and people could be easily bribed, similar to Zimbabwe, where things were far more organized. But we can overcome our problems in Uzbekistan. We just need more time and planning than for the first two operations."

"How about your end, Julia?" I asked.

"Finding a democratic alternative to the current government is difficult there. There is basically no opposition party, and there hasn't been for a while. Nor is there a strong freedom and democracy movement. Anyone who says anything in opposition is jailed or killed. They have a tight lid on everything."

"Is there anyone in exile?" I asked. "Or barring that, a former Uzbek, living outside the country, Western educated and successful, or at least charismatic, who might fit what we're looking for?"

"I've been checking around as much as I can," said Julia. "Clearly we can't go forward without a democratically minded individual or group of individuals to succeed into power. Otherwise, if we remove the government, we'd create a power vacuum, chaos, and probably civil war."

"Agreed," said James.

"I agree too. Sometimes we see democracy rise out of a long internal battle, but it's not the situation we aim to create. Our movement is a new idea. We cannot have failures at this point. The world needs to see that removing corrupt world leaders works. I realize that it won't always succeed – look at Iraq."

"Iraq was missing a democratic opposition," Julia said. "The U.S. basically took over and said, 'do it our way.' They didn't bother to solve the Sunni and Shiite divide until it was nearly civil war. In the two countries we've picked, Venezuela and Zimbabwe, there was no such divide. And we had a local opposition that was ready to take over."

"Let's look a little more," I said. "And if we don't find someone who can take over, then we'll switch to another target. It's not like we've got a shortage of corrupt leaders in the world."

"No doubt," said James, smiling into his beer.

"Right, let's convene tomorrow after my testimony."

50

Senate Testimony

"What you're proposing, Mr. Levy, is illegal and meddling in the affairs of sovereign countries," said gruff and overweight Senator Bradley, sitting behind a wood-paneled committee platform along with Senator Godfrey and the other senators on the committee, in SD-419, the room in which the United States Senate Committee on Foreign Relations meets.

"The U.S. is constantly meddling in the affairs of sovereign countries. That's not an argument," I said.

Senator Bradley grimaced. *I am not a good diplomat. Julia really should be doing this,* I thought to myself. "What I mean, sir, is that the United States is always pushing for what's best abroad, for democracy. At least, that is our goal. What my organization is proposing is stronger law enforcement."

"Arresting leaders of sovereign states is a radical idea. You do realize that?"

"Completely. It's a new world. Countries can no longer pretend that they're not part of a world community, no longer an isolated island unto themselves. Their actions affect us all. Corrupt leaders should no longer be allowed to act with impunity and be above the law. Yes, this is a new idea, but a good one, if done right. That's why I am here pushing for it."

"The committee's time on this matter has come to an end. We need to wrap up. We'll take your proposal into consideration. Thank you, Mr. Levy.

We're going to take a five-minute recess and then move on to the next item on our agenda," said Senator Bradley while putting on his reading glasses and examining the schedule in front of him. "Support for a children's art project to beautify trash receptacles around the world."

I gathered up my iPad, from which I read my materials. An overweight woman approached with three kids at her side, all dressed cutely in their new suits. They stood ready to take my place at the table. I passed through the gallery at the back of the room, where Julia rose from her seat and followed me out.

"How'd I do?" I asked Julia.

"More or less okay. You got a little emotional."

"Testifying before the Senate is not something I do every day. That should have been your job."

"You're the famous, rich entrepreneur in the United States, so it was better that you testified. Your testimony will make the news. No one cares about me. That's why Senator Godfrey wanted it this way."

Just as Julia was saying this, Senator Godfrey approached. "Great job, Mr. Levy! You are a natural at this." The senator wore a suit and a bowtie and was ebullient and red-cheeked. He shook my hand and patted me on the back a little too hard. "Hello, Julia," he said, bending over to kiss her on the cheek. She only barely tolerated him.

"What happens next?" I asked.

"I'll keep fighting to move your proposal along and working with my colleagues on this."

"How does it look?" I asked.

"This is a radical concept. You got a long fight ahead of you. But your ideas are gaining popular support. Sorry, it's time for me to run, Joe. I'll see you in Salt Lake City in a couple days, right?"

"I'll be there," I said.

"Great, thanks for coming, Joe." He patted me on the back again and thankfully didn't make another attempt to kiss Julia. He marched off down the hall.

"You don't really like him, do you?" I asked Julia.

"Not in the least," she said.

"Do we really have to deal with him?" I said.

"Unfortunately, you've started a political wing to push a political agenda. You have to deal with politicians."

"Yuck, now I know what everyone means when they say dealing with these guys makes you feel greasy. I don't want to fly up to Utah and endorse him."

"You have to. He's a powerful ally."

I sighed. "I feel like I'm selling my soul."

"I've dealt with these situations and people my whole career in the Foreign Office. It's a necessary evil. They are all a little dodgy, a little too political, and a little too bumptious."

"Are you sure about this guy? He lives an awfully lavish lifestyle for a senator."

"Most of these guys are independently wealthy to begin with. I told you he checked out with my contacts in the British Foreign Office, but I'll ask again when I meet with my U.S. contacts over the next couple days."

"Please do," I said. "I'm going to head off now. Keep in touch."

"Of course," said Julia.

51

Salt Lake City

As I sat scrunched into my economy seat, something was bothering me the entire flight out to Utah. My whole life I'd been bucking the bureaucratic system, finding it too intertwined, corrupt, self-serving. But Julia was right – I had formed a political wing to influence politicians, so I guess I had to deal with them, which meant horse trading. It was so different from being a businessman. With EasyData, I simply focused on making a good product and selling it. In politics, compromises and deals were reached. Not everyone was happy with these deals, but policy moved forward in incremental steps. This was what our founding fathers expected. Madison wrote about this in the *Federalist Papers*. Madison actually wanted government to move slowly, to be gridlocked, so that cooler heads would prevail and that all interests would be simultaneously butting heads against one another.

From Salt Lake City Airport, I took the train downtown to the Perry Hotel, a moderately priced business hotel not too far from the rally being held at the Calvin L. Rampton Salt Palace Convention Center. Soon after I checked in, the phone in my room rang. I picked it up; the voice on the other end stated, "Mr. Levy, this is Alice Lu from Senator Godfrey's office."

"Hi Alice, what can I do for you?"

"The senator asked me to show you around the city," said the voice curiously. "He might have mentioned it to you?"

"He did mention something about that. Sorry, I'm so busy hopping between appointments that I lose track of things. When are you coming by?"

"I'm in the lobby now."

"You are? I'm sorry. I'll be down in a moment."

I put my shoes back on and headed downstairs. Alice Lu was a tall, pretty woman in her late thirties. She had long black hair down to the middle of her back, wore black-rimmed glasses, and a black power suit with a skirt that showed her attractive legs, clearly fit from long-distance running. She had the air of an ambitious, cunning staffer, looking to move ahead working for a powerful senator.

"Welcome to Salt Lake City." Alice smiled. "Senator Godfrey wants me to show you the projects he's been working on in the state, so you can see what he's done locally."

"Is this the standard tour given to supporters?"

"Generally, but not always. He said you were skeptical of him."

"Really? I never said that to him."

"He senses it. The senator has a good feel for people. It's a good characteristic for a politician."

"Sounds like it."

"I have a car parked out front. Are you ready?"

"Sure," I said.

Alice led me outside to a Jeep Grand Cherokee. We spent the afternoon driving around the city, first going to a large building just outside the downtown area. "This is the senator's project for Native Americans. Native Americans have long been an important issue for Senator Godfrey – supporting their communities, helping to preserve their culture. Being a senator in the West, he feels strongly about the horror and oppression done to Native Americans. He blames a lot of the problems that the community faces modernly on what was done in the past. He wants to give them a fighting chance."

"I have to confess that I don't know much about Native Americans," I said. "My focus has always been on helping people in developing countries around the world."

"Senator Godfrey's is too, but he feels like there's been too much focus on what's going on outside America, forgetting that there are many people here in our own country who need our help. This is the richest country on earth. There's no excuse for us having people struggle. The senator believes in personal responsibility and self-determination, but that can only happen if people have the opportunity to succeed."

"Very interesting," I noted without anything to add.

A few minutes later we drove passed a large park located just outside of town. "The senator procured money for this land to be set aside as a wildlife preserve with hiking trails and picnic areas. It's been a great boon to Salt Lake City, which is full of outdoorsy people."

"Where are we going now? Is that a prison?" I asked.

"That's the Utah State Prison. Senator Godfrey focuses a lot on law enforcement. He's made sure that the prison system here has plenty of funding. Did you know that Utah is the only state in the Union that still has death by firing squad?"

"I didn't. That seems rather antiquated, like something I'd imagine at a French Foreign Legion fort in North Africa."

Alice laughed. "It does, now that you mention it. Death by firing squad was actually banned for a couple years, but Senator Godfrey was instrumental in bringing it back. He believes that the death penalty has been weakened. Drug companies are refusing to sell the drugs required for death by lethal injection. Senator Godfrey figured that if that's the case, they should bring back death by firing squad. There'll always be plenty of bullets and people to fire them."

"Are there enough people willing to be part of a firing squad?"

"Oh, you bet! The last time we had an execution, people lined up around the block to apply."

"Do they tie the condemned to a wooden post and give him a blindfold and a cigarette?"

"You're kind of funny, Mr. Levy. Can I call you Joe?"

"Of course."

"Joe, it's not like the old movies. It's much more clinical than that. It's done inside the prison in a special white room. The condemned is strapped into a chair that looks a lot like an electric chair. The feet are strapped in, the head is held by a brace. Around the chair are a number of sandbags to catch stray bullets. A hood is placed over the condemned's head and a target placed over his heart. There are five shooters, all police-officer trained. They use thirty-caliber Winchester rifles. One of the rifles is loaded with blanks so that no one knows for sure who fired a real bullet, defraying the responsibility among the shooters. The marksmen stand behind a screen with slots through which they can point their rifles."

"Have you witnessed an execution?"

"Almost – I was here at the prison once when one was happening, but not in the room where it took place. I know how it works. I was part of the senator's campaign to reinstate the death penalty, so I had to be familiar with the details."

Alice spent the afternoon taking me around the city, showing me local projects that were paid for with federal funds procured by the senator. At some point, I got a little tired of it.

"Alice, let's call it a day. This tour has gone on longer than I expected."

"Fair enough. We are done anyways. The senator asked me to take you to dinner."

"Dinner? So long as we don't have to talk about more politics and the greatness of Senator Godfrey."

Alice smiled. "It's a deal. Have you heard of Log Haven?"

"No."

"It's a Salt Lake City establishment. It's a log cabin that's been turned into a restaurant. It's an interesting experience if you haven't been."

We drove east into the foothills outside of town. The city turned quickly into mountain wilderness. The road curved till we arrived at a rustic-looking log mansion. It was a theme restaurant but interesting nonetheless.

The valet took the car. The place was crowded, but something told me this wouldn't be a problem. Alice approached the hostess and said, "We have a reservation under Senator Godfrey?"

The hostess, a girl in her mid-twenties with long brown hair, scanned her list of tables and, scribbling one off, said, "Come with me," grabbing two menus. She seated us at a table near the window.

Alice ordered us a bottle of wine. "No, thanks. I'd rather not drink," I said.

"Are you sure? It seems like you need to relax. And this is a good place to do so. The restaurant encourages people to take their time dining, enjoy themselves and their company. They don't rush you off."

"No, thank you. But you're welcome to have some."

Alice ordered a glass instead.

"Interesting place," I said. "Clearly the senator comes here a lot."

"He frequents a few places in order to form relationships and loyalty. You can see that it got us a table on a busy night. People are aware of how much he's done for the state."

"I saw the same thing dining with him in Switzerland. It sounds like you really believe in the senator's mission?" I asked.

"I guess I do," Alice said, almost surprised. "He does have his downsides."

"I'm surprised to hear you say that. I thought I would be getting more of the full-blown PR sales pitch from you."

"PR is only part the reason why I am here with you. You know." She smiled at me flirtatiously.

I swallowed. "What are these downsides you mentioned?"

"He's a good guy, but he's your consummate politician. He works his deals. He's an important man."

"This must be a great opportunity for you, then?"

"It is. I'm looking to run my own lobbying firm someday, and this is valuable experience. Anyways, you're becoming kind of famous. There's kind of a movement around you."

"I don't think that's true. A lot of people think I'm crazy, trying to hold world leaders accountable for their actions under the law. They think I lost it because of the murder of my wife. Maybe they're right."

"More and more people are attracted to your message. People are fed up with corruption and government officials who are above the law because of their position and connections, even here in the United States." Alice paused and sipped from the glass of wine.

"Tell me more about his downsides," I said.

Alice laughed. "You're really pushing this."

"I want to know whom I am endorsing. Besides, you're about a glass of wine in, so I figured now would be the time to press you about this."

"I mean, look, he likes his lavish lifestyle. You've seen it. Check out this place. You met with him in Switzerland. He lives in the nicest neighborhood in Salt Lake City. He lives large, but he does good things. I think he feels that this lifestyle is his due for being a good senator."

"Where does he get the money to live this way?"

"I'm not sure exactly. He comes from a rather wealthy old Utah family. They were involved in the construction of the railroads out here. You know, the Transcontinental Railroad, Promontory Point, et cetera."

"Do you think he's involved in any kickbacks, things like that?"

"Just political favors. But that's what all politicians do."

"My organization is about fighting corruption, as you know."

"You don't have to worry about Senator Godfrey. He's larger than life, but he's okay. Let's stop with politics."

The conversation turned to our mutual interest in long-distance running in the wilderness and to films. I had a rich and delicious dinner of grilled elk and mashed potatoes. The meal went on for a good two hours before the restaurant emptied of diners, and the waiter announced that they would be closing. We stepped outside into the moonless night; the valet brought our car. Alice drove me silently back to town.

Alice pulled the car up in front of the hotel, put it in park, and switched off the motor. "It was nice to finally meet you," she said, looking straight ahead out the windshield and then turning toward me.

I looked back at her. "You've been a great tour guide. And pleasant company," I added.

Alice leaned in and kissed me on the lips. I enjoyed the soft lips of a beautiful and charming girl against mine. It had been a long, long time. But I was suddenly struck by a horrible feeling. Guilt, repulsion, fear. That I was being unfaithful. I gently pressed Alice away from me. "I'm sorry, Alice, I can't," I said.

"I understand," Alice said, a bit surprised. "Maybe the wine is making me bold." She sat back and faced forward. "But I have a bit of a confession. It's no accident that I am the one giving you the tour today. I've had a crush on you from afar for a long time. You seem like a good guy, and what you're doing is inspiring."

"Thank you, and you are charming. But... It's just...I'm sorry, but I am just going to go to sleep now. Thank you for the evening."

Alice lowered her eyes, fidgeted a bit with her fingers, and then looked back up toward me with a half-smile. "One more thing I want to say before you go. That kiss..." she said.

"What about it?" I asked.

"It was nice."

52

Joe the Political Operative

The convention center was filled with Senator Godfrey supporters, wearing pins, hats, and t-shirts covered with campaign slogans. We were just a month before the election. This was the first political rally I had attended in person. And like the difference between a sporting event on television and a sporting event in person, it was a much different feeling, an overwhelming feeling. Nothing I had ever seen on television matched the energy in that convention hall, everyone on the same page, supporting the senator, venerating the senator. A rally for a candidate felt more like an apotheosis, rather than the hiring through an election of a representative who is truly and technically an employee of the people, there to serve us.

A few people spoke ahead of the senator, warming up and rallying the crowd. First, the mayor of Salt Lake City, offering his fervent support and adulation, enumerating all the things Senator Godfrey had done for the city, some of which I had seen yesterday. Followed by the governor of Utah, who was popularly received, the applause continuing for what seemed like ages. Not having followed American politics too closely, I was not familiar with the governor. Then again, this was not my home state. This place was an echo chamber because all these people were there in support of the senator; there would be no critical voices. The senator was all good, and his opponent was simply all evil. I wondered why I was getting involved in politics. This was not what I did, all this bullshit. If there were only some way we could just act like sane people, analyze the issues, and have each candidate propose solutions in a sober manner, not blindly supporting or opposing someone based on their party. Such allegiance was fine with sports. The result of a game was for fun, and so if your team did everything wrong, but you still shouted, "We're number one!" that was okay.

I was lost in thought, which seemed better than actually listening to the speeches. Finally, Senator Godfrey took the stage to massive applause, everyone listening to him, spellbound, for thirty minutes, speaking about his accomplishments, as well as the failures of his opponent. He finished up his speech and, as I stood in the wings offstage, waiting, he arrived at my introduction. "Today, I would like to introduce one of my newest supporters. You are all familiar with him. Joe Levy created the revolutionary and successful software company EasyData. Instead of living in luxury, he and his late wife spent their time and money on humanitarian issues." He went on for another five minutes about my accomplishments. The people around me smiled at me. I got very hot and began to sweat. I didn't want to make eye contact with anyone.

"Mr. Levy now continues to be a force in helping people around the world. He supports efforts in good governance and fighting corruption, something that y'all know I support as well. And now, without any further ado, please come out here, Joe."

There was thunderous applause, which I did not expect. I walked out onto the stage as confidently as I could, smiling uncomfortably at the audience and giving a meek wave. Senator Godfrey stood back from the dais, clapping for my arrival. I shook hands with him and then approached the microphone. The audience continued clapping. I said, "Thank you" into the microphone a couple times, waiting for the audience to quiet down. The applause died down. When it was quiet, one guy yelled "Yeah, Joe!" The audience laughed. I smiled and said, "Thank you for the enthusiastic applause. Getting involved in politics is a new thing for me. For years, my late wife, Liz, and I wanted to help people. It started almost twenty years ago in West Africa with clean water and sanitation. Even then, we were fighting corruption. We traveled the world for several years, seeing how people lived, how other cultures worked. It became apparent to us that people needed help from the outside world. It became even more clear that much of the suffering wouldn't exist in the first place if not for bad governance. Yet Liz and I still tried to help people directly, teaching them how to feed themselves, produce things, create profitable work. Bad government was an impediment for us but not something we wanted to take on, because, quite frankly, it was a can of worms we did not want to open. But then when my wife—" My voice broke. I felt Senator Godfrey put his hand on my back in support. I started again. "When my wife was killed by people exercising power under a corrupt authority, I realized that these countries didn't need money, they didn't need food, they needed good governance." The hall erupted in applause. I waited as people came to their feet. The rush of energy from the crowd was overwhelming. I could see how this could be addicting to politicians. "Senator Godfrey has long been a fighter in providing aid to developing countries overseas. As chairman of the Senate Foreign Relations Committee, his vote and his influence have directed American wealth to those who need it around the world. And now, I join forces with Senator Godfrey in pushing for reforms to hold world leaders accountable for their crimes, to eliminate kleptocracies, to make sure that countries and those who run those countries act as good citizens, and like you and me, if someone breaks the law, they will be subject to arrest and due process before a court of law and punished accordingly." Again, the crowd erupted. Pauses for these lengthy applauses were not something I accounted for when I was preparing my speech. "Senator Godfrey has a reputation for good governance. Working together for this cause makes the world better and our country better. And this is why I endorse Senator Horatio Godfrey for reelection to the United States Senate. Thank you." The crowd roared. I shook hands with Senator Godfrey and walked offstage.

"Thank you, Joe," I heard the senator say into the microphone.

I was greeted by Alice as I exited the stage. "Really good job, Joe."

"Thanks," I said.

"You came off sincere and personable. It really had an impact on the crowd and will play well on the news tonight. A lot of people have been touched by your story and what happened with your late wife. I'm very sorry, by the way. I can imagine that it's hard bringing this up."

"It's okay," I said. "As much as I hate politics, I hope this partnership with Senator Godfrey works out for our mutual benefit."

"I have one more question for you, if it's all right."

"Sure, what's that?"

"Are the rumors true?"

"What rumors?" I said.

"You know."

"No, I don't."

"That you had something to do with Zimbabwe and maybe Venezuela. A lot of people supporting you seem to think you're behind them. Don't get me wrong. If you were, I'd think that was cool."

"I had nothing to do with either event."

"Even if you were responsible, I wouldn't expect you to tell me anyways," she said with a smile.

53

An Interesting Call

"Your speech at the senator's rally went over well," said Julia over the phone.

I was back in my house in Denver, unpacking my bag, currently unfolding my suit and hanging it up in the closet. "Thank you," I said. For security, Julia and I only talked about our legitimate operations over the phone.

"I know you're not pleased working with a politician, but you did nicely."

"Senator Godfrey isn't that bad. Maybe I am drinking the Kool-Aid, but after seeing some of his work and attending his rally, I actually like him better."

"I asked some of my Foreign Office contacts about him. It is the same thing we knew about him already."

"His assistant said the same. She took me for the rote Senator-Godfrey-is-awesome tour around Salt Lake. I have to admit that I enjoyed speaking before a rally of a few thousand people."

"Don't ever go into politics," said Julia.

"I'm not even thinking about it. I'm just trying to push my political agenda. Anyways, I'm supposed to be interviewed a couple times over the next few days, Christiane Amanpour on Wednesday and on NPR on Thursday. Where are you off to?"

"I will be traveling to The Hague to discuss some of the practical issues with those who work with the World Court. I want to know how they feel about being given the authority to pursue and arrest sovereign leaders," said Julia.

"You'll have an uphill battle convincing them to favor the death penalty."

"I thought about that: let's not call it a death penalty."

"We're not weakening our stance?" I asked.

"Not our stance, just the way we sell it. Europe and much of the world are against the death penalty. Instead, we'll sell it as a necessary use of force in apprehending noncompliant criminals."

"I will defer to you on these matters. You're the former diplomat, and you're in charge of the political wing."

"As it should be. It's late here in the Netherlands, so I have to go."

I heard a beep over the phone. "I have another call coming in. Stay in touch, Julia, and let me know how it goes." I looked at my phone but didn't recognize the number. It was a Utah area code. I clicked over.

"Hello?" I said.

"Joe, it's Alice."

"Hi Alice, how are you?"

"I'm fine. I just want to say that I enjoyed our conversation the other night." Her voice was soft and hesitant. "I felt a lot of sympathy toward you, your movement, and what happened to your wife." I heard her swallow hard. "I have something to tell you... Look into the senator's ties to Zimbabwe."

"What?" I said. "What ties?"

"I don't want to say any more. Have a good night."

"Wait, Alice—" The line went dead. I thought about calling back but decided against it. I dropped the suit on and fell back onto my bed, the phone falling to the floor. I stared at the wall for a few minutes. I grabbed my phone and scrolled through my apps till I got to Skype. I looked at my watch and dialed the phone.

"Can you put me through to President Enati? It's Joe Levy."

54

A Turn for the Worse

"Why are you dragging me all the way down to Mexico when I have important meetings in the Netherlands?" asked Julia, storming into the bungalow next to the beach in Baja California. She was still dressed for a rainy day in Amsterdam.

"How do you walk in the sand in those high heels?" said James.

"Not funny today," I said to James. "Sit down, Julia. We have a big problem. James, get President Enati on the secured line if you could."

James had his heavy-duty, military-style laptop on the desk, secured in a rugged metal case with rubber bumpers on each corner as though this thing could take a direct bomb blast. A line ran from the computer off the table and out a sliding glass door to the small garden behind the bungalow, where a satellite transmitter sent and received signals to and from a clear sky.

"One moment," said James, typing something into the computer. A foreign-style ringtone emanated from the speakerphone.

"President Enati's office, special line," said a female voice from the speaker.

"It's Joe Levy. We've got a conference call scheduled with the president. Can you put us through?"

"Right away," said the friendly voice.

There was a click. "Hello, Joe," said the president.

"Hello, Tinashe," I said. "James is here, and so is Julia. I got your message.

I'm assuming the news isn't good."

"I'm sorry. It's not. Can I talk freely?"

"Go ahead," said James. "This is a secure line."

"I had some men investigate Senator Godfrey's connections with the old regime here in Zimbabwe. We spoke to some of President Shaw's old cronies. Many spoke to us freely, given their immunity under the truth and reconciliation agreements we have."

"What? What's this about Senator Godfrey?" said Julia.

"That's why we're here, Julia," I said. "Go on, Tinashe."

"Senator Godfrey arranged food and monetary aid for Zimbabwe. This we all knew. And we knew most of this money got funneled into the president's private accounts. But we found out that Senator Godfrey may have arranged for the aid specifically for the personal benefit of President Shaw and taken a cut. I have details of food aid and other equipment being sold on the black market with little of it reaching the people for whom it was intended."

"Good god," said Julia.

I winced. "Let Tinashe finish."

"The senator has been running similar rackets around the world in the countries where he pushed for aid," said President Enati.

"But my sources..." said Julia.

"It gets worse, Julia," said President Enati from the speakerphone. "Some of the witnesses said that the senator and President Shaw used violence to protect their monopoly, so that only their organization would receive the aid and the kickbacks. I can't prove this, but I was told by one of President Shaw's old aides that the senator pushed to have Liz killed because he wanted you out in particular. Apparently, you and your organization were causing problems for the senator's schemes all over the world. He was hoping that by offing your wife, you would 'learn your lesson' and not 'meddle' in their affairs. He called Liz 'nutsy.'"

We all sat in silence as President Enati finished his sentence. Julia looked around the room at our reactions. James puffed out his cheeks. I folded my arms.

"Are you there?" asked President Enati's voice from the phone.

"We're here," James said. "We're just taking things in. Can you get us the evidence of what you mentioned? We'll send over a special courier."

"I'll give you whatever I have. There's not much hard evidence, just testimony," said President Enati.

"Keep this quiet for now," added Julia. "We don't want to put the senator on alert."

"Got it," said Enati.

"Thank you," said James. "Signing off." He switched off the line and then hit a few buttons. "We're clear. The line's off."

"I can't believe it," said Julia. "I figured that he was a little crooked but—"

"—How could you two let me endorse him?" I yelled. "You two with your contacts around the world couldn't figure out that this guy was a complete crook? I knew it. I knew it. I knew it. I had a bad feeling about him from the beginning, from our first meeting in Geneva. You should have fucking known better, Julia. You've dealt with these assholes your whole life, and you got snowed, completely fucking snowed."

"Calm down, Joe," said James.

"Shut up," I said. "You with your mercenaries and informants. God damn it!"

"It might not be true," James said. "We've just talked to Enati. Let's look at his evidence, and I can investigate—"

"— Oh, come on James," I said. "You know damn well it's true. We're all a bunch of fools. To think that I've been hanging out with and endorsing the man who ordered my wife's, Liz's, death." I wiped the tears from my eyes. "God damn it!"

James and Julia sat, not saying a word.

"But why?" I added after a moment of silence. "Why is he working with me? Why is he now supporting us?"

The room was silent. "Keep your enemies close," said Julia.

"We have to kill him," I said. "James, get the plans in place."

"No!" Julia said. "We are not for personal vendettas. Let's collect evidence on the senator and turn him over to the FBI."

"Even if that happens, he'll get some sweetheart deal and spend a few years in jail, if at all. He might get away with it entirely. We have to take him out. That's our job. We assassinate corrupt world leaders. Senator Godfrey fits that category."

"Remember yourself, Joe," Julia said sternly. "We arrest corrupt leaders and have them prosecuted and jailed. Assassination is a last resort. We're trying to send a message to the world. This is about law and order, not blood feuds."

"How can you be so calm?" I said to Julia. "She was your fucking niece, practically your fucking daughter."

"I'm walking out in two seconds if you continue speaking to me that way," said Julia.

"Joe, it's time to calm down," said James. "We understand you're upset—"

"Upset?" I picked up the computer and threw it across the room, smashing it into the wall.

Julia looked at James, indicating that she was leaving. James nodded. Julia left the room. I approached the wet bar in the corner and swiped all the glasses off the shelves, smashing them to the floor and cutting my hand, blood now covering my fingers.

James grabbed me from behind, pressing my arms against my sides. I couldn't move.

"Let go, damnit!" I said.

"Dude, you gotta stop."

I struggled but couldn't get free from James's strength. I stopped resisting, falling to the ground, James letting me go.

* * *

A few hours later, James escorted Julia back into the conference room, still an angry look on her face. I sat at the end of the table playing with a pen and notepad in front of me. I raised my head up to look at her. "I'm sorry, Julia," I said. "You can imagine how I'm feeling."

"I can," said Julia. "If anything happens to Senator Godfrey, I'll report you to the authorities myself. I don't care if you were Liz's husband."

"Understood," I said. "You're right. We need to focus on the purpose of our organization. We need to get the senator in the proper way. Let's gather evidence on the man and turn him over to the FBI."

"That's the correct decision," said Julia. "If you are instrumental in his prosecution and removal from power, it gives us that much more credibility. The world knows you endorsed this man as your ally. By admitting error and working toward his conviction, we follow through on our principles."

"Here's our plan of attack," I said. "Julia, have your team locate where in the world Senator Godfrey has been directing aid. Those are the countries that we need to investigate. James, your team will follow up on the ground with any leads from Julia. Find me someone specialized who can delve into this."

"I'll get a courier down to Tinashe to pick up the evidence," said James.

"No need. I'll get it myself," I said.

55

Another Unhappy Revelation

I t was a pleasant surprise arriving in Harare. It was now two years after
the coup. At the airport, I found a clean facility and passport control
that operated efficiently. I was even able to apply for a visa online. The
officer scanned my passport, and when I offered to show him the printout
of my visa, he said, "It's okay, we got it on the computer."

ATMs operated in the arrivals area, offering me money in the new and
stable Zimbabwean dollar. I got a taxi from the airport and drove through
the clean, well-maintained streets that hummed with business. Shops were
open. Billboards abounded advertising cell phones, appliances, and fast
food. Foreign investment had returned, and the economy was thriving. A
police officer directed traffic professionally at a busy intersection. A road
crew worked to widen the road with modern equipment.

I arrived at the Jameson Hotel, a place I remembered well from that
important day. After I checked in and had a shower, I decided to walk to my
meeting to explore the streets of downtown Harare. I passed in front of the
building from where I'd fired the fatal shot that killed President Shaw. The
presidential offices were located in the Munhumutapa Building. The guard
asked for my ID, examined it, verified my name on a list, and waved me
through. "Wait inside," he said to me. "Someone will be right with you."

It was an old-fashioned lobby with marble benches for people to sit. I
sat on one, crossed my legs, and waited. Finding that uncomfortable, I put

both feet on the floor and leaned back against the wall. A woman with long blonde hair and blue eyes came out to meet me. "Joe Levy?" she said.

"Yep."

"Follow me. I'll show you to the president's office."

She led me up the marble stairs to the second floor, passed colonnades that each had the symbol of one of the various tribes of Zimbabwe accompanied by pictures of their famous figures throughout history. At the end of the hall toward the front of the building, the woman opened a door and sent me in. President Enati sat inside, typing away on his computer. "Mr. Levy is here," the woman said.

"Thank you, Maryanne. Joe, good to see you." He approached me, shaking my hand and patting me on the back.

"Hello, Tinashe. It's good to see that you're doing well."

"You look good, given what happened. I wish you had come to visit sooner and not for this reason."

"I know, but we've had other things to do and accomplish."

"I don't want to know anything about that."

Tinashe gestured toward a chair in front of his desk. "Please sit down." I took the satchel off my shoulder and sat in the elegant chair. Tinashe rounded his desk and sat in his executive chair, pushing the computer screen out of the way on its hinge so he could see me better. "What do you think of my new office?"

"It's exactly what you need."

"I think so too. I did exactly what I said. I turned the old presidential palace over to the people. Its grounds are now a public park. We hold concerts there, plays, outdoor exhibitions. The building itself is being converted into an art museum. We took inspiration from the Huntington Library, Art Collection, and Botanical Gardens just outside Los Angeles, where Henry Huntington's old residence was transformed into a botanical garden and world-class art museum. This building we're in now was the old colonial administrative building. It serves our needs. It is elegant enough to convey credibility on the world stage but not so extravagant as to burden the people. Plus, it's right in downtown Harare, making it accessible to them."

"I'm very impressed by your commitment to democracy. Julia can be overly tough, but I had the feeling we found the right guy in you to take over. I saw the statistics that the economy was thriving, but it really didn't hit me till arriving here and seeing just how far things have come."

"We still have a long way to go. Over twenty years of oppression to get rid of. We're still trying to change the culture of bribery and corruption. It's a slow process. My biggest concern is succession. I can serve two four-year terms, for a total of eight years, just like in the U.S., then I term out. I have a ways to go before that happens, but I hope to create an environment by then in which another honest president can be elected. Whoever it is, I will hand over power peacefully. That's the most important thing I can do."

"Good for you, Tinashe. I'm sure you realize what an example this sets, not just for Africa but for the rest of the world."

"Thank you." Tinashe smiled, but then his face turned serious. "Shall we get down to business?"

"Let's."

Tinashe got up from his desk and approached a file cabinet. He removed a key from his pocket, turned the lock, opened a drawer, and walked through the files with his fingers, pulling two, three, then four files out and stacking them on top of the cabinet. He scooped the pile from the top and carried them over to me.

"Here you are, Joe."

I looked at the labels on the files, my eyes straining. I recently realized that I needed reading glasses. I reached into my jacket pocket and pulled out the case, slipping the glasses over my eyes. I flipped through the files. I saw the written testimony, pictures of people, copies of documents.

"There's one more thing, Joe," said President Enati seriously.

I ceased flipping through the documents and focused on President Enati.

"I'm not sure I should tell you this, but we found the actual guy who killed Liz."

Black shadows encroached from the corners of my eyes and the room seemed to flip. "Who is he?" I asked.

"It's in that blue folder."

I opened it. Inside, on the first page, paperclipped to the top was a picture of the man I remembered from that night. "Tendai Chiri," I said, reading the name.

"That's he," Tinashe said.

"How do you know it was he?"

"It's all in the file. After I took power, I decided to implement a truth and reconciliation program, similar to what they had in South Africa after apartheid and in Rwanda after the genocide. I didn't want vendettas against people who carried out crimes for the old regime. Not only would our jails be full of people, but we would be unable to move forward as a country. Thus, everyone was given immunity so long as they told the truth and confessed their crimes under the old regime. Just like in South Africa and Rwanda, it was all documented as a warning to future generations. It proved so successful in those places that I wanted to do that here."

"And how has it worked out?" I asked.

"So far, it's been an amazing way of healing."

"Tendai Chiri confessed?"

"First those who had been in his gang of thugs told their stories and named him. He hadn't come forward voluntarily. The authorities went out and arrested him. We offered him the same deal we did everyone else: tell the truth, the whole truth, on record, and you will be granted immunity."

"Why didn't you tell me before that you found him?"

"I didn't know till I started looking into Senator Godfrey's file. I'm the president. I don't deal directly with local law-enforcement issues. This was all handled at a lower level."

"This Tendai Chiri is a free man?"

"He is."

"With complete immunity for killing my wife and other people he may have harmed?"

"That's the point of the truth and reconciliation committee. It's how we're able to move forward."

My fists tightened, and my stomach knotted. I clenched the photo. I looked up. "You're right, Tinashe. It's important to move forward. We're going to review this file and gather evidence on Senator Godfrey so that we can have him prosecuted. Keep this under your hat for now. Okay?"

"I'm happy to help. If you need anything else, let me know."

I stood up from my seat and offered my hand to Tinashe. He shook it and gave me a hug and said to me, "Joe, I can only imagine what this must be like, to see this man who killed your wife, but you're doing the right thing. Your organization pushing for law and justice is the right thing. Violence is the last resort."

"That is true, Tinashe."

I walked out of the office, saying goodbye to Maryanne on the way.

56

An Old Hunter

month later, the three of us met at the Waldorf Astoria in New York City. It was Julia picking these fancy places for us. She was a lady and enjoyed living that way. It was annoying to both James and me, who could really do without the fancy accouterments. I could see why Liz ended up living in a tent in West Africa, rebelling against the lifestyle she had grown up in.

I stayed in a more modest hotel in Manhattan. Yet even modest hotels in New York were expensive. I wondered if I should have just stayed at the Waldorf. It wasn't as though I didn't have the money. I took the subway to the Waldorf and made my way up to Julia's suite. Julia was in the salon, sitting properly in a chair, sipping from a cup of tea. James stood by a large oak conference table in the middle of the room with another man whom I did not recognize, a computer, and a large amount of paperwork spread out in front of them.

"Joe, you're late," said James.

"Sorry, the subway got held up at a station. Someone had jumped on the tracks."

"This is Jerry Weinberg," said James, introducing the man sitting at the table. He was in his seventies, a white man with bushy gray hair. He wore glasses and a suit without a tie, the top button undone.

"It's a pleasure," Jerry said in a strong accent without emotion.

"Jerry is from Israel," said James. "He used to hunt down Nazis around the world and bring them to justice. His reputation for gathering old evidence is stellar."

"There aren't many Nazis left, fortunately," said Jerry. "Most of them are in jail or dead. Now, I do freelance detective work."

"Jerry's been working on our case for the past month, coordinating the gathering of information on Senator Godfrey and speaking to witnesses. He's aware of the need to work quietly so as not to alert Senator Godfrey."

"What has he found?" I asked.

"Now that you're here, I'll show you," said Jerry. "Everyone please gather around."

Julia rose from her chair, carrying over her teacup in the saucer, and joined us at the conference table.

Jerry began in his accent thick. "This senator of yours is up to his neck in corruption. It seems that in every country to which he has sent aid, he was getting some sort of kickback. He was smart, or at least had a smart adviser on how to move his money. It was difficult to find any hard evidence. But he may have moved it originally through Swiss bank accounts, and when the secrecy laws there changed, he probably switched to Bermuda or the Cayman Islands, laundering it through many of the tax-free holding companies that operate there. Or he could have done it through a multinational corporation. The senator took a large percentage, sometimes sixty, seventy percent of the monetary aid. Accounting standards in these countries are not strict. Money tends to disappear. You probably heard how billions of dollars in aid went missing in Iraq.

"He built relationships with these leaders over the years. To hold on to his monopoly, we found that he had people threaten and intimidate other aid organizations operating in these countries. He worried that legitimate aid organizations would find out what he and the government were up to. It was a common strategy to have roaming gangs of thugs, unassociated with the government, attack aid organizations under the guise of robbery."

"How do we connect him to all this?" Julia asked.

"There's no smoking gun, nothing directly linking the senator. It's a lot of rumor, innuendo, and circumstantial evidence. He had direct relationships with these leaders, but no records were kept, and witnesses were few and well paid."

"How about recorded phone calls?" said James.

"None that I've come across."

"No one had caught on and was surveilling him?" I asked.

"As far as I can tell through my connections," Jerry said, "no law-enforcement agencies are working on this."

"Where do I fit in his plan?" I asked. "Why is he helping our organization?"

"Working with a sympathetic billionaire who lost his wife tragically trying to save the planet from corruption is the best cover in the world," said Jerry. "And, sadly, he probably doesn't think you'll succeed."

We all sat in silence.

"What do we do next?" I asked.

"Find evidence of direct communication with these leaders and how he moved his money," said Jerry. "I bet that he works through a large corporation. Find that corporate connection, and you got him."

"How do we do that?" I asked.

"We need to get him to confess," said Julia.

"Confess?" I said. "How?" I leaned back in my chair.

Julia turned toward Jerry and asked, "What is upcoming on the senator's official schedule?"

Jerry leaned forward into his laptop, clicking through a few screens. "Campaign stops and fundraisers. And then a one-week trip to Africa."

Everyone perked up. "What's that about?" James asked, looking over Jerry's shoulder at the laptop screen. "He's going to Harare. The description says it's a visit to aid projects that the senator has helped fund over the years."

"He's burnishing his reputation as a humanitarian as part of his reelection campaign," Julia said.

"Or," I said, "he's trying to establish a new 'investment' with Zimbabwe's new government. I have an idea. Let's speak to President Enati."

57

The Setup

I n 1869, the Meikles brothers emigrated from Scotland to Zimbabwe and moved to the town of Salisbury, now called Harare. They had the idea to build a grand hotel in the style of the day overlooking the main Cecil Square. In 1915, the Hotel Meikles opened with all its opulence. Two lion statues, sculpted in Italy, guarded the entrance, and legend had it that they would roar whenever a virgin walked past. Like other grand Victorian structures in English colonies around the world, the Meikles Hotel took its place among the Raffles in Singapore, the Stanley in Nairobi, and the Strand in Rangoon.

The colonial-style building is long gone, replaced by a modern hotel in the early 1970s. In the process, much of the history that can still be found at other Victorian hotel palaces was lost, but its reputation and allure remain.

Senator Godfrey and a young gentleman entered the lobby, followed by three men in black suits, his security detail. The lobby was elegant, with rich carpeting and furniture upholstered in plush red fabric on the front and a parchment-print design on the back. They entered the Explorer's Club bar, a throwback to the days of the great white hunters with a wood-paneled interior featuring wicker chairs and old photographs. It was late afternoon, and the bar was already partially filled with guests, some starting on their evening cocktails.

President Enati sat at a table in the corner drinking an old fashioned. He was accompanied by his economic advisor, Stephen Cairns, a squat, chubby African gentleman in his late forties who gave off a knowledgeable and approachable air. A group of security officers stood nearby. The president rose as the senator and his assistant approached, striding confidently across the bar.

"President Enati," said the senator charmingly.

"Good afternoon, Senator," said President Enati, smiling and shaking the senator's hand.

"This is Chad Buchholz, an economist for PRIMARY." Chad was in his mid-twenties, suit, no tie, Caucasian, brown hair parted neatly on the side. "Chad is a freshly minted MBA from Harvard Business School. He's accompanying me on this trip to provide analysis."

"Welcome," said the president in his catchy Zimbabwean accent. "Sit down. Would you like a drink?"

The waiter, who had been standing by, approached the table.

"Gin and tonic, on the rocks. What do you want, my boy?" asked the senator, turning to Chad.

"A Diet Coke, please."

The security detail stood off to the side to allow the three men to talk privately.

"Thank you for taking the time to meet with us," said Senator Godfrey. "I've been wanting to get in touch with you since you took office."

"Zimbabwe needs support to rebuild its infrastructure and economy after the previous two administrations let the country go to waste, so I figured that I would hear you out."

"I can see a lot of improvement."

"When were you here last?" asked President Enati.

"Five years, at least. Boy, how things have changed for the better since President Shaw."

"We don't miss him," said Enati.

"It's good that you're here. I would like to see what we can do to help Zimbabwe recover and become the breadbasket of Africa again. Shall we get down to business? In coordination with your office, we have designed some infrastructure proposals. Chad, show the president what you got."

Chad removed a giant pitch book from his leather satchel, opened it to a middle page showing a colorful drawing, and angled it toward the president. "We've laid out design proposals with drawings and time estimates. To meet the electrical needs of your growing country, we have engineered this hydroelectrical dam." Chad flipped a few pages to a professionally rendered image of what the dam would look like at the proposed site along the Zambezi River. "In addition, we've redesigned the electrical grid with the necessary capacity to distribute power throughout the country."

"Electrical loads will go up thirty times from what they are now," the senator chimed in. "With international restrictions lifted and a proper government in place, manufacturing will return, along with overseas investment. Zimbabwe will once again be the second-largest economy in Africa."

"I like your proposals, and we certainly need the new infrastructure. But let's talk costs," said Enati.

Chad pulled out another sheet and handed it to the president.

President Enati whistled. "That's a lot of money. Five times our GDP. How do you expect us to pay for this?"

"Chad, show them our economic projections," said the senator. Chad handed another spreadsheet to President Enati and to Stephen Cairns. "Chad has projected that without these improvements, GDP growth will be stagnant or negative due to the strains on the current outdated infrastructure, but if your country builds these new projects, you can expect growth of seven to fifteen percent. Isn't that fantastic?"

"As a result," Chad added, "the debt you take on to build these projects will become manageable as your economy grows."

"From where would we borrow the money for these projects?" President Enati asked.

"I'd help you, of course," said the senator. "The international banks and monetary funds are willing to lend Zimbabwe the money. Arranging these types of loans is what I do."

"Your numbers are way too high," said Stephen Cairns. "We don't need all these power plants, dams, and sewage treatment plants. Your projections are unrealistic."

"I assure you," said Chad, "they're all very reasonable."

"You don't want to sell the future of your country short, do you?" asked the senator.

"This feels like a shakedown," said President Enati. "You make wild economic projections to get us to build excessive infrastructure and pay for it with huge loans that we can never pay back."

"The projections are reasonable," Chad repeated.

Senator Godfrey held up his hand to quiet Chad. "President, can we talk a few minutes alone? Just you and me."

"Stephen, can you leave us?" said Enati. "Wait in the lobby. I'll have security get you when I'm ready."

"You too, Chad," said the senator. Chad started to collect his papers. "Leave them," said the senator. Chad just grabbed his cell phone and exited the bar.

Senator Godfrey and President Enati were now alone.

"Mr. President," began the senator. "How committed are you to the future of Zimbabwe?"

"What kind of question is that?"

"Don't get testy. I am trying to make a point here. Hear me out."

"Go ahead."

"You are aware of my standing in the U.S. Senate, with the international banks and monetary funds. I am in a unique position to help Zimbabwe obtain loans."

"I appreciate that, Senator. We want the loans, but for reasonable amounts."

"Let me say again that I am the only one who can get you the necessary loans to rebuild the infrastructure in Zimbabwe."

"There's the Chinese."

"You don't want to work with the Chinese. You think I am being demanding? Try dealing with an authoritarian government. You'll be a puppet."

"I'll be a puppet under your plan too."

"You won't. Listen to me. How about we structure the loans in stages? In other words, we build some of the projects now and fund as needed. Later, when certain economic benchmarks are hit, the rest of the projects will be built and more of the loans will be funded."

"That sounds very reasonable. What's the catch?"

"There's no catch."

"Then why did you send my economic advisor and your assistant out of the room?"

"I figured we could talk more easily man to man."

President Enati appeared skeptical.

The senator continued, "Zimbabwe will get its infrastructure projects, its economy will grow, and the future will be set. The only thing I am asking is that PRIMARY handle all the construction."

"Now I see what's happening here," said Enati. "You benefit, not Zimbabwe. The money from those loans goes to foreign companies like PRIMARY to build the projects. Very little of that money stays in Zimbabwe."

"Not true. The country ends up with dams, power plants, roads, bridges, and water treatment facilities."

"At inflated prices and Zimbabwe will be saddled with debt! Forget it," President Enati said.

The senator's smile faded. His faced contorted into anger. He scanned the room to see if anyone was listening and then he peered at Enati, his eyes turning deadly serious.

"I'm done fucking around. Either you go through me or Zimbabwe will be a backwater for the rest of your term. Your economy will fail, and you'll be ousted and probably hanged. Then we'll find another guy to take your place who will do exactly what we want."

"Things are going great, as you noted. The economy is already starting to recover. I have very high approval ratings."

"They won't remain high after you've been tried and found guilty of fraud and corruption."

"On what grounds?" Enati said angrily.

"We'll find something. We always get what we want. Play our game."

"What's your game?"

"Accept the project and the loans. In return, you'll be taken care of."

"And what about Zimbabwe?" President Enati asked. "I was elected as an anti-corruption president."

"The country will benefit from all the new infrastructure. This is going to happen with or without you. Choose to be a part of it or not."

"How would this work?... If I hypothetically said yes," asked Enati.

"Approve the projects on behalf of the government, and you'll stay in power as long as you like, or in your case, till you've termed out. We'll set up an account for you in the Cayman Islands, and you'll receive monthly transfers. That's all. When you leave office, the sinecure we've set up for you will justify the money you will have already received."

President Enati folded his arms in consternation. Suddenly he looked across the room at the door and smiled. "Look who's here," he said.

I was held up at the door of the lounge by security. The president signaled to his security men to let me into the Explorer's Club. As I approached, the senator and President Enati stood to greet me. The senator was uneasy, giving me only half a smile, something unusual for him.

"Joe," said President Enati. "So good to see you."

"I was in town doing work and I heard that you two were meeting," I said, "so I thought I'd drop by. I hope that's okay."

"You're always welcome," said the senator unconvincingly. "Please sit down."

I was wearing a business suit without the tie. I had a large black leather satchel with me, exploding with papers. I pulled up a seat and sat down. The waiter approached our table. "Would you like something to drink, sir?"

"Nothing for me right now. Come back when the senator and the president want more."

"So, Joe," began the senator, "what are you doing in town?"

"I'm here working on the nonprofit, checking on things."

"Right, you said that," said the senator.

"It's okay. I feel like I caught you guys in the middle of something."

"It's fine," said President Enati. "What exactly are you working on?"

"Our irrigation project in the south. There are several farms that want to grow crops requiring more water. We're assessing their needs and figuring out how to sustainably divert water to those areas. How are you, Senator? The election is coming up soon."

"Everything is going well. I have a sizable lead in the polls. Your endorsement really helped."

"I was happy to support you." I paused. "I can't help feeling like I am interrupting something. Perhaps I should go."

"We were discussing Zimbabwe's economic future," said President Enati. "The senator has presented me with a number of options for future infrastructure projects."

"That's great," I said. "Goodness knows that Zimbabwe needs it. I assume the senator is also helping secure loans."

"We were just discussing that," said the president.

"This is something you do a lot, Senator. Isn't that right?" I asked.

"What do you mean?" said the senator curiously. "You know I do. Helping developing countries receive loans to improve their infrastructure is what I do. It's why you are supporting me."

"I know. I was just giving you props...for all the good things you do. You've helped a lot of people. It seems like you should be getting something in return for all this altruism."

The senator's eyes narrowed. "Why are you here, Joe?"

"I think you've figured that out," I said. The table fell silent. I reached under my seat, picked up my satchel, unlatched the leather strap from the buckle, pulled out a pile of papers, and spread them out on the table.

"What's this?" the senator asked, looking toward President Enati for an explanation.

"This, Senator, is evidence that you've been shaking down governments of developing countries for the last thirty years, getting them loans, sending them aid, and getting kickbacks. Even worse, threatening their leaders if they don't comply."

"What is this bullshit?" said the senator. He picked up his gin and tonic, downing the rest, the ice cubes tinkling around the glass tumbler. "Waiter, get me another," he said loudly.

"I'll have a drink too," I said. "Ginger ale."

"Another one for me too," said Enati.

The waiter, who had been waiting patiently by the bar, disappeared to fetch our orders.

"Now, what exactly are you talking about?" asked the senator.

"All these papers show movements of money into and out of the Cayman Islands, coming from countries where you've secured loans for governments, governments known to be kleptocracies. Essentially a few thousand pages of evidence."

"Come on, Joe," said the senator. "This is ridiculous. Where did you get this stuff? I've made enemies over the years. One of them has gotten to you. You know about the good I've done. All this sounds flimsy."

"You're right. It was flimsy. But thankfully you arranged this meeting with President Enati. We suspected that you would try to shake him down like you did other heads of state. The president, being a friend, agreed to wear a wire. Up there is a camera. Your whole conversation was filmed and recorded. Throughout the years, you have done a good job avoiding direct involvement. We couldn't find any hard evidence tying you to the illegal movement of money. That is, until today. Now that we know you've been operating through PRIMARY, we have what we need to connect the dots."

"In other words, the jig is up," said President Enati.

The senator's face turned ashen. "Where's my drink? Waiter!" he yelled.

"Coming, sir," said the waiter nervously.

"Turn off the tape for a moment," said the senator, deadpan.

"Do it," I said into my mic.

"What do you want?" asked the senator.

"I don't want anything. I'm a billionaire," I said.

"You must want something."

"Truth and reconciliation," I said.

"What?" said the senator.

"I know you're familiar with the concept," I said. "It's what they did in

South Africa and Rwanda. And now here in Zimbabwe. You confess to your crimes and agree to stop, and we'll let you go."

"You must be nuts," said the senator.

"You have me mixed up with my wife. She was the nutsy one."

The senator winced.

"An investigation will be a big mess for you," I continued. "It's better if you confess, resign your seat in the Senate, and donate all your money to charity. We'll let you keep a small amount, enough to live out the rest of your life in comfort. Not luxury, but middle class."

"Ain't no way. And I suppose the charity you want me to give the money to is yours?"

"That would be a conflict. Give it to anyone else doing development in the third world. Or several of them."

"Fucking do-gooder," said the senator. The waiter arrived with the drinks. "Took you long enough." He looked at his drink, sniffed it, and took a sip. "This isn't a gin and tonic. Waiter, come back here." The waiter returned. "There's no gin in here. It's just ginger ale."

I sniffed my drink. "The waiter must've mixed them up. I smell gin in mine," I said. "Here you go, Senator." I slid his drink across the table.

"Thanks," he said indignantly.

"I'll bring you another, sir, since the gentleman already sipped his," the waiter said to me.

"Wait, before you go," said the senator to the waiter. The senator downed his drink in one gulp. "Bring me another one, and don't fuck it up this time." He stared at me with a look of hatred I'd never seen anyone give me before. "Do I confess publicly?"

"No, then you would have to go to jail. I couldn't stop anyone from prosecuting you. You confess now, to us, on tape. We'll keep the recording private, and if you ever break the deal, it'll be released."

"What if I refuse?"

"You don't have a choice. We'd go straight to the press. Your reputation would be ruined with all your life's work and you would go to jail. But we'd rather do it this way. It's less messy."

"Can I think about it?"

"No," I said.

Senator Godfrey stared into my eyes. It took all my will to hold his gaze.

"Fuck you," the senator said, breaking away. The senator rose from his chair and charged out of the bar, his security detail right behind.

"Good job, Joe," said Enati. "We got him."

"He's not going to like what happens next."

* * *

"Nice job," said Julia as I walked into our temporary control room in one of the hotel rooms.

"Thanks," I said.

"Why do you look so glum?" Julia asked.

"He may snake his way out of this," I said.

"If he tries, we're prepared," said Julia. "You did the right thing, Joe."

"I hope so," I said.

James stood by the window, his hands in his pockets, not saying anything.

"I'm going out for tea," said Julia. "I will see you both for dinner." Julia, elegantly dressed as always, grabbed her purse and walked out the door as lightly as I'd ever seen her move.

James watched her leave. As soon as the door shut, he turned to me and asked in a calm manner, "What'd you do, Joe?"

I set my bag down, took off my coat, and plopped into one of the recliners. "What do you mean?"

"What was the deal with the senator's drink?"

"The waiter mixed up the drinks, and we corrected the mistake."

"Come on, dude. Whom do you think you're talking to?"

"He killed my wife, James. He killed Liz. And he lied to me, used me, used us."

"What was the substance?" James asked.

"Polonium-210."

"Where on earth did you get that?"

348

"I'm a billionaire running a secret army of mercenaries. It wasn't a problem."

"You know that stuff is highly toxic. You better hope that you didn't poison yourself too."

"Don't worry, your guy told me how to handle it properly."

"Which guy?"

"I ain't telling you."

"The senator is going to suffer a slow, painful death."

"I'm well aware."

"That's what the Russians did to Alexander Litvinenko in 2006."

"Again, I know."

"I say this as your friend: that was stupid." James took a sip of water. "Not only is it against the principle of our organization, it is against everything you've worked for...that I've worked for." He walked to the window and pulled back the curtains. "You had him," he continued. "We had all the evidence. We did it in the right way. I just don't understand why..." James stopped himself from speaking.

"He killed Liz," I said.

James stared out the window at the street below and watched the afternoon pedestrians going about their business as normal. James continued, "I see your mistake. My mistake. Our mistake. The point of having a justice system is that it is a neutral party that administers justice on behalf of society and the victim. You were too emotionally involved. The victim shouldn't have to pursue his own justice."

"Are you going to turn me in?" I asked.

"I'm not. But you'd better watch out for Julia."

58

A Slow Death

A few days later, I returned to Denver and back to the normal work of managing my legitimate international aid organization, jogging, and meditating. We supplied our evidence to the press, and shortly thereafter, the news broke about the senator's criminal enterprise. It was a major headline in all the U.S. newspapers. On that same day, the senator fell violently ill during a Senate hearing. His election opponent fed upon the news. After two days in the hospital and just two weeks before the election, the senator released a statement through an aide that he was resigning his Senate seat and ending his reelection bid. It roiled political circles.

It was not long after that I received a note, through our usual channels, that Julia and James wanted to meet urgently. This time it was not going to be at some far-off destination but locally, for me at least, in the Brown Palace Hotel Denver.

I drove downtown one sunny fall afternoon in Colorado and left my car with the valet at the hotel. I walked through the lobby, caught an elevator, and took it up to the fifth floor. I walked down the plush carpeted hallway, arriving at the door of a conference room. I turned the handle, pushed the door open, and entered. Inside, James and Julia were sitting at a large oaken conference table with our secure speakerphone in the center.

"Hello, James, Julia," I said, trying to sound casual.

Julia looked down at the table without saying a word.

"How are you, Julia?" I said.

"Not well, it was a long flight," she said.

"What's going on?" I said.

"Sit down," said James sympathetically.

Julia turned toward the speakerphone. "Are you there, Tinashe?"

"I'm here," came President Enati's voice from the phone.

"Hello, Tinashe," I said.

"Hello, Joe," said Tinashe, not very nicely.

"Is someone going to tell me what's going on?" I said.

Julia picked up the *Denver Post* from the conference table. The headline read "FBI Alleges Senator Godfrey Assassinated, Dead from Polonium-210 Poisoning."

"I assume you've heard about this," said Julia.

"Good riddance," I said.

"What'd you have to do with this?" she asked.

James sat in the chair next to me, just looking at the table without making eye contact with me or anyone else.

"Are you thinking that I did it?" I asked.

"I'm entirely sure you did it," said Julia, throwing the paper across the room at me, it fluttering into pieces across the conference table and onto the floor before even reaching me.

I flinched.

"I had a feeling you did something odd with his drink that day. My instincts always tell me when there's something odd. But you promised. I gave you the benefit of the doubt."

"He was a killer, Julia," I said.

Julia didn't respond. She just glared at me with a hate like I had never seen from her before, a look worse than any word she could have spoken. She glanced at James, who was still staring at the table, running his fingers through the grooves. "You knew about this, didn't you?" she asked him.

James lifted his head slightly, barely meeting her eyes. "Not until afterward," he said.

Then, looking at the speakerphone, she said, "President Enati, you wanted to say something."

"Joe," said President Enati, "Tendai Chiri was found dead a few weeks ago."

"Who's that?" asked James, looking up suddenly at Julia and then me for an explanation.

"That's the man who killed Joe's wife," said President Enati.

"What? When did you find him?" James asked, turning to me for a response.

President Enati answered instead. "I found him and told Joe. Mr. Chiri had confessed his crimes before the Truth and Reconciliation Commission. I only discovered it myself after you asked me to look into Senator Godfrey's ties here in Zimbabwe."

James again looked at me. I said nothing.

The president continued, "Apparently, he was hit by a car a few weeks ago, right around the time you were here, Joe, after I showed you his file. I just found out about it randomly when one of the investigators brought it to my attention. Did you have anything to do with that, Joe?"

I felt everyone's gaze and took a deep breath. "After you showed me the file," I began, "I rented a car and drove down to Banket, the town near where Liz was killed. I just had to see what he looked like now. What he was doing. I had no intent to do anything. Maybe I did. I don't know. He was easy to find. The asshole was on Facebook. That smiling face. It said right there on his profile the name of the company he worked for, a warehouse, ironically. I drove there and waited outside that afternoon. I saw him leave work and walk down the road, listening to music on his earphones, leading a normal life. The warehouse was just outside of town, and there was a stretch of forest before the town began. There was no traffic. He walked alongside the road. It was just so easy. I drove up behind him and hit the gas. He was listening to music and so probably didn't even hear me coming. I just had to veer slightly onto the shoulder to run him down. I felt the thump and then saw him in my rearview mirror, lying on the side of the road, completely broken. I stopped for a moment but didn't get out. Then I just drove off."

The room was dead silent.

"What'd you do with the car?" James asked finally.

"A few towns over, I paid a guy to clean and repair it. I said that I hit a sable antelope. I'm sure he didn't believe me, but I gave him enough money to keep quiet."

"I have heard enough," said Julia. "So long, Joe."

"Julia, come on," I said.

She grabbed her purse and walked out.

"Joe," said President Enati from the phone. "I can't talk to you any longer. Goodbye." The line clicked off. A dial tone continued from the speakerphone. James reached across and switched it off.

I looked toward James. He folded his arms but didn't make eye contact with me.

"You get it, James. Don't you?" I said.

"I kind of get it. But I'm a soldier. I've killed a lot of people in my life. Some were justified. Others were questionable, but I was following orders. I don't need to tell you that we were going for something different with this organization. I'm still your friend, but you're on your own now." James pushed back the chair and stood up.

"You're leaving too?"

"I have to." James paused and looked at me as if he were going to say something more but then continued out of the room. The door shut. The room was silent. I was alone.

59

His Final Breath

Chris Billings could see the sky brightening through the cell window. Dawn was coming. Joe sat on his jail-cell bed looking pensive.

"What happened next?"

"A few hours later, the FBI showed up at my house. I was meditating. They actually rang the doorbell." Joe chuckled. "I opened it and let them in. There must have been a dozen men there. Flak jackets that said 'FBI' and black SUVs. The agent showed me his badge. Two men at his side put me in handcuffs. He said that I was being charged with the murder of Senator Horatio Godfrey."

"Did you ever think of denying it or going to trial?" Chris asked.

"Why bother? I confessed and accepted my punishment. My lawyer advised me to fight it, the death penalty part, but I didn't want to. My only request in agreeing to the guilty plea and accepting capital punishment was that it be done by a firing squad in Utah."

"Why a firing squad?"

"I grew up watching black and white films like *Beau Geste* and imagining a brave death in front of a firing squad in a desert fort in North Africa, wearing a blindfold and smoking a cigarette."

Chris typed away on his laptop. "You have a cavalier attitude. Is this a joke to you?"

"Hardly. Kind of. Maybe. Life is kind of a joke. I killed evil men, men responsible for the deaths and suffering of thousands of people, and I am the one being punished by the justice system."

"Whom do you think told the authorities on you?"

"I think we both know it was Julia."

"Does that bother you?"

"No, she warned me. She had higher principles than I did."

"Do you know where James and Julia are now?"

"I have no idea. I'm sure that James is fine. Julia is hiding in exile, probably not liking being away from her London flat. I imagine that she regrets that Liz even met me."

"What's going to happen to your organization?"

"My political and developmental organizations will go on."

"You have a lot of public support. There are thousands of protesters outside."

"Nobody likes corrupt leaders. We hate privileged, powerful people who abuse their power, especially when their duty is to be helping and working for the people." Joe smiled a bit. "I guess I fall into that category as well."

"There are rumors that you might get pardoned at the last minute. Are you hoping that happens?"

"I really don't care if it does or doesn't happen."

Chris stopped typing and looked at his screen and then asked Joe, "You said at the beginning of the interview that you had no regrets."

"I don't."

"You had Senator Godfrey caught in his crimes. You didn't have to kill him. You were a billionaire and could have led a nice life helping people, and maybe even remarried."

"It wasn't for me," I said.

"You were never able to move on, were you? You never got over Liz."

"Moving on and getting over someone are lies lovers tell themselves."

The bolt on the cell door clanked open, the door slid back, and the guard appeared in the doorway.

"Are we ready?" said Joe.

The guard said nothing but waved in two other guards carrying shackles.

Joe was compliant as the restraints were placed around his arms and ankles. His eyes and face reflected no fear. The sky was really beginning to lighten now, just ten minutes before the first rays of light would be cracking over the horizon.

"Stand up," one of the guards said to Joe. He rose to his feet. "Follow him," said the guard, motioning to the other guard.

Joe shuffled along the floor, his legs barely able to move in the shackles. Chris closed the lid of his laptop, stood, and watched Joe go by. "Good luck, Joe," Chris said. Joe just smiled back.

Joe and the three guards exited the cell into the hallway, where a guard shouted, "Dead man walking."

Chris followed the procession through a series of doors that opened into a new and unfamiliar hallway that led to the death chamber. It was a white room. A heavy wooden chair sat at the far end. Behind it was a dark wooden backdrop and sandbags stacked in two columns on both sides of the chair. Directly opposite was a wall with metal slots. On the side, across from where Chris stood at the door, there was a one-way mirror for those in the gallery to watch. The guards guided Joe to the chair. His shackles were removed, and he was told to sit down. Joe sat in the chair and put his legs into the binds. The guard wrapped the leather straps around his ankles, pulling them tight to the chair leg and fastening the buckles closed. Joe had already placed his arms on the rests, while the other guards tightened the wrist straps. "Are those okay?" the guard asked.

"They're fine, thanks," said Joe.

"Lean your head back," said one guard.

Joe leaned his head against the back of the chair. Lastly, a guard pinned a paper target over his heart.

"Do I get a blindfold and a cigarette?" Joe asked.

"You get a blindfold," said one of the guards, taking a hood and placing it over Joe's head.

When the two guards had finished their prepping, the head guard checked all the straps. "Are you comfortable?" he asked.

"Yes, thank you," said Joe.

"The prisoner is secured," said the head guard.

The guards exited the room, taking Chris out with them. "This way, sir," one said, leading Chris to the gallery. Even though the gallery was adjacent to the death chamber, the entrance was through another set of doors off an entirely different hallway.

Inside the gallery was a set of ten chairs. Some of which were already filled. There were a couple of other pool journalists. Five of the chairs were marked "Reserved for Family." In the back of the room stood the warden, a man wearing a dark blue suit and a red tie. He leaned against the back wall with his arms folded. Next to him were a set of phones, three of them: red, white, and blue, one connected to the Utah Supreme Court, the other to the governor, and the last internally to the prison. The warden stood steely at his post, waiting for a last-minute call stopping the execution. The chairs faced the darkened window looking in on the death chamber. There was Joe, hooded and strapped to the chair, seemingly all alone. The door to the gallery opened. Five people walked in, three men and two women. They were the senator's widow, daughter, and three sons. Traditionally, the victim's family were the last to arrive at the execution and the first to leave. A guard removed the paper "reserved" signs from their chairs and gestured for them to take their seats.

No one spoke in the gallery. One of the senator's adult sons held his mother's hand. The warden checked his watch, looked at the clock on the wall, and then glanced at the phones. The analog wall clock read 6:58 a.m., its second hand circling past the number one heading to the two. The execution would take place exactly at 7 a.m., dawn.

Chris checked his watch and flipped his laptop open. It was silent. Someone coughed. The other two reporters checked the clock frequently. The second hand now approached twelve, and the minute hand clicked one spot over to 6:59. The second hand sped past twelve and moved determinedly and interminably to the one, then the two.

Chris peered through the window into the death chamber. Joe sat completely still. Not even his fingers moved.

The clock's second hand reached the six. Thirty seconds until dawn. In the gallery, the sound of metal against metal was heard as the slots of the far wall opened. Through each of the five slots, a rifle barrel pushed through, their handlers unknown behind the wall. The warden again checked his watch, and then the telephones. They were silent. The second hand of the wall clock reached nine and continued inexorably on to ten, leaving that number behind and continuing to eleven, and finally reaching twelve. A loud bang startled everyone in the room.

Red blood spread through the target on Joe's chest and soaked his shirt. His head slumped forward against the restraint. Smoke wafted up from the rifle barrels. All five withdrew into the slots, which were promptly closed.

The door to the death chamber opened. A tall man in a dark suit with a stethoscope around his neck walked in with a medical bag. He was flanked by two guards. He approached Joe and put two fingers on his wrist. The doctor placed the stethoscope's listening pieces in his ears, unbuttoned Joe's shirt, and put the chestpiece inside the shirt and held it there for a couple ticks, moving it around to three or four spots. The doctor took the stethoscope off Joe's chest and removed the pieces from his ears. He looked toward the gallery and nodded his head.

The white phone in the gallery rang. The warden picked it up. In a very matter-of-fact way, the warden nodded and said, "Uh-uh," and then hung up. "It's done," he said to the senator's family in the gallery. The daughter began to cry. The family stood up and walked out the door while everyone else waited. Once they had left, the other visitors in the gallery got up to leave. Chris closed his laptop and started to walk out but then turned around.

"Warden?" Chris asked.

"What is it?" he said, looking distracted.

"Did the prisoner have any last words?"

The warden paused a moment before answering. "Yes. He simply said, 'Liz.'"

The End

About the Author

A native Californian, Marc Weitz runs a law practice in Downtown Los Angeles. He graduated from the University of Colorado with a degree in Finance and Environmental Conservation, lived in New York City, and attended Southwestern University School of Law in Los Angeles. His travels inspire his writing. As of 2019, he has traveled to over 114 countries and all fifty states. Marc travels to and writes about faraway places. He currently splits his time between Los Angeles, Paris, and anywhere in the world.

Also by Marc Weitz

If you liked this book, let Marc Weitz take you on more adventures with *For Freedom and Danger* and *Through the Cold and Gray*.

Through the Cold and Gray

Sophie Cutler, a young American journalist, is sent to Northern Europe to write a puff piece on a charitable hospital. But when the secretive doctors fail to explain a series of mysterious deaths, her investigation leads to the discovery of a plot of the most sinister kind. Will this be her big scoop or the end of her career?

For Freedom and Danger

1914, World War I, The African Front. Lt. Richard Parks, a British officer and iconoclast stationed in East Africa, accepts a dangerous covert mission to lead a small team of African soldiers to infiltrate German East Africa in order to blow up a railway bridge. But when the army's plan fails, Lt. Parks must improvise in one of the most hostile fronts of World War I.

www.ingramcontent.com/pod-product-compliance
Lightning Source LLC
Chambersburg PA
CBHW031608100726
47898CB00006B/1704